THE LORE *of* THE EVERMEN

The Evermen Saga, Book 4

OTHER TITLES IN THE EVERMEN SAGA:

THE LORE *of*
THE
EVERMEN

The Evermen Saga, Book 4

JAMES MAXWELL

Text copyright © 2014 James Maxwell

Published by 47North, Seattle

www.apub.com

Amazon, the Amazon logo, and 47North are trademarks of Amazon.com, Inc., or its affiliates.

ISBN-13: 9781477824610
ISBN-10: 1477824618

Cover design by Mecob

Library of Congress Control Number: 2014934607

Printed in the United States of America

This book is for my wife
Alicia
with all my love and gratitude
for our enchanted years together

THE TINGARAN EMPIRE

IN THE YEAR OF THE EVERMEN 546

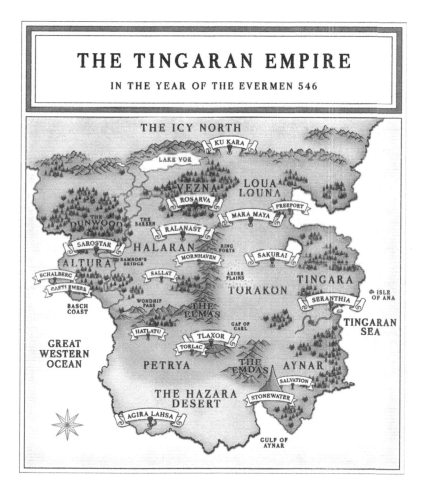

PROLOGUE

Gorain, pirate king of Nexos, steeled himself to kill his wife and only son.

Looking down from the battlements of his once proud island fortress, Gorain gauged how far he would need to throw them to ensure they struck water. The pounding of the surf on the rocks below combined with the thudding booms of the enemy's battering ram as it crashed against the last of his keep's inner gates. His heart sounded louder still, blood throbbing in his temples, swamping his senses.

Gorain ran a hand over his face and scanned the walled space at his keep's summit. A single soldier was on his knees, with eyes closed and palms pressed together in supplication. Gorain's wife, Sedah, stood nearby, with their son clutching her skirts and her eyes wide with terror. Below the fortress, clouds of smoke rolled up from the village. The island was tiny, and dominated entirely by the harbor, fort, and small town at the fort's base. Nexos had fallen. Gorain had tried, but nothing could defeat this foe.

Gorain crouched and held out his arms. His son ran forward, and Gorain clutched the terror-stricken boy to his breast. "Don't be afraid, Arsan," he whispered. His son shuddered in his arms. "This will all be over soon."

As he listened to the growls and snarls heard between the strikes of the battering ram, the cries of warriors brought back from the afterlife only served to strengthen Gorain's determination. They had come from Veldria, and they had crushed Gorain's island fortress of Nexos in a matter of hours. He'd had no warning; his scout ships never returned to raise the alarm. A sudden armada came over the horizon, undead men and women poured from their ships, and in moments the enemy seized his harbor and his fifty docked vessels. Gorain had learned their nature in the frenzied fighting and had even managed to destroy a few of the undead warriors himself. But the outcome of the battle for Nexos was never in dispute. Gorain and the last of his men had retreated to the summit of his fortress, guarded by one final set of sturdy gates.

Gorain felt his beloved son's tears as he held him close, and he wondered if he had the courage to do what must be done. There was no other option. If he couldn't save their lives, he had to save their souls.

He would cast his wife and son into the sea, before throwing himself off the battlements.

Gorain was an educated man, a minor noble who'd carved out his own kingdom, and though the Veldrins called him a pirate, Gorain was a wise leader. He could see that many of the undead were once ordinary people from Veldria, Gokan, and lands further north. Gorain would do anything to avoid those he loved experiencing this same fate, to become animated corpses, a fate far worse than death. He would throw them into the sea, their bodies would drift away with the tide, and Gorain would join them in the afterlife.

Looking over his son's shoulder, Gorain met his wife's eyes. "Sedah, come closer."

As Sedah stepped forward, Gorain thought about his wife. She looked as beautiful as the day they were married, and they'd shared over a decade of happy years. Her blonde hair still glowed with health, and her brown eyes never failed to melt Gorain's soul. Gorain felt such a squeezing on his heart that he thought it would burst in his chest.

Gorain wished he had poison, and time for a poison to do its work, but only moments remained until the last of the inner gates broke. Falling until they struck the sea would fill his wife and son's final moments with terror. No, the blade was better. Gorain was an experienced warrior, and he knew how to make a death as quick and painless as possible.

When Sedah was behind his small son and starting to crouch with arms wide to share the embrace, Gorain lunged forward, swift as a snake, even as he continued to clutch his son close to his chest. He slipped the dagger in between Sedah's ribs and pulled it out in one precise movement. The knife found its mark, and as the blade exited Sedah's heart, the life left her eyes. Gorain's wife fell down to the ground, finally sprawling out on her back.

Gorain continued to hold his son even as the dagger in his right hand trembled. Aisan tried to turn, but Gorain held him fast. With his left hand he stroked his son's soft pale hair before bringing his hand down to the base of his son's neck and further. Gorain made soothing sounds as he followed the contours of his son's back, finding the right place to plunge the knife in between the shoulders and ensure the boy had as quick a death as his mother.

Gorain heard a cry, and looking up, saw the last of his men run forward. The soldier's face was filled with terror, the crimson blood on his uniform contrasting with Gorain's colors: a pattern of checkered black and white squares. The soldier threw himself off the battlements, screaming as he fell, and then Gorain heard a distant splash.

Soon Gorain and his family would join the soldier in the sea, where the swift current would carry them away, and the dark arts of this unholy enemy could never touch them.

Gorain closed his eyes as he prepared to perform the most difficult task of his life. He brought the tip of the dagger in between his son's shoulder blades.

"I'm sorry, Arsan. I love you," Gorain murmured.

Gorain pushed the blade in, the sharp steel easily penetrating before Arsan knew what was happening. Tears welled at the corners of Gorain's eyes as he pushed at an angle to find the heart. It was as painless a death as Gorain could give him.

Arsan died.

Gorain dropped the dagger and rocked his son in his arms, but he knew his task was far from finished. He lowered his son before looking at his hands, wet with the blood of his family. He knew he'd had no other choice. Better that they died unaware of the moment death came. Gorain would be the only member of his family forced to look death in the eye.

Standing, Gorain once more looked out at the sea. He had to ensure they made it to the water, where they would slumber in peace, their souls departed to safety in the afterlife.

As the pounding of the battering ram at the last set of inner gates continued, Gorain looked down at the bodies of his wife and son, drinking in their faces, thinking about how much he loved them.

Gorain wondered which of them to throw first.

The tears finally came as he bent down and picked up his son's small body. At five years old, Arsan was surprisingly heavy. Gorain carried his son's body to the battlements and once more looked down. He was confident the boy would reach the water.

Gorain drew in a breath and heaved. He watched to make sure of the splash. The small body sailed through the air.

Gorain's eyes widened when he saw a man in black clothing standing on the rocky shore, looking up. The man's eyes met Gorain's, and then he did something incredible.

He rose into the air, and deftly caught Gorain's son by one of his little legs.

Gorain gasped with horror. He watched as the man continued to rise, his path taking him ever higher as he held Gorain's son. He reached the battlements and came to rest gently on his feet barely three paces from Gorain.

Gorain felt dread crawl up his spine as he looked at the man. He was slim and tall, with sculpted features and a sharp chin. He wore tailored black clothing, with diamonds set in chrome at his cuffs and a silver chain around his neck. His forehead showed cruel lines; his lips curled as if in perpetual displeasure. His hair was blood red, with streaks of black at his temples, and his eyes were the blue of a winter sky.

Gorain felt dread, but stronger still, he felt a sense of abject failure. He had no doubt that this was the man responsible for the terror. He was a demon, a wielder of powerful dark arts. The bodies of his wife and son were now in this man's power.

"I gave my men instructions to take you alive, Gorain of Nexos," the man in black said. The man's voice was emotionless, but behind it Gorain could detect a faint tone of irritation. "Your dead son?" the man inquired, holding the body higher. "Unfortunate. I also gave instructions for your family to be taken alive."

"Why?" Gorain said.

Gorain couldn't take his eyes off the body of his son, held casually in his enemy's grip. Seeing the direction of Gorain's gaze, the man in black threw the small body on top of Sedah's motionless form. Gorain's family now lay in a crumpled heap.

Gorain tensed. On the ground, near the bodies, he could see the dagger.

"I wouldn't," the man said. He muttered some strange words and shifted his hands. As symbols on the backs of the man's hands began to glow, Gorain felt the very air around him grow solid, pinning his arms to his sides.

"I have a proposition for you," the man said.

"A proposition?" Gorain said. "Kill me now." He fought to hold back the tears as he looked at the bodies. "I have nothing to live for."

"I agree," the man said in a flat voice.

He stepped forward until he stood close to Gorain, fixing the pirate king in place with an icy stare. His hand shot forward, and he clutched Gorain's throat. Gorain heard himself gasp as his lungs stretched for air. He made a rasping sound like the croak of a frog.

It was the last sound Gorain heard before he died.

"You are special," a voice spoke. "There are only two others like you, in all the world."

Gorain felt strange. Something was missing. He could remember his life, just as he could remember dying. Was this the afterlife?

"Open your eyes," the voice commanded.

Gorain's eyes opened. He had no choice in the matter; his body wasn't under his own control.

"Sit up."

Gorain's body followed the order. Through the dim haze of his broken awareness he saw he was on an iron table. The stone walls of his keep surrounded him, and Gorain saw he was in one of its lower chambers. The man in black regarded him intensely. A shudder swept through Gorain's body.

Suddenly, Gorain again felt the pain of his death. He moaned and gasped and clutched at his throat. The man in black waited patiently.

"Never fear, Gorain, the tremors will pass. I have brought you back myself, and I know these arts better than any."

Time passed, and then Gorain felt his body still.

"Now, before we begin, I must perform some tests. What is your name?"

"Gorain Delman," Gorain heard himself say.

"Good. We are within your island fortress. What is it called?"

"Nexos."

"Excellent. Now, I believe some introductions are in order. My name is Sentar Scythran. I am called the Lord of the Night. Who am I?"

"Sentar Scythran," Gorain said woodenly. "The Lord of the Night."

"Well done," said Sentar Scythran. "Now, as you probably know, you are dead. You are under my power and the power of my necromancers. However, you can also express your own thoughts. Speak freely, Gorain."

"Why have you done this to me?" Gorain moaned. Something inside his consciousness was missing. He was no longer a man. He was something else.

"An excellent question, my friend," said Sentar. "I am planning an invasion, and I have a great army fit for the task. My plan is simple, as all good plans are. I will take my army across the sea in my many ships and conquer the lands in the east."

"I don't understand," Gorain mumbled.

"Well, Gorain, great armies are led by capable commanders, and my necromancers know little of naval strategy or siege tactics. You are to become one of my commanders. I have brought you back, personally, with all of my skill set to the task. I have worked for three full days on you, and a large amount of my precious essence has been spent on the lore that enables you to sit here and speak with me. Look at your body," Sentar instructed.

Gorain examined himself. He was shirtless, and saw thousands of tiny glowing symbols covering every visible portion of his skin. Gorain felt power course through him. Even as he suffered through the missing parts of his awareness, Gorain felt strength and speed in his limbs and the complete absence of the living's problems of pain and fatigue.

"I will never serve you," Gorain said.

"Ah, but I think you will." Sentar Scythran nodded to a man in gray robes, who had been standing against the wall, watching the proceedings. The gray robed man disappeared through a door, returning a moment later with two followers.

Gorain's wife and son looked at him with dull eyes that were perfectly white. On the throat and hands of both woman and child were more of the strange runic symbols, glowing eerily blue where clothing didn't cover their pale skin.

"No," Gorain cried. He lunged forward.

"Sit and be still," Sentar commanded.

Try as he might, Gorain couldn't contradict the order.

"What is your son's name, Gorain?"

"Arsan," Gorain whispered.

"Arsan," Sentar said, as if tasting the words. "Now, Gorain, you can think; you can feel. How much of your little son do you think remains? Do you think his inner self screams with horror at the things done to him? Answer me, do you believe there is still a part of his soul, chained to his body?"

Sentar had asked Gorain a question, and even as he tried not to speak, Gorain answered. "Yes," he said hoarsely. "I want my son free."

"Necromancer Renrik, a demonstration, please. Take off Arsan's hand," Sentar instructed the man in gray robes.

The necromancer took out a long dagger and lifted one of Arsan's arms. Without hesitation Renrik hacked at the flesh, grimacing as blood splashed out and he was forced to push through the thin bones of the boy's wrist. Gorain's son didn't make a sound, but Gorain wanted to scream. The necromancer removed the hand and held it up, the stump of the limb dripping red blood to the stone in a steady patter.

Even as he raged at what was being done to his child, Gorain felt a greater horror at the fate of their souls. His eyes roved from Sedah's beautiful face to Arsan's sightless eyes. Trapped in some horrific semblance of life, Gorain's wife and son would never be free.

"Speak, Gorain," Sentar Scythran said.

"Destroy them. I beg you," Gorain said. "End it for them. I will do anything."

"I promise you I will do so, if you agree to serve." Sentar gazed directly into Gorain's eyes. "Although my necromancers and I can control you, we must give you some free will in order to make use of your skills as a commander. If you agree to serve, and serve well, I swear to you that I will set your wife and son free, even if you fall in the battlefield. I have extended this same offer to Farix of Torian and Diemos of Rendar, and both have accepted. You are special, Gorain, and I have done this to you at great cost. Will you join the two kings who were once your rivals and enter my service? What do you say?"

Gorain bowed his head. He felt his eyes burn, but he couldn't weep. "I will serve," Gorain said.

"Excellent. Renrik, take charge of our new commander and begin his instruction immediately."

Renrik bowed. "Master."

"Gorain, we will bring back many of your men to serve you, and you can be in charge of your own ships. Do you plan to honor our agreement?"

Gorain's lips moved. "I do."

"Then we will leave this rock as soon as possible. We have an unbeatable host of warriors and the commanders to lead them. We have the essence we need to bring my brothers home."

The Lord of the Night smiled. Somehow, it made his visage even more sinister.

"The gods will soon resume their rightful place."

1

Miro Torresante, high lord of Altura, strode with purpose through the streets of Seranthia. The district of market houses passed him in a blur.

Four bladesingers scanned the crowd for threats while another twenty of the elite palace guard struggled to keep up with their young high lord.

Miro was thankful for the cold of Seranthia's winter. The high lord's robe he wore was silk, but the glistening folds and stiff collar gave the material weight. It was covered with protective runes, and as part of his ascension Miro had learned the language of single-activation sequences, but he longed for the armorsilk of a bladesinger. A bladesinger had never been high lord before, and even with all the robe's power, it was no match for armorsilk. Single activations could only do so much; the most powerful lore always required continuous chanting.

Yet the robe was a sign of his office, and Miro was on official business.

Miro scowled as he walked, and barely registered the merchants and couriers who drew away from his glare. It wasn't just the sword and flower *raj hada* on his striking robe, nor the deadly warriors who surrounded him. They'd all heard of the tall man with the long black hair, currently tied back with a clasp of gold and emerald. They saw the thin scar running from under one eye to his jaw line, and whispered his name, bowing down before him like water cresting at the front of a ship. Even with so many influential rulers in Seranthia for the Chorum, the power of this man was palpable.

Unaware of his effect on the passersby and consumed with his purpose, Miro muttered to the man walking beside him. He looked at Beorn as he spoke and wondered if he looked as uncomfortable in his regalia as Beorn did in his.

Beorn, a veteran of the Rebellion, was nearly twice Miro's age. In comparison to Miro's lithe grace, Beorn's boots stomped heavily as he shifted in his formal attire, his *raj hada* proclaiming him the lord marshal of Altura. Beorn had resisted the promotion, but Miro wouldn't have it any other way.

"Two days to get an audience," Miro said. "Two days!"

"The Louans are busy," Beorn said, scratching at his salt-and-pepper beard. "Everyone wants what they have."

"To be concerned about gilden at a time like this. Sentar Scythran is coming to destroy us all, and all the Louans care for is money."

"It's their way."

"It's greed. Pure and simple."

"Here we are," Beorn said as they came to a halt outside the Louan market house, a huge, cube-shaped structure. Blue trim decorated the building's paintwork, and the Louan device, a spinning wheel, hung prominently above the door. Miro glanced up and saw the device move; the silver wheel was actually turning.

The double doors stood wide open and guarded by a handful of Louan grenadiers. Miro had an appointment, and it was clear who he was; yet even so, he was forced to wait impatiently as one of his men stepped forward and announced his arrival.

"High Lord Miro Torresante of Altura to see High Lord Ramon Stouk of Loua Louna."

"Please wait here," one of the Louan guards said.

Miro fumed as he was made to wait outside the Louan market house. He remembered when he'd come to Seranthia as a younger man, and the elaborate courtesy the Halrana displayed to Tessolar. Now he was required to wait outside the Louan market house like a common supplicant.

"Calm," Beorn said under his breath. "We need what they have."

Finally a woman emerged from the entrance and stood at the top of the steps, bowing from the waist in the eastern manner. She was short and middle-aged, with close-cropped sandy hair and an intelligent cast to her eyes. Her tailored blue clothing was well made and expensive, and her *raj hada* proclaimed her an artificer as well as a senior merchant of House Loua Louna.

"High Lord," she said, "my apologies for keeping you waiting. I am Touana Mosas. Please follow me. Your bladesingers may come, but I'm afraid the rest of your retinue will have to wait outside."

Miro waited as Beorn spoke to the men, issuing instructions. Beorn then nodded and fell in behind Miro as Touana led the group through the market house. Passing several closed doors, Miro heard strange buzzing sounds and a scraping similar to the effect a saw makes on wood. Miro wondered what was happening inside, but returned his thoughts to the task ahead.

Touana gestured for them to follow her into a large wood-paneled chamber. The bladesingers ranged the walls, radiating comforting strength, as Miro and Beorn took a seat at a long table. Miro wondered when the Louan high lord would be joining them as Touana seated herself, clasping her hands on the table in front of her.

"Now, High Lord, what can I help you with?"

Miro struggled to stay calm. "Where is High Lord Ramon?"
Touana gave an apologetic smile. "I'm afraid he's busy."

"Busy?" Miro growled. "With what?"

"Not with *what*, High Lord—with *whom*. He is with the emperor and was unable to make this meeting. My apologies, but—well . . . he is the emperor, and with the Chorum in five days there is much to discuss. I am sorry for any offense, and please trust I am fully authorized to negotiate on behalf of my house. Now, what can I do for you?"

"You know what we need," Miro said. "Prismatic orbs. Mortars. Dirigibles. The tools of war. The enemy is coming."

"Yes, I do understand, High Lord. As I'm sure you can imagine, this new threat from the west has sown the seeds of fear among the houses. We can only produce so much, and prices have come up accordingly. How much are you looking to spend?"

"Spend?" Miro said. He caught a warning look from Beorn. "We're asking for your help, and you're worried about gilden?"

"High Lord, I don't mean to patronize, but let me give you a lesson in basic economics," Touana said. "Even in times of war—in fact, especially in times of war—the rules of finance must hold sway. Every high lord believes his land is at risk. The only fair way to allocate our resources is by the market forces of supply and demand, and their effect on prices. Tell me what you can spend, and I will do my best to ensure your order is fulfilled."

Beorn laid a cautioning hand on Miro's shoulder. "We've been busy fighting a war, a war that freed your house, among others, from the primate's evil. Since discovering this new threat, we've been pouring gilden into bolstering Altura's defenses, which unfortunately aren't as strong as the other houses', and Altura lies directly in our enemy's path."

"You say," Touana said, shocking Miro with her bluntness as she met his gaze. "Yet by your own admission, High Lord, this enemy's eventual goal is the relic housed inside the Sentinel, and they come by ship. Who is to say they won't bypass Altura altogether and make landfall at some other part of the Empire?"

Miro had to acknowledge she had a point, even as seething rage burned within him. "Yes, I'll admit there is no way of knowing where they'll make landfall, but it's logical that it will either be the free cities, Castlemere and Schalberg, or Seranthia. Last year we found a new continent across the Great Western Ocean, only to see it fall. Trust me, our enemy won't stop there. The entire reason for the assault on the new lands to the west was to form an army and to gather the ships to carry it here. The closest ports are the two free cities, and Castlemere borders Altura itself. I can understand the desire to strengthen Seranthia, and I applaud it, but if they gain a foothold in Altura, their forces will grow in power to the point where the rest of the Empire will never be able to hold them off."

"It's a matter of fairness, High Lord. If Grigori Orlov of Vezna wants to defend his house, and can pay, it is not for us to turn him down. The gilden he provides goes to our merchants, who efficiently allocate orders to our workshops, who pay their workers, who turn up to work to earn their pay. Without gilden, the whole system falls apart, and I'm sorry, but I cannot give you what you want without payment."

Miro clenched his fists, and Beorn shot him a cautioning look.

Touana fixed Miro with a penetrating stare, interrupting him before he could speak. "Tell me, High Lord, how many enchanted swords are you exporting from Altura, for free? How many sets of armor?"

Miro sighed in exasperation. He had a sudden thought, and reaching into the bag lying at his feet that he'd brought with him, he pulled out a pyramid-shaped prism of quartz. He set it down on the table in front of Touana with a heavy clunk and then crossed his arms in front of his chest.

"What's this?" Touana frowned as she looked at the device. She picked it up in her hands and inspected the matrices of runes. "Whatever it is, I can see it is not a complex device."

"No," Miro said. "It's not as complex as the things your artificers make. It's not a timepiece, or a seeker, or a child's toy. It does require a fearful amount of essence to construct, however."

"Go on."

"It's a single link in a chain. Our enchanters are making these devices—we call them reflectors—in numbers. Artificer Touana, what we have devised is a signaling system. We're mounting the reflectors on top of towers, spaced at regular intervals, to connect every capital. That includes Stonewater, and we're even linking up with the icy north. Each device does one thing, and it does it well. When a source reflector in a capital is activated, the prism lights up with that house's color. It then sparks the next reflector, and so on in a chain, until everyone in the Empire knows that nation is under threat. The devices are made to be indestructible. You ask me if we're giving up our resources for the greater good of the Empire and I say, yes, and here is the proof. When we're finished, we'll have a system that will enable reinforcements to go and help those in danger. The essence we're using could be used to buy the orbs we need or build more enchanted weapons, but I believe this is more important."

"It's an intriguing idea, High Lord," Touana said, "and I applaud your dedication. However I cannot change my position. We cannot give you what you need without payment."

"Can you offer terms of credit?" Beorn asked.

"Coin only, I'm afraid." Touana smiled and spread her hands.

Miro stood up out of his chair, knocking it back behind him. Touana didn't even flinch when he leaned forward. "They're coming for Altura. And if we fall, so will you. Be it on your head."

"I can only advise you to state your case at the Chorum, High Lord. The emperor's new agreement allocates essence evenly among the nine houses. Perhaps you can have the agreement changed in your favor."

Miro shook his head, at a loss for words. Beorn scooped up the reflector and waved to the bladesingers, hurrying to follow the high lord as he stormed out of the Louan market house.

Miro soon stood back in the open air, but his shadowed eyes saw something altogether different from the busy streets of Seranthia.

"That went well," Beorn said.

Miro turned and looked at Beorn. "I was there," he whispered. "I saw what will happen to Altura."

"I don't think we can count on getting any more Louan weapons anytime soon."

Miro growled, "She talks about fairness. Why should Petrya get the same essence as Altura when it's we who will bear the brunt of Sentar's invasion? What's fair about that?"

"We have five days until the Chorum," Beorn said.

Miro nodded. "We need to prepare."

2

"All of our hopes depend on these devices," Ella said.

Ada, the eldest daughter of Dain Barden of the Akari, turned the pyramid-shaped prism in her hands. Ada frowned as she examined the device, seeing the holes on each corner of its base, where it could be mounted, and noting the myriad of tiny symbols covering each of the three other faces.

Perhaps five years older than Ella, Ada's hair was even paler than Ella's, near white to Ella's gold. She wore it in a thick braid she occasionally tossed when irritated. Ada now tugged on her braid, her expression thoughtful rather than fierce.

Ella had invited Ada to this meeting in the Alturan market house in Seranthia. She'd had conversations like this with lords and templars, Tingaran melders, and Torak builders. This was now Ella's chance to convince the Akari about Altura's strategy for dealing with the coming storm.

The device Ella called a reflector was made of quartz, and Ella had drawn the runes herself, using a lens to aid her vision. Ada passed it to the three other Akari seated around the broad table as Ella shivered; it was late winter in Seranthia, and the heating system in the cavernous market house struggled to fight the chill. For once the Akari didn't look out of place in their heavy furs.

"We're building them to connect all the capitals and we're even connecting Stonewater. Our enchanters mount them on towers, and as long as the next reflector in the chain is in sight of the previous one, the light carries from one to the next."

"So there will be a tower with one of these at its summit in Ku Kara?"

"Unfortunately, in your case, no," Ella said, "much as I might like it to be otherwise. As far north as Ku Kara is, we're only able to extend the chain to Lake Vor. We simply don't have the resources to continue farther into the icy north."

"So you need us to keep watch on the tower at Lake Vor?" Ada said, glancing up to meet Ella's eyes.

"Exactly. If a reflector is activated in Seranthia, for example, it will shine purple. If the Petryans in Tlaxor were to activate theirs, it would shine red, the color of Petrya, to show they require assistance. The colors will spark along the chain until every device is lit up with that color, and everyone knows that a house is requesting help. It's a simple system, but we hope it will be effective. We're asking all the houses to pledge their assistance and to come if one of us calls."

"I understand," Ada said. "I'll explain the system to the Dain. How many of these towers have you built so far?"

"We've traveled to Seranthia by ship, but after the Chorum we'll be heading back home over land. Our enchanters will build them as we go, although the station at Lake Vor will necessarily be one of the last constructed."

"Excuse me, Enchantress. Two messages for you."

Turning, Ella saw a courier in Alturan green standing just inside the doorway. She didn't recognize him, but that wasn't surprising; there were so many new faces in the market house these days.

Ada stood as Ella took the two notes the courier handed her. "I see you have work to do," Ada said. "I also have other business to take care of. Thank you for the demonstration. I'm sure my father will agree to help."

Ella rose and touched her fingers to her heart, lips, and forehead as Ada and her retinue gave a short bow and departed.

Ella opened the first of the folded notes and frowned.

It was from Ilathor, kalif of House Hazara, written with the flowery prose the desert men favored. Ilathor greeted Ella and asked her about her well-being. He said he wanted to see her at her earliest convenience.

Ella thought about the time she'd spent in Petrya with Ilathor after she'd helped the desert prince conquer Tlaxor, the Petryan capital, a city guarded by a volcanic lake. Lord of the Sky, it felt like eons had passed since. She set the note aside and opened the second message.

There was just one written word. *Tonight.*

Ella smiled and felt a flush of pleasure. It was already growing dark, and she wouldn't have long to wait. Ella glanced around to make sure she was alone before exiting the meeting chamber and heading deeper into the Alturan market house. She passed through the great hall, weaving through the merchants and soldiers she encountered on the way to the stairs. She checked over her shoulder to make sure she wasn't being watched before she began to climb. The set of stairs led her up two levels before she reached her personal chambers at the end of a corridor.

Her heart raced with excitement.

Entering her chambers and gently shutting the door behind her, Ella threw a heavy cloak with a furred collar and hood over her shoulders before pulling on two soft gloves. She crossed the room and pulled open the doors leading to the balcony.

The fierce biting wind struck her with force, and she grimaced at the chill on her exposed cheeks. Stepping out onto the balcony, she tried to close the doors softly behind her, but they were torn from her grip and slammed shut.

It was freezing out on the balcony, but even so, Ella placed two gloved hands on the rail and looked out at the grand skyline of the Imperial capital Seranthia and the golden glow of the windows, which gave the city a softened beauty in darkness that it never had in light.

There were so many buildings pressed close together that it was difficult to encompass them all. Block-shaped structures clustered around her: the market houses of the other eight houses. Nearby, snowy gardens surrounded the manses of Fortune's wealthy merchants. A long line where the distant buildings ahead terminated could only signal the length of the Grand Boulevard. The Imperial Palace rose above it all, easily the highest structure around, dominating the city with its lofty size.

Seranthia was now so peaceful, but Ella feared the tranquility would soon be shattered by the coming darkness. In a way she'd come to love this city, a difficult place in many ways, where it was easy to feel like a stranger, yet filled with infinite variety. Rich and poor mingled together in Seranthia, even though the difference in their stations was greater here than anywhere else. Many of the city's inhabitants seemed to think of Seranthians as separate from Tingarans, and even the individual neighborhoods were renowned, with each projecting its own charisma and the citizens of each fiercely proud of the district they called home.

An emperor now lived in the Imperial Palace. Seranthia's pride had returned.

Time passed as Ella looked out at the city, her thoughts turning from one thing to another. If anything, it grew colder, and Ella fought to control a shiver. The message was vague about the time, so she didn't know if she was too early. Deciding to head back inside, at least for a while, she turned away, but then she caught a flicker of motion on a nearby building.

Ella frowned and tried to peer through the flurries of wind and snow. All she could see was a figure: a dark shadow.

Ella watched the figure, a man, climb from one roof to another, leaping and bounding with incredible agility. He ran and leapt from one building to the next, flying through the air for tense heartbeats before landing with catlike grace. A wide gap separated the Alturan market house from the surrounding buildings, but the figure didn't pause. He dashed forward and threw himself into the air.

Ella stiffened as she waited for him to plummet to his death, but at the end he hovered as if floating, coming to rest gently beside her on the balcony.

Seemingly impervious to the cold, Killian pulled back his hood and grinned. The night was clouded, but the shimmering lights of the city poured from countless windows to light up his face. His wild red hair, down to his collar, framed a strong masculine face with a sharp nose and square jaw. Ella couldn't help smiling when she saw the twinkle in his deep blue eyes.

"You couldn't use the front door?" Ella said.

Her heart rate increased. Killian had a way of looking at her that made her feel there was nothing else to rest his eyes on.

"Easier said than done. You have no idea how hard it is to get away," he said. "I have people by my side from the moment I wake to the last thing at night. Lords and ladies compete for the honor of having breakfast with me, and as for lunch and dinner . . ." He shook his head. "And then leaving the palace is a major event. There are the formalities. When the emperor travels to the Alturan market house, people speculate—particularly the Tingarans— that I'm showing preference to Altura. Every action is analyzed. I sometimes . . ."

"Shh," Ella said. "You look well." She smiled.

"I've missed you. First, the coronation, and now with just a few days to go until the Chorum . . ."

"I've missed you too," Ella said.

She drank in the sight of him. He wore a regal purple cloak with black trim, and underneath, his embroidered collared shirt was tucked into black trousers. A silver belt bore the image of a nine-pointed-star, matching the silver buckles on his black boots. She saw both sides of him: the boy he was and the man he had become.

"Ella?"

"Yes?"

"Can we not talk about the future tonight? I mean, I'm happy to talk about *our* future. I'd like to talk about our future. Just not the war. I mean . . ."

"I'd like that," Ella said. "I'd like that a lot."

The night passed as Ella and Killian talked about Alise, Killian's mother, and his joy at finally having the family he'd always searched for. Ella couldn't help but think of her own mother, Katherine.

"You're lucky you knew her," Killian said, "even if you didn't know who she was."

Ella found herself looking into Killian's eyes as they spoke, and they stood close together, so that Ella forgot all about the cold.

Without talking about the threat from across the sea, Ella told Killian how worried she was about her brother. Miro's zeal kept him up at night, the desperation in his eyes evident every time Ella saw him.

Killian listened as no one else did, and he took Ella's hands in his warm, comforting grip.

He then spoke about the things Evrin was teaching him. Killian had the powers of the Evermen, but Evrin had warned Killian that if he confronted Sentar Scythran, he would face the most dangerous opponent imaginable.

"Evrin says he doesn't have time to teach me everything so he's just concentrating on doing a few things well. I also have the knowledge from my time in Shar. I'm nearly ready," he said.

Ella was glad he'd brought up the subject of his unique abilities, for it gave her an opportunity to ask the question she'd been burning to have answered.

"Killian," Ella said, tilting her head to look up at his face. He looked just a couple of years older than she. "I need to ask you something, and I want you to tell me the truth. Evrin Evenstar and Sentar Scythran are both over a thousand years old. Will you live forever?"

"No one lives forever," Killian said with a wry smile.

"I'm being serious. Will you live for a long time, like Evrin?"

"I . . . I can't say. I honestly don't know."

"And I'll grow old and gray while you tire of me. Then you'll watch me die."

"Ella, please don't . . ."

"We'd be foolish not to speak of it."

"Not now. Not tonight. Let's just be together."

As the hours passed and the occasional star shone through the speeding clouds overhead, Ella felt her furred cloak struggle to hold off the night's chill.

Inside, her warm bedchamber beckoned.

As Ella made a decision, she felt her breath come short. She was going to invite Killian inside. They'd never been together. Not in that way.

Ella opened her mouth, and Killian suddenly looked up at the sky.

"Scratch it," he cursed, "I was supposed to be back in time to have dinner with the Council of Lords." He grinned sheepishly. "My mother will kill me."

"Do you have to go?" Ella asked.

"I can't tell you how much I want to stay," he said. Ella thought she saw his eyes flicker to the balcony doors.

But he sighed and drew away. It hit her with force; she didn't want him to leave. "Don't go." Ella pulled him close.

"I wish I could stay. Will you come and see me?"

"At the palace? Are you sure?"

Killian stroked Ella's cheek as he held her. "I'm sure."

"When?"

"The day after tomorrow. In the evening. We can have dinner, the two of us and my mother. She likes you, Ella."

Ella shook her head as she smiled. "She's only met me twice."

"Will you come?"

Killian tilted Ella's head, and they kissed.

Ella had kissed Killian back in Sarostar, in another time, when life was simpler, and no one knew about the darkness to come. This kiss sent a tingle through her lips as their two bodies fitted together perfectly, with his head at just the right height.

The kiss went on for a long time, but eventually Ella and Killian's lips parted.

"The day after tomorrow," Ella said. "In the evening."

"I'll wait for you," said Killian. "I promise."

Ella nodded. "I'll come," she said.

Killian spread his arms at his sides and chanted under his breath as he rose into the air.

And then he was gone.

Two days later, Ella arrived at the Imperial Palace in her best dress, a figure-hugging garment of soft yellow Alturan silk. She'd taken special care with her appearance, lining her eyes with the dark paste Shani used, chewing bitter peppermint for her breath, and selecting emerald jewelry to match her green eyes. She was glad for the cloak she wore over her snug dress; she'd had to pass dozens of guards to get to this point, and of course they were all men.

As the weather closed in and the howling wind scattered sleet through the air, Ella wished she had some easier method of communicating with Killian. Perhaps she could build some kind of signaling system for the two of them, she thought wryly.

She thought about their future together. As always, the thoughts filled her with both excitement and apprehension. She looked up at the grand façade of the Imperial Palace. How would she fit in here?

Ella wondered which of the several entrances to use and decided on the main gate. Killian hadn't mentioned another entrance, so the main entrance made the most sense. She wore no *raj hada* and had no guards with her. No one here knew who she was.

Ella ascended marble steps broad enough for a hundred men to walk forward together and not touch shoulders. The arched entrance loomed impossibly tall, the massive double doors closed to the weather. Ella spotted a small entry portal set into one of the doors and turned the handle.

Ella entered a cavernous hall and quickly closed the door behind her, mindful of the frowns the scurrying courtiers sent her way. She glanced around and wondered whom she should approach; all she could see were rushing officials and cushioned benches lining the walls. She'd come this way before, but she knew she couldn't just start scouting around for Killian.

"Yes?" a well-dressed man approached, looking down his long nose at Ella. His thin hair was combed over a bald patch on the top of his head. Ella didn't recognize him. "I'm Lord Osker, the emperor's steward. Can I direct you?"

"I'm here to see the emperor," Ella said.

"I see." Lord Osker looked Ella up and down. She regretted wearing emeralds now; they marked her out as Alturan. "What is your name, and what is it regarding?"

Ella flushed. She'd expected Killian or perhaps Lady Alise to be waiting for her. Should she tell Osker she'd been summoned for a private dinner with the emperor and his mother?

"I'm Enchantress Ella Torresante. The high lord of Altura is my brother. It's about a private matter. The emperor is expecting me."

"Of course," Lord Osker said. "Please make yourself comfortable." He indicated one of the benches.

Ella nodded and sat down.

———————

Lord Osker left shaking his head. Another Alturan who thought she could simply walk up and ask for the emperor, currently in a critical meeting with the new primate and running well over time.

Osker could have consulted the arrivals list but he had a knack for sensing a bold attempt to get an audience with the emperor. No doubt she was here to press her brother's demands for more essence for Altura. Osker had his own position on the matter, and those he gave his allegiance to required him to control the emperor, and always attain the best outcome for Tingara.

If Altura's high lord wanted more essence, he would have to press his case at the Imperial Chorum. Lord Osker knew from experience that if he kept a supplicant waiting long enough, he or she would eventually leave, and the problem would resolve itself.

One of Osker's small army of clerks and servants came hurrying forward. "My Lord, we have a problem. Rats are escaping the cold and coming into the cellars."

"Oh my," Lord Osker exclaimed.

He promptly forgot all about the Alturan girl, and scurried off with his man.

3

Ella had never seen so many garish costumes. Adjoining the Imperial Palace, the interior of the great hall set aside for the Imperial Chorum was a rainbow of color. There were so many symbols and designs that it was difficult to appreciate them all.

On the tiers surrounding the central podium, the contingents of the houses sat in sections of crimson, emerald, orange, and an array of other hues. Ranged along the walls, the *raj hadas* of the nine houses competed with each other. The addition of the withered tree of the Akari and the black sun of the templars meant there were eleven sections, and high on the ceiling, the nine-pointed star of the Empire spread across a huge flag of black silk.

Long ago, in this very room, Emperor Xenovere V announced the annexation of Torakon, precipitating the great war that shattered the old Tingaran Empire and led to the demise of Primate Melovar Aspen. Here, only a few weeks ago, the high lords crowned the new emperor, Killian Alderon.

Now it was time to hear about the new threat that High Lord Miro Torresante of Altura said was coming from across the sea.

Ella watched, her heart in her mouth, as Miro made his impassioned speech. She was shocked when some of the Tingarans,

Petryans, and Veznans hissed at his request for more essence for Altura.

Ella exchanged glances with Shani, a splash of red among the green of the Alturan section. The Petryan elementalist scowled. Seated on her other side she felt Amber, Miro's wife, tense, and Ella reached out to squeeze the hand of her childhood friend.

Miro, standing on the high disc-shaped podium that rotated infinitely slowly as he spoke, looked all alone.

Ella heard Amber whisper. "After everything he's done . . . everything we've seen."

Miro's arms fell at his sides at the end of his speech, and he left the podium. The new primate, a plump and soft-skinned old man who was as different from Melovar Aspen as two men could be, stepped up in his place and held out placating hands. He asked for a vote, and the leaders of the nine houses touched a tablet in front of them. With his own source of essence, the Dain of the Akari would abstain from this vote.

Ella felt her eyes burn as the response was overwhelming. Each house would have the same essence allocation, regardless of the scale of the perceived threat. Part of her knew it had been a foregone conclusion; yet even so, she felt disappointment. Miro had worked so hard to gain their support.

Then Ella frowned as she noticed the pattern of the voting. She made a quick calculation before coming to a realization. There was no denying the truth.

The emperor had voted against Miro.

Just a couple of days ago, Ella had left the Imperial Palace hurt and confused. Killian had invited her to dinner; yet every time she had tried to announce herself, she had been turned away. It was as if the officious Lord Osker had spread a warning to his staff. Ella had finally given up trying. If Killian wanted to see her, he could come to her.

Now Killian had just voted against helping Miro.

Miro returned to the podium, his shoulders slumped and defeated. He thanked the houses for responding to the current crisis. He then held up one of the shining reflectors and once more explained that the system was for the benefit of all the houses. Miro asked them to agree that if one of the houses called, the other houses would send help, and he vowed to do the same.

Then Miro cleared his throat. "I'm sure you've all heard my story now, and I won't tell it again. But please, I beg you, don't doubt my words. Speak with my wife, Amber, and the people of the once great nation of Veldria that I've brought here with me. Speak with my sister, Ella."

Ella saw the long-nosed Lord Osker sitting across the hall with the other Tingarans. Osker's head turned when he heard her name, and as their eyes met across the room, Ella fixed her best scowl on him.

"I didn't just meet Sentar Scythran," Miro said in a voice filled with emotion. "He held me captive. He . . . tortured me." Miro paused and then looked up, his gaze sweeping the hall from one side to the other. The resolve in his eyes was frightening. "This enemy thinks nothing of us. Nothing!" Miro almost spat. "He thinks himself a god and slaughters men, women, and children like cattle to feed his war machine. When we take an army to war, we must do everything we can to risk as few of our sons and daughters as possible. The self-styled Lord of the Night can throw away as many of his revenants as he likes. He doesn't care how many we grind into the dust, just as he doesn't care about his own followers, those who see that their own best chance of survival is to join with him."

Ella felt Amber's grip on her hand tighten and returned the clasp. Across the hall, some of the Tingarans had the decency to look down rather than meet Miro's eyes.

"He cares about one thing, and that is to restore the place of the Evermen at the top of the chain. The last time this happened, the Evermen made us their slaves. Long ago, we, the nations of the Empire, banded together and pooled our resources to throw off the shackles and be free. This time, the Evermen won't treat us as their slaves. The only humans walking Merralya will be the dead."

Ella let out a breath. Miro's depiction of the future was terrifying, and all the more so because she knew how likely it was. Sentar Scythran possessed incredible powers, and even with Evrin's training, Killian was young and inexperienced. Sentar possessed a ruthless determination and would by now have turned his revenant army to building ships as well as seizing vessels from the lands he'd conquered. Ella believed Miro when he said Sentar would come for Altura first.

Miro finished by saying that if anyone required further explanation on the reflectors and their use, to please speak with an enchanter at the Alturan market house. He again vowed to come if an ally called. This time his unspoken request for the other houses to make the same promise hung in the air as he stood down.

A Tingaran lord rose to the podium to speak. He expressed doubts about Miro's story and questioned the wisdom of the Imperial Legion answering the call of the Alturan devices, when the Alturan high lord himself stated that the Sentinel was the enemy's final goal.

After several more speeches, the Chorum was over.

As the horde of delegates dispersed out the various exits, Ella found herself outside the hall in the more spacious gallery, feeling the need for air. She saw a familiar face, someone who could help her, and called out.

"Rogan!"

Rogan Jarvish turned and smiled at Ella, though his smile was strained and didn't reach his eyes. His hair was entirely gray, the last vestiges of black vanished. The responsibilities of his time as lord regent and now as adviser to the emperor had aged Rogan where the strains of combat never had. He touched his lips and then his forehead in greeting—it would be inappropriate to do more—but his eyes were warm as he walked forward.

"Enchantress," Rogan said.

"Please, Rogan. I need to see Killian. He must convince the other houses to do more for Altura. The Legion is strong here in Seranthia, but Altura can't hold out alone. Halaran will help us, but Petrya and Vezna must do more."

Rogan paused and then nodded. "I'll see what I can do. This could be a good time; for once the Tingarans don't have him boxed up in the palace."

"Tell him I'll be up in the gallery." Ella pointed up at the second level. She could see a wide-open window, and there were no people around.

Rogan nodded and walked away. Taller than the men around him, he still cut a daunting figure. Miro said that even the Tingarans found it difficult to argue with Rogan's scarred face.

Ella walked up the steps and leaned out the window, inhaling slowly, a deep breath that filled her chest. From here she looked out on an expanse of manicured gardens, one of many between the palace's various subsections.

She heard a throat clear behind her, and even as she rehearsed the words she would say, Ella smoothed her expression and turned with a smile on her face. She drew back in surprise when she saw the man who stood facing her.

Ilathor Shanti, kalif of House Hazara, wore a costume both exotic and regal. His loose robe of black and yellow fell away at both sides, revealing a ceremonial dagger stuck into a golden belt. His hair was shorter than Ella remembered, and his sculpted beard was longer. He smiled at Ella, teeth white against his dark skin, but his burning eyes displayed emotion.

"Ella," Ilathor said, "I need to speak with you. Away from your brother, and away from all these other people."

"Please, not now," Ella said.

"Then when?" His brow furrowed, and his voice became firm. "When, Ella?"

"Another time."

"You have said that before, and this time I will not accept it." Ilathor shook his head, and then the anger went out of him, and he sighed. "Did you not receive my message? I have a proposition for you, if that is the correct word. I am kalif now, and I have brought my people to greatness. Agira Lahsa is becoming a city to rival any of the other houses. I can give you the life you deserve."

Ella covered her mouth. "Ilathor . . ."

"Ever since I met you, I have not been able to stop thinking about you. Even amid the madness of the war, you were at the forefront of my mind. I have seen you grow, and I am awed by everything you are and everything you do." Ella had never seen him like this; Ilathor was a stern man, and this confession must be costing him greatly.

"Since my father died," he continued, "I have been alone against the world. I need you. I can sense you find it hard to love, but love is a risk. The night we shared in Petrya . . . I have never experienced anything like it . . ."

Ella looked past Ilathor's shoulder and felt every vestige of blood drain from her face. A man in regal clothing stood behind the kalif of the desert tribes: Killian.

Ella had never seen the expression Killian now wore. The thief from Salvation had a thousand faces. Now she was seeing him raw.

"Is that true?" Killian asked. His eyes narrowed.

Anguish hit her with force, like a stone dropped into her stomach, plummeting through her chest, tearing at her insides.

Ilathor whirled as he heard Killian's voice. Ella couldn't register Ilathor's reaction; her eyes were on Killian's face.

"I will leave you two to talk," Ilathor said stiffly. He left without another word.

Ella opened her mouth and then closed it.

"Is it true?" Killian demanded. His face was close to hers. His expression was frightening.

"Why would you care?" Ella said. "You couldn't even make time to see me."

"My meeting ran over! It's true, isn't it?"

"How could you vote against my brother?"

"You're avoiding the issue."

"This is more important than us!"

Killian scowled. "What do you want from me? You want me to dedicate everything we have to Altura's defense? There's no guarantee they'll make landing there. It's the Sentinel he wants. I can't look after you. I have to worry about the needs of all the houses. That's what an emperor does. I can't be seen to favor one house over another." He shook his head, and his red locks tossed from side to side. "How could you? And now you're asking more of me?"

"You don't understand," Ella cried.

"You're right," Killian said. "I don't."

Miro found Ella sitting with Shani on the stairs in a secluded part of the gallery, their heads close together.

"Ella," he said softly.

Ella glanced up, and Miro saw that her eyes were red. "What is it?" she asked.

"Kalif Ilathor . . . he's spoken to me."

Ella raised her voice. "About what?"

Miro shrugged. "He wants my permission to ask for your hand."

Ella drew in a sharp breath. "And what did you say?"

Miro smiled. "What do you think I said? It's your decision to make."

"She doesn't love him," Shani said.

Miro nodded. "Ella, I have to ask something of you, though, and if that's the case, you aren't going to like it."

"What is it?" Shani demanded.

"Ilathor's sailing home to Agira Lahsa tomorrow. We have yet to connect Agira Lahsa through the desert to Wondhip Pass so they can be part of our signaling system." Miro turned his gaze on Shani. "I need Ella to go with Ilathor and see it done."

"Send someone else," Shani said flatly.

"I can't," Miro said. "Ella," he implored, "we are in desperate need of allies, and Ilathor is a proud man. Now isn't the time to refuse him. There's next to no chance Sentar will make landing in the desert, and we need the Hazarans to agree to come to our aid in Altura. I'm sorry to ask this of you, but I need you to ensure Ilathor's help. You have to go with him. You won't have to stay long—just long enough to build the station in Agira Lahsa and continue the chain north to Wondhip Pass. You'll also need to connect Tlaxor, Petrya's capital. Please, will you do it—for me?"

Shani frowned, but Ella nodded. "I understand. Of course I'll go."

"Thank you," Miro said.

"I don't want to spend any more time in Seranthia anyway."

4

Agira Lahsa, the hidden city, was hidden no more. Ella watched as it materialized out of the hazy desert sky, rising from the sands as the swift Buchalanti ship approached.

Ella had seen this city when it was little more than a series of blocks jutting out of the sand. Now the walls were complete, the great amphitheater rebuilt, bigger than any arena in Sarostar. An enormous archway with a tower on each side framed the paved road to the city's entrance, splitting as it left the city, with a fork heading down to the sturdy dock and a second road wandering out into the desert.

It was getting dark, and the palms that marked the low oases dotting the landscape around Agira Lahsa became silhouetted by crimson rays. The first stars appeared in the sky, and Ella breathed in the cool, dry air as she tilted her head back and looked up at the sky. Nowhere in Merralya, not even in the icy north, were there stars like those in the Hazara Desert. They pricked the night's curtain in ones and twos, and then in their hundreds. Soon a swath of constellations swept from one horizon to the other.

Ilathor joined Ella at the rail. "Beautiful, is it not?"

The six-week journey from Seranthia had been smooth, with fair weather and pleasant conversation. Ilathor never finished the proposal Killian's arrival had interrupted, and it hung in the air between them. Ella had departed Seranthia swiftly and didn't see Killian again.

If he'd tried to find out at all, Killian would know she'd left in Ilathor's company.

"Glorious," Ella said in response to Ilathor. She knew she couldn't do anything to endanger the kalif's help. If Altura called, the desert warriors' speed on horseback meant they would be able to respond to a distress call faster than anyone except the Alturans and Halrana who would already be there.

As the Buchalanti ship tied up at the dock, Ella again examined Agira Lahsa, awed at how much it had changed since the last time she'd seen it. Spires and minarets clustered around a series of domes, structures as exotic as the desert men themselves. She squinted against the failing light and saw a band of riders coming down from the city gate, all the figures perfectly spaced from one another.

The riders sped down to the dock and drew up, the group halting as a single Hazaran rode forward. He drew his scimitar and held it in the air in salute. Ella smiled when she saw his lean form and long black hair, the ship's lights glinting from the silver circlet at his brow.

"Jehral! Come aboard, you rogue!" Ilathor called. Ella saw the warmth in his eyes that she only saw when he was with his most loyal aide.

Jehral slipped gracefully off his horse and was first up the gangway as the ship made fast and the Buchalanti sailmaster called out instructions for unloading.

Jehral embraced Ilathor and then Ella. "It's good to see you, Enchantress," he said.

"You too, Jehral."

Ella saw Jehral shoot a look of inquiry at Ilathor, who shook his head imperceptibly. "Ella is here to build a new signaling system the Alturans have devised," the kalif said.

"Your presence here is most welcome." Jehral bowed with a flourish. "Shall I call a palanquin?"

"A horse is fine with me."

"Always one to do anything a man can do," Jehral said, grinning. "You've been missed, Ella."

They soon disembarked, Ilathor leading the column up the road, passing between the towers and heading into the city, raising his arm and waving as Hazaran men and women called out and bowed as he rode past. Ella smiled and shook her head. She couldn't help but wonder whether Killian accepted the same treatment. Killian was the emperor and had the powers of the Evermen, but somehow Ella couldn't picture Killian smiling as people bowed down to him.

The column of riders headed directly for Ilathor's new palace, through a series of grand arches to a sandy circular area with a central fountain. Grooms ran forward to hold their horses' halters. Ilathor leapt down and crouched to kiss the floor at his feet. "I have returned!"

Ella exchanged glances with Jehral, who was grinning from ear to ear. "Come, Ella," he finally said. "I'm sure you are tired from your long journey. Follow me."

Broad steps led up through more arches to an expansive area of stone, the columns spaced far apart and rugged desert palms lit up by torches on the far walls. Ilathor's new palace was as grand as the Crystal Palace but infinitely different, made to gain maximum exposure to breezes, with gardens and fountains in the center and mezzanine levels at all sides.

Passing a column, Ella's mouth dropped open when she saw the marble inlaid with precious stones: turquoise, amber, obsidian, and rose quartz. Shining silk carpets lined the inner squares. The spilling water in the fountains could only be powered by Louan lore. It all must have cost a fortune.

Ilathor's eyes sparkled when he saw Ella's reaction. "Ella, I must leave you now," he said. "My tarn leaders and I have much to discuss; they will be anxious to hear about the Imperial Chorum." He hesitated. "Please, will you think on what I've said?"

The kalif departed with a flourish, and Jehral touched Ella's shoulder. "Enchantress Ella, I would like you to meet my sister, Zohra."

A young woman came forward to stand by Jehral's shoulder. Her hair was a rich, deep black and her eyes had the smoky amber color Ella had only seen among the Hazarans and some of the Veldrins. Zohra was as lean as Jehral but blossomed with youth, and Ella felt suddenly self-conscious, knowing she was travel stained and pale skinned when compared with Zohra's flawless olive complexion. Zohra had high cheekbones and a wide, full-lipped mouth, but it was her eyes that were striking. Ella knew men would fall for those eyes.

Ella smiled, keen to make a favorable impression on Jehral's sister. "It is a pleasure." Ella bowed and touched her fingers to her heart, lips, and forehead, but it was clumsy compared with Zohra's graceful curtsy.

"Enchantress," Zohra said, "you must be weary from your journey, and I am sure you wish to get out of those clothes. Chambers have been prepared. Please come."

"I will see you later," Jehral whispered.

Zohra led Ella up some stairs to a set of chambers at the side of the first mezzanine level. True to the rest of Ilathor's palace, Ella's chambers were beyond even those she'd seen in the Imperial Palace in Seranthia, with an antechamber, a receiving room, a dining area, a dressing chamber, a bedchamber, and two baths.

"Jehral has told me of you many times," Zohra said. "He is very fond of you."

"And I, him," Ella said.

"Kalif Ilathor Shanti is also very fond of you."

"I am flattered by the kalif's attention," Ella said, uncertain what else to say. "I didn't meet you the last time I was in Agira Lahsa . . . ?"

"I am young," Zohra said, with a small smile and a shrug. "I have only just reached my nineteenth birthday. Among my people, an unmarried woman of rank is kept from the men until this age, when we are allowed to serve the men. Already some have asked my brother for my hand."

On uncertain ground, Ella said, "Are there any among them you care for?"

"No," Zohra said, "and Jehral will not force my hand. For that, I love him. Here are your chambers. Rest tonight and tomorrow. Tomorrow, in the early evening, there will be a banquet."

Ella touched Zohra's arm. "I've come here to do something important and it can't wait. I'd be honored to join you at the banquet after I'm done, however."

Zohra shrugged. "As you wish," she said.

The next morning, Ella woke tired, yet anxious to leave Agira Lahsa and make her way to Altura. There was so much work to do there, yet Miro had her far from her home, doing something any enchanter could do.

Ella dressed in a plain, functional dress and roamed the palace until a steward found her and asked if he could help. Ella felt relief when he fetched Jehral, who strode up to Ella with a smile on his face.

"Eager to get to work, Enchantress?" he said, noting the satchel at her shoulder.

"I don't have much time here," Ella said apologetically. "I have to get back to Sarostar."

"Don't worry, I understand. What do you need?"

"Do you have a high point in the palace? Somewhere with a commanding view of the desert? Perhaps a lookout or a watch tower?"

Jehral nodded. "The astronomical observatory. It is the perfect place. I can show it to you. What else do you require?"

"At least two of your elders. I have to explain to them how the lore functions."

"Of course." Jehral clicked his fingers, and a steward came scurrying forward. "Please show the enchantress where to find the observatory. Ella, I must get back to discussions with the kalif, but I'll make sure the elders find you. Rest assured, we know how important this is."

"Thank you," Ella said. "I don't know what I'd do without you."

"You would achieve your task, with or without me," Jehral said. As he walked away he turned and looked over his shoulder and grinned. "You always do."

The steward led Ella up a winding windowless staircase to the observatory, the tallest tower in the palace. It was open to the sky on all sides but covered with a domed ceiling, a wide slit in the dome showing a strip of blue sky. As Jehral said, it was perfect.

Ella was relieved. She knew her work would progress much faster without having to construct a tower: the lore depended on a fair line of sight. She took a pyramid of quartz from her workbag: a primary reflector that could be activated rather than a link in the chain. Ella then removed essence, gloves, and a scrill for fusing the reflector in place, and set to work.

The observatory was lit on all sides by the fierce afternoon sun by the time Ella was finished and had completed her tests. The Hazaran elders—the keepers of their lore—were quick to grasp the way the reflectors functioned. At any rate, they would only need to know the activation sequences to call for help. If another house called, the color that sparked within the pyramid-shaped prism would say enough.

With a relieved sigh, Ella thanked the elders and put her tools away as they left.

Only then did she remember the banquet.

"Scratch it," Ella said under her breath. She was playing two roles at once: enchantress and diplomat. She couldn't let one suffer for the other.

Another steward encountered Ella at the bottom of the steps leading down from the observatory tower. "Ah, Enchantress, we've been looking for you. The kalif awaits your presence."

Ella groaned and glanced down at her plain clothing. With a sigh, she followed the steward through the palace to a raised terrace overlooking the bustling city below. Even from this height Ella could hear the cries of the hawkers in the streets, though the sound was partly drowned by men's laughter and the clinking of plates and glasses. She wished she wasn't late; all eyes would be on her.

A long banquet table stretched to fill the terrace. Servants poured red wine and whirled away with empty dishes. As she approached from behind, Ella saw Ilathor's broad back while Jehral sat at his right hand. On Jehral's other side a woman turned and Ella caught Zohra's eyes on her. Ella smiled in greeting, but Zohra didn't smile back.

The steward indicated the empty seat at Ilathor's left hand. Evidently this was where Ella was supposed to sit.

Ilathor and Jehral stood as they noticed Ella's arrival, and she blushed when the rest of the Hazaran men followed suit.

Seeing their elaborate costumes, with the men looking regal in black and yellow silk and the women beautiful in sweeping pale dresses, Ella wished she'd taken the time to return to her chambers to change, even at the risk of being further late. Here she was, hot and sweating, coming straight from the endless observatory steps.

"May I present Ella Torresante of Altura, the sister of the high lord and an Academy-trained enchantress," the kalif said. "We owe her everything, for she helped us regain our lore and take back our rightful place among the houses. We owe our conquest of Petrya to Ella, and I ask that everyone make her welcome."

Ella smiled, feeling her cheeks flush as she took the seat proffered to her while the men resumed their places. The kalif rattled off a series of introductions, with Ella nodding so many times she felt like a puppet on strings, knowing she would never remember any of the names.

The man to her left, a heavyset tarn leader with curled moustaches, spoke as if resuming a heated discussion. "As I said, Kalif, we have finally achieved stability. If this force comes from across the sea, what use would they have for the desert?" He turned to Ella. "Perhaps, Enchantress, you could shed light for us?"

"Saran, please," Ilathor smiled, "leave her alone. This is supposed to be a banquet."

"No," another man spoke. "I want to hear what she has to say." Ilathor sighed wearily and nodded to Ella.

Ella chose her words carefully, thinking of reasoning these practical men would understand. She'd evidently arrived at an important time. "First, let me ask you a question," she addressed Saran, the man on her left. "Are you entirely self-sufficient in the desert?"

"Well," Saran harrumphed, "not entirely. We mine gold, and gold buys much."

"As I understand it a lot of your trade comes from the free cities," Ella said. "My brother, the high lord, doesn't believe Castlemere and Schalberg *might* fall. He believes they will undoubtedly fall."

Silence followed Ella's assertion. Finally Saran spoke again.

"That is one man's opinion. The Empire is strong."

"No." Ella shook her head. She felt heat rise to her face. "The Empire is weak. We're too fractured to pool our strength and deploy it where it's most needed. Without your aid, Altura will fall, and if Altura falls, the rest of the Empire will follow. Without trade, your people will starve, this city will crumble, and you'll go back to being a splintered group of tribes. Eventually, you'll be hunted down, and even if your people are the last to perish, your days will be numbered."

Zohra gasped, and the other men and women at the table looked uncomfortable. Ella hadn't meant to be so direct, but seeing these men feast and talk when she knew how much work had to be done in Altura upset her. Agira Lahsa didn't look like a city preparing for war.

"I don't see how you can be so certain . . ."

Ella stood up from her chair. "Please excuse me," she said. "I have work to do."

Ella left the terrace and tried to calm herself as she looked for somewhere she could be alone. Ilathor found her with her hands resting on the rail of a small balcony, gazing out at the desert and inhaling the spicy scent of the city carried forward on the dry breeze.

"Ella?" Ilathor said.

Ella turned to the kalif, and rather than avoid him, this time she met his eyes directly. "Ilathor," she said, using his first name, "can I count on you if Altura calls?"

"Yes . . . of course. I am the kalif. My men will follow."

"Will you promise?"

Ilathor reached forward and took Ella's hands. "I promise."

"Thank you," Ella said, letting out a breath. She leaned forward and kissed his smooth cheek.

Ilathor suddenly put his arm around her waist and pulled her close to him.

Ella put her hands flat on his chest. "Ilathor," she said. "Ilathor! I can't. I must go. You love your land with an incredible passion. I feel the same way about mine. I can't feast here when I know how much needs to be done to protect my homeland. I have to go."

"I understand," Ilathor said. He was breathing hard. "You are a strong woman, and you are resisting your passions, where I cannot. I should take note from your example."

Ella chose to ignore the comment. "Your elders know all they need to about the reflectors. Listen to them. I have a long journey ahead of me. It will take time to build the towers and mount the reflectors as I travel back to Altura."

"Of course," Ilathor said. "When you arrive home, will you send word?"

"I will."

"Ella, I . . ."

"I know," Ella said, smiling.

Ilathor returned her smile. "I will send Jehral to take care of you until you reach Alturan lands. I wish you did not have to leave so soon after arriving, but I understand. Fare you well, Ella. Until we next meet."

"Farewell, Kalif," Ella said.

5

Killian wiped at his eyes, feeling the familiar onset of fatigue. He avoided looking at the timepiece high on the wall; he knew the afternoon meeting had run well into the night.

He still wore the thick clothing he'd worn all season. Though it was supposed to be spring, winter was reluctant to release Tingara quite yet. The wind howled outside the barred windows, and Killian heard the shutters tremble.

The grim weather echoed his mood. Several weeks had passed since the Imperial Chorum and Ella's hasty departure, yet still Killian couldn't get the events of that day out of his mind. Killian had expected Miro's impassioned plea for more essence for Altura to fail. He hadn't expected to discover that Ella and Ilathor had once shared a bed.

Killian was jealous.

She acted like she loved him, but he knew there was something between her and the kalif, and even when Killian innocuously brought up Ilathor in conversation with her, she never explained a thing.

He now sat in the war rooms, high in the Imperial Palace, his palms resting on the rune-covered surface of a simulator. Rogan was speaking in his deep, rumbling voice—something about the Imperial Legion.

He needed to concentrate. He knew how important these discussions were.

But Killian couldn't stop thinking about Ella.

He'd seen it in her eyes; the ruler of the desert had been speaking the truth. Did she love Ilathor? He cast his mind back to the chamber inside the Sentinel, on the day of the primate's death, when she'd entered with Ilathor by her side. He'd seen the protective way the handsome Hazaran held her back from danger.

Ella had risked everything to bring Killian home from the wasteland that was Shar, and he'd thought that what was between them was powerful enough to keep them together through any adversity. Killian had thought Ella loved him.

Yet Ella left the day after the Chorum without a word of explanation. She'd left in the same ship as the kalif of House Hazara.

"You're far away," Rogan said. "Am I boring you?"

"No, I'm sorry," Killian said, returning his gaze to the simulator as he realized he'd been staring at the wall. "There's something on my mind."

"Well set your mind on this. As I was saying, the signaling system is a good idea, but it doesn't change one key fact. If Altura calls, you're going to have to make a choice. Do you head for the west, leaving Seranthia exposed? Or do you leave Altura to her fate?"

"What should I do?"

"You can't leave us defenseless," said Marshal Trask, a staunchly loyal Tingaran.

"Either way," Rogan said, "you should prepare your strategy before the moment itself comes."

"I'll think about it," Killian said. "Please leave me now."

The marshals swiftly bowed and departed, leaving Killian alone in the room. He looked down at the simulator in disgust; he knew the map in every detail. He knew how his men were deployed and the travel times from one place to another. He didn't need further reminding.

Deciding to find a place where he could be alone with his thoughts, Killian deactivated the simulator and left the war rooms.

He climbed a staircase and entered an empty sitting room with antique cushioned sofas and low tables. Looking at the furniture, he wondered how previous generations had managed to seat themselves on something so uncomfortable. Killian found the balcony doors and pulled them wide. Heedless of the biting wind tearing at his clothing, he stepped out and gazed at his city.

From his vantage, Killian could see the common people below as they passed through Imperial Square. They all deserved his protection. Could he leave them exposed? He knew Sentar Scythran would come for Seranthia, even if it was just to remove the city as an obstacle as he entered the Sentinel and opened the way to Shar. It was an outcome Killian had to do everything in his power to avoid.

But Killian also knew that if Altura called, Ella would be in the thick of the fighting, and she would be battling revenants. How could he abandon her homeland to its fate? Even if Ella managed to survive, he knew she would never forgive him.

Additionally, if the enemy gained a foothold in Altura, their numbers would swell in size, like a plague of locusts feasting on the fields at harvest time. Killian had faith in Miro, but surely Altura couldn't hold out alone?

Were his feelings for Ella clouding his judgment?

Perhaps he could split his forces if Altura called, as Miro seemed to think was certain. Would a smaller force be enough?

Killian looked down at his hands, the silver symbols decorating the palms only barely visible in the low light of Seranthia at night. Who would challenge Sentar, if not Killian? Staying in Seranthia and sending someone else to the west—say, Rogan Jarvish—even with the majority of the Legion, still might not turn the tide.

Killian's heart told him the future of the Empire would come down to a battle between Sentar and himself.

He wished Evrin Evenstar wasn't leaving. Evrin wasn't aligned to any particular house, and the old man was perhaps the only one Killian could trust for impartial advice. Evrin was wise, and he'd seen and experienced things Killian struggled to imagine.

But Evrin was now leaving for Altura. Like everyone else, Evrin didn't know if Sentar Scythran would choose to land at Altura, the shortest journey from the new world to the Empire, or travel by ship to Seranthia, his ultimate destination.

Evrin was helping both Tingara and Altura, and Killian wished he could do the same. He had a duty to protect all of the Empire, not just Tingara. If Altura called, what would he do?

Sighing, Killian looked down from the balcony, deciding to watch the people for a while longer. He stood and let the wind buffet him, as if it could scour his mind and bring clarity to his thoughts. He rested his eyes on various folk and wondered where they were going and what their business was. He followed a Halrana merchant sitting atop a drudge-pulled cart and calling out to clear passage through the square. He next settled on a group of revelers, soldiers most likely from the way they walked, though they wore street clothes.

Killian's gaze settled on a solitary woman standing outside the iron-barred fence that separated the grounds of the palace from the square.

He realized she hadn't moved the whole time he'd been watching. What was she doing, standing out in the cold? Was she waiting for someone?

He wondered who she was. Her cloak looked to be of decent quality, though unembroidered and without decoration, evidently not expensive. It didn't have a hood, and though it wasn't snowing, the wind blew her raven-black hair in a wild tangle about her face. The white skin of her oval face gave way to a sharp nose.

She tilted her head, scanning the upper windows of the palace, and Killian saw that she seemed expectant. Was she waiting for someone from the palace to go out and fetch her? Why didn't she talk to the guards?

She turned slightly and Killian could now see her more clearly.

His blood ran cold when he saw her face.

Killian gripped the rail tightly. His breath caught as he peered down at her face; she hadn't seen him, but he could see her clearly.

He felt his heart rate increase to a thundering gallop.

Killian bolted from the chamber, dashing down the steps that would take him on the fastest route to the main palace entrance. He threw himself down the passageways and servants' corridors, knocking stewards and courtiers out of the way, ignoring their questioning looks and hasty following bows as they realized who he was.

Killian reached the heavy doors at the main entrance and heaved them open with all the rune-enhanced strength in his limbs. The wind poured through the sudden opening with force, sending the palace staff scurrying as papers flew everywhere.

The guards outside—Tingara's elite—brought their pole-arms crashing down, and Killian went through them as if they weren't there, the sharp steel barely registering on his forearms.

The guards shouted, uncertain what to do. Was the emperor under attack? They scanned all directions in alarm, but they couldn't perceive any threat.

Killian ran for the iron fence and gripped the bars with white knuckles. He stared into the face he hadn't seen in an eternity as the blood throbbed in his veins. His breath came short, and without realizing, the iron bent and twisted in his hands as he examined every aspect of her visage.

"It's you," Killian breathed.

Remembrance thrust his consciousness back in time, to a time when he'd been happy, truly happy, for the first time in his life.

***

The show was over, and tomorrow there would be another, so the circus tent was left standing, the seating gallery erected, the trapeze swinging high, the animals fed, their cages scrubbed. And as usual, Marney was already worrying about tomorrow night's routine, rehearsing in his head every last detail of the performance they'd given a thousand times.

It was the perfect opportunity for Killian and Carla to get away.

He held her hand as they ran through fields of summer flowers while stars sparkled overhead. The encampment was just outside Seranthia, a ten-minute walk from the wide road that led from Seranthia to Salvation. Marney had chosen the place well; though the long grass was dry, there was fresh water for the animals nearby as well as thickets of trees for fires and hunting.

Killian wanted to see one of the night shows he'd heard Jak the mime talk about. He raced across the fields, his lover's hand held firmly in his own, bounding over the uneven ground, feeling his limbs burn with the fire of youth.

Carla laughed beside him and pulled him up. "Slow down! We'll trip up in a rabbit hole."

The bright night was lit up by scattered stars and a full moon. Killian glanced at Carla, seeing her raven-black hair glow, her teeth shining white against her skin, and he grinned. "Can't you smell the rabbits out?"

"Nothing to smell. They'll run when they see the light cast by the human torch."

Killian laughed. He and Carla teased each other endlessly about their most striking feature: her long nose and his wild red hair.

"Come on," Killian said. "Hurry up! We'll miss the shows."

"I'm hurrying!"

"You run like a girl." Killian grinned.

"You'd rather I ran like a man?" Carla followed the comment with a fist-pumping, grimacing run, like an athlete at the Imperial Games.

"I prefer it when you walk," Killian said. "Particularly if I'm standing behind you, where the view is best. Actually, when I'm holding you on the trapeze . . ."

Carla pulled him up short and yanked her arm from his, placing both hands on her hips. "That's enough from you. I'll face you when I walk."

She came at him with solid, lumbering steps, like an animal tamer intimidating his beast—she was an excellent mimic—and held a finger up at Killian's chin. He realized the finger was a distraction only when she hooked a leg behind his and pushed forward so that they both fell down.

Carla was now on top of Killian's chest, looking down at him, their faces close together.

"And this is how I like you," she said.

Carla leaned down and brushed her lips across his, sending fire through his chest and deep into his stomach. Her long hair tickled his face as it brushed across his skin.

"The night's warm," Carla breathed as she leaned in to kiss him. Killian felt her hands on his belt. "Seranthia can wait."

The night passed like a dream.

The two lovers returned from Seranthia with less energy than they'd left with, strolling rather than running, but laughing just as much. It was late, nearly dawn, and Marney Beldara, Carla's father, would be angry, but Killian didn't care, and neither did Carla. Marney was as much of a father to Killian as he was to her, and Killian knew he had a bright future with the troupe.

Nevertheless, Killian and Carla hurried along the stretch of road leading back to the camp. Killian was partway through a joke he'd heard from the fire-eater twins when Carla suddenly grabbed Killian's hand and pulled him off the road.

"What . . .?"

"Shh," Carla said, hauling him far from the road as she pointed. "Look."

A large column of men marched back in the direction of Seranthia. Carla pulled harder on Killian's hand and began to run, continuing until they were out in the fields, and then she made Killian lie beside her on the ground.

"Shh," she said. "Don't make a sound."

Killian felt her tense beside him. He started to wonder what such a large group of men were doing out so late at night.

The sound of heavy boots grew louder, and Killian saw they were Tingaran legionnaires: strong, terrifying men with shaved heads and sharp weapons.

There was something strange about them. As they passed the place where Killian and Carla lay in hiding, Killian saw their faces were covered in soot.

He made to stand, but Carla pulled him back down.

"Something might be wrong," Killian hissed to Carla. "There could be a fire. They might need our help."

"Do not let them see you," Carla whispered. "Why would legionnaires be fighting a fire in the middle of the night? Perhaps in the city—but out here?"

Killian watched them go with a puzzled expression on his face. He'd heard rumors of the emperor's growing madness. He hoped no one was hurt.

"We'll stay off the road from now on," Carla said.

As they walked through the fields, Killian decided to wake Marney and tell him what they'd seen. Marney would be angry, but he'd know what to do, and they could see if anyone needed help.

It would soon be light, and the first rays of dawn crept into the sky, revealing the hills and grassy fields with the trees just behind. The camp was just ahead.

Killian smelled smoke.

Carla grabbed Killian's arm, pinching his shoulder with sharp fingers.

"No, Lord of the Earth, no," she moaned.

The radiant dawn revealed a plume of dark smoke ahead.

The next hours were a blur for Killian, and even when he tried to remember what happened next, he couldn't. He later reasoned that perhaps his consciousness had removed the worst of the memories, though fragments still remained.

He remembered running through the field and roaring, screaming like a man running into his first battle. The fire had swept through the dry plain, though swords and pikes had also done grisly work.

His two strongest surviving memories were finding the animals burned to death in their cages, and an old woman—to this day Killian had no idea who she was—telling him someone from the crowd had reported Marney for spreading sedition against the emperor. Killian could only remember Marney saying something about helping Seranthia's street urchins.

Killian and Carla didn't find Marney's body, or the fire-eater twins, or Jak the mime and several others. They raced back to Seranthia, arriving outside the Wall just in time.

The emperor's men had them lined up on top of the Wall.

Killian saw they'd been cut by the whip, Marney worst of all. He remembered Carla sobbing beside him, and then Killian's colleagues—his family—were pushed.

Marney was last, and Killian could swear their eyes met, and then the only man who'd ever been kind to him fell from the impossible height. Like the others, his body made a little puff of dust when he hit the ground.

It was the last time Killian saw Carla. He didn't know if he helped her in her grief, or was too stricken himself to be of any use. The memories simply weren't there. He knew he'd carried the bodies back to the forest and spent days burying them all, even the animals.

Killian never sought Carla out. He went back to Salvation.

And there he met Primate Melovar Aspen and heard about a plan to end the emperor's rule.

———————

Killian forced himself to let go of the iron bars as the memories came rushing back. He now stared at her; she'd changed, but then he supposed so had he.

"Hello, Killian," Carla said with the same lopsided grin she always had.

"Hello, Carla," Killian whispered.

"Are you going to invite me into your palace?"

The rushing guards finally caught up to Killian. "Open the gate," he ordered.

The iron drew apart, and Carla stepped through.

Killian's lost love had returned.

6

Flurries of frigid air dashed themselves against the window, almost causing Miro to flinch, as if some ghostly enemy rattled at the glass. He wondered when this cursed cold weather would end: warmth would make things much more difficult for a revenant army.

Unfortunately, Tingara's cold spell had carried through Torakon and the Azure Plains, to Mara Maya and even all the way to Ralanast. Winter was reluctant to give way to spring. Miro and Amber's journey overland from Seranthia to Ralanast had been an ordeal of constant shivering.

As he paced the length of High Lord Tiesto Telmarran's private dining hall in Rialan Palace, home of the Halrana high lord, Miro wondered what had transpired back in Sarostar and the free cities in his absence. He'd left people back home he could count on: Amelia, Bartolo, and Deniz, to name a few. But he itched to get back home to Altura. He'd scanned the missives from Sarostar, but there was still no word of the enemy. Even so, no message was instantaneous, not with the signal towers still being built. Miro could only hope the enemy had yet to be sighted.

He was basing so much on hope.

Miro clenched and unclenched his fists as he thought about Ella, wondering if she'd arrived in Agira Lahsa. He hoped she was safe.

He hated having to use the people close to him, but whom else could he trust?

And with his arrival in Ralanast, he was now about to give Amber an impossible task, when all she wanted was to go home to their son, Tomas, currently being looked after by Rogan's wife, Amelia. With Amber gone, Miro knew he would feel like he was missing a limb.

Miro's pacing took him back to the window, and once more he looked through the glass, seeing Ralanast, capital of Halaran, spread out before his eyes, stretching in all directions. His eye was drawn to the magnificent Terra Cathedral, and he remembered spending his first night with Amber near the great dome, after the liberation of Ralanast.

Lord of the Sky, that felt like an eon ago.

Miro glanced at Tiesto. He would once have described the Halrana high lord as fresh faced, though his frequent worried expression made him look older than he was. Yet Tiesto had grown into his position and looked every inch a high lord. Perhaps it was that Tiesto's worried face had grown tighter still.

"I fear it won't be long now," Miro said to Tiesto. "It will have taken Sentar Scythran time to gather the essence he needs, and the ships, but he's in a hurry. Are your constructs ready? And your men?"

"I'd like another week . . ."

"We might not have another week."

"I realize that, Miro, but . . ."

"We need you now!" Miro glared.

Tiesto flinched as if Miro had punched him.

Miro dropped his gaze. "My apologies, High Lord. My plea at the Chorum was an utter failure. We still have many cities to connect to the signaling system, including Sarostar itself. No one will pledge assistance. I wonder if the essence cost to build the system is worth it at all."

"We voted for you," Tiesto said. "But they think it's more fair . . ."

"Fair?" Miro's tone was bitter. "What's not fair is that Loua Louna is protected on all sides. Vezna is protected by us. Yet if we fall, so will they."

"I'm sorry," Tiesto said.

Miro sighed. "No, Tiesto. I should apologize. You've supported us every step of the way. I've heard the rumors; some of them say I've invented all this. It doesn't matter what we did in the war against the primate."

"A few stupid people . . ."

"Yes, but some of those people have power." Miro tried to force himself to relax. "How soon can your forces be ready? Please give me some good news."

"Is anyone ever ready? You know better than anyone that war takes time and is as much about logistics as brave hearts. The best I can give you is two days."

Miro breathed with relief. "Two days?"

"In two days we'll take the bulk of our constructs and fighting men to Altura. I'll give the order tonight."

Miro turned to Tiesto and spoke with sincerity. "High Lord, thank you. With the other houses worrying only about themselves, I can't tell you how much I appreciate your support."

"My people owe you an eternal debt. We'll fight with you to the end."

"I just hope that isn't what happens," Miro muttered.

He wiped a hand over his face, feeling a level of tiredness he'd never felt before, not even in the last war—and the real struggle hadn't even started yet.

"The Veznans will appreciate you sending your wife. It's a strong statement," Tiesto said.

"Yes, but will they promise aid?"

"We can only hope."

Miro pondered. Amber would soon leave to connect Rosarva, the Veznan capital, to the signaling system, with her most important objective being to convince the isolationist Veznans to support whoever called.

Whoever called.

Miro was the only man in the Empire who'd spoken to Sentai Scythran at length. While in the lands across the sea, he'd been captured and beaten, and he'd heard the Lord of the Night's plans.

He knew it was going to be Altura.

Back in Seranthia, Ella's friend Shani had promised to do her best to convince Petrya to help, but Miro had heard the apprehension in the elementalist's voice. The war was over, wasn't it? No one wanted to think about a new one.

"He's coming," Miro whispered.

"What did you say, High Lord?" Tiesto asked.

"I said he's coming," Miro said. "It won't be long now."

"High Lord, can I give you some advice, much as you won't appreciate hearing it?"

Miro smiled wryly. "Go on."

"Get some rest. We've gone through the plans a dozen times. You're desperate to get back to Altura, I can see, but unless you have a few horses from the desert tucked away, you can't run all that way. We're in constant communication, and we'd have heard if a fleet had been sighted. Let tomorrow worry about tomorrow."

Miro grinned, realizing he was getting advice about worrying from Tiesto Telmarran. "Thank you, High Lord. I'll take your advice in the spirit it was given. What time is it?"

"Four hours before dawn."

"Perfect." Miro smiled. "I thank you for your hospitality. A warm bed and a good Halrana meal in my belly. A solid night's rest for once. We'll leave at dawn, and I'll see you in Sarostar."

———◆———

Ella and Jehral drew up as they reached the heights just below Wondhip Pass. Behind them, harnesses jingled and the swarthy men who made up Jehral's guard called out to one another.

The air was dry and cool up here, high in the mountains, and the view, all encompassing. In the north, Ella could now see glimpses of the forests and farmland of Altura. Behind the company of guards, to the south, the rugged red land of Petrya gave way to the yellow expanse of the Hazara desert. To the east, the peaks of the Elmas formed an indomitable barrier, stretching as far as the eye could see. Looking westward, the blue ocean filled her vision, as unbroken and unchanging as the sky.

"We're nearly there," Ella said. "It's not much farther."

Jehral grunted as he kicked his gelding forward, but this final leg to Wondhip Pass, the precarious route connecting Altura and Halaran to Petrya and the Hazara Desert, was treacherous and strewn with loose rubble.

"I'm going to have to dismount," Jehral said. "Your horse might be able to keep going, but Burin here does not like carrying my weight while rolling around on the rocks."

"Yet another thing women are better at," Ella said, grinning. "We're lighter and make better riders."

"You sound like my sister," Jehral said. "She also insists on riding like a man." Jehral slipped off his horse as he called back to the company of desert men. "Dismount!"

As she waited for the Hazarans, Ella looked back the way they'd come. They'd covered an incredible distance in the past weeks; horses gave the Hazarans a decisive advantage when it came to travel. Ella had now built her towers in a long line from Agira Lahsa through the desert, keeping each in sight of the next but able to space them far apart because of the lack of intervening trees and mountains.

Making a detour east, she'd also connected the Petryan capital, Tlaxor, to the chain, and when she built this final station high in the Elmas, at Wondhip Pass, Jehral would return home, having escorted Ella to Altura's border. Ella's task with the reflectors was nearly done.

Ella wished she could have spent longer with Shani in Tlaxor, but she was still pleased to have been able to see her friend. Shani was doing all she could to convince the Petryan high lord to promise aid. Shani seemed determined, but not hopeful.

Ella patted the letter she carried in a pocket of her dress, for Bartolo, currently training soldiers at the Pens in Sarostar, from his wife. Ella knew Shani was sad that the two of them were apart. They regularly traveled back and forth, but both had strong ties with their homelands. She wondered if they'd ever choose to live together in either Altura or Petrya.

Jehral and his troops now led their horses by the reins as they picked their way over the rocks, and the company's journey into the mountain pass continued. Soon the path leveled off to enter a cleft in the rock, with high walls rising on both sides. Ahead Ella saw more of the green land to the north revealed in the view. Drinking in the sight of the emerald forests and blue ribbons of the Sarsen's tributaries, she felt an intense longing to return to her homeland. Turning and checking her position, she made sure she could still see the red earth of Petrya behind her.

She was at the absolute middle of the pass.

"This is the place," Ella said.

Jehral nodded and ordered his men turned out in a defensive formation. Ella reached into her satchel and removed three thin rods, as thick as her wrist and as long as her arm, placing them on the ground.

She reached into her bag again and took out one of the triangular prisms. Keeping the reflector covered by her body, Ella whispered a series of activation sequences and watched with satisfaction as the prism cycled through one hue after another. When her tests were complete, she took out a triangular piece of flat metal and fitted each of the rods into holes on the corners of the steel base.

Ella placed the pyramid-shaped prism on top of the metal triangle. The prism now stood on three legs.

When she was just a young girl, Ella had seen an enchanter rescue her brother from certain death when Miro fell through a platform of thin ice. This enchanter, as some did, carried a staff, and he could lengthen and shorten it using a series of activation runes. The enchanter used his staff to rescue Miro, and from that day Ella had wanted to become an enchantress.

Ella had applied a similar concept to the legs of the reflector's tower. She'd chosen a good place; she was high, with a view of both Altura's south and Petrya's northwest, and there were no trees or other obstacles in the way. Even so, the tower should be tall, and she began to chant softly to the legs, speaking to each in turn, lengthening them evenly, watching the rune-covered metal grow longer.

When the legs were as long as three men were tall, Jehral and his men helped Ella mount the tower at the center of the pass. They stuck each foot of the three legs firmly against the walls so that anyone passing this way would have to pass under the prism. Ella used her wand to fuse each foot to the surrounding rock. It took some time before she was satisfied: This tower wouldn't go anywhere, not even in the strongest storm.

"There," Ella said, looking at Jehral. "The tower is complete." Sadness hit her with sudden force. "I suppose this is where we part ways."

Jehral opened his arms and they embraced.

"I don't know why," Ella said into his chest, "but I don't think we can win."

Jehral pushed her away and looked into her eyes. "Have hope."

"If we call, will you answer? Please, Jehral, you're closest to him. Make sure he comes."

"We will come."

Jehral glanced away and then turned back, his expression anxious. "Ella, I know about the kalif's desire. I wish to say: do what your heart demands. I will always be your friend regardless, and the kalif will help your people if you call."

Ella knew that to Jehral these weren't just words. The Hazaran's strong sense of honor gave weight to the statement. She stammered a reply.

"My orders are to turn back now, but I don't like leaving you like this," Jehral said.

"I'll be fine," Ella said. One of Jehral's men held Ella's horse. "Thank you for the horse. It's hard being out of touch."

"Fare you well, and salut, Ella," Jehral said. He called to his men. "Draw up! We'll lead our horses back down the mountain until we're past the rocks."

"Wait, Jehral," Ella said. "I almost forgot."

She once more reached into her workbag and took out the scabbard lying beside the rods. Walking over, she handed it to a surprised Jehral.

"This is for you."

A sword rested snugly in the long scabbard like a hand in a glove. Jehral held the hilt of the curved scimitar in one hand and the scabbard in the other as he drew the blade six inches, his eyes widening in surprise when he saw the symbols on the shining steel.

"I had Ilathor find the blade for me. He said it's as fine as his own. Do you know the Larbi word for the desert rose?"

Jehral opened his mouth.

"No, don't say it now," Ella said.

"Al-maia," she knew he'd been about to say.

"Say this word to activate the sword. To deactivate it, say the Larbi name for the dust storm." Ella grinned. "Some Larbi words are derived from the runic language. I hope that it keeps you safe. I don't know when we will next meet, but I hope it will be under favorable circumstances. Farewell!"

Ella inserted a foot into her stirrup and grabbed hold of the pommel to pull herself up onto her horse's back. She looked out over her forested home and past; the distant ocean filled her with dread.

Ella kicked her horse forward and waved.

As she rode, Ella pictured the devastation of Shar and recalled Miro's vivid descriptions of the fates of Veldria and Gokan. The enemy would come with an armada of ships. They would have black powder, and they would have revenants.

It had been too long since Ella had been to the Academy of Enchanters. She'd been busy building the new machines at Mornhaven and then in Seranthia for Killian's coronation and the Chorum. Though she wasn't on the best terms with High Enchanter Merlon, she looked forward to once more seeing the Green Tower and the Great Court.

It was time for Ella to do her part and to create some weapons of her own.

7

Tapel ducked a blow from the son of a prosperous merchant and then countered with a clumsy thrust. He tried to shut out the calls of encouragement and derision from the boys circled around him but was conscious of their watching eyes. Tapel was desperate to make a good impression.

All the boys training at the Pens in Sarostar knew Rogan Jarvish was married to Tapel's mother. He couldn't think of anything worse than embarrassing himself, but these boys had all been training ever since they could hold a sword. If it weren't for Bladesinger Bartolo's private instruction, he wouldn't have lasted as long as the four blows struck so far in this spar.

Tapel took a step back, shifting one foot behind the other in the way he'd been taught. His opponent came forward to meet him and raised his sword as if to strike. Tapel lifted his practice sword to parry, but instead of striking, the merchant's son kicked Tapel hard in the side of his knee.

Tapel winced but managed to stay on his feet. Another feint then became a real blow, and Tapel's arm numbed at the shock of the two wooden swords colliding. Tapel couldn't believe the strength of the blow. His opponent was three years younger than him.

Some of the boys jeered at Tapel. He was a foreigner with a Halrana accent, and they resented his private instruction and life of privilege. He couldn't see what was so privileged about it; he slept in the same barracks as the other boys, only returning home on Lordsdays for dinner with his mother, Amelia. Tapel could still remember starving in war-torn Ralanast when these boys had been well fed in Sarostar.

Tapel blinked sweat out of his eyes and looked for an opportunity to strike through his opponent's defenses. The guard of the merchant's son was high . . . perhaps he could make a false pass at his head and cut low . . .

Tapel took a step forward and feinted into the face of the merchant's son, then dropped to one knee and smashed his wooden sword where the boy's thigh should have been. Unfortunately, it wasn't.

His opponent had deftly sidestepped around the clumsy attack, and with Tapel's footing uncertain, the merchant's son charged.

Tapel dropped and rolled to avoid the charge, then returned to his feet, panting and gasping. His opponent skewered the air where he'd been. Tapel shook droplets of sweat from his mousy hair. He hadn't thought he would regret winter's passing, but now, on spring's doorstep, the sweat was becoming a problem.

"Never give up the advantage of solid footing unless you're absolutely sure of yourself," Bladesinger Bartolo said to the ringed boys. "Tapel's roll was the only move available to him, but a better opponent would have bested him anyway."

Tapel's light wooden sword felt like it was made of solid iron. He waited for the next attack, knowing it was only a matter of time until he was beaten, and knowing it would hurt.

He looked around at the boys circling the sandy floor of the arena and wished there weren't so many watching. Distracted, he almost missed his opponent coming forward. Tapel raised his sword with both hands on the hilt to ward off the overhead swing in the nick of time.

"Concentrate!" Bladesinger Bartolo called.

Tapel tried, but he couldn't forget that Bartolo himself, as well as Miro, the high lord, had trained in this very arena and gone on to become the world's finest swordsmen. And the man who'd trained them was Rogan, Tapel's stepfather. Tapel didn't want to let Rogan down.

Tapel moved to dodge the next attack but instead felt a dulled wooden sword point smash into his left bicep. He fought the urge to cry out, even though the blow was agonizing.

"Fight on," Bladesinger Bartolo called out. "Tapel, hold your sword one-handed now. Your left arm is limp."

Tapel lifted the sword, now as heavy as a sack of grain, and tried to ward off the next flurry of blows. There was a sound like a cracking whip, and he felt a sharp whack on his temple; suddenly, he was on his back on the ground, staring up at the sky.

"Tapel, stand," Bladesinger Bartolo said.

Lord of the Earth, it was an effort, but Tapel climbed to his feet.

"Now bow to your opponent. Good, both of you. It's time for the sixth form now. Steel swords. Tapel, go to the infirmary and get that head seen to."

Swaying on his feet as he left the arena, Tapel put his fingers to his temple and looked with surprise as they came away tinged with red. He couldn't even remember the skin being split. He wondered if that was what it was like in real combat—whether you kept fighting even when you'd been cut deeply, or whether you felt the pain right away and struggled to go on. Perhaps it depended on the wound.

Some of the youths made way for Tapel to get past, chuckling and shaking their heads, but Tapel turned back to the arena as two sixth-form students with sharp steel swords stepped in. Now fifteen years old, he wanted to watch the older boys fight.

The best to watch were the young men four and five years older than him. Once, he even saw Bladesinger Bartolo enter the arena with Dorian. Their swords whirled so fast, Tapel couldn't even follow. Not long after that Dorian went into the Dunwood for secret training. Dorian returned with the zenblade and armorsilk of a bladesinger, and half an ear. He never told anyone what had occurred in the Dunwood, although Tapel heard rumors that the Halrana were somehow involved. Dorian had half an ear, but Tapel could feel the envy washing off every other student.

Bladesinger Bartolo took his eyes momentarily off the ring to frown at Tapel and incline his head sharply in the direction of the infirmary. Tapel sighed and walked away from the arena, wishing he'd been able to start his training as early as all the Alturan boys. He wondered if he'd ever get rid of his Halrana accent. At least he was staying in the barracks, where his mother couldn't keep an eye on him.

Unfortunately, today was Lordsday, and after practice he had to make his way to the Crystal Palace, so his mother could fuss over him.

Anything was better than that.

Fergus the ferryman gazed out at his city as he navigated the Sarsen.

White snow turned translucent as it warmed in the afternoon sun and dripped from the trees with a steady patter. The ice in the Sarsen was gone; fish were spawning in pools far from the city; and singing birds flashed into the green water, emerging with little wriggling prey downed with gusto.

Flowers dotted the riverside gardens in the Woltenplats and on the banks below the Crystal Palace: yellow daisies and shimmering summerglens, dainty white dewdrops and scarlet passionflowers. Bees buzzed as they flitted from one petal to another, and the hum of insects in the nearby Dunwood formed a melodious backdrop to any conversation away from the city center.

Mornings were misty and evenings cool, but at this time of year, at this time of day, there was no place better to be than Sarostar.

Fergus knew Sarostar like the back of his hand. He knew the histories of all the nine bridges and the stories of intrigue and politicking from the many years of the Crystal Palace's turbulent history. He knew the names of each of the buried souls who occupied the Heroes' Cemetery near the Academy of Enchanters, and he knew the best place to have a mug of cherl or buy a length of Alturan silk.

But most of all, Fergus enjoyed knowing the people. He loved Sarostar, and he made it his business to get to know as many of her residents as he could, something his job as ferryman facilitated. He knew when to talk and when to listen. He knew the right questions to ask, and how to nod and keep his mouth shut. His wife said he was too curious, but Fergus thought there was nothing wrong with being interested in people.

A city's heart wasn't just in her beautiful buildings and the tales that made up her history. It was in her people: the humdrum details of their daily lives; how they interacted with the city, buying and working and eating and loving. If Fergus the ferryman could live forever, he would never tire of his favorite people in all the world, the people of Sarostar, capital of Altura.

Yet Sarostar had changed.

Though ferryboats were again traveling the river after a cold winter, for once, Fergus the ferryman wasn't enjoying the spring. He pulled on his oars, hauling against the Sarsen's strong current, and scowled.

Fergus had never in all his life seen so many strangers in Sarostar. Over the last months the city had become a scene of intense activity; Sarostar's nine bridges thronged with travelers from sunup to sundown. The demand for the services of the ferryboats was endless. Not only was half of Halaran traveling back and forth between the free cities and Ralanast, but there were also these people from across the sea, the Veldrins. Even Dunfolk now scurried through the city so frequently that people barely registered their presence anymore.

It was all so different.

There were so many newcomers, and so many of them looked suspicious! He looked at his current passenger, a prime example. Fergus had tried engaging the man in conversation, but his passenger stayed silent as a clam. The man's manners were strange and his skin swarthy. He looked around the boat as if it were dirty, and sniffed disdainfully, looking pointedly at the pipe stuffed into Fergus's belt. He was definitely a Veldrin.

Some of them settled in well, but many still pined for their home. Lady Amber, the high lord's wife, had performed miracles, and a new district appeared in Sarostar's north: the Veldonplats it was coming to be called. The people there had beds to sleep in and nightlamps to fill their houses with light, but it was a running joke in the city that there was an excess of nightlamps in the Poloplats market and a shortage of plain candles and oil lanterns. The Veldrins hadn't taken well to enchantment.

One thing was for certain: they worked hard to perform to the high lord's demanding schedule for fortifications. They knew what was coming, and their feverish stories had the whole city on edge. Just two days past, a Veldrin named Deniz had told Fergus about the fleet that would come from the west. When the time came, Fergus would fight.

Yes, some had settled in well, but not this one.

Fergus rowed hard against the current, the muscles in his shoulders and back straining with effort. As the afternoon began to fade to evening, Fergus's passenger stared in dread at the Crystal Palace's cycling colors. When the high lord opened the way home, this one would be happy to go.

"There we go," Fergus said as the flat-bottomed boat gently nudged the dock near the Pens. "Two copper cendeens that'll be."

With a grunt the Veldrin handed Fergus a couple of coins and disembarked.

Fergus knew the high lord was doing the right thing, but that didn't mean he didn't long for the old days, when he knew every face in Sarostar.

"Ho, Fergus."

Fergus looked up when he heard a boy's voice, and broke out in a smile when he saw who it was. "Tapel! Lord of the Sky, lad, another beating, eh?"

"I gave a bit back," Tapel said.

"I'm sure you did. Here, get in. Next stop, the Crystal Palace."

"Was that last man a Veldrin?" Tapel asked as he hopped into the boat.

"Why do you ask?"

"He sniffed when he passed me. I hate it when they do that."

"Some of them think we're barbarians," Fergus said, pushing off. "Don't mind them, lad. A lot of strangers in Sarostar, though."

"You've noticed too?"

"Eh?" Fergus grunted as he put his back into the oars. "Noticed what?"

"Oh, nothing. Well, tell me, do you think this is strange? I saw a one-eyed man a few weeks ago. He was walking through the Poloplats market, dressed as a wealthy merchant. He was buying goods in the section where they sell stores. You know, salted meat, biscuits, that sort of thing."

"What of it?"

"I swear I saw the same man again, just yesterday," Tapel said. "This time he was dressed as a beggar."

"Are you sure?"

"Not really."

"You should say something to someone at the palace. Or perhaps your instructor."

Tapel shuddered. "Bladesinger Bartolo? I couldn't."

"Well, sometimes people like you and me notice things that others don't. We'll keep an eye out, eh?"

Tapel gave a weak smile as he touched a red mark on his head, and Fergus saw a boy struggling with the expectations that had been placed on him. "All right. Thanks, Fergus."

"Your mother's well?"

"Yes, she's fine. I miss Ralanast, though."

"I used to visit family there, did I tell you?" Fergus said.

"What district do they live in?"

"They're dead. Killed in the war."

"Oh, I'm sorry."

"Don't be sorry, lad. I lost my cousins, but you lost your pa. Do you miss him?"

"He used to yell at my mother," Tapel said. "Rogan's good to her."

"I'm glad to hear it. Used to scare the daylights out of me, Rogan did. I like hearing about him from you, though. We all have our softer side, and it's nice to know he's no exception."

"He's not that soft," Tapel said wryly.

"I'm sure he's not." Fergus chuckled. "But don't you worry, Tapel."

Fergus pulled up at the dock near the Crystal Palace.

"You'll make him proud."

8

Miro rubbed sleep from his eyes as he examined the new wall outside Sarostar. In the long series of defenses between Castlemere and Sarostar, this was the final bulwark. If he didn't hold them here, Altura's capital was doomed.

It was early dawn, and the distant treetops in the direction of the coast were tinged with golden light. Behind Miro the city was waking, merchants taking goods to the Poloplats markets and officials hurrying to appointments that simply couldn't wait. Already the sound of chisels and hammers filled the air, soldiers-turned-workmen muttering as they fitted blocks and dug trenches, lifted cannon and felled trees. The fresh scent of the forest wafted in on a cool breeze, banishing the smell of stone and upturned earth.

Miro kicked the tall wall with a booted foot as he looked up at its summit. The thick barrier was made of solid stone, the blocks tightly fitted together and bound by strong mortar. The wall curved slightly, its arc covering the final approach from Castlemere. At regular intervals Miro's men had built round towers, and on each tower a brass cannon pointed at the sole road from the free cities.

Commodore Deniz, the Veldrin naval commander who had led his people to safety in Altura, had helped Miro place and sight these cannon. Miro was reluctant to take too many cannon from Deniz's fourteen Veldrin warships—all needed for the naval struggle—and he and Deniz had settled with Miro taking a third of their original complement. Miro and Beorn then distributed their cannon evenly between these defenses at Sarostar and those at Castlemere. Miro had a few mortars, but too few, and just one solitary dirigible.

In the last war, archers had provided Miro with a decisive advantage, but he knew the coming fight would depend on weaponry with much greater destructive power. Miro's men would be battling revenants, and the only way to defeat those already dead was to crush the brain, remove the head, or literally tear the bodies to pieces. In order to survive, Miro needed bladesingers and elite swordsman, prismatic orbs, black powder, runebombs, and dirigibles. He had too little of everything.

Miro and Beorn walked from one end of the curving wall to the other, examining the ditches at the ends, the towers and cannon, and the strong iron gate in the center. Miro had liberated cities in Halaran, and he himself had been under siege at Wengwai. He knew the weakest points would be the gate and the extremities. He kept the workers building, but he would never have time to encircle Sarostar. High Enchanter Merlon had reinforced the central gate with the little he knew of the lore of the builders. Miro had done all he could, but would it be enough?

Miro praised his men as he passed; they were hard at work digging and lifting, and when a group of bare-chested soldiers saw their high lord and paused to touch their fingers to their foreheads, Miro shook his head.

"Please, don't stop, keep going. I'm proud of all of you. Many lives will depend on the work you do today."

Finally, Miro and Beorn stood outside the iron gate and looked at the approach. The road stretching from Sarostar to Castlemere was broad enough for three wagons to pass side by side, and the surrounding forest was thick, close to impenetrable. The vast majority of Altura's trade passed along either this route or back via Samson's Bridge to Halaran, in the east.

"We're lucky," Beorn said.

Miro smiled without humor. "How so?"

"The forest is our ally. We know they're going to travel along this road. If the free cities fall, we know this is where we'll stop them."

Miro turned back and looked at the city he'd called home his entire life. "I agree with you on one point. This is where we'll make our final stand."

"How does this compare with the defenses at Wengwai?"

"In a word? It's a good effort, but Wengwai's defenses were well beyond anything we've done."

"That's more than a word."

Miro barked a laugh. "So it is."

"But we've got something the Gokani didn't have," Beorn said. He peered at the road to Castlemere as if trying to divine the future. "Lore."

Miro and Beorn were both pensive for a time as they wondered what effect their weapons and defenses would have on the enemy.

Miro spoke into the silence. "And yet Sentar Scythran has lore of his own, and his power is the one thing we don't have a counter for."

"Overwhelm him with numbers? Perhaps bladesingers?"

"We can try." Miro shrugged. "But it isn't going to work."

Miro heard someone call out his name and, turning, saw an older woman with flaxen hair approaching. Never one to use his title, Amelia strode forward briskly as Miro briefly raised his eyes to the heavens.

"Miro," Amelia said again. "You need to rest. I can't believe you've just arrived from Ralanast and didn't even stop by the palace.

You're no good to anyone exhausted." She caught Beorn grinning at Miro's discomfort. "The same applies to you, Beorn."

Miro and Beorn exchanged rueful glances.

"How is my husband?" Amelia said.

"Rogan is well," Miro said. "He misses you and Tapel both. Here,"—he handed Amelia a letter—"this is for you."

Amelia snatched the letter, clutching it to her chest. "He's getting too old for this. And the Halrana? What did Tiesto say?"

"High Lord Tiesto is three days behind us. He's brought everything he could: colossi, ironmen, woodmen and golems . . . as well as regular infantry, pikemen, and their animators of course. Amelia, could you . . . ?"

Amelia let out a breath. "Quarter-master to the army . . ." She shook her head. "Who would've thought?" Her expression softened. "Of course, Miro. Beorn can help me. We'll see they're fed and housed."

"Thank you," Miro said.

"Speaking of being fed . . ." Amelia said.

"We'll finish up here in a few hours, and then I promise you, we'll go back to the Crystal Palace for a meal."

"I'll expect you there," Amelia said. "No excuses."

Evening found Miro at the Crystal Palace, sitting with his Council of Lords, trying to find gilden for the Louans. They examined every aspect of Altura's finances, from the storehouses of grain to the stocks of enchanted weapons and armor. They were revisiting old ground; there simply wasn't any money left.

Miro dismissed his lords and rubbed at his temples. His next task would be to go to the coast to inspect the defenses at Castlemere, a journey of several days. He was relieved to be back in

Altura; if Sentar came now, at least Miro was close. But being back simply reminded him how much there was to do.

And it wouldn't end. Even if they waited month after month, Miro would have to keep building, training, feeding, housing, trading, governing . . . It wouldn't end, not until they came.

And then the end might be all too near.

"You look exhausted," a voice said.

Miro glanced up and saw Ella standing beside the white stone table, looking down at him, her face registering concern.

"You don't look too rested yourself," Miro said. "I'm glad you're back safely. How did it go?"

"The kalif has promised to come to our aid if we call. Agira Lahsa and Tlaxor are both connected through Wondhip Pass. The Petryans and Hazarans will see our signal if we call."

"Thank you, Ella. I mean that. I know it can't have been easy."

"Are you getting any sleep?"

"Some." Miro blinked and wiped at the corners of his eyes before once more looking up at his sister. "What did Shani say about Petrya?"

Ella's expression turned grim. "She's trying. Petrya and Altura were never friends. If another house calls, it might be a different story."

Miro sighed. "So it comes to three houses: Halaran, Altura, and Hazara."

"Don't forget the Buchalanti. And Amber will come through with the Veznans, I'm sure of it. Also, I hear the Veldrins are hard at work both here and at the free cities. They know what's coming. Perhaps the Tingarans are right; we still don't know if Sentar will pass Altura by altogether. Perhaps it's we who will find ourselves answering another's call."

"He held me captive, Ella. We spoke. He'll come here, I'm sure of it."

"I have some good news," Ella said. She held up a scroll. "This was waiting for me here. It's from Evrin. He's leaving Seranthia and coming here to help."

"I hope he has something up his sleeve," Miro said. "Sentar . . . our best are no match for him. He took me down with barely an effort. And what will the Imperial Legion do if we call? They're still the most powerful force we have."

"We just have to hope. Come with me. I want to show you something."

Ella took Miro's hand and pulled him out of his seat. He let her drag him to his feet reluctantly. Still holding his hand, she led him through one of the translucent corridors of the Crystal Palace, along another hall, and to a lucent door. In his fatigued haze, Miro didn't recognize the door.

"What are you showing . . .?"

"Shh," Ella said, holding a finger to her lips.

Ella gently pushed the door open and led Miro inside.

A small child was asleep, curled up against a pile of cushions, the three-year-old Tomas barely taking up space on the massive bed. Miro's son looked carefree and innocent, his tousled locks of hair a perfect match to Amber's auburn.

"It's called a bed," Ella whispered with a smile. "No one will find you here. Everyone's depending on you, it's true, but you're no good to anyone if you're not thinking clearly. Don't worry, Miro; you'll get us through."

Ella slid Miro's shirt off his back and pulled off his boots as he sat on the bed. He fell down into the soft mattress, infinitely comfortable, and closed his eyes.

"I have faith in you," Ella whispered.

Miro didn't hear her.

He was already asleep.

9

Far away in the north, verdant spring hit the wild forests of Vezna with a spurt of growth unmatched at any other place in Merralya. The burst of new life touched nowhere so much as the living city of Rosarva, a place where every structure, from houses to halls, workshops to temples, to the defensive barrier of thorns surrounding the city, was grown rather than built. Gnarled trunks leaned against each other at odd angles, and twisted branches formed roofs overhead, yet it was all done to a rigid framework, for Veznans were a thorough, methodical people. And more than any of the other houses, they just wanted to be left alone.

In the Lyceum, the spurt of growth was welcome, for the rains and sunlight were needed for the cultivators' creations to reach their promise. The guardian plants, thornshrubs, highwalls, and nightshades would soon be awakened, and a new generation of plants would fill their creators with a satisfaction that only a Veznan could appreciate.

The most learned of the cultivators carefully pruned back the Juno Bridge, leading to the Borlag, where the high lord made his residence. It wouldn't do for those poisonous, grasping thorns to accidentally brush the wrong person.

And in the Borlag itself, an island of land surrounded by a weed-filled moat, the only building in the living city made of stone rose to dominate its land mass. The many chambers of the high lord's palace mostly stayed empty: High Lord Grigori Orlov, the man who'd replaced the deposed Dimitri Corazon, received few visitors from outside.

Amber sat at a table of rose-colored wood in an upper hall of the high lord's palace. Across from her was Sergei Rugar, lord marshal of Vezna, a slim man who appeared to be Amber's only friend among his people. Sergei had a cap of light blonde hair, fashionably curled, and a charming smile.

High Lord Grigori himself brooded at the far end of the table, several places away, where it was difficult for Amber to meet his eyes. He was short and stocky, with wide-spaced eyes and extremely short, close-cropped dark hair. Grigori Orlov had so far been a man of few words.

Amber put her fingers to her temples as she felt the approach of another headache. She now regularly dreamt of three-legged towers and triangular prisms of quartz. She'd sent the other enchanters and her guards onward, north to Lake Vor, where they would build the final station and ensure the Akari would keep watch. Amber was alone in Rosarva.

And now she had the most difficult task of all. She had to convince the Veznans to promise support, to come to the aid of whoever called, in the event of a bright light shining from the city's tower.

This wasn't her first meeting, and she could tell she wasn't making much progress. She'd told the story of her and Miro's voyage to the land across the Great Western Ocean. Her descriptions had been vivid and compelling; she'd worked on her speech ever since she'd left Miro in Ralanast. Grigori Orlov had only shown mild interest. It was none of his concern.

Amber looked at Grigori, and he frowned.

"The enemy's main strength isn't just the power of the revenants we will be facing," Amber said. "It's in the way Sentar Scythran's army feeds on humans like a plague. When he destroys a town, or an army, or a city like Rosarva," she stressed the name of the living city, "he leaves none alive, for he wants corpses in the way other conquerors might lust after gold. He takes those who were strongest in life, particularly warriors, for revenants still possess much of their skill-memories and can follow complex instructions. The strongest he brings back, adding their numbers to his army, which swells in size as a result."

Amber took a deep breath, wondering if she was getting through to Grigori.

"The children and the weak, the elderly and the infirm, are slaughtered out of hand. Sentar's necromancers make them line up, and at the end of the line lies death. There's nothing complex about it; it's slaughter." Amber bit the words off.

"Hmm," High Lord Grigori said.

"The bodies of the weak are then thrown into the vats to distill essence from their life force. The essence is used to make more revenants. Do you understand, High Lord, what I am saying? An army of a thousand can swiftly become two thousand. Soon it is four thousand. The growth only stops when Sentar runs out of bodies. As we grow weaker and our numbers thin, he grows stronger."

Grigori tapped his fingers on the table.

Amber struggled to hold down her frustration. She had to win him with logic, not emotion. She needed him to see that Vezna's safety was also at risk.

"He won't be coming with an army of a thousand," Amber said. "Across the sea is a continent as big as all the lands of the Empire put together. When we left, he'd conquered Emirald, the capital of Veldria, but much of the surrounding land was unconquered. Entire populations would have been added to his army since we left, and harbors would have been taken, their ships added to his armada. It's a long journey across the sea, but we expect him to arrive at any moment. He has had the time he needs since the destruction of the ships at Emirald. The free cities, Castlemere and Schalberg, and Altura itself, are the closest lands. Once he makes a foothold, he will sweep the Empire clean, and he won't stop until he's at Seranthia."

"But he may land at Seranthia itself?"

"Yes, he may—which is why the signaling system isn't biased to any one house. We've pledged to come to the aid of whoever calls. We're asking that House Vezna make the same pledge."

"If Sentar conquers Altura, or Tingara, or both, why would he then come to Vezna?"

"Would you really sit back and allow the rest of the Empire to fall into darkness?" Amber countered. "Is that a beneficial outcome, do you think?" She couldn't keep the tone of accusation from her voice. She breathed slowly in and then out to calm herself.

"Leave me for a moment," High Lord Grigori said. Sergei met Amber's eyes and indicated the terrace doors with his chin.

"Lady Amber, if you'd like to join me on the terrace? Perhaps you would like some fresh air?" Sergei inquired.

Amber nodded; she craved the open air. In contrast to the rest of Rosarva, she found the Borlag an oppressive place.

"Of course, Lord Marshal," she said, noting to herself that only Sergei had the courtesy to use her name or title.

As Amber rose from her seat, the door burst open, and a small girl raced into the room, her sparkling eyes on the high lord. The girl wore a thick white tunic with orange trim, the material supple and expensive. At her neck she wore the Veznan *raj hada* on a pendant, the silver sprouting seed at her neck matching the green seedling she held in her cupped palms.

"Look, Father!" the girl cried.

She displayed her handful of dirt, and the small sprout with two leaves poked up about four fingers in height. "They're growing!"

Grigori Orlov opened his arms and pulled the child onto his lap. "Show me, Katerina. That's incredible!" The dour high lord beamed. "In such a short time too?"

"The high lord's daughter," Sergei murmured to Amber.

Both Katerina and her father ignored the dirt spilling out onto the floor. Grigori scooped the dirt and sprout from his daughter's hands and then gently shook out the soil, adding to the mess. "Look at the roots. A strong plant needs good roots. They're thick and wide, see?" He laid the sprout flat on his palm and pulled his daughter close. "If they're all like this, you've done an excellent job."

"Really?" Katerina squirmed.

"Come," Sergei said to Amber, leading her to the balcony and closing the doors behind them.

Amber breathed in the fresh springtime air wafting from the city across the moat. She realized her hands were shaking, and she clasped them, one inside the other.

"I'm sorry," Sergei said. "I've tried to convince the high lord to agree to your proposal, but he only cares for Vezna and for watching his daughter grow."

Amber looked out at the Juno Bridge, a tall arch spanning the moat. The high lord had conceded to let her mount her reflector on a single rod fixed to the living bridge. Amber had placed the device in the center of the bridge so that the prism was high in the sky, above the tops of the trees, but also visible in the palace.

Amber took relief from the fact that the reflector was dark. The chain of towers reached all the way to Sarostar via Samson's Bridge. It stretched to Ralanast and to Seranthia. No distress call had been sent.

"What else can I say?" Amber said. "I was there. I saw what's coming with my own eyes. Vezna isn't safe. If Altura falls, your lands will too."

"Perhaps you should go home, my Lady," Sergei said gently.

Amber shook her head. "I can't leave without a promise of aid. I'll stay for as long as it takes."

"The high lord's hospitality only extends so far."

"Then he'll have to lock me up." Amber lifted her chin. "He can try to cast me out, but I'll just come back."

Sergei let out a breath. "You are determined." He gave her his charming smile. "I will continue to work on your behalf."

———◆———

The next day, at mid-morning, Amber walked around the Borlag, following the thin strip of land surrounding the high lord's palace. She felt cooped in the brooding interior and needed to stretch her legs.

Katerina, the high lord's daughter, sat playing in a puddle, her golden hair in a wild tangle. She pulled at the weeds on the edge of the puddle, clearing a space around a single solitary summerglen.

Amber sighed. As always, she missed Tomas. She crouched at Katerina's side.

"Hello, Katerina, isn't it? I'm Amber," she said warmly. "What are you doing there?"

"I'm saving this flower's life," Katerina said loftily. "My father says healthy plants must be encouraged, and weeds rooflessly destroyed."

"Ruthlessly," Amber corrected, smiling. "Your father is a wise man," she added.

"Papa says I'm going to be high lady one day," Katerina said, pausing to beam at Amber. "Then I won't have to do lessons, and I can make better plants than anyone ever."

"That's wonderful," Amber said.

As Katerina returned to her weeds Amber's brow furrowed. Vezna was famed for its court intrigues. What would the conservative Veznans think of a woman ruling their house?

"Your rings are pretty," Katerina said. "I like that one best." She pointed to the emerald-set ring Miro had presented to Amber the day he'd proposed. "It's green, like a tree!"

"Green's my favorite color," Amber said. "Is it yours too?" Katerina nodded. "This ring belonged to my husband's mother, and my husband gave it to me when we were married."

"Will I have to marry?" Katerina asked, turning to Amber with serious eyes as she plucked at the weeds. "I don't want to."

"That's your choice," Amber said. She hoped it would be, at any rate.

On a whim, Amber pulled off the pale silver ring with a small ruby she wore on the smallest finger of her right hand. It was tight and took some yanking, but she managed to get it off.

"I'd like to give you this as a gift. It's not as pretty as my emerald ring, but it's just as special."

"Why?" Katerina asked.

"It has a special power. Do you want to see?"

Katerina immediately lost interest in her weeding, staring in fascination at the ring. "Show me!"

Amber held the ring out carefully in two fingers, looking at the tiny symbols spanning the circle. It was simple, but she'd made it herself, and was quite proud of it.

Amber spoke the activation sequence. *"Tuhlanas."*

The symbols glowed softly and the ruby began to shine. "Put your hand close to the ring with your palm out. No, don't touch it."

"It's hot!" Katerina exclaimed.

"It's lore," Amber said. "When you say the special word, the ruby lights up and gets hot." Katerina looked on in awe as Amber named the deactivation rune. *"Tuhlanar."*

The runes faded, and the ruby dimmed. Amber handed Katerina the ring.

"You have to be very careful. If you use it as a light, be careful about the heat, and if you use it to make a fire, make sure you are far away from other trees and buildings. Do you understand?"

"I understand," Katerina said gravely. "They teach us about fire. Vezna has a lot of trees."

"Good," Amber said. "Can you remember the special word?"

"*Tuhl . . .*" Katerina struggled with the strange pronunciation, but she eventually got it right. "*Tuhlanas.*"

The ring came to life.

"Now, how do you make it stop? It's the same but with an 'ah' sound at the end."

"*Tuhlanar!*" Katerina said, looking at Amber proudly. The ruby went dark.

"Well done," Amber said. "Now, if ever you can't remember how to turn it off, just throw the ring in a bucket of water. It isn't strong enough to make all that water hot. Can you remember that?"

"Yes." Katerina grinned as she placed the ring on her middle finger. Amber didn't have big hands, and the ring fit.

"You're a good girl," Amber said. "You're nearly grown up, aren't you? I have a son, but he isn't as old as you."

"What's his name?"

"Tomas," Amber said.

"Tomas," Katerina said. "That's a funny name."

Amber laughed. "Don't say that to him. You might hurt his feelings."

As Amber sat with Katerina, she saw movement on a distant third-story balcony. Sergei Rugar stepped out dressed in somber dark clothing with orange trim. Another man in uniform was at his side, and they were deep in conversation.

Spying Amber, Sergei waved, and Amber waved back.

Katerina soon forgot about her ring and went back to her weeding.

"Katerina? Where are you my love?"

High Lord Grigori appeared from behind a wall, his boots and hands dirty from spending time with his plants. He stopped in his tracks when he saw Amber with his daughter. "My Lady," Grigori said, nodding.

"High Lord." Amber returned his nod, feeling foolish at the mud on her knees, but realizing the Veznan high lord was just as dirty.

"Look, Papa!" Katerina cried. "Amber gave me a gift." She displayed the ring proudly.

"I hope you thanked the lady," Grigori said.

Katerina's mouth popped open, and she turned. "Thank you, Lady Amber," she said earnestly.

"You're welcome, Princess," Amber said. "I should be going now. I've had a lot of fun playing with you."

"See you at dinner!" Katerina called, turning back to her weeds.

Amber stood and walked back toward the palace, feeling the high lord's eyes on her back.

10

"Someone to see you, Your Imperial Majesty," Lord Osker intoned as if speaking a eulogy.

Killian took his eyes off the rows and columns of carefully written figures and closed the book, thankful for the interruption. When he saw who it was, he rose to his feet, grinning.

"Carla. How are you?"

"I am well, Your Imperial Majesty," she said with a twinkle in her eye. Lord Osker frowned; she hadn't hidden the mockery in her tone.

"Please leave us," Killian said to Osker.

He waited until Osker had left the room. "Not you too." He sighed in exasperation. "Call me Killian, Carla. I'll have you on charges if you don't."

Carla came forward and they awkwardly embraced. She held his palm a little longer than was necessary, squeezing it as their hands parted.

"Please sit down," Killian said, indicating the cushioned sofa across from his own. "How did you get past Osker? You haven't lost your charm. He normally doesn't let anyone past."

"Brrr," Carla said, ignoring Killian's question. She looked at the cold hearth, occupying an entire wall of the cavernous sitting room. "It's warm outside. Why is it always cold in your palace?"

"It's big," Killian said with a grin.

"If you can't afford heating stones, surely you can afford a fire?"

"Budget cuts." Killian laughed.

"You look weary. You need to relax. What are you reading?" She picked up the book and flicked through the pages. "'Province of Aspar,'" she read, "'granary stores at seven thousand imperial drams.' Exciting."

"Terribly," Killian said. "How goes the search?"

Carla's expression grew pained. "A drinking house in the Tenamet is looking for waitresses."

"Sounds promising."

"Required skills are dancing, long legs, easy morals, and"—she tapped her long nose—"a pretty face."

"Don't say your face isn't pretty," Killian said. "I like it just the way it is."

"I'm not doing that kind of work." Carla laughed. "Still, I need to do something."

He was surprised at how easily they'd fallen back into the old repartee. Since her arrival at the palace, their friendship had resumed something of its former shape. Killian had told Carla his story—somewhat abbreviated, with his involvement with the primate left out—and Carla had told him hers.

After her father's death, she'd finally joined another troupe, but had to leave when the troupe leader's attentions became . . . forced. She didn't elaborate much, and Killian didn't ask her to. He'd kept his secrets, and he couldn't blame her for keeping hers. The world was a harsh place for someone on her own, and Tingara harsher than most.

"Well, let's see. You've been an actor, an acrobat, and more recently a merchant's assistant and a helper at a school for spoiled children. Do I have it right?"

Carla grinned. "You do."

"So you are a lady of many talents. Would you . . . do you want me to get you work?"

"No," Carla said, lifting her chin. "I can do this on my own."

"Well said," Killian said. "Where are you staying?"

"With a friend," Carla said. "But he says I have to move out. He wants his floor back. He's been saying it for weeks."

Killian frowned.

"The expression on your face!" Carla chuckled. "Don't tell me you don't like me living with a man. We haven't seen in each other in how long? What about you? I'll bet you have a mistress or two tucked away around town, and a special sally gate for sneaking out at night. The privileges of power." She grinned.

Killian thought immediately of Ella. He banished the image of her heart-shaped face. He found he was getting good at that lately.

"Nothing like that," Killian said. "To be honest, being emperor takes up all my time. I don't know who thought of wrapping up high lord of Tingara and leader of the Empire into one position. So what are you going to do? You need to stay somewhere." Carla sighed and Killian saw real concern cross her face.

Killian hesitated. He could see that Carla needed help. He'd lost a mentor when Marney Beldara was murdered. But she'd lost a father.

"What if I found you rooms here?" Killian said.

Carla glanced up. "You'd do that?"

Killian wondered what his mother would say. "Of course."

"I'm glad I found you," Carla said. "Killian Alderon, emperor of Merralya." She shook her head; then, leaning forward, she kissed Killian's cheek, and he smelled her perfume, rich and floral. "It would only be until I can find work."

"For as long as you need it," Killian said.

"I still can't believe it," Carla said, shaking her head. "From orphan of Salvation to emperor. Is it hard?" she asked him frankly.

"Yes." Killian sighed. "It's hard."

"Everyone is talking about an invading army coming from across the Great Western Ocean. Is it true?"

"I'm afraid it is."

"And there's a new signaling system so the houses can request aid."

"You're well informed," Killian said.

"It's hardly a secret. What will you do with the Legion if someone requests aid—say, Altura?"

"Please, Carla, not you too. The fact is, I don't know. I'm thinking about it."

"I'm sure you'll do what's right. You always were a kind soul. We're lucky to have you as emperor."

"A kind soul?" Killian smiled. "I've never heard myself referred to like that before."

"Look at what you've done for me," Carla said.

There was space next to Killian on his sofa, and Carla stood up and moved to sit next to him, curling up on the seat so that her knees touched his thigh. She was very close, and Killian tensed when he once more smelled her perfume. Her raven-black hair shone, pulled back from her oval face but with a few loose strands falling past her eyes.

"Where do you sleep?" she said, raising an eyebrow. "Are you going to place me close by?"

"I'll . . . I'll leave that for the chamberlains to decide," Killian said.

Carla moistened her lips, and Killian remembered how soft they'd once felt, a long time ago. "I'll bet you have a huge bed."

Killian grinned and stood up. "Stay here."

He strode out of the room and called out, "Lord Osker!"

It didn't take him long to find the officious steward. "Yes, Your Imperial Majesty? Can I be of service?"

Killian led Osker back into the sitting room. "Please find Lady Carla here some chambers. She's going to be staying in the palace for a time. Please inform the rest of the staff, and have someone fetch her belongings from the city."

Osker's eyes flickered to Carla, who clapped her hands together. "Of course. I will see it done," he said.

Lord Osker left the room, and Killian returned to Carla's side, leaving some space between them as he sat.

"Lady Carla," she said. "I like the sound of that."

A chamberlain entered the room. "Go with him," Killian said. "He'll show you to your new chambers."

Carla again kissed Killian's cheek, just to the side of his mouth. "Thank you," she whispered. "I want to talk more and hear more about what you've been doing. You've changed so much!"

"I suppose we're both older."

"Not too much older, I hope?" Carla smiled at him over her shoulder as she followed the chamberlain from the room.

Killian sat for a long time after she'd departed, staring without seeing in the direction she'd gone, and then he heard a throat clear behind him.

Lady Alise, Killian's mother, stood with her hands on her hips, disapproval written across every line of her face. She was slim and fine boned, and still beautiful despite the gray streaks in her long brown hair. She never followed Tingaran fashion, letting her hair cascade down her back when the other ladies were in curls and foregoing embroidered purple for plain brown dresses.

Lady Alise was a force to be reckoned with in the palace, and even Rogan Jarvish gave her as much time as she asked of him. She'd initially stepped reluctantly into her new role, but Alise now saw it as her duty to keep Killian abreast of the various machinations within the court. She loved Killian fiercely, sometimes in a way that frightened him, but he loved her in return.

"She has nowhere to stay," Killian protested. Why did he always sound like a whining child when he was with her?

"You don't know her," Alise said flatly.

"I've told you about what she's been through. We're old friends."

"You haven't seen her in many years. She left you without a care for your fate."

Killian scowled. "Mother, we were once very close. I can't leave her out in the cold. This is my city, and I have a responsibility to everyone who was affected by the war. The economy is shaky—you always say that—and it's hard for many."

"Yes, charity is an important part of your mandate," Alise said, "but focused charity, intended to help the most people with a sustainable solution for their plight. She has her eye on you, my son. I thought your heart was with another."

Killian flushed. He could still remember Carla's warmth beside him on the sofa.

"I can't turn her away," Killian said. "She needs my help. It's only temporary."

"Be careful. That's all I ask. You need to know those you trust to their core. You are the emperor, but you are young and inexperienced. I have seen the way Ella looks at you. Think well before you break her heart."

With a final stern look, Killian's mother turned and left him.

Killian watched her go, and then wondered where Carla's new chambers were.

He could still smell perfume in his nostrils.

11

The Academy of Enchanters in Sarostar was the scene of intense activity. A series of buildings that clustered around the Great Court, with an archway at one end of the Court facing the Green Tower at the other, the Academy was grand in a way the Crystal Palace could never be. Where the palace was ethereal, the Academy was solid. The Crystal Palace was a place of beauty, a demonstration of the things enchantment could do. In contrast, powerful works of lore came out of the Academy. Lore was serious business, and this place demanded it be treated as such.

At noon, springtime in Altura, the glow of runes in the Great Court competed with the bright light of the sun. The workshops of the masters and qualified enchanters were busy, but not as frantic as the grassy expanse at the Academy's heart.

The things being built in the Great Court were too big for any workshop. This lore was too dangerous to be confined.

Enchanters, assisted by their students, constructed zenblades, armorsilk, rail bows, and runebombs. By a strict designation, the faculty demanded there be significant distance between the workbenches, for both access and safety, yet no space was as clear as where Ella worked in the very center.

Ella was sad to see the centurion trees all gone, but once the decision was made to utilize the Great Court with its ideal location, they'd all been cleared away. One day new trees might grow, but they would take hundreds of years to reach the majestic beauty of their ancestors. As a student Ella had sat under the shade of the centurion trees, reading and learning. She'd made friends with Amber here, and this was where her brother had watched her graduate. When Tomas was poisoned, Ella had passed under the tall branches to pray to the statue of Evora Guinestor, still sternly watching the activity below from her lofty height. The centurion trees were gone, but even so, Ella felt at home here more than at any other place.

Ella stood with Luca Angelo, a Halrana animator, beside his colossus. The gigantic construct, as tall as the buildings around it, slumped dejectedly, deactivated. Beside the colossus, resting on a long bench at waist height, was a sword.

The length of three men, it was single-edged and sharp as a razor. The runes Ella had drawn would make it sharper still, as well as lighter, harder to see, and capable of burning with fiery energy. It wasn't a single-activation sword; this lore would need regular chanting from an expert. Miro had told Ella that Luca was one of the best, and it was time for Ella to find out whether Luca was up to the challenge of controlling both the colossus and the sword simultaneously.

"Are you ready?" Ella said.

Besider her, Luca took a deep breath. "I'm ready." His voice shook.

"Remember, we're just here to grasp the sword and pick it up. Nothing more."

Luca let out his breath with a whoosh, making his dark locks shake. "I know."

"Enchantress." A voice sounded at Ella's elbow. Turning, she saw High Enchanter Merlon, looking stern in a sparkling robe decorated with a myriad of spidery symbols. "Please perform your test away from the rest of us. Do I make myself clear?"

Ella fought the urge to groan. "High Enchanter," she said, "how do you propose to move the sword? It's as heavy as . . ."—she looked around for inspiration—"as heavy as a block of iron the length of three men! I just need to make this simple test. When the colossus can carry the sword, we can move down to the fields."

High Enchanter Merlon, a plump and usually jovial man with shaggy eyebrows, grunted. He finally turned and walked away, muttering and shaking his head.

Ella was actually eager to get to the fields, where she and Luca could give the colossus its first real test. At least Ella didn't have to worry about the crystal trees, as sad as that was. The small grove of rare glossy trees in the fields below the Academy was gone. The constant explosions and ground-trembling quakes had shaken all their shards to the ground. The crystal trees died soon after.

"It's all right," Ella reassured the young animator. "Go ahead."

Luca looked up at the colossus and called out. The slumped construct came to life, symbols glowing and sparking, spiraling out from its chest in a multitude of colors: crimsons, blues, emeralds, and golds. The colossus straightened, and when Luca named a second series of activations, it went down to one knee and lowered its head.

The cage on top was open, and Luca climbed the ridges on the leg, walked along the bent knee, and nimbly jumped up to the shoulder. He pulled himself into the cage, seating himself on a fixed stool and touching the tablet in front of him. The colossus once more stood tall.

Ella was mindful of the enchanters who'd stopped working and now watched. There were fifty paces of cleared space around the colossus, but she still saw one or two onlookers take several steps back.

Animator Luca touched the tablet and chanted in a sonorous tone. The colossus opened a fist and reached for the hilt of the sword.

In one swift motion the huge manufactured creature made of iron and wood picked up the sword and held it high.

Ella felt a surge of excitement run through her. Throwing all caution to the wind, she pointed at one of the gaps in the enchanters' workbenches. "Head to the fields! That way!" she cried.

As eager as Ella, Luca took his colossus with bold strides through the gap, sending enchanters dashing to either side. The ground trembled with each step, and Ella spurred herself into motion, chasing the colossus through the grand archway and in the direction of the fields. The colossus swiftly outpaced her, and she stopped to watch.

"I wonder that you even need my help," Ella heard a voice behind her say.

Whirling, Ella saw an old man with gray hair flecked with ginger and a soft beard. His eyes were kind and colored an intense, vivid blue.

"Evrin!" Ella said. She grabbed hold of him and hugged him.

"Careful, dear," Evrin said. "I'm an old man."

"Hold on a moment," Ella said. "Luca!" she cried. "Luca!"

The animator didn't hear her. He was busy taking huge swings at the air, joyfully waving the sword like a child playing at soldier. At least he hadn't tried to activate the blade.

"I don't think he can hear you," Evrin said.

Ella laughed. "It doesn't matter. It looks like he's enjoying himself. Did you just arrive now?"

"Just this very moment." Evrin rolled his shoulder to show the ragged knapsack on his back.

"Here, let me show you around. I can explain what we're doing here, and then we can find you some rooms. Would you rather stay here or at the palace?"

"Wherever you need me," Evrin said.

"I'm staying here at the Academy, in the Green Tower. It's comfortable in there. You'll like it."

"Ella!" Ella heard High Enchanter Merlon's voice calling her name.

"Quick, let's go. Here, let me carry your bag," Ella said.

Ella led Evrin around the outside of the buildings, skirting the Great Court at first, not wanting to re-enter so soon after her dramatic departure. She asked Evrin about his journey and then told him about her voyage to Agira Lahsa.

"How is Killian?" Ella asked.

"He's well. Extremely busy. I have taught him enough, I think, and if I showed him more, he would have too much to practice and likely be proficient at none of it."

"Can he stand up to Sentar Scythran?"

Evrin shook his head. "There is no way of knowing. He was always powerful, Sentar, and extremely cunning."

"Where will he land, do you think? The fact that you're here . . ."

"Ella, I don't know. I'm here because your brother possesses a strong conviction it will be Altura, and he's a smart man. I'm also here because Seranthia possesses the Imperial Legion, the fleet, storehouses full of prismatic orbs, and dirigibles. I'm here because Seranthia has Killian. It doesn't matter where Sentar lands. Even if he takes his ships to Aynar and rouses the templars, he must be stopped where he is."

"How long will we have you?" Ella asked as they strolled around the far side of the Green Tower.

"I'll stay here until a signal lights to send me elsewhere. An ingenious idea of yours, by the way."

Ella blushed at the compliment. Coming from Evrin, it was high praise indeed.

"Come on," Ella said. "Luca doesn't need me for the moment. Let me show you what we're doing here."

Ella took Evrin up a set of stairs and skirted Ash Building to reach the lecture halls they'd repurposed. Immediately she smelled sulfur, a terrible stench of rotten eggs that grew worse as they approached.

Inside, some knowledgeable Veldrins and open-minded enchanters mixed chemicals. Ella explained the process. They purified the raw sulfur that miners carried from the mountainous south, until it was a bright yellow powder. Miro's men also mined saltpeter from the hills in the east. Finally, black powder resulted when they combined the sulfur and saltpeter with ground iron.

Liquid in clear glass bottles bubbled on heatplates with glowing runes. The new Veldrin alchemists loved heatplates; they said they could control the temperature must better than with flame.

"I have to say," Evrin said, "I understand none of this."

"Fascinating, though, isn't it?" Ella said, her eyes shining. "Amber gave me a book from one of the masters of the Alchemists' Guild. Since then we've found cures for many common ailments and learned more about the physical world than we ever understood before. Our knowledge is moving forward in leaps and bounds."

"Is everyone at the Academy as enthusiastic?"

Ella frowned. "No, not everyone. I'd like it if the Academy kept studying these things, even after we no longer need to produce black powder in quantity. But if they won't, I have a plan."

"Tell me about it," Evrin said as Ella led him back out to the open air. They both inhaled deeply, happy to be outside and away from the sulfur; the former lecture halls were all high ceilinged, but even so, the air was noxious.

"I'd like to found an academy of my own," Ella said. "I haven't actually said anything about it to anyone. Perhaps it's a foolish dream."

"No, Ella. It's not foolish. Go on; I want to hear more."

"It should be somewhere central. Perhaps Mornhaven— that's where the essence is, after all—or Seranthia. I'd like to get the loremasters of all the houses together for a meeting, similar to a Chorum, with everyone from the high animator to the high cultivator present. We could bring all the Lexicons together and share knowledge. We could discover where essence's power really comes from, and we could learn the things even the Alchemists' Guild never knew. Who knows where the knowledge could take us?"

"It's a lovely dream," Evrin said. "Please don't let it stay that way."

Ella smiled at Evrin as she led him to the workbenches spread throughout the Great Court. She didn't introduce him—he was uncomfortable with reverence—and he received only the occasional curious glance. Old men weren't hard to find around the Academy.

Ella showed him the armorsilk and the new runebombs—some designed to roll, others to adhere to a wall or patch of ground and project a controlled explosion. She then showed him the catapults—purely mechanical devices—intended to throw barrels of black powder and clusters of prismatic orbs.

"We're trying everything," she said. "We've tried to get cannon to shoot runebombs, but so far it isn't working. Do you think you could help?"

"With cannon? It's not really my forte, my dear."

"Whatever you'd like to do, then." Ella smiled and gave Evrin a quick squeeze. "It's good to have you here."

Ella and Evrin continued talking, but the mood turned somber as they found themselves in the Heroes' Cemetery, looking down at the rows of grave markers. Many of the heroes were bladesingers from the last war, but the graves went back to the Rebellion and beyond, to a time when there were no bladesingers, just excellent swordsmen with single-activation blades.

"Bladesinger Huron Gower," Ella said softly as she read a marker, as if to speak too loud would indicate disrespect. "I wonder who he was?"

"A brave man, no doubt," Evrin said, "who died for his homeland."

Ella surprised herself with the relief she felt that Evrin was here. There was no one she could share her fears with: Miro was worried enough as it was; Amber was far away in Vezna; Shani was back in Petrya lobbying the high lord. Ella had felt friendless and alone.

"Evrin," Ella said as she looked at the graves. "I'm afraid. I don't want to lose the ones I love. I couldn't bear it if I lost Miro or Amber or Shani, or someone else I love."

"We all must die some time, my dear. Contrary to what many believe, it's how we face life, not how we die, that is the important thing. People never remember how someone died. In a way, it's not important. When they tell each other stories about a lost friend's life or catch a scent that reminds them of a face, they aren't thinking of death. They're bringing a piece of that person back to life, if only for a time."

"What do you think happens when we die?" Ella thought about Katherine, her mother, and Serosa, her father. Where were her parents now?

"Honestly? I don't know. Personally, I like the Dunfolk's beliefs the best—that we're all connected, and nothing is destroyed, only changed. When a tree falls and decays into the ground, it feeds the life around it. When a tree is burned and smoke rises into the air, it's absorbed by raindrops or gathers on the wings of birds. Nothing is ever lost."

"I like that," Ella said. She looked around the Heroes' Cemetery, and beyond, to the green fields, the winding river, and Sarostar's western quarter. Fragments of her mother were in those blades of grass and in that swirling water. Part of Ella's mother was in Ella herself.

"Don't be afraid," Evrin said as they turned away from the graveyard and began to walk back up toward the sandstone buildings of the Academy of Enchanters. "Face your fears like you always have, and everything will be well."

Ella nodded and felt Evrin's words soothe her frayed nerves. They were both silent for a time before Ella voiced something else that was on her mind.

"Evrin, do you know of any specific weaknesses in the Evermen? Something that could be exploited in Sentar's powers?"

"Weaknesses? Eventually loredrain will conquer even Sentar, but he must possess a great deal of essence by now."

Ella pondered. "The alchemist whose book I have . . . he said something to Amber and Miro. He believed the Evermen have a weakness, but he wasn't certain. His last words were, 'Remember, everything is toxic, it is the dose that makes a thing a poison.' Something like that. Does it mean anything to you?"

Evrin shook his head. "I'm afraid it doesn't."

"Could you . . . could you teach me something about the things you taught Killian? I might see something."

"Of course." Evrin hesitated as they walked, and then took Ella's arm. "Now there's something I must tell you."

"What is it?"

"For much of my life I've kept secrets. I've hidden who I was, and I stayed silent as the people of Merralya came to worship those who once enslaved them. I now believe I was wrong. Only when armed with the truth can people make the right decisions. I want to tell you the truth now, Ella. I no longer enjoy keeping secrets."

Ella looked at Evrin with concern. "What is it?"

"Just before I left Seranthia, a woman came to the palace. She is a former . . . acquaintance . . . of Killian's."

"Acquaintance? Who is she?"

"I hear she is his former lover."

A tight feeling gripped Ella's chest as she remembered Killian's story. "Carla?"

"Yes," Evrin said. He looked quizzically at Ella. "You know her?"

"I know of her."

"He was joyful to see her. I knew you would want to know, and I can't stand here with you and not say anything."

"It doesn't matter," Ella said. She tried to believe what she was saying. "Come on, we're here at the Green Tower." Ella tried to smile. "Now let's find you some lodgings."

———◆———

The middle of the night saw the frantic activity in the Great Court calm somewhat, though the occasional enchanter or Veldrin hurried from one building to another, perhaps to find a tome in the libraries or to fetch essence from the dwindling reserve.

Evrin stepped out onto his private balcony and sighed. Had he done the right thing in telling Ella about Carla? Was it better she didn't know?

He looked out at the Great Court and wondered if he was even needed.

Evrin was depressed.

Without his powers, what could he do against Sentar? He'd brought this horror on the world by keeping the people ignorant of the truth. He should have known the relic would never stay hidden; the Sentinel was too great a mystery.

The relic was impervious to harm, as was the statue itself, although somehow the essence in the pool had melted the surrounding wall like butter. The Sentinel was now walled up, but it was only a bare measure of protection from cannon, orbs, and Sentar's own power.

And what did it matter if the portal stayed closed, if Sentar conquered the Empire on his own?

Once Sentar had the world under his boot heel, he could take his time about opening up the portal. Only Killian could challenge Sentar.

What use was an old man?

12

The burning sun shone fierce rays on the yellow expanse of the Hazara Desert. A growing wind blew sand off the rolling dunes, sending it flying through the air. The sand caught in hair and clothing; it entered noses and mouths, ears and throats. Jehral pulled his headscarf up to cover his nose and mouth, leaving his eyes exposed to the coarse grains.

He'd taken to leading some of the regular patrols personally, and without being asked, he concentrated on the rugged coast. Day after day he led his men along the cliffs and coves, camping under the stars at night, watering horses at scarce oases. His men were tough *shalaran*, unmarried warriors. They made no complaint, though some spoiled for a fight and questioned his persistence to his face.

A rider made his way up the column, overtaking the men behind Jehral to draw up alongside his leader.

"Salut, Jehral," Rashine said.

More big than tall, Rashine rode his horse like an old man on a donkey, legs flapping to the sides. He made a formidable warrior, but his thoughts were slow. He tugged on his earring as he spoke, holding the reins with his other hand.

"Rashine," Jehral said. "What is it?"

"How long must we continue following this coast? There is nothing here."

Jehral looked to the left, scanning the deep blue ocean even as he replied. They were following a long escarpment, with the breakers below the cliffs barely audible.

"Until I say otherwise, Rashine. That is how long."

"The men grow impatient."

"And I grow impatient with the men. We are not rabble. We are Hazarans in the service of our kalif. I do not lead by consent. I lead because I have the trust of the kalif."

"There is nothing here. The land is empty. Nothing but sand and rock. Little water. No enemies."

"Enough, Rashine," Jehral growled. "If you prefer, we can settle the question of leadership the old way." Jehral rested his hand on the hilt of the sword at his side.

"No, Jehral." Rashine blanched. "I bow to your wisdom."

Rashine dropped back and Jehral sighed. He couldn't keep them much longer on this endless patrol, but the sea frightened him. Jehral once more swept his gaze across the whitecaps scattered throughout the once endless Great Western Ocean. It was as barren as the desert. More so.

Perhaps it was time to go home. Jehral's wife would have a bath waiting when he returned. Ah, but then he would have to listen to her nagging about how long he'd been away. The longer he patrolled, the worse she would get, but while he was here, he could delay the inevitable just a little bit longer.

One more day, Jehral decided. Lord of Fire, all right— perhaps two.

"There is something below the cliff ahead," the scout reported. He coughed as he wiped sand from his lips and shrugged. "It is probably nothing."

"Show me," Jehral said.

He kicked his horse into a canter, lunging up a dune and feeling the soft sand give way beneath his gelding's hooves. Cresting the ridge, he shielded his eyes against the glare as he descended the other side.

The cliffs were jagged and broken, and Jehral could make out a thin strip of sand following the coast. He saw nothing.

"Where?" he called out to the scout.

"Up ahead. I was close to the escarpment or I would not have seen it."

As their path took Jehral and the scout closer to the cliffs, the sound of the horses took on a satisfying rumble as the ground became more solid. Behind them the column made faster headway, catching up as the scout reined in only twenty paces from the sheer cliff edge.

"Look." The scout pointed. "There, at the base of the cliff. It isn't a rock."

Jehral squinted against the sun.

Rashine pulled up beside him. "It is nothing," he said.

Jehral's sharp eyes saw a crumbling ruin of some sort, brown in color and half-in, half-out of the breakers washing over it with each surge of the tide.

"We will investigate," Jehral said.

"How do you plan to get down the cliffs?" Rashine said.

Jehral fixed Rashine with a level stare. "We climb."

He left half his men to guard the horses and had the remainder strip down to trousers only, removing the loose white over-garments made to ward off the worst of the sun's rays. Fetching coils of rope from the baggage animals, Jehral then led his designated climbers to a broken low point in the cliff.

"Tie the ropes together," Jehral instructed as he looked for somewhere to fix the end. By the time the tying was complete, he'd spied a promising promontory of rock.

"We will descend one at a time," Jehral said as he fastened the rope around the rock. "Rashine and you two, help me pull on the end of the rope to test it."

Finally satisfied, Jehral tossed the coiled rope over the side of the cliff. It would be long enough.

"I will go first," Jehral said. "Wait for the count of one hundred, and then the next man will follow."

"I will be next," Rashine said. He may have been a grumbling fool, but he was a brave fool.

Jehral took a deep breath and then, without thinking too much about what he was doing, began to descend. At first it was easy, but then his arms began to tire and his sword got in the way. The muscles in his shoulders strained, and his bare chest scraped across the rock. Blinking sweat from his eyes, he tried not to look down and was almost surprised when he reached the bottom and his feet once more touched solid ground.

Eight more men followed while Jehral watched from below. Soon a chorus of advice rolled up from the watchers at the base of the cliff.

And then one of Jehral's men fell.

With a cry he plummeted from high on the cliff, his body twisting and limbs flailing at the air. He hit the rocky ground with a sickening crunch only half a dozen paces from the onlookers.

Jehral cried out in shock, calling a warning far too late. "Keep an eye on the next man! Warn me if he looks like he's falling." Jehral hurried forward and crouched at the body. He combed the long dark hair from the swarthy face. "Alhaf," he murmured, "I am sorry you had to die like this."

Jehral took Alhaf's body under the armpits and dragged him away from the base of the cliff, arranging the limbs on the hard sand of the beach. The rest of Jehral's men made it down unscathed, but each blanched when they saw the body.

"We will take Alhaf's body home with us," Jehral called, "and he will be buried with honor. Let us now see what his sacrifice was for."

Jehral drew his sword, and his men followed suit. He once again marveled at the symbols painstakingly drawn along its curved length by Ella's own hand.

"Come," he called.

They traveled along the narrow beach while the breakers roared beside them. The cool wind smelled of salt and took the edge off the fierce heat. Jehral rounded a corner of the cliff, and there it was.

He stopped in his tracks as he beheld the remnants of a once mighty ship. Jehral's heart thudded in his chest. "Please, let it not be," he whispered.

Jehral reluctantly placed one foot in front of the other and sensed the same trepidation in his men. "A leader leads from the front," he reminded himself and picked up his pace.

The vessel must have been huge when intact. The curved beams of dark wood could only have come from mighty trees. Splashes of color here and there showed where the exterior had been painted in garish hues.

The part of the ship in the water was crumbled and in disrepair, though the sides were still high. Knowing nothing about ships, Jehral could only guess how long it had been here.

The front was still mostly whole.

"Be on your guard," Jehral called.

He reached the ship and walked to a gaping hole in its side. Rashine elbowed him aside and peered in.

"Ahh!" Rashine cried, drawing back.

Immediately the desert warriors tensed, bared swords at the ready.

"What is it?" Jehral said. He stepped forward, summoning his courage as he poked his head into the hole.

The ship was crammed full of bodies.

Hundreds of them lay bloated and waterlogged, with a putrid stench clogging the air so strongly that only the stiff ocean breeze had prevented Jehrel's men from smelling the bodies before.

Jehral took a deep breath and pushed his head in again. The corpses were all shapes and sizes, some pale skinned and others dark as night. Women were among their number, and some were dressed in the fitted clothing of city folk, whereas others wore furs and barbaric horned helmets. There were as many weapons as there were bodies, with axes and daggers, two-handed swords, and strange barreled sticks tossed to and fro with the surging water.

The bodies were all covered in arcane symbols, macabre blue tattoos covering their skin.

Jehral removed his head from the hole. He inhaled slowly to steady himself.

Revenants.

Jehral's men looked to him for orders.

Urgency coursed through Jehral's blood with sudden force. Fighting the revulsion, he became cold and efficient as he stepped away from the vessel and addressed his men. "Men of House Hazara, you are looking at a ship of our enemy from across the sea. You fought revenants in the war, and we are fortunate this ship foundered, or right now we would be facing several hundred of them. Their bodies are in there," he said, pointing to the ship, "and we can only hope that this is all of them; that right now survivors of this wreck are not loose in our lands."

"What orders?" Rashine asked.

As Jehral opened his mouth, another of the desert warriors walked over to the hole and stuck his head inside.

Taking them all by surprise, something grabbed hold of the swarthy warrior, pulling him by the neck and dragging him into the hole.

The Hazaran warriors cried out and froze with terror. A moment later, a wrinkled hand took hold of the hole's rim. A face came up, a decayed grimace with green splotches around an open mouth. Momentarily stunned, the Hazarans watched in horror as a bare-chested man with long, scraggly hair climbed out of the hole. He tumbled out onto the beach and then rose to stand.

"Revenant!" one of Jehral's men cried.

"Attack!" Jehral roared.

The closest to the ship, Rashine swung his heavy scimitar at the revenant. The curved blade bit deep into the creature's shoulder, and it snarled, making a jerky movement as it looked at the wound.

Then the creature moved. And it was fast.

Its arm whipped up as it struck Rashine across the face with terrible force. A solid crunch accompanied the blow. The big warrior crumpled to the ground and lay still.

Jehral lunged forward and hacked at the exposed neck, but the revenant moved quickly and dodged, twisting out of the way. It came at him with gaping teeth and clutching fingers, hitting the center of Jehral's chest and knocking him onto his back. The stench washed over him as the creature's face loomed over his, the teeth mere inches from his neck. Jehral's sword fell out of his hands.

As one of Jehral's men leapt forward to heave the creature away, the revenant casually struck back with the same terrifying speed, lunging forward to grab the warrior by the throat and squeeze. Jehral heard a crack, and the Hazaran crumpled.

Jehral took advantage of the distraction to return to his feet and pick up his sword. As another of his men fell, Jehral swung at the revenant's exposed back, cutting into it with all the force he could muster. The scimitar almost came out of his hands as the blade cut deeply between the shoulder blades and stubbornly refused to come out. The revenant turned and growled as Jehral finally pulled his scimitar free, dark liquid spilling from the wound to the sand.

The living corpse's eyes were entirely white.

As three of the warriors rushed it together, Jehral suddenly remembered.

"Al-maia," he cried, the name of the desert rose, hoping he had it right.

The runes on Jehral's shining blade lit up with fierce shades of crimson, and the heavy scimitar suddenly felt lighter as it came alive in Jehral's hands. He felt heat washing off the blade, and set his brow in determination.

Another of Jehral's men died at the revenant's hands as it tore out his throat, and with a cry Jehral swung blindly at the macabre creature.

He put all his strength into the blow, and the glowing blade passed through the solid body without slowing.

The revenant fell down in two halves as Jehral's blow separated the torso from the waist, but it was still twitching, and its arms spasmed as it tried to pull itself along the ground. Jehral cut down again, a precise blow at the neck, and removed the head from its shoulders.

The monster lay still.

Jehral panted, his chest heaving. *"Khamsin,"* he said, and the scimitar went dark. Jehral examined the steel in surprise. Whatever Ella had done, the blade wasn't even dirty.

Jehral panted and then looked to his men. Only half a dozen lived. Jehral moved to Rashine's still body and felt for a pulse at Rashine's neck; there was none.

"Lord of Fire," someone said.

One of Jehral's warriors walked from body to body, checking each for signs of life. He looked at Jehral and shook his head.

Jehral drew in a deep breath. He looked at the hole, but there didn't appear to be any more of the creatures stirring. His thoughts returned to action as he addressed his men.

"Fire," Jehral said, "that's the solution. Marhaba," he addressed the warrior, "I am going to leave you in charge here. The kalif must know about this, and I am a better rider than any of you. I will make the journey myself. Listen to me well. Keep an eye out for more of them, and quickly burn the whole ship. I don't care if it takes you days to dry out every last piece of wood and burn every bone to ash. I will send the rest of the men down to you with tinder. Do you understand?"

"Yes, Jehral," Marhaba said. His face was white. "I understand."

"Stand guard here. Help will arrive soon, even if the men have to slide down the rope until their hands bleed. If another one comes, use fire, and use your scimitars to remove the head. Does anyone question my decision?"

"No, Jehral."

"Good. You have your orders. Burn it all."

Jehral climbed back to the summit of the cliff and sent the rest of the men down to the wrecked ship. He then took two spare horses, and digging his heels into his gelding, he launched the horse into an immediate gallop.

Jehral raced through the desert, lunging over the dunes, speeding across the sand and changing horses regularly. He didn't eat or sleep; every thought was on the urgency of his ride.

He reached Agira Lahsa haggard and worn, covered in dust, and went immediately to the palace.

As he reached the sanded area, grooms rushed forward, and Jehral threw them the reins, ignoring their startled expressions. He bounded up the steps and ran through the palace, leaving brown footsteps in the shining silk carpets.

"Zohra!" Jehral cried out when he saw his sister.

"Jehral," Zohra said, her eyes registering her surprise. "You are returned." She looked him up and down. "You cannot see the kalif like that."

"Where is he?" Jehral said, ignoring her.

"Taking lunch on the terrace, but . . ."

Jehral dashed through the palace, calling out for the kalif, breaking the serenity, leaving stewards staring after him in surprise. He found the kalif with two of his tarn leaders seated on the long table on the terrace.

"Kalif, I have urgent news."

Ilathor turned and looked up in surprise. He shot to his feet when he took in Jehral's appearance. "Jehral, what is it?"

Jehral paused to gather his breath. "We found a ship wrecked on our western coast. It was filled with revenants. We thought they were all just corpses, but one was still alive and killed four of my men. I left the men to burn everything and came here as quickly as I could."

Ilathor swiftly stood, knocking his chair back as Jehral spoke. The two tarn leaders also rose, exchanging fearful glances.

"Ships—Jehral, did you see any more ships?"

"No." Jehral shook his head. "No more. But where there is one, there will be more."

Ilathor uncharacteristically swore.

"Kalif, we must warn the Alturans," Jehral said.

"The signaling system," one of the tarn leaders said.

The kalif made a cutting motion with his hand. "It won't serve us. It's designed only to call for aid."

"Kalif, I request permission to ride to Altura."

Ilathor hesitated before finally nodding. "All right, Jehral. I will also send word to the Petyrans."

"I must get fresh horses," Jehral said. "By your leave?"

"Be safe, my friend," Ilathor said. "Stay alive."

"I will." Jehral bowed quickly and turned on his heel.

During the frantic ride to Agira Lahsa, Jehral had tried to make sense of it. The ship must have blown off course. Unfortunately, Jehral didn't know whether the enemy ship had lost its way while sailing to Altura or while heading further south, where a fleet could round the cape and head east to Tingara.

One thing he did know, however, was that where there was one ship, there would be more. And if Miro was correct, Altura would soon be under attack.

13

Miro surveyed the greatest stretch of defenses he'd ever constructed. The low wall stretched in a long line following the ridge where the beaches met the forest. From behind Castlemere, it continued eastward as far as the cliffs, where the enemy would never land, and westward halfway to Schalberg, the smaller of the free cities. Most importantly, the walls and towers covered the road to Sarostar.

Miro's decision to fortify the ridge rather than the cities themselves had been unpopular but necessary. He could never cover the entire coastline, nor could he simultaneously defend Castlemere and Schalberg in the face of an enemy landing at any place they chose, while also defending the road to Sarostar. Miro, Beorn, Tiesto, and the subcommanders all agreed: it was better to defend the ridge, where they had the cover of thick forest behind them and could fight from a higher position.

Miro was thankful there was only the one road from the free cities to Sarostar. Of course, the enemy could land anywhere, but the forests were too thick for them to penetrate through easily, and Sentar would never attempt a time-consuming push through the tangled trees. No, Sentar's way was to take his opponents head-on, overwhelm any defenses, add the dead to his army, and push on.

If Miro were attacking the Empire, he would land at these beaches, push through the defenses on the road to Sarostar, and the way to the Empire's heart would be open.

Miro had cleared the land in front of the wall, creating a huge killing ground. Below him, past the killing ground, the city of Castlemere looked weak and defenseless. Built to encircle a natural harbor, Castlemere barely had a wall; it was more of a wooden fence. The forest had stretched nearly all the way to that wall, but now it was gone. In its place were hidden ditches marked with cautioning red flags: the flags would be removed when the enemy came. Red and black markers indicated buried runebombs and big barrels of black powder. Rounded, heavy boulders painted white allowed Miro to gauge distances for his cannon, mortars, and archers.

The defensive wall was high and broad, but unlike the wall outside Sarostar, there were no ramparts; the men would fight from behind the wall rather than on top. It now took Miro over an hour to walk from one end to the other, and he'd piled tree trunks at each end all the way to the forest and even continued the barrier of logs inside. Only a colossus could lift those trunks.

He wanted the enemy to hit him from the front.

Castlemere was usually a bustling place, the larger of the two trader cities, but aside from the dock, filled with ships and sailors, the small city below was eerily quiet. The populations of the two cities had been evacuating ever since Miro's story became common knowledge, straining Sarostar's already stretched resources even further. Of course, even in Castlemere and Schalberg, stubborn citizens always remained.

In the distance, Miro watched as a huge Veldrin warship tacked back and forth to enter Castlemere's harbor. The fourteen Veldrin ships were all here, as were several Buchalanti vessels. Only the Buchalanti storm riders were scouting—they were faster than any other vessel— while the Veldrin ships stayed in harbor, crews at the ready.

Miro thought about his naval strategy. He was aware that he knew little about fighting on the sea, and so he would leave it to those he trusted with his homeland's fate. As if on cue, Miro saw Commodore Deniz and Sailmaster Scherlic weaving through the deadly defenses of the killing ground as they approached.

"Sailmaster," Miro said, clasping Scherlic's hand and then turning to Deniz. "Commodore. It's good to see you both."

Deniz and Scherlic had as many similarities as they had differences. Both had the weather-beaten skin of men who had spent most of their lives at sea, with leathery faces and rugged features. Both were tall, but Deniz wore an elegant uniform of blue and brown, whereas Scherlic wore a belted coral-pink robe. Of the two, only Deniz was armed, wearing a fine sword at his belt, with a gem-crusted hilt. As always, Deniz had a three-cornered hat with a blue feather on his head. Deniz was friendly, but his eyes were penetrating. Scherlic was dour and intimidating, one of the few men who made Miro uncomfortable.

"What news?" Miro asked.

"Still nothing," Scherlic said. "Our three storm riders scour the seas. Well, two storm riders at the moment. The *Infinity* is at harbor." He made the final statement sound like an accusation. "As soon as I finish here, we'll leave once more."

"Is it worth sending out Veldrin ships as well?" Miro asked.

"No," Deniz said. "The Buchalanti ships are much faster than ours. Our warships are powerful, but we can't risk a single vessel. Better that we leave the scouting to the Buchalanti."

Miro nodded. "When the time comes, I'd like to send a bladesinger with each of you."

"To what end?" said Scherlic.

"Essence," Miro said. "If I know our enemy, he's impatient. He'll have gathered the essence he needs to open the portal before leaving. If there's a ship we can identify as holding a great deal of essence, my bladesingers have orders to do anything they can to see it sunk . . . even if it means their lives. Defeating one of the Evermen will be hard enough without facing more. We can't allow the portal to be opened."

"As long as your bladesingers don't get in the way," Scherlic said.

"They know their business," Miro responded.

He wished he had more bladesingers, and he hated to risk two in this way, but success would be worth the risk. Bartolo was busy training the recruits at the Pens, but only one of Bartolo's recruits had been deemed good enough to be elevated, and even then he'd lost half an ear in testing. Miro touched the scar on his face. He supposed half an ear wasn't a bad outcome.

"Commodore, tell me again about how many ships they might have."

"Impossible to say," Deniz said, "but I can name four cities south of Emirald, each with a small navy the enemy could have captured. Then there are the pirate kings."

"Pirate kings?" Scherlic raised an eyebrow.

"Renegade nobles." Deniz shrugged. "Self-proclaimed kings who built their own navy and declared their borders separate to Veldria. All educated men, trained from birth in combat, and ruling by force as much as right of blood. I was always hunting them down; they captured our merchant shipping and plundered our coastal towns. Added together, their navies could have rivaled the Emir's. Fortunately, they fought each other as much as us. They may have suffered the same fate as Veldria."

"Let's just worry about what we know," Miro said. "How are your men, Commodore?"

"Anxious, but disciplined," Deniz said. "Ready as they'll ever be."

"Sailmaster?"

"We don't work in formation like the Veldrins," Scherlic said. "But here in Castlemere we have the three storm riders and two blue cruisers. In Schalberg we have another blue cruiser and two dreadnoughts—eight Buchalanti vessels in total. If the enemy fleet is in these seas, we'll find them."

"We've performed some tests," Deniz said. Scherlic scowled. "The Buchalanti ships are fast and well armed, particularly the dreadnoughts. But their armor won't stop cannon." Deniz looked at Scherlic somewhat apologetically.

Miro gazed along the fortifications. "If we can stop them in the sea, I won't consider all this to be wasted time. I'll consider your people the greatest heroes of our age. Thank you, both of you. I'll leave you to the business you know best."

The men of Halaran and Altura cheered as Miro walked in his armorsilk, his new zenblade on his back, following the outside of the defensive wall. He nodded at soldiers as he passed, greeting many by name and thanking them for their efforts. Miro checked the cannon emplacements at the forts and inspected the gaps he'd left to allow men and constructs to make sorties. Upon exiting these gaps, Miro's men all knew they had to immediately turn to the left. Every other direction, including the place in front of each gap, was marked by red warning flags.

He walked through one of the openings to the inside of the wall and checked the racks of spare weapons, the covered shelves where prismatic orbs and barrels of black powder waited, ready to be used.

Looking up, Miro could see the great carts in the forest where the constructs were housed. The heads of colossi poked above the treetops.

More than anything, Miro wished he had more orbs and dirigibles.

When he'd finished inspecting the defenses, he was halfway to Schalberg as the setting sun melted into the horizon. At mealtime he decided to go through the battle plan once more with his commanders.

Still no word from Amber.

———•———

That night Miro organized a feast. The quartermasters from the army and remaining tavern keepers from the free cities joined forces to give the men a better meal than the usual monotonous fare.

Miro knew he would have at least two days' notice from the Buchalanti scouts, and morale was important. He spent the last of his gilden on the feast. It was probably one of the best meals many of these people had ever had.

Bonfires dotted the pale white sands to the east of Schalberg, far from the defenses, the fires banishing the darkness and continuing into the night. The men drank weak beer, but it didn't stop them from singing. They toasted Miro and hid their fear behind jokes and tall stories about the women in Tingara.

Miro didn't join in.

He stood alone near the water's edge, looking up at the sky. A comet passed overhead, leaving a sparkling tail in the afterimage.

"An omen," a voice came from behind him.

Miro glanced at Commodore Deniz. "Do you believe in such things?"

"No," Deniz said, and both men chuckled.

"I feel it, though," Miro said. "Something tells me it won't be long now."

Deniz nodded, his face clearly visible in the starlight. "I feel it too."

"Tell me, Deniz. With all this talk of omens and Evermen, what do you believe?" Miro asked.

Deniz shrugged. "My people believe in gods who live under the sea and in the sky. They shoot lightning bolts at each other when they fight, like a bickering husband and wife."

"And you?"

"I don't know what I believe. I know, though, that I will fight this darkness with every ounce of strength I possess, even to my own death. Though the navy has always been my family, my homeland was ruined, and even if my people return and rebuild, Veldria will never be the same again."

"Don't lose hope," Miro said.

"I have found something else to hold on to," Deniz said. "Vengeance."

For a time there was silence between them before Deniz spoke again. "And you, Miro of Altura, the man from across the sea, whom I once took captive, what do you fight for?"

"I fight for my homeland and for the lives of those I love. I fight so that my son, Tomas, can grow up in a free world."

"A worthy cause," Deniz said, "perhaps much more so than revenge. Tell me, are you ready to die?"

Miro paused. "I am," he finally said.

Deniz nodded as he gazed at the dark seas.

"But I'll try not to."

14

The Poloplats market in Sarostar was a place where items both ordinary and strange could be found. It was never the same from one day to the next, and scouring the market day after day could yield results, if one knew where to look.

Ella had once worked in the market selling flowers. She still recognized many of the merchants, and this morning she'd already enjoyed startling Harry Maloney, an unscrupulous buyer she'd once had to work with, with a cheery greeting. He'd sputtered hot cherl all over his jerkin. Ella didn't feel bad: his clothes were always filthy.

Just like the other merchants and buyers, Ella asked Harry about the things she needed—sometimes people without scruples could get hold of goods that others couldn't—but so far she hadn't had any luck. She needed more of everything: beakers and vials, bars of iron, and any swords she could lay her hands on. She needed things she didn't even know she needed. Already Ella had found slow-burning oil, and flicking through the alchemist's book, she found a formula for naphtha. She bought all the merchant had and instructed him to send the flasks to the Academy.

Ella would have liked to send someone else to the market, but she knew she had to come herself. She wasn't paying with gilden; she paid using the letters of credit Miro had given her. The merchants always hesitated when she presented them, but Ella wouldn't accept their refusal. They knew who she was and didn't dare say no to her face, especially when she gave them a certain stare.

Tungawa's book contained formulas for poisonous fumes and fiery liquids, and Ella kept an eye out for anything interesting. The book always made her think of the alchemist's dying words, words Ella thought were intended for her. It is the dose that makes a thing a poison. What had he meant?

The lore Evrin had taught Killian didn't give Ella any hint at the truth, as fascinating as it was. When Sentar came, how could they ever hope to defeat him? Would Killian come to their aid if Altura called?

Walking along the aisles, Ella scanned the low tables. She emerged back onto the road, and as she was about to re-enter the next aisle of stalls, she overheard two merchants talking.

"Look who it is," a vendor with a jewelry display said to the fat man next to him, a seller of pots and pans. "You wouldn't know it to look at him, but he's probably wealthier than the emperor himself. What do you do with that much gilden?"

"What do you think you'd do?" said the fat man. "You'd get out of here and head east, or maybe south. Anywhere but here. Any fool can tell this isn't a place to stay."

"What are you going to do if you have to flee?"

"Where would I flee to? This is my home."

Ella scanned the road in the direction the two men were looking, curious to see the subject of their attention. A convoy of three wagons stood pulled up at the side of the main road, near the section where stores and supplies were sold. Surrounded by a cluster of guards, the driver of the foremost wagon stood negotiating with a seller of vegetables.

Ella squinted but a group of soldiers passed by, obscuring her vision. When they'd passed, she quickly crossed the busy road, speeding up as she recognized the squat figure with broad shoulders and close-cropped hair.

"Hermen!" Ella called. "Hermen Tosch!"

Hermen turned at the sound of his name, revealing a round face and deep-set eyes. The free cities trader, who turned up in the most unlikely places, looked uncomfortable, as if he didn't want to see her. Ella had first met Hermen when she'd helped the Hazarans rediscover their lore. She'd last seen him in the ice city, Ku Kara, and though they weren't close, she now considered him a friend.

As Ella passed the wagons, she saw two young men, one in each of the driving seats of the two other carts. A woman sat next to the youngest, and both of the young men had Hermen's features.

"Enchantress." Hermen nodded. He rarely smiled, but Ella had learned he possessed an acerbic wit. "No surprise to find you here," he said in his thick, guttural accent.

"Where are you going?" Ella asked.

Hermen sighed. "East, Ella. East and north. There's virgin land north of Loua Louna. I'm taking my family and making a fresh start."

"I didn't know you had a family." Ella turned and smiled at the woman and the two young men.

"That's my wife, Greta, and my two sons, Thorsten and Rolf," Hermen said.

"Pleased to meet you," Ella called to Greta.

"And you," Greta replied, but she didn't smile. "Hermen, we must go."

"What's in the wagons?" Ella asked.

Hermen hesitated. "My life's work," he said.

Ella wondered what he meant. She looked at the way the wagons' axles were bowed under the weight of their loads; whatever Hermen had with him was heavy.

Then Ella had a sudden thought, and realization dawned. She frowned and strode around to the back of Hermen's wagon. Hermen left his haggling to chase her. Pulling the flaps at the back of Hermen's wagon wide, Ella saw chests, dozens of them.

"You're taking your money and running?" Ella said, letting go of the coverings and turning back to Hermen.

"Not all of us are fighters," Hermen said. He looked down at the ground. "I'm a trader, Ella, and I have a family to take care of."

"What about him?" Ella said, indicating with her chin an old man passing by.

The old man's wrinkled face peered at the world from under a fringe of thin white hair. He wore faded Alturan livery, the sword and flower on his chest barely discernible. He carried a worn scabbard strapped to his waist and traveled with a group of all ages under the supervision of a middle-aged officer. All carried sacks over their shoulders as they walked in the direction of Castlemere.

Castlemere: Hermen's home.

"Do you think he doesn't have a family? Children? Grandchildren?"

"It's not my way," Hermen said. "We can't all fight."

"No, obviously it's not." Ella fought to control her anger. Part of her knew she wasn't being fair to Hermen, but the sight of the chests, no doubt filled with gilden, filled her with anger at the unfairness of it all.

"I must be going."

"Good-bye, Hermen. I wish you a successful new start," Ella said. She stuck out her hand, and he slowly returned the handshake before letting his hand fall away. Ella wondered if she'd ever see him again.

Hermen looked sad. "Good-bye, Ella."

Ella crossed the road back to the market, promising herself she would forget about him, though she felt Hermen's eyes on her back.

———◆———

"You can't blame him," Evrin said to Ella as they walked through the grassy fields surrounding the Academy. "People will always act true to their nature. It is the way of the world. We can't expect more from people than they can give."

"I guess I thought he was better that that."

"Has he ever shown you his nature was any different?"

Ella thought about the first time she'd met Hermen, in the shadows of Ilathor's tent, deep in the Hazara desert. He'd seen an opportunity in the Hazarans' growing power, and he'd most likely profited greatly.

She remembered when they'd met in Ku Kara. Once again, Hermen had been opening ties with a people formerly lost to the trade of the Empire. He'd always spoken of profit and customers and trade routes.

"I suppose not," Ella said. "But how can he leave his home so callously?"

"His family is his home. As long as he has his family by his side, he can protect them and create a new home somewhere else. We all have ties to our homeland, but the ties of family are stronger still."

"I don't see Miro taking Amber and Tomas to some place far away."

"That's not Miro's nature," Evrin said. "But even your brother doesn't just fight for some rocks and rivers, forests and fields. He fights for the people he protects. He knows that even if all of Altura were evacuated, the enemy would still have to be faced. He has chosen this place to make his stand."

"What about you?" Ella said. "Where is your home?"

Evrin smiled sadly. "I lost my home when I saw something greater. I once ruled over thousands of people from a glorious palace. My love . . . she showed me something altogether more important. I thought my brother Evermen were my family, but she showed me we weren't brothers; we were allies, united by our arrogance and our lust for power. She became my family, and I fought for her and others like her. I fought for you, Ella, and I will continue to fight."

"That makes me sad. Are you saying you don't have a home?"

"I have places where I spend time. But yes, I suppose you're right; I have no home. It was lost to me long ago, but the trade was worth it. Every human is my family, whether I know the person or I don't."

"You put Hermen Tosch to shame."

"He is just acting true to his nature." Evrin looked into the distance, and Ella wondered what he was seeing. "Just as I must face what I once did and act true to mine."

15

As Carla left the Imperial Palace, she looked up at the great timepiece on the face of the tallest tower. *Slow down,* she reminded herself. She had time. She was out looking for work, and she needed to walk with purpose, but not with frantic worry.

She strolled toward Fortune and the Tenamet; it would make sense for her to seek employment in the boutiques of the city's wealthiest district, or perhaps the eating and drinking houses of the place where Seranthians went for pleasure. Heading along the Grand Boulevard also gave Carla a chance to see if anyone was following her. She'd caught the sidelong looks from Alise, Killian's mother; the woman was definitely keeping an eye on her.

Carla pretended to read the inscription on one of the statues lining the side of the Grand Boulevard closest to the park. It was difficult to establish whether any of the multitudes walking along the avenue were watching her, but she was trained at these things, trained and talented. Looking back at the palace, Carla continued to wait. Anyone following her would have to loiter when they were uncertain where she was going. Carla was satisfied, for now, but she couldn't let down her guard.

She turned back into the warren of streets and alleys when she reached Fortune. So far, her actions hadn't given away any purpose other than a young woman looking for work.

Carla passed a series of dressmakers and resisted the urge to glance in. She loved fine dresses and had a wonderful wardrobe, but her current guise had her wearing basic clothing. She'd chosen this set carefully and had some nicely snug bodices and fashionably short skirts, but she knew she could be much more beautiful in a lovely dress. As always, it was a matter of striking the right balance, in this case between poor and pretty, careworn and clean. She needed to evoke the right amount of sympathy, yet not be pathetic. She needed to be attractive.

Next Carla walked past a row of manses, and now she was truly envious. One day she wanted to have the biggest manse in Seranthia, but though she sometimes spent time in the company of Seranthia's lords, she didn't want to achieve her ambition—to become rich—because of a marriage to some powerful man. She wanted to do it on her own. Carla shuddered at the thought of being given an allowance and told how she should spend her time. Nothing was more valuable than freedom.

Carla felt absolutely no remorse at using Killian. She supposed that in some strange locked-up part of her mind, she blamed him for her father's death. She knew that didn't quite make sense, which was also strange to her: that she could think that and still feel the same. Shouldn't logic prevail over emotion? Carla thought of herself as a logical person. But one couldn't be perfect all the time.

Savory aromas wafted toward her as she walked past a pastry shop. Carla entered and ordered a scroll, sitting down and taking her time to enjoy it. She liked the fancy food they served in the palace, but sometimes simple food was just as good.

She'd chosen the shop well, and she knew that any watcher would have to keep an eye on the shop from the street. Carla exited, and straight away she saw him.

He was good, to have escaped her notice so far. A professional, obviously. His tailored clothing—rich enough to get him into most places, but not ostentatious enough to stand out—gave that away. Even his face was bland, with two little moustaches his only distinguishing feature.

Looking down at the ground, as if disappointed by the results of a luckless job hunt, Carla continued into the Tenamet.

She passed through a section of storehouses with spiked fences, quiet streets where a young girl needed to keep her wits about her, and pretended to scan the alleys fearfully, though Carla knew this area well and could handle herself; her search was more to keep an eye on her follower. Then the number of passersby increased, and though it was early evening, revelers began to fill the streets and alleys in numbers.

Raucous music blared from doorways, and lopsided façades in need of new paint invited anyone with gilden to enjoy a meal, a few mugs of beer, or something more. Carla entered The Gilded Remedy and waited for the space of twenty breaths and then exited again, once more looking dejected. A few doors down she walked into The Hornet's Nest and nodded at the barkeeper. Giving him the sign, Carla went to the door at the back and knocked three times, paused, and then knocked twice more.

The door opened, and a huge man with a spiked iron club looked her up and down. Carla gave him the sign, and he made way. "Just passing through," she murmured.

This was where she would lose her pursuer.

Carla descended a set of stairs and walked along a narrow hall, passing doorway after doorway; she knew each contained a bed and little else. Some were open, and shone the wan red light of faded nightlamps in lukewarm invitation, whereas others were closed, grunting sounds coming from within.

Carla reached the door at the back and nodded at the guard. He recognized her, but she made the sign anyway, and he pushed the rear door open, revealing a dark alleyway.

Carla wrinkled her nose at the stench and stepped around the piles of refuse. The alleyway popped her out onto the streets again, a block away from where she'd started, and now she hurried, taking a series of turns and then finally breathing freely as she left the Tenamet behind altogether.

There. She'd shaken him.

Able to hurry for the first time, Carla headed down to the harbor as the sun set and evening turned to night. Arriving at the docks, she looked out at the strange tower-like shape of the walled Sentinel, covered from base to top. She'd asked Killian about it, but he'd been evasive. Carla hadn't pressed him, and she didn't really care; her purpose had nothing to do with whatever his reasons were for walling up the majestic statue.

Carla followed the wharves to the farthest end. She reached back and pulled her hood over her head so that her face was shadowed. It was quiet here and dark. Carla waited and hoped she wasn't late.

Sensing movement behind her, Carla started to turn, but rough hands grabbed her arms, pinning them at her sides. Before she could cry out, someone stuffed a gag in her mouth and placed a blindfold over her eyes, tied over her hood.

"Move," a low voice said, putting pressure on her back.

Carla took a hesitant step forward and felt the pressure increase. She nearly stumbled, but her captor guided her and she heard the splash of water. She fought down her panic, and then she was physically lifted and felt rocking beneath her feet as she was set down in a boat.

Soon the sound of wood scraping on wood, followed by a regular splash, told Carla she was moving. She tried to count the minutes, but it was difficult, for she struggled to breathe through the gag, and her senses were heightened, her hearing conjuring up images of impending death by drowning or a blade in the chest.

The rowing ceased and the boat coasted forward for a time before hitting wood with a clunk, nearly propelling Carla out of her seat. She was again picked up and set down, and she felt solid planking beneath her feet. Wherever she was, it must be close to the docks. She speculated about her location. Perhaps one of the shipyards? One of the houses of the rich merchant families who could afford their own pier?

"Keep walking—don't stop," the voice said again.

Carla took several steps forward.

"Stairs ahead."

Carla lifted one foot and placed it down, then tested the next step. Getting their measure, she reached the top of a stone stairway and continued ahead. She heard the creaking of a door, and then she was seated in a chair.

Carla felt hands fumbling at the knots of her blindfold, and then with a sense of relief, she felt it removed. Her hood stayed in place, hanging low over her face.

Carla was in a low-ceilinged room with very little light. She sat at a long table with several other figures, all with hoods over their faces like her. It was impossible to see anyone's features.

Carla was ranked high in the Melin Tortho, the most powerful of the streetclans, but even she didn't know where she was, nor did she know the identity of the man who sat at the head of the table, carefully placed where the shadows were deepest.

Scanning the other figures, Carla did have an idea who one of them was. She recognized the hunched build and lanky frame of the emperor's steward. Neither Carla nor Lord Osker acknowledged each other, but she'd made the sign in the Imperial Palace and seen him return the countersign.

In addition to Carla, Osker, and the man at the table's head, three other figures sat at the table. Whoever they were, their faces were shadowed, but they must be powerful to be seated at the same table as the man at the head.

Carla pricked her ears as the man at the head now spoke. She tried to pick up the cadence of his speech or the timbre of his voice—she was good at such things—but a man in his position must be cunning indeed, and a voice could be disguised. Still, knowing the identity of the Tortho himself would be a valuable secret to possess. Carla planned to supplant him one day.

"Those here are united by a common purpose," the Tortho said. "We work together to increase Tingara's power and keep our city safe from our enemies. Some of you are from the streetclans, and some are not. Speaking for the Melin Tortho, we wish neither to depose the emperor, nor to be the cause of conflict in the city. We like things just the way they are. We also have no wish to see the city fall to invaders, something the high lord of Altura warns us about. What do the nobles say?"

One of the men opposite Carla spoke. "We wish to keep Tingara safe. We wish to protect our lands and resources from those who would take them, whether from inside the Empire or without. We don't want the houses taking the protection that is rightfully ours."

"And the merchants?" the Tortho asked.

Another figure spread his hands; his voice was smooth as silk. "You've said it all already."

"Let us be more plainspoken, then," the Tortho said. "After mad Xenovere and the crazed primate, this new emperor may be the best thing to happen to Tingara in a very long time. But he has spent much of his time living as a foreigner, and his loyalty to Tingara is untested. He has friends in Altura and Petrya and among the Hazarans. Speaking simply, we cannot afford to lose the Legion. If Altura calls, and the emperor decides to send away those who should rightfully be protecting Tingara, then the emperor's decision must not stand. We have sent men to the west to isolate Altura, but here at home we must prepare for a signal still reaching the emperor."

Carla gulped. This was where she came into the plan, she knew. She'd fought hard to take her seat at the secret circles of power in Seranthia: a Halrana by birth, she'd had to prove herself time and again before she'd earned her new family's trust. After the death of her father, the streetclans were the natural home for someone who despised the mad emperor, someone who had no family, no home, and no other place to go. She had to fulfill her duty.

"Though we come from different backgrounds and share different interests, we are united patriots, all of us. Desperate times call for desperate measures. Although our last rulers were despots, they nonetheless gave rightful precedence to Tingara above all others. We are uncertain about the new emperor. If he cares more for the other houses than he does for Tingara, he threatens everything."

A chorus of assent came from the room.

And then they told Carla what she must do.

16

Jehral rode through the desert as only a horseman born and bred could do, lunging up the soft sand of the dunes and scrabbling down the reverse sides as he spurred his horses to ever greater efforts. Carrying only enough water for a few days, he strictly rationed himself to tiny sips, hoping the speed of his journey would get him through.

Taking advantage of the glittering starlight shining through the clear night skies, he rode through the days and into the nights, rotating mounts as he went, speeding past the strange rock formations and finally seeing red boulders replace the yellow sands as he entered Petrya.

As he left the desert behind, he was able to make better headway, spurring his horse into a gallop, with his two remounts trailing behind. The sound of hooves clattering on rock filled his consciousness, providing an unceasing rhythm to his journey so that even in the small snatches of sleep, he dreamt of the patter of horse feet.

Winding through Petrya's northwest, skirting the forests of rust-colored trees, he found the thin trail leading up to the mountains, and called forth ever greater efforts from his mounts as the slope steepened and the trail carved a zigzag path up the face of the mighty Elmas.

Jehral cursed when the treacherous Wondhip Pass again forced him to dismount. Leading all three of his horses, he walked as fast as he was able over the loose scree and treacherous gravel, navigating his way around fallen boulders and into the gully that was the pass's highest point.

As Jehral was about to pass under Ella's tower, he looked up at the prism, seeing it was still dark and unlit. The enemy fleet must still be missing. Only Jehral knew it was close. Miro needed to send every man to Castlemere and prepare for the worst.

He thought about what he'd seen. The wrecked revenant ship told a story better than any written account. He remembered the way the single animated corpse had destroyed his men. The urgency of his mission spurred him on. Altura must know.

One of Jehral's horses, a young and inexperienced mare, stumbled and whinnied in pain as Jehral heard a terrible crack that sent a shiver crawling up his back. The horse drew to a halt, and Jehral saw her lift her leg, eyes wide and body trembling. Splinters of bone protruded from the broken leg; the horse would never make it down from the mountain.

Jehral cursed and felt the animal's pain and terror as if it were his own. He led his other two mounts forward through the gully and to the other side. They wouldn't want to see this.

He hobbled the two horses and turned back into the gully. The wounded mare was in terrible agony, and Jehral's heart reached out to her.

"You have done well," he whispered in soothing tones. The mare looked at him and rolled her eyes while she shivered. Jehral drew his sword and rested his hand on the horse's neck as he found the right place to make his strike, behind her foreleg. He continued to speak in a soft voice, and then with one swift move he plunged the blade into the horse's side, driving hard to reach the heart. She died instantly as Jehral stood back and hung his head.

The blood dripped off the enchanted blade. In a matter of heartbeats, the steel shone bright and silver once more. Jehral sheathed the sword and again walked through the gully to reach his other two mounts.

Sighing, he took the reins and again led them forward over the treacherous down slope, exhausted but determined as he headed for his final destination.

Jehral had promised Ella to do anything he could to help, and he was a man who lived by his word.

Sarostar beckoned.

———————◆———————

Jehral's journey took him along a winding road past fallow fields and through lush forests. He changed horses regularly but could see they were blown, both of his mounts foaming white at the mouth.

As he rode, he pictured the bloated bodies of the revenants and again saw the single revenant kill four of his men, all armed, with nothing but its hands. He remembered the last war, when a small army of Akari revenants had crushed the Hazarans at the Gap of Garl. He needed to hurry.

He looked up at the sun. It was perhaps midday. He was close to Sarostar now and could see a bridge spanning one of the Sarsen's many tributaries. Jehral kicked into a gallop. Below the bridge he saw a mighty waterfall, and in awe of the great drop, he was distracted by the plummeting cascade.

As he reached the far side of the bridge, Jehral was attacked.

He saw a flicker of movement but was too slow to react as a spear point thrust up at his chest from somewhere below. Part of his consciousness told him it was an ambush, even as the spear hit the center of his chest, throwing him out of the saddle and sending him catapulting through the air to land heavily on the ground. Only the leather cuirass he wore under his clothing saved him for being impaled.

Adrenalin surged through Jehral's body as he shook his head to clear it. Behind him he heard the roar of men rushing to the attack. Jehral leapt to his feet and drew his sword; thankfully the scabbard was still at his side.

His opponents halted their mad charge as Jehral shifted, head scanning to keep them all in his vision.

There were four of them. They wore light armor and no insignia, and at first Jehral thought they were bandits, but then he saw their features looked Tingaran. These men had tattoos, but they also didn't look like military; they had the swagger of men from the street.

"You fool, Pedron," a lean man, evidently the leader, said to one of his fellows, the warrior holding a spear. "We could have let him ride past."

The accent was definitely Tingaran. What would Tingarans be doing here, close to Sarostar?

"I don't care, Dan. I want his horses," Pedron said.

"You imbecile! You can't even ride!"

"I'm hungry. I haven't had meat in weeks."

Jehral watched the exchange in bemusement. He took the opportunity to activate his scimitar. *"Al-maia,"* Jehral spoke softly. The runes on the shining steel lit up with fiery colors.

The leader, Dan, swore. "He's got an enchanted blade."

"It's worth a lot more than they're paying us," Pedron said. "Whoever kills him gets it!"

Pedron rushed Jehral with the spear while the others circled to the left and right. Jehral pretended to look uncertain, taking a few steps backward, but then he dashed forward and knocked aside the thrusting spear to whip his scimitar across Pedron's throat.

Jehral spun, and before the leader could slash at his back, he took the scimitar through the backswing and into the leader's attack. His opponent raised his sword to block, but Jehral's blade cut through the steel, shearing it in two. Dan was suddenly holding half a sword, with a stricken expression on his face.

Jehral waited again, panting as he once more stepped back to keep his three opponents in sight. He feinted at the Tingaran on his left but turned right, and his superior swordsmanship immediately showed as they all took the bait. A slashing blow took a swordsman in the chest, and the man went down.

Jehral blocked a thrust, swiping the blade out of the way, and then shifted to stab at the leader's abdomen. His opponent nimbly drew back, but even so, the blade bit into his side. The leader went down.

The last of the ambushers came at Jehral, but defeat was already in his eyes. He looked in surprise at the gash the scimitar left across his chest and then fell to his knees, blood welling around him as he died.

Jehral deactivated the sword, and his chest heaved as fatigue set in. He was exhausted from the frantic ride, and the fight had taken still more of his energy. The leader, Dan, looked up at him with wide eyes as Jehral approached.

"What are you doing here?" Jehral demanded, crouching beside him.

"We . . ." the leader coughed and choked. "We . . ."

The man's eyes rolled back in his head, and his chest shuddered as the life went out of him.

The lands around Sarostar were supposed to be safe, yet here these men were, on the outskirts of Altura's capital itself.

Jehral cursed when he saw his horses had bolted. Still, as tired as they were, they wouldn't go far.

Jehral decided to leave the bandits—if that was what they were—where they'd fallen. He cast in circles, looking for hoof prints, and finally found a circular imprint in the soft earth.

Jehral began to walk.

17

Tapel darted from street corner to street corner as he watched the one-eyed man buying stores in the Poloplats market. He was sure he'd seen this man dressed as a beggar before, and now here he was in plain but well-cut clothing. Who was he? And why did he keep buying supplies?

Tapel skirted the stalls, hiding among some hanging tapestries, keeping the one-eyed man in sight. A Veldrin walked past, a swarthy man with an elegant doublet and tight blue leggings.

"Excuse me," Tapel whispered.

"Yes?" the Veldrin looked down his nose.

"Is he one of you?" Tapel indicated the one-eyed man.

"One of whom, my boy?"

"One of you. A Veldrin."

The Veldrin shook his head. "No, I can tell at a glance. He isn't one of us."

Tapel thanked the Veldrin and then scurried to keep up with the one-eyed man. Could he be Halrana? Perhaps from the free cities?

The one-eyed man reached forward to hand over some coins to a merchant and Tapel saw a tattoo at his wrist. Alturans and

Halrana didn't commonly have tattoos, but people from the free cities sometimes did, particularly sailors. Tapel decided to get close and hear the one-eyed man's voice.

Tapel's darting figure drew some glances, but few people took note of a fifteen-year-old boy, even if he was flitting from one stall to another. A few merchants fixed Tapel with baleful stares.

"Salt beef," the one-eyed man was saying. "And wine."

"It's quite a journey you're provisioning," the vendor said.

"Mouths need feeding," the one-eyed man said with a shrug.

The accent certainly wasn't from the free cities. Tapel had been to Tingara and he thought perhaps it was Tingaran. What would a Tingaran be doing here in Altura?

Tapel wondered if he should go to Bladesinger Bartolo, or perhaps to his mother. But what would he say? And if he lost the one-eyed man now, who could say Tapel would find him again?

Tapel decided to follow him.

The one-eyed man finished his business and hefted a heavy knapsack onto his shoulder. Tapel trailed him out of the market, hiding in the crowd as his quarry traveled over the Long Bridge, heading east.

The crowds thinned as the one-eyed man traveled through the district of workshops and storehouses. Tapel found it difficult to keep up, darting behind walls and breathing heavily whenever he thought he might be spotted.

The one-eyed man's stride opened up as he reached the road to Samson's Bridge, and the trees at the city's outskirts gave Tapel useful cover. Tapel couldn't lose him now; this road led to only one place: the bridge, and the border with Halaran.

Tapel poked his head from around a tree and saw the man still lumbering along ahead. He felt foolish. Perhaps the man was camping with friends; there was certainly little space in the city. Tapel weaved through the trees, deciding to head deeper into the forest as he followed the road, staying in cover, where he could move faster without worrying about being spotted.

There were plenty of campsites around, so why was the man still traveling as if he had a long journey ahead of him?

Tapel followed the one-eyed man for mile after mile, and soon he started to tire, although his quarry showed no sign of halting. Now that he'd come so far, Tapel stubbornly refused to give up. He would find the one-eyed man's camp, and then he would know. If they were up to no good, Tapel would tell his mother. Amelia would know what to do.

Hours passed, and Tapel knew he was due at the Pens, and he would now be in trouble. Still the one-eyed man kept plodding along. Finally the trees began to thin, and ahead Tapel saw tall columns, the supports holding up Samson's Bridge.

A tall three-legged tower stood beside the bridge, and at the apex Tapel saw the pyramid of quartz. He knew all about the signaling system, and he knew that this junction at the bridge was an important place. From here towers in the east would connect Altura to Tingara, and towers in the north would extend the chain all the way to Vezna and beyond.

Tapel's brow furrowed.

He reached the edge of the trees and peered out. Where had the one-eyed man gone?

Tapel waited and moved silently forward, scanning the bank where the cliffs plunged to the surging river below, checking each tree in turn. His face fell as he realized he'd lost his quarry.

Tapel turned as he heard sudden movement behind him.

He jumped as a hand clapped over his mouth. Suddenly a face pressed close to his, the whiskers rubbing against his cheek, and a voice spoke with stinking breath. "What are you doing, eh, lad? How long've you been following me?"

The hand came off his mouth, and Tapel wondered if he should scream. Looking out at the bridge, he saw a drudge-pulled cart crossing the bridge, heading for Altura. Tapel drew in a breath when he felt a sharp point press into his side.

"Don't even think about it," the one-eyed man said, his empty eye socket so close that Tapel couldn't look away from the puckered skin. "Well? What's your story?"

"I was just hunting in the forest. For mushrooms," Tapel said. "That's all."

The man nodded. His eye-socket was wrinkled and wept fluid. "Hunting mushrooms. And where's your bag? Show me some mushrooms."

"I . . . I haven't found any yet," Tapel said weakly.

"Who are you? Who's going to miss you?"

"No one," Tapel whimpered. "I'm nobody."

"Good," said the one-eyed man.

He clapped his hand back over Tapel's mouth and dragged him through the forest while Tapel writhed and wriggled. Tapel's heart threatened to leap out of his chest, it was pounding so strongly. Fear filled his limbs, and he felt weak as he was hauled forcefully through the trees, heading downriver, in a southerly direction following the riverbank. Soon Tapel smelled smoke and saw a campsite in the trees.

Two rough-looking men sat around a fire while a third man with a tattoo on his neck tended it, adding fuel. One of the seated men had a sword across his knees that he was sharpening with slow circular movements. The other seated figure was a scrawny brigand with a shaved head.

The tattooed man at the fire looked up. "You bring the wine . . . Whoa! What've you got there?"

"Street kid followed me here," the one-eyed man said, gripping Tapel tightly.

"What's he, dinner?" said the man sharpening his sword.

The tattooed man at the fire barked a laugh.

"He's going to have to stay with us, at least 'til the job's done," said the one-eyed man.

"Just kill him." The swordsman shrugged.

"Hold on there," said the scrawny man. "I'm not in the business of killing children."

"It's not so hard after the first one," said the swordsman.

Tapel felt ragged terror course through him, sending shivers down his spine.

"Benji, throw me some rope," said the one-eyed man. The man at the fire, Benji, rummaged around the campsite and then tossed over a hemp rope. The one-eyed man deftly caught the length of twine in the air.

The one-eyed man bound Tapel's wrists and then threw him to the ground. Pushing down on Tapel's back, he also tied Tapel's ankles together. Tapel could scream, but out here no one would hear.

Tapel wriggled until he could rest his back against a fallen tree trunk. "Who . . . who are you?" he asked.

"Your worst nightmare," Benji said, grinning at Tapel as he pulled a dagger from his belt, brandishing his weapon.

"Seriously, Brin," said the swordsman to the one-eyed man. "We should kill him. What are you planning on doing, feeding him? Feel like adopting an urchin?"

"He can earn his keep," the one-eyed man, Brin, said.

"How?" asked the seated scrawny man.

"Our job is to keep an eye on the tower. If it lights up, we knock it down. Right?"

"Yeah."

"Well I've got a better idea. Check this out. I've got a surprise." Brin rummaged in his knapsack and withdrew a glass pyramid. "I ordered this when I was last in Sarostar and picked it up today. If we swap the real prism for a false one, our job is done."

"Our orders are to watch and only knock it down if it lights green," the scrawny man growled. "Who's to say they won't know as soon as we've broken the chain? What do we know of lore?"

"Hang on, Sebastian," Benji said to the scrawny man. "I want to hear this out." Benji left the fire and came over to crouch beside Tapel. "How's your climbing, boy?" he said.

Tapel realized his life hung in the balance. "Good."

"See?" Brin said. "We've been sleeping in shifts to keep an eye on the tower. Dan's bringing three more men, but that won't help much. If we swap the prisms, no one will be the wiser, and we can get some proper sleep for a change. The boy can help. Tonight."

"All right, Brin," the swordsman said. "We'll try it your way. Tonight."

The swordsman kicked Tapel awake well before dawn. The night was as black as pitch. Tapel groaned. Tied as he was, he'd had the most uncomfortable night of his life. His back ached and now his stomach hurt from the kick. If he'd eaten, he would have been sick.

"Go easy on the lad," he heard Brin's voice say. "He needs to climb. Come on, boy. Don't try anything foolish, or we'll carve you up."

Brin cut the twine around Tapel's wrists and ankles and then grabbed Tapel's wrist in a grip of iron, twisting the boy's arm behind his back and marching him forward. The four men took him out of the trees and down to the water's edge. As they took Tapel back upriver, he heard the Sarsen slosh and gurgle and saw the nearby supports of Samson's Bridge silhouetted against the night sky.

No one was crossing the bridge at this hour, and they had the area to themselves. Brin marched Tapel to the three-legged tower, where the thin supports held the prism higher than any of them could reach.

"Boy. Look." Tapel heard a creaking sound, and turning in alarm, he saw the scrawny man, Benji, holding a drawn bow, the pointed arrow glinting, aimed right at him. "Just so you don't try to run."

"You understand your task?" Brin asked, crouching down so he was at eye level with Tapel. "You're to shinny up this pole here 'til you're at the top. Remove the glass thing up there. Then call down. Got it?"

Tapel gulped. He knew the towers were important, and he didn't know who these men were, but he'd gathered their purpose. They wanted to break the chain of reflectors heading east. If Altura called, these men didn't want the lands of Loua Louna, Torakon, or Tingara sending help.

"Climb!" Brin said, emphasizing his point by shoving Tapel in the back, so he fell down.

Tapel slowly climbed back to his feet and wondered if he could run to summon help. He met the eyes of the man with the bow. He'd heard the swordsman's words; he'd killed children before, and these men wouldn't stop at killing him. If Tapel died, they'd just find another way.

Tapel grabbed hold of the thin pole and pulled himself up. Fighting at the Pens had made him strong, and though the metal was glossy, it wasn't slippery. Soon he had both hands on the tower's leg and his ankles twisted around the base. His arms on fire, he pulled himself up and managed to climb until he was at the apex, gazing down at the men standing below, heads tilted back as they looked up.

"He's up," Brin said. "Boy! Take off the prism, then toss it down." In a whisper to his friends he said, "We'll take it far from here and bury it."

Hanging by one hand and ignoring the drop below, gripping the tower's support with his wrapped legs, Tapel yanked and pushed at the prism. It took several tries, but he finally heard a click and felt it come away in his hands.

"Throw it down!" Brin called.

Tapel instead leaned back, the muscles in his arm burning to hold him in place, and threw with all his strength.

The prism curved through the air, looking like it would hit the bridge, but it missed. Instead it sailed past the steep riverbank and landed in the turbulent river with a splash.

"What did you do that for, insolent pup?" one of the watchers growled.

"What does it mean, Brin?"

"It doesn't matter," Brin said. "Think about it. Why mount the thing on a tower if you don't need to? It must need to be placed high."

"Sorry—I thought that was what you wanted me to do," Tapel called down.

Brin growled up to Tapel. "Keep your voice down. Just don't mess this part up, or I'll kill you myself. I'm going to throw you the replacement. Reckon you can catch it?"

"Not really." Tapel was holding on to his place at the apex of the tower with both arms and legs, but he didn't think he could hold much longer.

"Out of the way," one of the others said. He carried a long tree branch from the forest, forked at the end. He took the false prism from Brin and settled it in the fork before carefully lifting the prism up to Tapel's height.

"Place it at the top," Brin called.

Tapel released one of his arms and reached for the prism. His limbs were growing weak, and he was worried he'd fall at any instant, knowing these men wouldn't shed any tears. He placed the glass pyramid on the flat triangle of metal where the last had been. It wasn't quite the same size as the real one had been, but it settled comfortably, if a little loosely.

"Try to move it," someone said.

Tapel nudged the prism and it rocked side to side.

"Don't worry," Brin said. "I'll head back to the market and get some resin. That'll hold it fast. You can come down now, boy."

Tapel slid back down the metal leg of the tower and came to rest on his feet before sagging down to the ground.

"Well done," Brin said, clapping him on the back. The man with the bow relaxed the string.

Tapel sighed. He felt dirty, cowardly. But what value would there be in sacrificing his life? The thought didn't provide any comfort.

Tapel knew that he'd done it because he was scared. Despite himself, he felt tears well in his eyes.

"Come, boy," Brin said. "You've earned some food."

As they walked away from the tower, now rendered useless, Tapel knew he'd let everyone down. If these men killed him, Tapel hoped Rogan would never find out about the part he'd played.

His only hope was to bide his time and try to escape.

If Altura called, none of the eastern lands would come.

18

Beorn handed Miro a rectangular stone and Miro heaved, his honed muscles straining as he set the block on top of the fresh mortar, fixing it firmly in place before reaching to take the next.

Miro was bare chested in the sun, sweating in the ever warmer weather, but he found he was glad to be doing something physical. He was a man of action—planning gave him headaches and kept him awake at night. At Ella's suggestion he'd started helping out with the building, digging, clearing, and carrying. At Amelia's insistence he began to take a half hour out of each day—sometimes more—to play with Tomas, digging up the gardens outside the Crystal Palace and making a general mess. Physical fatigue helped him sleep, whereas mental fatigue never could.

Miro and Beorn were working at the defenses just outside Sarostar, where the arc of wall guarding the road from Castlemere now stood one foot taller. Unlike the wall outside Castlemere itself, this wall had ramparts, places where the defenders could stand high above a foe and rain down destruction. The wall was complete, but it could always be higher, stouter, and stronger. Miro paused to wipe sweat from his eyes while Beorn leaned back with a hand on his hip, his spine making a sound like a whip.

"I'm too old for this," Beorn grumbled, wiping dust from his beard.

"It's good for a man your age to get out and about," Miro said, grinning.

"Age means experience. Before I arrived, your brickwork was all over the place," Beorn said.

"What's that sound?" one of the soldiers said to a fellow.

Miro raised his head when he heard the last sound he'd been expecting to hear: the pounding of hooves signaling a horse at full gallop.

The rider came into view an instant later, skirting the wall until he reached Miro and then pulling his horse to a stop with a savage tug on the reins. The face of Jehral of House Hazara was flushed, and his chest heaved as he looked down at Miro.

The men around stopped work, and suddenly all eyes were on the desert warrior, his exotic garb of flowing black and yellow incongruous among all the shirtless workers. Miro's eyes took in Jehral's haggard face and the frothing mouths of the horses. There was blood on Jehral's chest, and though Miro didn't know horses, he could see that Jehral's mount was done in. The second horse, evidently a remount, was even worse, staggering with exhaustion.

Jehral held himself awkwardly, and Miro saw bruises on his chin and a torn sleeve on his left arm. He looked like he'd taken a bad fall.

As his eyes met Jehral's, Miro went rigid. Jehral must have ridden through the city to come here, galloping directly to the defenses. He would have had ample opportunity to stop at the Crystal Palace and refresh himself, yet here he was.

"Jehral," Miro said. "Lord of the Sky, did you just ride all the way from the desert? What happened to you?"

"It's nothing," Jehral said. He took several breaths to calm himself. "High Lord, I bring news. We discovered a wrecked ship off the coast of our lands. It must have blown off course and gone astray. The enemy can't be far."

"Describe the ship," Beorn demanded.

"It was filled with revenants," Jehral said.

The men around gasped in chorus. Miro's stomach clenched.

"It was huge, bigger than any vessel I've seen. The ship's foundering had taken a toll, but it was once painted with bright colors."

Miro closed his eyes. A ship full of revenants, wrecked on the coastline off the Hazara desert. It could only mean one thing. They were here.

"What happened to you?" Beorn asked.

"I was ambushed by four men on the way. I think they were Tingaran."

"Tingaran?" Miro lifted his gaze. "Where?"

"Not far from Sarostar, near the river."

"The signals," Beorn said. "We need to make the call."

"Scratch it!" Miro said. "We can't."

"Every hour that goes by . . ."

"Beorn, the ship was wrecked in Hazaran lands. It doesn't tell us anything other than that they're close."

"We fought one of the revenants," Jehral said. "They were still and unmoving, bodies decayed, but one was . . . alive. It killed four of my men."

"What do we do?" Beorn asked.

Miro made a decision and snapped into action, almost with a sense of relief to finally be doing something.

"It's time to mobilize. The only part of the plan that must wait is the lighting of the signals, and we won't evacuate Sarostar until we have final confirmation. Beorn, I want you to leave a skeleton force here and take the rest of the men from Altura to the defenses at the free cities. Send word to Scherlic. He must find the enemy fleet."

"What about the men who ambushed Jehral?" Beorn said.

Miro turned to Jehral. "Did you leave any alive?"

"No, High Lord. I was unable to question them."

"Then we have to trust they were just brigands; there's always some around. Beorn, tell our scouts in the vicinity of Sarostar to be vigilant. Jehral, I need you to . . ." Miro halted. "My apologies, Jehral, I realize you're not Alturan . . ."

"Do not apologize, High Lord. Just tell me what I can do."

"Are you well? Do you need attention?"

"Scrapes only." Jehral grinned.

"Good man. Go to the Academy of Enchanters and find my sister. Tell her we're putting the plan into action. She needs to stop work and move everything to our defenses at the free cities. I need every enchanter, every blade, and every trick she's devised sent west."

Jehral wheeled and rode away.

"Where will you be?" Beorn asked.

"I'll head directly for Castlemere while you round up the last of our men here and see to Sarostar. Come quickly, Lord Marshal, I will need you."

Beorn nodded. "I'll see you there."

A brisk wind blew from the west, carrying the scent of salt. A fine mist of spray filled the air as the bow of the graceful vessel smashed through one cresting wave after another. High in the crow's nest, in the rigging, and on the decks, rugged sailors scanned the horizon, always searching, each man privately fearing what the crew of the scouting vessel would uncover in the void of ocean west of Altura.

Sailmaster Scherlic called out orders and chanted activation sequences, lighting up the shimmering sails and feeling the deck heel beneath his feet. The *Infinity* was far from shore, and the horizon clear in all directions. With the blazing sun at a perfect midpoint high in the sky, it was noon, and only the seekers at the helm and mainmast told him which way was east and which west. Scherlic kept the symbols lined up in one clear direction as he traveled east, his path taking him further and further into the deep blue waters of the Great Western Ocean.

The slim ship rode the peaks of the waves, carving the water as she rose up and down, hitting the troughs with a regular series of resounding booms. With the wind gusting strong behind him, Scherlic turned the *Infinity* across the wind to head in a more northerly direction. He chanted in a deep voice, calling on the lore of the Buchalanti to pocket the main sail and catch more wind, tightening other sails, feeling his beloved vessel pick up speed until she flew like a bird.

"Ship, ho!" the man in the crow's nest called down. Without waiting for a response he called again. "Sails." After the space of ten heartbeats he cried out again. "Sails! Many of them!"

Scherlic frowned as the sailor's voice fell away in what could only be astonishment; he'd never heard one of the disciplined men and women that made up his crew react in such a way.

"Where away?" Scherlic called up.

"Dead ahead!" the sailor cried.

Scherlic was unable to leave his place at the ship's helm; he was the sailmaster, and every turn was a chanted rune, every close-hauling of the sails required his attention. There were fail-safes, of course, but to Scherlic the spokes of the huge wheel at the helm were decorative only.

He wished he could rush to the front of the ship and peer ahead, but made do with the Louan seeing device he carried at his belt. Scherlic activated the lens and turned it in his hands, bringing the distant horizon into focus.

He couldn't see anything.

The sailors in the rigging ceased moving as every man and woman stared ahead, usually a terrible breach in discipline, but even Scherlic had ceased chanting and let the symbols on the sails begin to grow dim.

He scanned the horizon to the left and right, waiting with pent breath, willing the *Infinity* forward, but dreading what would be revealed.

Then he saw them.

At first he thought it was a dark cloud, or perhaps he'd come across a new land, with a series of buildings rising from the ocean from one end of the horizon to the other. Surely these could not be ships?

There were just too many of them.

Scherlic took his eyes away from the seeing device and now he could see the armada with his own unaided vision. It was beyond anything he could have imagined, an uncountable array of ships of all shapes and sizes. As the *Infinity* grew ever nearer, Scherlic's experienced gaze saw that these vessels sat low in the water, as if carrying heavy cargo. He tried to count them, but he could only see the length of the line, not the depth; there was no purpose in trying to gauge their numbers from this limited perspective.

He kept his distance but drew close enough to see their direction of travel. He'd been warned about this enemy's capabilities, and he and Commodore Deniz had experimented with the range and power of cannon. Scherlic knew his mission: the important thing was to escape the armada unscathed and bring warning.

He was now close enough to see that the enemy fleet traveled straight, lumbering forward slowly, but inevitably, heading directly for the free cities.

A puff of smoke came from one of the closest ships, and four or five vessels broke free to give chase. Scherlic's lips curved in a smile; he'd like to see them try to catch the *Infinity*.

Then Scherlic could wait no more.

"Make all sail!" he roared. "Turn about. We're getting away from them."

Sailmaster Scherlic called power to his vessel, and the *Infinity* heeled over sharply as she came about. He focused all his energy on getting every bit of speed from the racing ship, and the *Infinity* shot forward as one of the fastest ships the world had ever seen sped across the waves.

The armada was coming, and they were coming for Altura.

Scherlic had to give warning to the high lord.

Miro had been right all along.

After a week's frantic journey, Miro was nearly at Castlemere. He was on the road from Sarostar to the free cities, leading a long column of soldiers, when the courier found him.

"High Lord," the man in green panted, "urgent message."

Miro realized his hands were shaking as he waited impatiently for the courier to catch his breath. "Tell me," he demanded, but he knew what was coming.

"The enemy fleet has been sighted. Here," he said, handing over the dispatch.

Miro swiftly broke the seal and scanned the message from Scherlic. The sailmaster described the fleet as huge, an armada, more ships in one place than he'd ever thought possible.

He said they were undeniably heading for the free cities.

Miro's homeland was under attack.

"What's your name?" Miro said to the courier.

"Faron, High Lord."

"Faron, I am going to entrust you with a vital mission. Can you handle it?"

"Yes, High Lord." The young man trembled.

"Get to Sarostar as quickly as you can. Do not rest." Miro bit the words off. "If you see Beorn, tell him the news, but more than anything, get to the Crystal Palace. Find Amelia. Give her the message, and tell her I'm instructing her to light the green signal. Do you understand?"

"Yes, High Lord."

"Here," Miro said. He tugged the signet ring off the fourth finger of his right hand. "You now have my seal. Let nothing stop you."

"You can count on me, High Lord."

"Good man. Now go."

Miro was about to face the most important battle of his lifetime. He remembered the devastation of Wengwai, the ravaging of Veldria, the swarming might of the revenant horde.

Miro's heart pounded in his chest. He began to run.

The free cities beckoned as Miro raced to defend his homeland against the Lord of the Night.

19

Bartolo strode briskly from the Pens to the Crystal Palace, walking along streets of cobblestones and following the river for a time, taking in the scene of organized chaos that was Sarostar entering its final stage of readiness. He knew about Jehral's discovery of the wrecked ship, but as far as Bartolo was aware, they still knew nothing about their enemy's present location. Sarostar was busy now, but if and when they sighted the fleet, the city would enter a new state of readiness. At the moment, Bartolo had something else on his mind.

The guards made way for the tall, dark-haired bladesinger at the main gates and then stood aside at the marble steps to let him inside the palace itself, welcoming him with a nod. Bartolo tried to wipe the scowl from his face, but it kept returning, and he soon gave up.

Bartolo found Amelia sitting at a table with some of the overseers of the granaries. She glanced up as he approached, and her expression immediately grew worried when she caught sight of his face.

"What is it?" Amelia said.

"It's Tapel," Bartolo said. "Your son needs training. I thought we'd all agreed to it." He tried to keep the anger from his voice.

"I know the training's hard, but I want to talk to him. Tell him to come out."

"He's not at the barracks?" Amelia said.

Bartolo snorted. "He certainly isn't. You know he hasn't shown up in days. This isn't the first time he's disappeared, and this time we're going to talk."

"Please leave us," Amelia said to the men at the table. They swiftly touched fingers to lips and foreheads and departed. "Now, just wait a moment, Bartolo. Start at the beginning. I thought he was with you."

"He's not here? You're sure?" Bartolo said. His anger swiftly became replaced with concern. "I assumed he's been here all this time. I haven't seen him in three days. Where's he been sleeping?"

Amelia sighed in exasperation. "It's probably nothing. This is Tapel we're talking about."

"Yes, but three days? Is that like him?"

"I'm starting to worry . . ." Amelia said, turning suddenly frantic eyes on Bartolo.

"It's probably nothing." Bartolo exhaled. "Scratch that boy. I don't have time to organize a search."

As Amelia rose from the table, Bartolo heard the sound of a throat clearing, and he and Amelia both turned to see a steward standing just inside the doorway. By the steward's side was a sturdy, round-faced man with a bald pate.

"My apologies," the steward said, "but this man has been asking to see either you, Bladesinger Bartolo, or you, Lady Amelia. Knowing you were both here . . ."

"We're busy," Bartolo said, scowling.

"It's . . . it's about Tapel," the bald man said.

Amelia and Bartolo exchanged glances.

"Who are you? How do you know my son?" Amelia demanded.

The bald man looked nervous. His clothing was plain and faded, but well mended, and his features were Alturan.

"I'm Fergus, a ferryman," he said, twirling a woolen cap in his hands.

"Do you know where my son is?" Amelia said.

"I'm not sure," he said.

"Well, do you know where he is, or don't you?" Bartolo asked.

"Well . . . no, I don't . . . but, you see, I've gotten to know the boy. He often takes a boat from the Pens to the Crystal Palace on Lordsdays. He didn't come by last Lordsday . . ."

"Let me ask you one more time," Bartolo interrupted. "Do you know where Tapel is?"

"I think I might have an idea where he's gotten to," Fergus said. "That's why I came, actually. You see, he told me about a one-eyed man . . ."

"What one-eyed man?" Amelia demanded.

"Let him finish!" Bartolo glared.

Amelia's eyebrows went up and she opened her mouth. "Why, you hypocritical . . ."

"If you keep interrupting, we'll never hear what he has to say," Bartolo said. He frowned at Amelia one last time before turning back to Fergus.

"Tapel saw a one-eyed man in the market," Fergus said. "He said he saw something suspicious about him. I told him to say something to one of you, but he didn't want to. Then, well, I waited for him on Lordsday—I've been keeping an eye on him, you see—and when I didn't see him . . ."

"So you think his disappearance is something to do with this one-eyed man?" Bartolo said.

"I think it might, yes."

"How can we find this man?" Amelia said.

"Well, you see, that's the thing . . ."

"Out with it, man," Bartolo growled.

"Well, I saw him, today—the one-eyed man, that is. He was buying resin in the Poloplats market. So I followed him all the way to Samson's Bridge, but then I lost him. I can tell you he didn't cross the bridge, though."

"What does he look like?" Bartolo asked.

"Well, he's got one eye . . ."

Bartolo's hands moved as though to strangle someone, and he fought to control himself. "Where does it look like he's from?"

"I wouldn't say he's from 'round here, that's for sure. Even with all the newcomers, I know my Sarostar. I'd say, at a guess, Tingara?"

"And you lost him near Samson's Bridge?"

"That's right. Near the big three-legged tower."

"The signal tower," Bartolo said, his eyes meeting Amelia's. "Jehral said he was ambushed by Tingarans near the river."

"Lord of the Earth," Amelia gasped, clasping her hands together. "What should we do?"

Bartolo felt his heart race. "Amelia, I need you to go to the Pens. Tell every boy and recruit you can find to head to Samson's Bridge. Get them to bring my zenblade and armorsilk. Fergus, come with me."

Bartolo and Fergus crept along the road. Bartolo was uncertain how many enemies he might face, and he knew that above all else, with Tapel potentially in enemy hands, he and Fergus couldn't be seen.

Samson's Bridge lay ahead, and just in front of the supports, on the Alturan side, Bartolo saw the tall tower with its shining prism mounted at the apex. He breathed a sigh of relief to see the tower still standing; whatever had befallen Tapel, it wasn't related to the signaling system.

"Here's where I lost 'em," Fergus whispered.

The two men stood side by side among the trees, peering ahead. Fergus had said Tapel's one-eyed man didn't cross the bridge, which meant he would be either downriver or upriver. For some reason these men were in hiding; there was a surfeit of campsites closer to the city. Where would this man go if he didn't want to be seen? A camp used a lot of water, and occasionally left flotsam to float downstream. If this man—or men, more likely—were clever, they would have made their camp down from the bridge, where any leavings would float away from the people crossing.

Hearing the sound of voices behind him, Bartolo whirled and saw a group of seven youths heading up the road. Their ages ranged from seventeen to nineteen, and all carried steel swords and wore determined expressions. Leading them was Dorian, the recently elevated bladesinger. Bartolo waved his arms to get their attention and made a cutting motion with his hand across his throat. Immediately, they were silent. Bartolo could only pray they hadn't been heard.

Seeing how Bartolo was pressed in among the trees, the recruits, led by the yellow-haired Dorian, followed suit. The young bladesinger approached, and Bartolo leaned forward to whisper into Dorian's good ear.

"I figure they'll be camped downriver," Bartolo murmured, "but it's prudent to check in both directions. I'll take Fergus and two of the recruits—say, Martin and Timo—and start searching downriver. You take the others upriver. They'll be in the trees, so keep a sharp eye out. The lads are under your protection; use them for scouting, but do the fighting yourself."

"Understood," Dorian said. "Also, this is for you."

Dorian handed Bartolo a bag and a scabbarded sword. Reaching into the bag Bartolo pulled out garments of shining green silk. Bartolo gripped Dorian's shoulder in thanks, and swiftly donned his armorsilk before fixing his scabbarded zenblade at his waist.

"From now on we stay silent," Bartolo said. "Keep your ears open. If either of us hears sounds of a fight, come to the other's aid."

Bartolo motioned Fergus and two of the youths to follow. He led his small group through the trees that followed the riverbank south, walking with Fergus on his right and the two boys on his left, closer to the water. Martin was a sturdy lad of seventeen, with broad shoulders and flaxen hair. Timo was a year older, and though he looked reedy, he'd been training with a sword for well over a decade.

Bartolo sniffed the air as he walked. If they were clever, he wouldn't be able to smell their smoke, but not everyone was skilled with woodcraft, and Tingarans least of all.

He tried to keep his movements steady and graceful, making no sound through the forest mat, but Bartolo kept tensing as his thoughts turned to Tapel.

What had they done with the boy? What would he say to Amelia if Tapel were dead? What would he say to Rogan?

The lad deserved a better fate than to die at the hands of some brigands. Tapel had been brave, but foolish, to follow this one-eyed man. Even if there were brigands camped here, it wasn't so important that it was worth Tapel's life. Any day now they were expecting the Buchalanti scouts to announce they'd sighted enemy ships. With Altura clear in the enemy's path, it would be a cruel joke indeed to lose Tapel to bandits before the battle even started. Even if Tapel were unharmed, it was a distraction Bartolo could do without.

"Foolish boy," Bartolo whispered under his breath.

Bartolo stopped. He smelled smoke.

He waved his arms until he had the attention of his whole group. Bartolo pointed at himself and then made an inverted vee with his index fingers. The others fell back while Bartolo moved ahead so that he was the point of their wedge.

Bartolo activated his armorsilk.

Chanting under his breath, he started to name activation sequences and felt the armorsilk tighten around his shoulders, the material shifting to the texture that could turn away steel. Bartolo was practiced at this, and to a man standing a few paces away, he would make no sound. He was in tune with his armorsilk and knew how to call forth its power in a way no one would hear.

He gave the armorsilk strength and shadow, and glancing at his forearm, he could soon see the leaves of the forest floor through the material.

Bartolo drew his zenblade, slowly, until he held it out in front of him in a scarred hand.

Continuing the near silent chant, Bartolo again crept forward.

The smell of smoke grew stronger, and Bartolo thought he saw an encampment ahead, but the trees weren't as thick as he might have liked this close to the river, and his vision was impaired as he was forced to flit from one tree to the next like a bird. If it was a camp, without the shadow effect of the armorsilk, he would have already been seen.

He hoped the others had the good sense to stay back.

Bartolo heard voices; it was definitely a camp, and he was now perhaps twenty paces from the fire. He had his back to a tree, but he now poked his head around. Two tents surrounded a low circle of embers, and Bartolo smelled grilling meat.

Bartolo flitted to one more tree, and then he could make out their words.

"We're low on food again," a gruff voice said.

"The city's in chaos. It's not a good time to go in," an assertive voice spoke.

"How long have we got, eh, Brin? How much food?" a higher pitched speaker asked.

The second, assertive voice spoke again—Brin, the other man had called him. "If we're careful . . . two weeks at the current rate."

"Two weeks," the gruff voice said. "That's not long."

"Think about it like this," Brin said. "If the city calms down, we can get more food. If it doesn't, and they're attacked, they'll light the signal, and we can watch to see they don't catch onto the ruse. Then we can go."

Ruse? Bartolo felt a shiver course through his body.

"Either way, Brin, our supply of food is limited," the gruff voice said. "We should kill the boy."

Bartolo's blood ran cold.

"He's just a boy," Brin said.

"We can't let him go," the high-pitched voice said. "Kill him."

"Fine," Brin said. "But I'm not going to watch. Throw the body in the river."

Bartolo heard the sound of scraping steel.

20

Bartolo took a deep breath, and forgetting about silence, he whirled around the tree and shot forward. He immediately took in the scene. Four men sat around a fire. Tapel lay trussed on the ground, bound and gagged. Bartolo called on the power of his zenblade, seeing the symbols inscribed in the metal spark along its length.

The bandits shot to their feet.

"Bladesinger!" a man with a sword cried.

Bartolo dashed in and easily dodged a clumsy blow from the swordsman to strike at the man's chest. The zenblade barely paused as it carved through from the man's armpit to the other side of his body. Bartolo then ducked a blow from an axe to thrust into a second, scrawny man's throat. He saw a one-eyed man look at Tapel and then turn and run.

"Stop him!" Bartolo called.

The fourth bandit knelt at the fire and picked up a burning brand. He came at Bartolo with wild eyes, swinging as he sent sparks flying through the air. Bartolo tried to counter without killing his opponent, but the man's clumsy attack brought him too close, and he went down with a cry as Bartolo's blade sliced his side.

The one-eyed man ran with arms pumping, darting through the trees, and then Bartolo saw the ferryman, Fergus, rush to intercept him. Both went down in a tangle of limbs.

"Keep him alive!" Bartolo cried.

Fergus struggled with the bandit but was knocked back. The one-eyed man's fist smashed into Fergus's cheek, and Fergus lost him as he sped away once more.

Bartolo dashed after him and saw his two recruits ahead as they sped after the bandit, following the river. The boys were young, and at the peak of fitness. The one-eyed man looked over his shoulder and saw them gaining on him.

The bandit veered to the left, but Timo rushed in to meet him. He then tried dashing to the right, but Martin was coming in fast. Turning back to the left, he had his eyes on Timo and not on where his wild run was taking him.

With a cry the one-eyed man plunged over the cliff, falling headlong into the river. His flailing body vanished from sight.

Bartolo groaned; even if the bandit survived, they would never find him. He rushed back to the camp and knelt beside Tapel's bound form. "Lad, are you hurt?"

Tapel groaned and Bartolo scowled when he saw bruises on the boy's face. He cut through the bonds and swiftly checked Tapel for wounds.

"The signaling tower," Tapel gasped. "They switched the prism. They made me help."

"Slow down," Bartolo said.

Fergus, Martin, and Timo arrived at the fire. The two recruits began to search the camp.

"There are four pallets. That's all of them," Martin said.

Tapel rubbed at his wrists. "They said more would be coming, but none did."

Bartolo thought about the four men who'd ambushed Jehral. The Hazaran had said he'd killed them all. "Tell me about the prism."

"The crystal on the tower is made of glass. It's a fake."

Bartolo swore. Hearing movement behind him, he turned and saw Dorian approach with his three recruits.

"What happened?" Dorian said.

"We got them." Bartolo indicated the bodies. "One jumped into the river."

"Who were they?"

"Tapel?" Bartolo asked.

"They were Tingarans," Tapel said, "from Seranthia. They didn't say who they worked for, but they weren't from the Legion. I think they might have had something to do with the streetclans. They didn't want Altura getting aid from Tingara. They wanted to prevent a distress call from getting through."

"But why do it here?" Dorian said. "Why not closer to Tingara?"

"I think I know why," Bartolo said grimly. "There are two critical stations: this one at Samson's Bridge and the tower at Wondhip Pass. The one here links Altura to all of the lands in the north and the east: Halaran, Vezna, Torakon, Loua Louna, Tingara, and Aynar—even the Akari via the station at Lake Vor. The station at Wondhip Pass links Altura to Petrya and the Hazara Desert. If a signal reached Torakon or even Halaran, word might still have reached Tingara by courier. That's why here."

"What do we do?" Dorian asked.

"They've no doubt hidden the real device someplace we'll never find it. We'll have to run back to Sarostar as quickly as we can. If Miro activates the device at the Crystal Palace, word needs to get out soon as possible. Scratch it! This is going to add days. We're going to need an enchanter . . ."

"Actually," Tapel said, "the real prism wasn't hidden."

Bartolo stared at Tapel. "What did you say?"

"It's in the river, near the bridge."

"Why there?" Dorian asked.

"They made me climb the tower and help them swap the fake prism for the real one. But I didn't give them the real one. Instead, I threw it in the river."

Bartolo looked at Tapel in surprise. "Well done, lad," he said. "Come on! Leave the bodies for the crows. Quickly, to the bridge!"

The group of two bladesingers, five recruits, a ferryman, and Tapel hurried back they way they'd come, to stand near the support columns at Samson's Bridge. The three-legged tower loomed over them.

The water surged below the stone arch of the bridge itself, turbulent and frothing.

"It's hopeless," Fergus said. "I know water, and you'll never find it."

At that moment, a fiery green light shone brightly from somewhere in the water below the bridge.

The chill that ran through Bartolo's spine was like nothing he'd ever felt before. Miro had activated the reflector at the Crystal Palace. Looking back toward Sarostar in the west, Bartolo could see a distant green light, high in the sky. The device in the water had responded to this reflector.

But looking east, across the bridge to the land of Halaran, there was no onward signal. With the prism in the water, the chain was broken.

The fleet had been sighted. Sentar Scythran was here, and he was coming for Altura.

Bartolo took a deep breath and began to strip off his clothing.

"No," Tapel said.

"You'll never make it," said Dorian.

"Do you know what our strategy is?" Bartolo asked as he disrobed. "All the high lord's planning and effort has one objective, and one objective only. It's to delay the enemy. Not to win; Miro doesn't think we can. It's to hold them until help arrives. Every moment counts, and even if I die here, I'm going to try."

Soon Bartolo stood in just undershorts, the muscles in his abdomen rippling as he drew deep breaths to flood his lungs with air.

Without thinking too hard about what he was about to do, Bartolo fixed his gaze on the shining green light welling from the deep water below. He ran to the edge of the bridge and stared down into the depths.

Bartolo drew in a breath as he climbed up onto the rail.

He dived, head first, into the surging water.

It was the middle of spring, but the water from the north was cold, so cold it sent icy needles stabbing into Bartolo's flesh. The current immediately fought to drag him downriver as his arms and legs clawed against it, his vision firmly set on the green light. He fought the water like an enemy, feeling the muscles he'd hardened over years of training and countless battles come to his aid.

He knew he had to keep his eyes open, but the force of the river made it nearly impossible. He concentrated on the color green, focusing on the glimmers that came through his eyelids. The current tried to pry open his mouth, and with each stroke of his arms and kick of his legs he felt the breath in his lungs grow short.

Bartolo was running out of air.

Summoning reserves of strength, he opened his eyes wide, and there it was in front of him, a shining green prism, too bright to look at.

A dozen more strokes should take him close enough to touch it.

Bartolo screamed underwater and kicked harder, fighting his own buoyancy as his body desperately tried to return him to the surface where he could breathe again, and live. Instead, he pulled hard, clawing at the water as if gouging out the eyes of a vicious enemy.

Bartolo reached out with his hands, and he touched the prism.

The surge of victory was short lived as the river pushed him half a dozen paces again.

He couldn't breathe anymore; his brain was starved for air, and he felt his vision closing in.

Bartolo knew that if he couldn't succeed, he wouldn't be able to try again. Dorian was young, and he would try, but he would drown. This was his one chance. Only he could do this.

Bartolo channeled the last of his energy into one final surge. His body dipped deeper into the water as an unpredictable current twisted him over. Turning back around, he felt a rock under his arms and hooked a wrist underneath. Bartolo used the leverage to gain the last distance, and he took hold of the shining prism.

The rock moved, rolling, and suddenly Bartolo's arm was stuck under the boulder.

Bartolo clutched the prism to his chest with one arm and tried to move the rock, to free his trapped arm and return to the surface. His chest heaved and his mouth opened. Water flooded into his chest as his body fought his mind and won, gasping in whatever substance it could find in the space around it.

There was movement. Someone was in the water with him.

Strong arms moved the rock and freed Bartolo's arm. He felt himself taken under the armpits and heaved forcefully upward. Bartolo felt himself pop to the surface, but he was dazed, his vision dark, his lungs filled with water. Drifting down the river now, the newcomer rolled Bartolo onto his side and heaved at his stomach. Water gushed out of Bartolo's mouth and he felt his body squeezed again.

Bartolo twisted and rolled his way down the river until the current slowed near a bend. Bartolo heard voices and felt many hands on him, hauling him out of the river to land, his body flopping onto the bank like a hard-won fish.

Bartolo opened his eyes and felt hands prying at his own, struggling to release his grip.

"Let go," he heard Dorian's voice. "I've got it."

Bartolo felt a surge of relief when he realized he still held the prism.

Another figure leaned over him. Scraggly wet hair revealed a bald pate and a round, sturdy face. "You're lucky I'm a good swimmer, bladesinger," Fergus said.

Bartolo grinned, and then coughed again, ejecting another stream of water.

Bartolo lay on his back, recovering from his swim as Tapel disappeared with the prism. He sat up as Tapel returned.

"It's done. I returned the prism to the top of the tower," Tapel said.

"Well done, lad," Bartolo said, coughing and shaking water from his dark locks.

"I saw an answering light in the east," said the boy.

"Here, help me up," Bartolo said. Tapel took hold of his wrist and hauled the bigger man to his feet. "Listen, Tapel. You did well. If you hadn't found these men, we wouldn't have known about the deception. Your mother would be proud, as would Rogan Jarvish."

Tapel's eyes misted. "I thought I'd betrayed us all."

"Nothing could be further from the truth. Now where's my armorsilk?" Bartolo glanced about. One of the recruits came forward, and Bartolo stood, weaving slightly, but eventually gathering himself and taking several deep breaths.

Bartolo smiled at Fergus. "I owe you my life," the bladesinger said simply. "It's a debt I won't take lightly."

Fergus grinned and shrugged.

"Gather round!" Bartolo called. Soon the group stood ringed around him. Gazing back at Samson's Bridge, Bartolo saw the reflector at the apex of the tower, shining bright green, lending urgency to every action.

"As you can see, Altura is in need. Our task at this point should be to head to the defenses at the free cities, where our high lord has built a series of fortifications on the ridge behind Castlemere."

The recruits nodded.

"However, we now have a more important task. Our high lord needs these signals to get through. We can see the light from the next link in the chain in the east, but Derrick and Roscoe, I need you to head over the bridge and confirm that the chain is whole. You'll be working on your own initiative, and you know what your mission is. We've planned for many things, but treachery wasn't one of them."

"We understand," Derrick said. The two recruits nodded to each other.

"The rest of you will be coming with me to Wondhip Pass. I know it's a long journey, but we know how critical the station there is. We don't need to travel all the way to the pass, just close enough to see the light, which should be visible from below. We simply need to confirm that the station in the pass is functioning. We'll be traveling fast, and we'll be traveling with little food, just whatever we can take from the bandits' camp. Everything depends on us."

"What about me?" Fergus said.

"I need you to go to Castlemere. Find the high lord and tell him what happened here. Tell him we'll make sure the chain is complete, and then we'll find him, wherever he is."

"And me?" Tapel said.

Bartolo knelt. "Tapel, you've been brave beyond any imagining. You saw something suspicious and acted on it. If you hadn't, we wouldn't have known the chain was broken. I need you to go to your mother at the palace. She's worried sick about you and needs to know you're not hurt."

"I want to come with you."

Bartolo shook his head. "We'll be setting a grueling pace. Those at the palace need to know, just like the high lord at the free cities. Now that we know about the danger, we can make sure the chain is functioning. Can you help me, lad?"

"I will." Tapel nodded.

"You have your tasks. See to it!"

Bartolo had to use his head. He wished he were with Miro, who would soon be facing the enemy.

But Miro's plan depended on support from the other houses. Bartolo had his own part to play.

21

Green lights traveled through the lands of the Empire. Each tower sparked the next, from Samson's Bridge through Carnathion to Ralanast, then from Ralanast through thick forest to Rosarva. The reflectors in Halaran sparked the tower at the Louan border town of Mourie before traveling on into Mara Maya itself. Green flared up at Sakurai, capital of Torakon, and then the fire passed along the chain to the Imperial capital of Seranthia.

Killian was alone in his private study when he heard a knock on the door. He looked up from the report in front of him, one of many in a thick pile, and called out, "Enter."

A melder in a purple robe—one of those who replaced lost limbs with rune-enhanced metal and transformed the direst cases into avengers—walked hesitantly in. The robed man's face was downcast, as if he were the bearer of bad news.

Killian's eyebrows went up. He seldom spoke to the melders, other than to ensure they had what they needed for their arts.

"What is it?"

"Emperor, we've been keeping a watch on the device the Alturans placed in the High Tower."

Killian's heart missed a beat as he recalled that he'd entrusted the Alturan devices to his own masters of lore. "What of it? Come on, out with it!"

"The reflector . . . it's shining. It's very bright."

"What color?" Killian said, though he knew the answer before it came.

"Green." The melder licked his lips.

Killian's hands clenched in frustration; he was barely conscious of his sudden tight grip on the paper in his hands. "Tell Lord Osker no one is to see me. No one! I need some time to think."

The melder closed the door behind him, and Killian put his head in his hands. He finally stood and looked down at the reports and then swung his arm, sending the papers scattering over the floor.

Altura had called, and they wouldn't have called without need. Miro had been right all along: Sentar had targeted Ella's homeland. Now Killian had to decide what to do.

Killian left the study and strode briskly to his personal quarters, sending clerks, stewards, couriers, and soldiers scurrying out of the way. They might interrupt him at his study, but they would leave him alone in his chambers. He entered his bedchamber, closing the door behind him and slumping heavily onto the first seat he found, a long bench with curved legs.

Even if he left immediately, the Legion would take several weeks to reach Sarostar. Could Miro hold that long? Could Killian leave Seranthia's defenses weakened?

Killian spent long moments running through the options in his mind. Looking down at the symbols on his palms, he saw that his hands were shaking.

The door opened and Killian glanced up in surprise. "I told Lord Osker . . ."

Carla entered the room, a bottle of amber liquid and two heavy-bottomed glasses in her hand. She smiled at Killian, but her eyes were creased with concern.

"I heard the news," she said. "You have a difficult decision to make."

"That's an understatement," Killian said.

Carla sat close to Killian on the bench and placed the glasses on a nearby side table. She pulled the cork from the bottle and poured two glasses of brown spirit while Killian stared at the floor.

"I think you need this," Carla said, holding out a glass.

Killian shook his head. "What I need is to think clearly."

"Killian, take it. I know you. I can tell the pressure is killing you."

Killian took the proffered glass and swirled the liquid in the bottom, hesitating, and then finally he took a long sip, feeling the alcohol slide down his throat.

Not a regular drinker of spirits, he coughed and frowned when he tasted a strange note—mint?—but he assumed it must be a flavor of the drink. The warmth of the spirit spread throughout his chest, warming him, but it didn't help him decide.

"What is this?" he asked.

"Petryan firebrand," said Carla, smiling. "Don't worry. I'm not here to pressure you; I'm just here to help. We all need a shoulder to lean on sometimes."

"Altura . . . they need help. I know Miro; he wouldn't request it without reason," Killian said.

"What will you do?" Carla asked.

Killian suddenly felt tired. His eyelids drooped, and he felt sluggish, unable to think. He set his glass back onto the side table and regretted drinking the spirit.

Responsibility weighed on his shoulders. If he answered Altura's call and left with the full strength of the Legion, he would leave

Seranthia defenseless. If he took only part of the Legion, it might not be enough. If Killian stayed in Seranthia, there would be no one to challenge the powers of Sentar Scythran.

If he didn't go, not only would he be dooming Ella and everything she loved, he would be giving his enemy a chance to gain a foothold that the Empire might never push him back from.

Killian made his decision. "I'm going to go," he said. "My responsibility isn't just to Tingara, it's to the Empire as a whole. I need to show the houses I will defend their borders as staunchly as my own. For good or ill, this is what I'm going to do." His voice strengthened as he spoke. "I'll leave a force here, but I'm going to take the Legion to Altura."

"I wish you hadn't said that," Carla murmured.

Everything happened very quickly.

Carla had a knife in her hand, and all thoughts of tiredness vanished as Killian felt adrenalin surge through his limbs. The knife was short, but silver symbols decorated the blade, and as Carla spoke an activation sequence, Killian knew it must be enchanted.

His mind whirled as he also saw a black paste smeared along the blade. Carla was taking no chances.

Carla lunged at him and Killian tried to dodge the blow, but she was fast and the knife scraped his arm, leaving a trail of dark poison. The runes on Killian's skin flared brightly but the knife didn't break the skin. Killian was surprised to see the blade still dark, as if Carla's spoken rune had no effect at all.

Carla cursed and thrust again, but now Killian was more alert, and he warded her blow easily, grabbing hold of her wrist until she grimaced. Without thinking, Killian felt power surge through his limbs as he threw the young woman across the room. Carla crumpled against the wall, sending a shudder through the timber.

Killian came to his feet, confused, but knowing he was under attack.

Carla crouched on the floor, staring down at the knife in her hand and frowning. She glared at Killian, her eyes dark with malevolence.

Killian glanced at the empty glass on the side table. "You . . . drugged me?"

"How are you still moving?" she demanded. "They told me . . ."

"Who, Carla? Who is making you do this?"

She lifted her chin. "No one. It's my choice!"

"Why?" Killian pleaded.

The door to Killian's bedchamber opened.

Lady Alise stood in the doorway. With an acrobat's agility Carla shot up, and her thoughts evidently turned to escape, for she lunged with the knife at Killian's mother.

"No!" Killian cried.

Killian's training at Evrin's hands came to the fore, overriding all other thoughts, and he chanted runes in quick breaths. He pointed his fingers at Carla and felt the power well within him as symbols shone with blinding brightness on his hands. Twisted threads of blue lightning bathed his former lover before she could strike his mother. Carla writhed as the energy strengthened and thickened, ripping at her body until she screamed in agony. Finally, she collapsed on the ground and was still. Smoke rose from her clothes, and her eyes stared without seeing.

Killian dropped his hands.

"What have I done?" he whispered. "Mother." Killian rushed to her side, stopping in surprise when Alise held him back, instead moving over to Carla and plucking the blade from her dead fingers.

Killian's mystified eyes went from his mother, to Carla's body, and back again. He crouched beside the young woman with the sharp nose and raven-black hair as the silence dragged out, but Carla was dead.

Alise drew in a shuddering breath. "I came as soon as I heard the news, but it seems she beat me to it."

"I don't understand."

"Look at the knife," Alise said.

Killian tried not to look at Carla's body as his mother handed him the knife. He expected it to be hot, burning with the power of enchantment. Instead it was cool.

As he held the knife out flat in his palm, Killian saw the symbols weren't actual runes, they were mockeries of lore, and would do nothing at all. He'd heard Carla name an activation sequence, but the blade didn't respond.

Alise took the knife back from her son, holding it by the hilt. She ran her finger along the black smear.

"Stop, the poison," Killian cried, but then he stopped in wonder as his mother put her finger in her mouth.

"It's only treacle," Alise said. "I thought this might be when she made her move."

"You knew?"

"I knew something, but not much, and no, I wasn't certain. When I found an enchanted knife in her possession, along with two jars of strange liquid, one green and one black, then I had my suspicions."

"Why didn't you say anything?"

"I am sorry, but I did what I had to do. I had to let you discover her treachery on your own. If I'd said anything, it would have created a divide between us, and I would have showed my hand, leaving her and whomever she works for to find some other way to strike. No, don't protest—you would have resented me, dear. I have been dealing with treachery a lot longer than you have. I was raised amid plots and whispered conversation, I am familiar with such intrigues."

"Why her?" Killian whispered. Events slowly caught up in his mind. His eyes misted as he looked at the body of the woman he'd once loved.

"I replaced her enchanted knife with a normal blade, knowing she would likely not know the difference. I exchanged her liquids for others. Did you notice an unusual taste in the spirit? Something like peppermint? I had to find something green on short notice."

Killian remembered the strange taste in the firebrand. "But why?"

"Many reasons. You're going to have to get used to this now. It's a hard lesson, and I'm so sorry it had to come at this difficult time, from one you once loved. The only friends you can count on are those you know as well as you know yourself."

Killian thought of Ella.

He returned his gaze to Carla's body and then looked at his mother. He needed to be strong now, more than at any other time of his life.

Killian drew in a deep breath before speaking.

"Altura's in trouble," he said. "I'm going to help."

22

Amber somehow managed to drink too much at dinner with Grigori Orlov and Sergei Rugar. Her head started spinning, and pleading fatigue, she had to leave the meal before the dessert course was served. It was unlike her; she thought she'd only had two glasses of wine.

She barely made it back to her chambers, collapsing fully clothed in her bed. The throbbing in her head filled her consciousness with dizzying lights, though her eyes were closed, and her mouth was dry, as if she'd spent a week in the desert.

Finally sleep took her, yet that night she had terrible nightmares. Her sleeping awareness told her someone was in her bedchamber, moving around, and Amber was completely and utterly helpless. She fought to wake herself, imagining her fingernails pressing into her palms and legs twitching, but knowing she made no movement. What was happening?

The nightmares finally went away, and Amber once more fell into darkness and the blessed unconsciousness of normal sleep. As light filtered in through the wooden slats of the window and touched Amber's eyelids, she began to dream again; this time there was a hand, shaking her roughly.

Amber opened her eyes. It wasn't a dream.

Her tongue was thick and her mind foggy.

"What . . . ?"

"Get up," a voice said.

Amber struggled to make sense of what was happening. A palace guard pinched her shoulder painfully as he shook her. Looking past the guard Amber saw Lord Marshal Sergei Rugar rummaging around in her drawers. He upended her undergarments onto the floor before moving onto the next.

Amber tried to pull herself up and fend the soldier away but could only manage a weak movement. "What are you doing?" she gasped.

Several other palace guards in orange tabards stood watching Amber. She felt a terrible violation; this was her bedchamber, a place for her alone. She was the wife of the high lord of Altura!

"Let go of me!" She managed to sit up and push the soldier's clawing hands away.

"Aha!" Sergei said triumphantly. He held up a pendant on a silver chain.

Amber's heart finally began to pump, filling her lethargic limbs with much needed blood. She tried to stand, to make some sense of what was happening, but the guards pushed her back down to the bed, looming over her with menace.

"High lord approaching!"

The palace guards straightened, drawing back and saluting as High Lord Grigori stormed into the room.

"Well?" the high lord demanded.

"It's the child's necklace." Sergei displayed the pendant.

"Dear Lord of the Earth," the high lord breathed. He rounded on Amber. "Where is she? What have you done with her?"

Amber once more tried to rise from the bed—she still wore last night's clothes and had slept on top of the blankets—but the palace guards again stepped forward and held her back, pressing down on her shoulders, keeping her seated.

"I don't know what you're talking about," Amber gasped. "I don't even know what's happening!"

"There's more," said Sergei. He held up a piece of paper. "High Lord, I think you should see this."

Grigori snatched the note from Sergei and scanned it swiftly. Red splotches came to his cheeks as he read.

"Your ploy will not succeed," the high lord said. He crumpled the note and threw it at Amber.

Amber struggled to make sense of events. She must have been drugged. Her mind was still clouded—she could barely think.

"I don't know what you think I did!" Amber protested

She picked up the crumpled piece of paper off the bed, recognizing the paper as her own. As she reformed the note, she felt her breath quicken. She'd been writing letters to Miro, and the handwriting matched her own, but this message was faked.

It was a demand for ransom, written in Amber's flowing cursive. It proposed an exchange: the life of Katerina Orlov, the high lord's daughter, in return for military support for Altura.

Amber looked pleadingly at the high lord. "This is not mine, and it also makes no sense. Why would I do such a thing? I'm not stupid, and I have a child myself. As you know, I wasn't asking for aid for Altura. We're simply asking the houses to help whoever calls!"

"Your motive is clear. If you thought this would work, you are gravely mistaken. No one will help your house now. Where is my daughter?" the high lord demanded.

Amber looked from one man to the other. "Sergei," she said, "you know I wouldn't do this."

"Do not presume to use my first name," Lord Marshal Sergei said coldly.

High Lord Grigori leaned over and shook Amber's shoulders. "You thought this would get my help? Where is my daughter?"

"I don't know!" Amber cried. "This evidence is false."

"We intercepted your other letters," the high lord said. "We've known the entire time you've been here. Do not try to lie. You've planned this from the beginning. Fortunately, Sergei is not as trusting as I am."

"It isn't true." Amber fought the urge to sob, even as another part of her raged. Whoever had made this plot knew their business; the high lord's wits appeared to leave him where his daughter was concerned.

"Lord Marshal, take her to the deep dungeons underneath the Borlag," the high lord commanded. "Find out all you can. She knows where my daughter is. Do whatever it takes."

Amber's mind tried to grasp the ploy even as the palace guards picked her up, holding her roughly by the arms. Sergei's men began to march her through the palace while servants looked on with wide eyes. Amber fought to defend herself and communicate her innocence, but her mind was refusing to clear, and she pinched herself to see if she was truly awake.

She was, and this nightmare wouldn't end.

They weren't gentle with her, and she stumbled more than once as the guards dragged her through the great hall to a part of the palace she hadn't seen before. A heavy door requiring two men to open led down several flights of stairs. The stone grew colder and the air danker the further down she went. The walls became rough and moldy. The only light down here was cast by an occasional nightlamp. All else was shadowed.

Amber was aware of metal doors clanging open, and then she was in a dungeon, a terrible place where hoops of rusted iron stuck out of the walls, and individual cells were placed far apart from each other. This was a place where dark deeds were done.

The palace guards threw Amber into one of the cells, and her head hit the wall. The floor was slimy with mildew, and a wooden bucket in the corner was the only item in the cell.

"Leave us," Sergei instructed.

As Amber looked with fear at the flaxen-haired, usually genial lord marshal, the palace guards retreated, leaving the two of them alone.

"I don't understand," Amber said, wincing as she touched her head. She wished she had something else to say.

"It's simple," Sergei said, suddenly flourishing his usual, charismatic smile.

Sergei waited until the last footsteps were gone. Amber wondered how a straightforward plan to enlist support could go so wrong.

"I'm sorry you got involved, but your arrival was too well timed not to use. You see, I plan to be high lord when Grigori is gone—he has no male children—and then he spoiled my plans by naming Katerina his successor."

Sergei frowned, his face twisting with disgust. "Who would follow a woman? A female high lord? The very idea is repulsive. My plan is to remove two annoyances at once. I can get rid of Katerina, the spoiled monster, and at the same time I'll make sure Grigori will never send our men in support of Altura. Our soldiers and night-shades will stay here, where they belong. The high lord was quite close to promising aid, I'll have you know. It's taken a lot of work to keep him reluctant."

As the last of the cobwebs fell away and Amber could finally think clearly, she looked up at the once charming lord marshal. "You're using me to become high lord? Think carefully, Sergei. My husband is a dangerous man."

"Think carefully? My dear, that's exactly what I've done. And I think your husband has bigger concerns. I wouldn't expect any help from him anytime soon. By the way, your device, on Juno Bridge? The reflector, or whatever you call it? It's been shining all night."

Dread hit Amber forcefully, like a punch in the stomach. "What color?" she whispered.

"Green," Sergei said with relish. "It's a lovely color, but I've taken it down; no one need wonder at it anymore, and it's quite bright. We all need our night's sleep."

Amber hung her head. Miro had activated the distress signal. Her homeland needed help. Miro needed her.

"Why are you telling me all this?" Amber said.

"I have a proposition for you, *Lady* Amber." He said her title sardonically. "If you admit to taking the high lord's daughter, I will ensure you leave Rosarva alive. As you have learned," he shrugged, "I am not without influence."

Amber thought about the high lord's golden-haired daughter. "And what will happen to Katerina?"

"Unfortunately, the current heir to Vezna will not be returning to the palace."

"No." Amber shook her head. "I won't do it."

"I'm sure some time in here will change your mind."

Sergei's clumping boots sounded, and he vanished for a time, leaving Amber alone with her predicament. Just when Amber thought he'd never come back, he returned, and she looked on in horror as Sergei held a shining green prism in his hands, glowing fiercely, nearly too bright to look at. "As for your reflector, this is a better place for it, don't you think?"

Sergei grunted and threw the quartz pyramid, sending it tumbling down the corridor. "Good-bye, Lady Amber. Don't try to escape. The Juno Bridge is hungry this time of year."

Sergei tossed the last words over his shoulder as he departed, his footsteps echoing from the dank walls of the dungeons below the Borlag.

Even with the prism far down the corridor, Amber could still see the glow of green light. In the darkness of her cell it was the only thing Amber could focus on. Everything was washed with green: the walls, the bars, the floor, even the bucket. The color of Altura told Amber her homeland was under attack.

The light continued to shine. Though the device required a reasonable line of sight to activate, now that it had, it would continue to glow.

Amber put her head in her hands.

23

Miro stood at the wooden dock of Castlemere's harbor, feeling the sea breeze cool on his skin and watching Deniz as he tacked back and forth, bringing the *Seekrieger* into the harbor against the wind. He heard the Veldrin commodore's crisp commands as he barked orders, the crew reefing the sails and taking them in all the way, bringing the ship up against the dock with a gentle nudge.

Deniz's men lowered a gangway, and Miro walked up to the foot of the ramp, waiting impatiently. "What news?" Miro demanded as the commodore came down to meet him.

"They're two day's sailing away," Deniz said. "We could see the command ships—they're the ones flying golden pennants—but we stayed clear of them. We had a brief engagement."

"You were supposed to wait for support . . ." Miro interrupted.

"We know what we're doing," Deniz stated. "Some of their ships were drifting. Easy pickings. We sank two, and we took a prisoner."

Deniz motioned and two of his men dragged a struggling, disheveled, pale-skinned man in a gray robe down the gangway. Miro's eyed widened when he recognized an Akari necromancer. The pale-skinned man glared at Miro and spat a curse. Miro heard something about the Nightlord taking him but closed his ears to the rest.

"You want him?" Deniz said.

Miro smiled grimly. "Apologies," he said. "Well done. We certainly do."

Miro gestured and two bladesingers came forward to take the necromancer from the Veldrins. "Take him up to the main camp, behind the killing ground," Miro said to the two men in green armorsilk.

"Be careful," Deniz said. "He's a handful."

"Don't worry," Miro said. He grinned at Deniz. "We know what we're doing."

Miro left the prisoner in Beorn's capable hands while he discussed strategy with Scherlic and Deniz. When dawn came, the two men would lead their forces against the armada.

In just a few hours, the naval defense of the Empire would begin.

Miro kept turning to ask Beorn's opinion, forgetting he was absent. He tried not to think about the grisly task he'd assigned his loyal commander.

"Our chances are not good," Scherlic said. "We have eight Buchalanti vessels, and the commodore here has fourteen Veldrin warships. Twenty-two in our two squadrons all told, fighting an opposing force five or six times that number."

"We have a few advantages," Deniz said. "Their ships are heavy in the water. When we sank the two ships today, revenants spilled out; each ship carries hundreds of them. We were able to outsail them and broadside them with our cannon before they could react. They are heavily armed, though, and their warships have more cannon than ours. They sail in proper formation, with fast scouts at the sides and cruisers deployed around the warships. The occasional ship drifts, but someone among them knows naval tactics."

"How is that possible?" Miro said. "I can understand using revenants to man the cannon, but naval strategy?"

"I don't know." Deniz shrugged. "But we'll soon find out."

"Do you think we can stop them in the sea?"

Commodore Deniz hesitated. "No. Scherlic is correct. They'll wear us down with sheer numbers."

Miro looked from one face to the other. Both men were stone-faced. "I understand," Miro said.

He knew what he was asking these two brave men and their crews to do. They all knew that every ship sunk meant several hundred revenants the enemy would lose to the ocean. Even so, Miro didn't know if the Buchalanti and the Veldrins would fight to the end; it was something only they could decide for themselves.

"High Lord." Miro turned when he heard a voice. Beorn entered the command tent with his mouth set in a thin line, blood staining his lord marshal's uniform.

"What news?" Miro said.

"He's dead," Beorn said flatly. "He lasted to the end, the wretched creature. Fanaticism like that makes me sick. I hope his soul rots wherever it is now."

"So you found out nothing?"

"He gave us something, but I have no doubt he was holding a great deal back. There are over a hundred vessels in the armada. Among them are different factions from across the sea: Sentar Scythran has enlisted three kings into his service. Each brings his own ships, along with his own men. One has a red flag with blue crossed swords. Another device is a white trident on a field of blue. The third king's flag is black-and-white checked."

"Farix, the pirate king of Torian," Deniz said. "He is the first, the one with the red flag and blue swords. Diemos of Rendar is the one with the white trident on blue, and the black-checkered flag can only be Gorain, the king of Nexos."

"What do you mean 'enlisted?'" Miro asked. "Why would anyone in their right mind follow the Lord of the Night?"

"They're revenants, just like the others, but under duress the necromancer said Sentar personally brought them back. They're almost the men they were in life, and can give orders and plan strategy. Sentar has made promises in return for their service."

"What promises?" Miro wondered.

"Does it matter?" Beorn said.

"My guess is Sentar Scythran says what he needs to in order to control his subordinates," Deniz said. "These men will be dangerous opponents."

"What else?" Miro asked Beorn.

"The necromancer said Sentar plans to drive all the way through from Sarostar to Seranthia overland," Beorn said, scratching at his beard. "He ranted a lot about the Lord of the Night's rightful place as god of all Merralya. You know, the usual stuff."

"It doesn't change anything," Deniz said. He glanced at the Buchalanti sailmaster. "We face the hardest day of our lives tomorrow. I must rejoin my men."

"Deniz," Miro said. "Before you go"—he paused, not knowing what to say—"I'll see your people returned to Veldria. You have my word."

"Thank you, Miro," Deniz said. "But for me Veldria is dead."

The fourteen Veldrin warships left Castlemere in a precise line, each captain knowing his duty, and every crewman leaping to follow orders. The faster Buchalanti ships would follow on their heels.

As Deniz left the placid waters of the sheltered harbor behind, he felt a strange sense of calm and pleasure as the *Seekrieger* easily met the larger waves, and looking up, he saw the great sails snapping in the wind. It was a good day for a fight.

The dawn sky was brilliant and beautiful, with shades of peach and orange spreading across to banish the last of nighttime blue as the rising sun in the east shone on the *Seekrieger*'s stern. Deniz's ship flew the blue and brown colors of Veldria tall and proud, with a second gold flag indicating this was the squadron's flagship, with the commodore as effective admiral.

Deniz had been denied a naval engagement when the revenants came to Veldria. Emirald had been taken by surprise. Today he would show his enemy what they'd missed.

The wind came across his beam, and when he turned to meet the armada, he would have the all-important wind gauge. Deniz's ships would be able to broadside the enemy with impunity for the first moments of the battle. The guns were out, and the weather was good. His marines were ready with grapples and muskets, and he even had a bladesinger, one of the fierce Alturan swordsmen he'd heard so many rumors about, standing tall and proud with his hands on the rail.

Deniz heard a cheer and saw his crew look to the left. The Buchalanti ships flew past him as if he were standing still, and Deniz raised a fist into the air and cheered along with his men. The three storm riders led the graceful vessels, with the *Infinity* foremost, sails blazing as runes activated and deactivated, and Deniz could swear he heard the sounds of sonorous chanting from the sailmasters.

Two blue cruisers followed the storm riders: these were bigger than the *Infinity*, and Deniz classed them as merchantmen, somewhere between a cargo ship and a war vessel.

Finally, the dreadnoughts passed by close on the *Seekrieger*'s port side.

The two lumbering ships, each nearly as big as a Veldrin warship, followed in the wake of the Buchalanti blue cruisers. Deniz corrected himself: they weren't lumbering; they easily out-distanced the *Seekrieger*, but in comparison with the storm riders, they were slow. Deniz had yet to see the dreadnoughts in action. Scherlic said they needed to conserve their power.

The nimbler Buchalanti ships would approach the enemy from the rear. It was deemed best for the two fleets not to get in each other's way, and when the enemy came to meet the Veldrin fleet, the Buchalanti would hopefully surprise them from the other side.

Deniz watched as the Buchalanti vessels grew smaller and finally disappeared into the distance. Hours passed by in a blur, the ocean beckoned, and Deniz tacked to gain speed, noting each of the following warships tack behind him in perfect synchronization. The waves grew in size, and the color of the water changed until it was the deep blue of the open zone. Deniz put on all sail and felt his ship lean forward like a Narean racing horse at the gate.

"Sails, ho!" the lookout called.

"Where away?"

"Dead north, Commodore!"

Deniz risked one more tack, drawing close at an oblique angle to confuse the enemy, and he watched the incredible vision of countless sails appear out of the horizon. He checked the line behind him and nodded, then returned to watching the armada.

He could now make out individual ships on the fringes; these were smaller scouts, faster than Deniz's warships, and they fled as he approached, heading for the safety of the larger cruisers and warships, huddling close to the bigger ships like a duckling seeking its mother's protection.

"Send the order! Close ranks!" Deniz cried.

He turned a point closer to the wind and bled speed to give his fleet time to draw up into battle formation. Deniz didn't want any gaps in his line when he fired the cannon.

Deniz was now close enough to make out individual men, and he gasped.

Every ship, large and small, swarmed with men. They were in the rigging and clustered on the decks, the vessels wallowing so heavily they no doubt filled the holds. As Deniz's Veldrin squadron approached, he could now make out the glow of runes on the enemy ships' planking, though he didn't know what the purpose of the lore was. He put it out of his mind; there was nothing he could do about it now.

Their cargoes of revenants would make these ships slow, and the warriors on the decks would get in the way of the sailors, Deniz reminded himself. The advantage was his.

"Ready . . . Tack!" Deniz cried.

The *Seekrieger* heeled over, and the snapping mainsail swung the heavy boom from one side of the ship to the other with deadly force. The sound of more sails resounded like the cracking of whips, and Deniz almost laughed with the beauty of it; these men were the best crew he'd ever sailed with. With perfect precision, every following warship in Deniz's line tacked at just the right moment, turning hard from one keel to the other, close enough now that a daring man could leap from one Veldrin warship to the next. The ships now traveled bow to stern, moving past the prows of the enemy vessels, the cannon murderously facing just where they needed to be.

There was no point in parlay. This army was the same force that had destroyed Veldria. This was war.

"Fire!" Deniz roared.

The report of the cannon crashed through the air, a booming thunder that shook the *Seekrieger* and sent her heeling before she righted herself.

Behind him he heard another boom, and then after a heartbeat's pause, another growl of thunder. If they'd fired together, their strength would have been wasted; the task was to launch each salvo one after the next. Deniz's captains knew exactly what to do.

Deniz watched the terrible destruction as the heavy iron cannon balls tore through the enemy vessels.

The air filled with the whiz of hurtling balls, and the subsequent crashes sounded like twigs snapping under the foot of a giant. Splinters flew in the air; masts and rigging came crashing down; and smoke obscured Deniz's vision so that he cursed. Then a breeze carried the black clouds away, and Deniz saw a cluster of enemy ships sinking. Fires raged and bodies filled the water. An enemy warship exploded as her magazine caught, the detonation so massive it took down two clustered scout ships.

Deniz saw a number of enemy ships behind those he'd destroyed. Dodging the return fire, he called out to tack again, and circled around for another strike.

24

Scherlic caught a puff of smoke through his seeing glass, far away on the other side of the huge fleet: Deniz had made contact with the enemy. Scherlic saw the heart of the armada still moving inexorably forward, and marking an enemy flagship by its cluster of gold and red flags, Scherlic called out a series of runes, singing constantly as he sent the *Infinity* surging ahead.

The eight Buchalanti ships sailed forward together, and unlike the Veldrin and enemy ships, their weapons didn't point from their sides in long rows. A ship faced forward, so its weaponry should face the same way.

The three storm riders led the pack like hounds on a scent, with the blue cruisers guarding the flanks and the dread-noughts lagging behind. Two mortars jutted from the front of the storm riders, whereas each blue cruiser carried four of the Louan devices. The dreadnoughts' weaponry was of an altogether different nature.

Scherlic glanced at the bladesinger standing on the deck, with one hand on the mast and the other shading his eyes. Scherlic knew the man's goal: to find which ship or ships contained the enemy's essence and to do all he could to sink it. Scherlic had been searching, but so far he hadn't seen any sign of a vessel being especially protected.

Scherlic returned his attention to his course. The point of a wedge, the *Infinity* struck directly into the armada's core.

Realizing the threat from the deeper sea, the enemy vessels came around, rotating slowly to bring their cannon to bear. Clouds of smoke rose from the enemy warships and cruisers, the smoke seen a split second before Scherlic heard the thunderous roar that followed.

The cannons' range was greater than the mortars, and Scherlic's voice rose as he called on the runes built into the very fabric of his ship. The deck lit up and the *Infinity* came alive from planks to sails in a splash of vibrant color. A series of balls smashed into the storm rider's side. Scherlic winced as he felt his beloved ship tremble beneath his feet.

Sparks followed each strike, but the lore held, and the heavy balls didn't penetrate the *Infinity's* enhanced superstructure.

Scherlic now led the Buchalanti vessels deep into the armada's soft belly. Each of these enemy vessels stole wind from the other, but the lore built into the *Infinity* and her sister ships meant they could sail with impunity through the clusters. Scherlic's voice rose as he used every bit of his skill to keep his ship moving, to turn away from the broadsides and navigate around the smaller ships.

He set his eyes on a warship directly ahead; he was chasing this ship's stern and would easily catch up to the slower vessel.

Scherlic's weapon master lined up the twin mortars and fired a salvo of orbs.

The glowing spheres sailed through the air. One struck the warship on the outside, just below the waterline; another landed in the mass of grotesque revenants. Taking sight as he fired, the weapon master launched more orbs at the rigging.

The enemy ship burst apart with a series of detonations as the prismatic orbs exploded. Clouds of flame flung up splinters of wood and pieces of bodies. In seconds the vessel sank below the waves.

Scherlic's crew didn't cheer, but set their sights on the next enemy ship. Risking a glance around him, Scherlic saw more warships destroyed in the hail of prismatic orbs from the storm riders and blue cruisers.

Scherlic's breath came ragged, but he chanted through the roar of blood in his ears, fear coursing through his body as his weapon master fired a salvo at an enemy cruiser. The sailmaster called on every rune carved into his ship's hull to ward off the growing frequency of cannon fire. Another enemy warship exploded, and then Scherlic nearly cried out as he saw the storm rider on his right flank break up under a direct volley of leaden balls.

A blue cruiser came up to fill the gap, and yet another enemy warship went down, but Scherlic could see the blue cruiser's runes had faded on half the decking. The lore was failing.

Scherlic looked for the Veldrin fleet but couldn't see Deniz or his naval force. Then he forgot all about Deniz when he saw one of the biggest enemy warships he'd yet seen emerge from behind a screen of smaller vessels. Most of the enemy ships were painted in the garish hues the Veldrins seemed to prefer, but this ship was painted with black pitch. A small golden flag indicated it was a flagship. High on the mast a second flag displayed a black withered tree on a field of white.

Scherlic signaled and one of his men bellowed, "Brace yourselves! Ramming speed!"

Forgetting about the formation, Scherlic pointed the *Infinity's* prow at the black warship. Below the waterline, the storm rider's steel ram carved the sea, ready to plunge into the vulnerable planking of its enemy. Scherlic chanted the runes in quick succession, singing with all his strength, feeling his wondrous ship alive beneath him in the way a Hazaran rider must feel his mount.

Scherlic would strike from an angle so the enemy couldn't broadside him. The black ship was doomed.

Then Scherlic saw a figure on the deck, calmly watching the approaching storm rider. He wore black clothing with embroidered silver thread, and his hair was the color of blood, slicked back to his head with streaks of black at the temples.

Scherlic felt red come to his vision as he roared the activation sequences now.

The black ship loomed over the smaller Buchalanti vessel.

The *Infinity* struck with a sickening crunch.

Scherlic lashed out a hand, grabbing hold of the mast to arrest his motion as the collision flung him forward. Buchalanti sailors fell from the rigging to land on the deck with shattering force.

Scherlic watched the figure in black rise into the air and disappear into the haze of the gun smoke. With satisfaction Scherlic saw he'd mortally wounded the black ship. It began to sink while the revenants swarming the decks launched themselves forward, running for the *Infinity*'s deck.

Scherlic called out more activations as he felt his ship tremble. A third of the symbols on the storm rider's deck went dark. Finally the *Infinity* pulled away from its crippled enemy, but Scherlic's eyes widened as he saw three revenants throw themselves into the air to land, sprawling, on the decks.

The Alturan bladesinger went into action.

His armorsilk flared up faster than the time it took Scherlic to take a breath, and his zenblade was suddenly alive in his hands. He threw Scherlic's men aside as he lunged forward and before the first revenant, a woman in ragged clothing, could stand, he'd taken her head from her shoulders. The next snarling monster climbed to its feet and charged at the bladesinger, but the man somehow rolled under the blow, and his backswing cut the revenant in two. The third revenant, a big barbarian with a horned helmet, now faced the bladesinger and growled as it launched itself forward. It moved at a speed that belied its size, a blur of motion.

But the bladesinger was faster, and three successive blows sent putrid flesh flying in all directions. Panting, the Alturan checked his enemies by prodding them with the tip of his blazing sword. Finally, he threw the larger pieces off the ship.

The Buchalanti sailors cheered the Alturan.

Finally free from the grip of the sinking black ship, Scherlic willed the *Infinity* forward again as another enemy warship closed in, turning in a tight circle to present a row of cannon mouths. As Scherlic saw the unfolding disaster, a Buchalanti dreadnought appeared in the distance.

Scherlic called on his ship's speed as he gave as much strength as possible to the weakened planking. He started to move away, but then the enemy broadside smashed the *Infinity*.

Splinters of polished wood flew in all directions as the cannon tore holes in sails and took chunks out of the deck. Scherlic prayed a hole hadn't been opened up below the waterline, but though there was damage at all quarters, the storm rider could still sail.

Scherlic's weapon master attempted a salvo of orbs, but the enemy warship's range was greater; it was too far away.

The dreadnought fired.

A wide beam of golden light launched from the mighty vessel, striking into the heart of the enemy warship. The beam carved through the ship, instantly splitting it into two halves down the middle. In moments the warship was sunk, its clawing cargo of revenants dotting the water before they too sank.

Scherlic drew in a shaky breath, and the *Infinity* came up to support the dreadnought.

25

Deniz led his squadron down the line of enemy ships for the third time, but he knew this time he wouldn't be as lucky as he had been thus far. The enemy had reduced his fleet down to eight warships, and though he'd sunk too many of the enemy vessels to count, still more targets presented themselves. Bodies filled the ocean, and the smoke of cannon fire and burning ships clouded the sea in a dark haze.

"Fire!" Deniz cried, and once more the *Seekrieger* lurched to the side as every gun in her port side fired together.

An enemy warship fired at the same time, and both ships trembled as they took crippling damage. Bodies and splinters of wood flew into the air on both sides. The *Seekrieger* shivered, and Deniz felt an immediate heaviness when he tried to keep an even keel steady to the wind, telling him that a hole had opened below the waterline.

Behind him the clustering Veldrin warships fired their own salvos, but it was ragged now as the loss of men and damage from responding fire took its toll.

Deniz wondered if he could tack once more and disengage, but then he saw ships flying enemy flags on both sides. He was embroiled, and his ship would soon sink. It would be a fight to the death.

Ahead of the *Seekrieger* a brightly-colored warship flew a golden pennant and a red flag with blue crossed swords. The ship was undamaged, and Deniz frowned when he saw a man calling out orders, standing with legs apart on the deck. The commander wore a three-cornered red hat and bellowed instructions to his crew.

Deniz remembered Beorn's interrogation of the necromancer. He knew the standard, and he knew who the man was: Farix, the pirate king of Torian.

The *Seekrieger* wallowed and groaned as she took on more water.

"Bladesinger," Deniz called to the Alturan who stood with one arm on a mast and the other holding a bared sword of shining steel. "It appears you may soon get a chance to use your weapon."

The bladesinger turned and nodded. "I am ready."

"Grapples!" Deniz called. "Prepare yourselves! We're going to hold the enemy's broadside and board her!"

Deniz could now feel the decks dropping beneath his feet as his ship sunk. But the enemy vessel was close. He fixed his gaze on the man in the three-cornered hat and urged the *Seekrieger* forward.

Commodore Deniz thought about his homeland. Better to die on a Veldrin ship than on foreign soil.

Farix called out an order, and a ragged blast of cannon fire tore into the crippled *Seekrieger*. Still Deniz's ship came on, sluggish but moving, on a direct path for the pirate king's flagship.

The crackle of musket fire sounded on both sides, and the air filled with whizzing balls. Deniz was now close enough to see the glowing runes on Farix's neck and hands. Revenants snarled as the Veldrins threw grapples and hauled the two ships together.

"Make fast!" Deniz cried.

With a roar Deniz drew his straight sword and led his men forward, the bladesinger at his side. He leapt over the side of the

Seekrieger and landed nimbly on the deck of the enemy warship, immediately ducking under the blow of a warrior with mottled skin and a thin line across his throat. Deniz countered and weaved around a second blow before slashing deep into his opponent's neck, severing the spine so that the head lolled to the side.

Cannon on both sides continued to fire and muskets cracked. Warriors screamed with swords held high. Limbs were shattered by the flying balls.

The bladesinger reached the pirate king first. Farix turned white eyes tinged with pink on his new enemy and dropped into a practiced stance. Both swordsmen held blades blazing with the glow of activated runes. In contrast, Deniz's sword was made of quality steel, but steel was all it was. Deniz now regretted turning down Miro's offer of an enchanted blade.

Farix launched a series of blows as the eerie sound of the bladesinger's song filled the air, audible even over the thunder of muskets and cannon fire. When the zenblade met Farix's enhanced sword, sparks scattered into the air.

The bladesinger moved quickly; the zenblade flickered to meet each blow. Searching for his own opportunity, Deniz couldn't fault a single strike.

Farix moved faster.

The two combatants moved in a dance of death, and Deniz could see they were both formidable swordsmen, their skills honed by years of practice. A strike from the pirate king smashed into the bladesinger's armorsilk but was deflected by the supple material. The bladesinger thrust into the pirate king's chest, tearing a fist-sized hole at the precise location of his heart.

But Farix kept going.

Around Deniz, Veldrin marines and sailors battled revenants while smoke filled the air, making it hard for Deniz to see anything but the bladesinger's struggle. Timing his attack, Deniz came up behind the pirate king and hacked at a limb, but when his steel sword came forward, Farix simply wasn't where he'd been a moment ago.

Another blow from the pirate king struck the bladesinger's neck. The hood protected him from some of the blow, but a splash of blood dripped down the green material. Deniz struck at the pirate king's leg, but Farix danced out of the way, and his backswing cut across Deniz's cheek, opening up a wide gash from his ear to his chin. Deniz narrowly avoided the next blow, rolling out of the way an instant before the pirate king's blade sliced the air.

The whirling swords increased speed until they could hardly be seen. Suddenly, the bladesinger was on the ground, gasping. Farix held his sword with both hands and thrust into the Alturan's mouth. Blood gushed out, and then the bladesinger shuddered and died.

Deniz roared and launched his own series of blows, ignoring the battle around him, fighting with the skill that had seen him destroy his foes time and again when battling other pirates for the Emir.

Farix's enchanted sword flickered out, almost contemptuously, and Deniz felt the burning blade slice across his throat.

He coughed and pressed his left hand to his neck. Blood spurted out and Deniz suddenly found himself on his knees, head lolling back, eyes looking up at the sky.

The smoke parted for a moment, and Commodore Deniz saw the blue and brown flag of Veldria, flying tall and proud from the mast of the *Seekrieger*.

Deniz pushed himself up onto one knee. He'd lost his sword. Where was it?

The crumpled body of the bladesinger was just near his feet. The bladesinger's chant had only just stopped. The zenblade still sparked with red and blue fire.

Still holding his throat as his life force left his body, Deniz picked up the zenblade. It felt made for his hand.

Farix had his back to Deniz.

Holding the zenblade with one hand, the other clutching his throat, Deniz put all of his remaining strength into his strike. At the last moment Farix dodged, as if sensing the coming blow, but Deniz moved with him. The commodore felt the sword meet resistance as it struck the pirate king's neck.

In the battle of lore, the zenblade won. Farix's head came cleanly from his shoulders. The body fell down to the deck.

Deniz stumbled and then fell back to his knees, and finally onto his back. He once more stared at the sky. This time he only saw clouds.

He was tired. It was time to sleep.

26

High in the sky, winds tossed a solitary dirigible to and fro in unpredictable air currents as the pilot struggled to keep the vessel afloat. A boatlike tub hung under the rune-covered cylinder by wires as the vessel's two occupants clutched onto the rails with white knuckles.

Miro had been told it was dangerous to fly so high, but he'd instructed the pilot to take him up anyway. In his heart he knew it was foolish to risk their sole dirigible, not to mention the lives of its occupants, but below, in the deep sea, the brave Veldrins and Buchalanti fought a battle that made the risk pale in comparison.

He felt a surge of joy as he saw the Veldrins' first pass, watching the warships shatter the enemy vessels one after the other. As Deniz circled around, Miro saw the Buchalanti charge into the armada from behind, and then a haze of smoke clouded the vista while he struggled to make sense of the battle.

"So many," the pilot whispered. "There are just so many of them."

Deniz destroyed more than a dozen ships with his second pass, but this time the enemy was ready for him, and he lost four of his own Veldrin warships. The commodore disengaged, and the Veldrin fleet sped away.

The *Infinity* led the point of a wedge deep into the armada. Launching their salvos ahead of them, the Buchalanti smashed ship after ship, and Miro soon realized the black specks in the water were bodies. Every revenant lost to the sea was a revenant he wouldn't have to face on the beaches.

Miro saw the *Infinity* crash into a big black warship.

Then, on the other side of the armada, Deniz became embroiled in close fighting, smoke clouding the scene as the Veldrins became encircled. Miro's fists clenched at the dirigible's rail as he wondered what was happening inside the cloud of gray haze.

The smoke cleared for an instant, and Miro saw the *Seekrieger* dangerously engaged, grappled to an enemy flagship. Miro felt his heart race, and he pinched his palms. Then Miro's heart leapt out of time as he saw the *Seekrieger* slowly sink into the water.

"High Lord, I must take us down," the pilot said.

"Soon!" Miro barked.

Fighting at the heart of the armada, the Buchalanti vessels fell to the enemy one after another. Miro saw the *Infinity* crippled with a battering broadside. A dreadnought took fire and returned with a fierce energy weapon, blasting vessels into halves. Then the dreadnought broke up under a sustained barrage.

Two Veldrin warships tried to break free of the encirclement, but the enemy shattered them with blasts of cannon. Smoke clouded the air once more, and Miro felt the blood drain from his face as he waited for it to clear.

The armada burst free from the smoke, leaving their sinking ships behind. Moving inexorably forward, the enemy left the destruction of the naval battle behind.

It was over.

"Take us down," Miro whispered.

The pilot struggled against the wind and for a moment almost lost control, but he managed to descend, and the passenger tub steadied.

The pilot turned them back toward Castlemere, and Miro soon saw the harbor come into view.

"Back behind the defenses," Miro instructed.

The dirigible descended and soon hovered over the ground as Miro threw down the ladder. He scurried down and then stood weaving on the ground as the pilot took his vessel back to safety. Miro was shaken.

"What news?" Beorn rushed up. His expression registered Miro's white face.

Miro looked around to make sure he couldn't be heard.

"The naval engagement is lost," Miro said. "The Veldrins and the Buchalanti . . . they're gone . . . all of them." He took a deep breath. "We destroyed a great number of enemy ships, perhaps half their force. But it wasn't enough. The rest will soon be landing."

"Miro," Beorn growled, "pull yourself together. We will mourn them later. Scherlic and Deniz . . . all those who fought . . . we will mourn them. But now is not the time."

Miro nodded. He took a deep breath and straightened, aware of his men's eyes on him. He pulled the mask of the high lord back over his face.

"You know what has to happen now," Beorn said, his face grim.

"I haven't agreed . . ."

"Miro," Beorn interrupted. "Listen to me. There's no other way. We've talked about this. It's a lord marshal's duty to speak the truth when it needs to be told, and I'm speaking it now. We must evacuate the last people from the free cities. Then we need to burn them."

"How can I tell the leaders of Castlemere and Schalberg we need to destroy their cities?"

"Let me tell them," Beorn said. He gripped Miro's shoulder. "It doesn't always have to be you, Miro, who must tell the awful truth."

"Is there no other way?"

"You know there isn't."

"Lord of the Sky." Miro muttered. "What a thing to have to tell someone."

"They knew it might come to this," Beorn said.

Miro sighed and nodded to Beorn. The two men walked back to the wall, and Miro found a courier.

"Summon Councilor Marcel of Castlemere and Councilor Lauren of Schalberg," Miro said.

He gazed out at the city of Castlemere as he waited. The killing ground extended ahead of him as far as the feeble city walls.

"Yes, High Lord?" a tall man spoke in a guttural accent. Beside him an attractive woman waited anxiously.

"Councilors," Miro said. "The naval engagement is lost. The brave men of Veldria and House Buchalantas took many of the enemy with them, but it is now time to put into action the next part of the plan. You know this is what we agreed to do. Only you can give the order. There is no other option."

Beorn opened his mouth, but Miro spoke first. "We must burn Castlemere and Schalberg. We can't give the enemy an easy harbor or a place to fortify. We need them to land on the beaches. We can't defend your cities, and we can't leave them standing."

Beorn glanced at Miro and sighed.

Both Councilors paled. The leaders of the free cities had little experience of war.

"No," Councilor Lauren said, shaking her head, "I won't agree to it."

"Listen to me," Miro said. "Even if we destroyed your docks but left the rest standing, the enemy would still make landing in your harbors and use your buildings as cover. Your cities are perfect targets—we know our enemy is always eager to find more of the living to add to their numbers, and they will have no desire to be exposed on the beaches. Landing is a time of weakness for them and we need to force them out into the open. Burning the cities will create wreckage, ash, and heat—an environment they won't want to disembark thousands of revenants into. If we can make them land on the beaches, we can hit them while they're exposed."

"We must do this?" Councilor Lauren's eyes brimmed with tears.

"We must," Miro said. "I swear to you, by everything I hold dear, if there were another option I would take it."

"I believe you," said Councilor Marcel. He slowly released a breath, and then nodded. "Give the order. Burn them."

The tears now fell from the corners of Councilor Lauren's eyes. "If we must," she whispered.

"I promise you, when this is all over, we will rebuild your cities. I swear to you, that you will always be free."

Councilor Marcel led a weeping Councilor Lauren away.

"You could have let me do that," Beorn said.

"The responsibility is mine," Miro said, "though I appreciate it, I really do. Give the order."

Miro wiped a hand over his face as soldiers ran for Castlemere while another group headed further west in the direction of Schalberg.

"Keep an eye on the coast," Miro said, "and tell that pilot to keep his dirigible in the sky. We need to know where they plan to land."

27

Bartolo, Dorian, and the five recruits were all exhausted, but they'd cut the journey to the lands of Altura's south down to days.

They'd just passed the last signaling tower before Wondhip Pass, seeing the prism shining bright and lustrous. Now the farmland and forests gave way to barren rock, the land gaining a gradual slope as Bartolo stared up at the Elmas, his eye following the winding mountain path that led to the pass. He placed his hands on his knees as he walked uphill, forcing fatigued limbs to continue the harrowing pace.

Bartolo rested briefly, glancing behind him and scanning the faces of his men. With no time to find others, these youths were all he had. He'd thought he might have to leave some of the recruits behind, but they'd stayed with him, even through the last few grueling, climbing miles. They were fit and well trained, but even so, Bartolo wondered if he'd been wise to bring them. If it came to fighting, the recruits had no armor.

Bartolo's gaze returned ahead, and he spotted a nearby rise where some boulders clustered to form a hill. He leapt from rock to rock until he was at the summit, before shading his eyes and gazing once more up at the mountain. Hearing movement behind him, he turned and saw Dorian climbing up the rocks to meet him. The young yellow-haired bladesinger moved with grace, and wore his armorsilk like it fitted him, Bartolo noted with approval.

"What do you think?" Dorian said.

"Nothing," said Bartolo. "No light."

"Why would Tingarans stop the light at Wondhip Pass? I can understand their motivation in blocking our call to the east, cruel as it is, but to prevent our signal going south? Do they really hate us so much?"

"I don't understand it either," Bartolo said. "After what happened at the bridge, I had to check. And here we are, and there's no light at the pass."

Inwardly, Bartolo seethed. Altura was under attack. His homeland needed him.

Miro needed the signal to get through.

"So you think there'll be four of them, like last time?" Dorian asked.

"Tapel said that last bunch was waiting for four more men to join them—the ones Jehral met. So, at a guess, I'd say between four and eight."

"You think the recruits are up to it?"

"Eight bandits against us two and five lads who've trained at the Pens most of their lives? I can't see them putting up much of a fight. The last station was guarded by rogues, not warriors," Bartolo said. "This one shouldn't be any different."

Bartolo stretched, hearing his back crack as the recruits caught up. He felt confident, but a thought kept nagging him.

Why would these men in the pass, Tingarans, care whether or not Hazarans and Petryans helped Altura?

Loki had only the barest idea where he was.

After the shipwreck, he'd taken his surviving draugar and finally found a way up from the beach to the high cliffs above. That was only the beginning of his ordeal, for Loki was confronted by a terrible expanse of desert.

He knew this must be the Hazara Desert he'd been told about. The storm had turned the ship around before casting it against the shore, but this land could be no other place. He also knew his draugar wouldn't last long: the Lord of the Night had cooled the air aboard the ships with lore, but the sun here was fierce, and rot would soon take them.

Loki headed north and struck success when he found a Petryan town called Hatlatu. He used his wretched draugar from across the sea to destroy the town and kill the townsfolk, first questioning some screaming women, checking his location, and finding out about the route to his fellow necromancers in Altura via the mountain pass.

Loki used his essence to make new draugar from the dead of Hatlatu to replace those he'd lost, but making a draug took time, and he only made a dozen.

Now these dozen were all he had left.

Loki's goal was to find cooler lands and meet up with his fellow necromancers, and so he kept heading north. Finally Loki found the mountain pass.

The pass was guarded by a strange tower.

Loki tried to decipher the lore, but it was foreign to him. He didn't let any of his draugar pass beneath the three-legged tower, and particularly he stayed clear of the triangular prism.

But there was only the one way through.

Finally Loki decided to take a risk, and sent a draug to pull at one of the tower's three legs. The whole thing finally came crashing down, and Loki made his draugar send the tower tumbling down the mountainside, back the way he'd come. The strange glossy pyramid was buried in a rockslide, and Loki was pleased when the way through the pass was made clear.

He made camp in the gully. It was a good, defensible position, with a sweeping view of the land on all sides. Looking through the pass to the north, he now saw lush forests and knew this must be the land of Altura.

Loki frowned when he saw movement on the mountain. He quickly set an ambush and waited to see who was coming.

———◄►———

"This is one of the worst approaches I've ever seen," Bartolo muttered. He finally made a decision. "I'm going to scout ahead. Bladesinger Dorian, you're in charge. Bring them forward, but shadow the rocks, and don't enter the pass."

Bartolo scampered ahead, keeping his body close to the ground. He left the path and climbed up the steep mountainside, gripping loose boulders and pulling himself forward and up. He felt sweat dripping down his brow and shook droplets from the dark locks of his hair.

Up ahead, he could see a cleft in the mountain: Wondhip Pass. He veered off, climbing vertically now, taking his weight on his legs and pushing hard, only using his arms to steady himself. He kicked a rock loose and sent it tumbling down the mountain. Soon he was twenty paces high, and he felt his arms and legs burn as he kept going, refusing to look down. He now skirted the rock face, heading toward the pass but maintaining height so he could look down.

Bartolo cursed inwardly when he saw the cleft was too steep for him to look into, the walls too high.

He would have to climb down.

Bartolo's feet scrabbled at empty air as he descended for a time without being able to see what lay below him. His heart beat loudly in his ears as blood coursed through his limbs. Finally his left foot found a ridge in the rock, and he wedged it in tight. Moving slowly and fighting the fatigue in his limbs, he shifted down inch by inch, and then Bartolo could look down, though he was still a hundred feet away.

His heart hammered as he saw a gray-robed necromancer and a dozen revenants waiting in ambush.

Bartolo closed his eyes. He would be sending recruits—well trained but hardly battle hardened—against revenants. They were outnumbered two to one. The lads didn't even have armor.

He climbed back up and shifted again along the mountain; it was easier when he could see where he was climbing. His urgency spurred him on, but he was forced to take a different route on his return journey, climbing higher still, ascending the steep face until he was precariously perched hundreds of feet above solid ground.

Bartolo clutched at a rock but felt it fall away from his hands. He winced at the clatter as more stone fell, and then he heard a rumble above his head.

A huge boulder bounced along, gathering speed as it fell. Bartolo looked frantically for somewhere to lunge to, but he couldn't find any handholds, and in a heartbeat the boulder would smash into his head, crushing his skull and throwing him from the cliff face to plummet to his death.

As Bartolo cringed, awaiting the inevitable, he heard a howling wind.

Without warning a great gust shoved him hard up against the mountain, and he couldn't have moved even if he'd wanted to.

The sound of the crashing boulder as it rolled along the stone suddenly stopped. Bartolo looked around him in amazement, wondering where it was; he hadn't seen or heard the huge stone fall.

Glancing up, he saw one of the strangest sights of his life.

The boulder hovered in the air, directly above his head. Wind howled in his ears, an eerie gust unlike any force of nature. The boulder . . . moved. It traveled horizontally along the cliff, though Bartolo knew the movement was impossible, and when it was a safe distance from Bartolo, the stone once more dropped and resumed its crashing charge.

The wind fell away, and Bartolo was once more able to move his limbs.

Knowing the sound of the boulder would disturb the revenants, Bartolo lunged for another outcrop and grabbed hold to pull his body to a safer position. He began to make his way down a cleft, heading back toward the waiting recruits, and he'd soon descended the mountain face, to once more reach the winding trail.

Dorian waited with the recruits, their backs to a large boulder as they drank water and rested in the shade. Bartolo decided against mentioning his experience with the boulder; he could hardly believe it himself.

Dorian rose as Bartolo approached, and as the two men put their heads together, Bartolo thanked the wisdom that had led them to elevate the young man.

"Bad news," Bartolo said. He shook his head; the term didn't do their plight justice.

"What is it? Ambush? How many?"

"Revenants," Bartolo said.

Dorian's eyes widened and he blanched. "How?"

"I don't know how, but they're here. Come on. I need to talk to all the lads."

Bartolo crouched down on his haunches as he scanned each face in turn. Timo regarded him with intelligent eyes. Martin looked strong and sturdy, ready to face anything.

"Listen," Bartolo said. "The tower in the pass is gone. Unless we can raise it again, our signal to the lands in the south won't get through. A force waits in ambush. I must fight, and Dorian will help me, but it's time for the rest of you to go home."

"Go home?" Martin said. "No, we're here to help you."

"No." Bartolo shook his head. "You can't. There are a dozen revenants waiting in ambush. The seven of us . . . well . . . we're outnumbered. Our force isn't enough."

"Then how do you plan to restore the tower?" Timo said.

"I'm going to fight," Bartolo said.

"But I thought you said there are too many of them?" Timo pressed.

"There are," Dorian said, looking at Bartolo. "But we're going to try anyway."

"Then I'm trying too," Martin said, crossing his arms in front of his chest.

"Me too."

"So am I."

"I'm not going home now."

"We won't leave you."

Bartolo drew in a slow breath and let it out in one strong stream of air. "I appreciate your bravery, and your loyalty. I really do. But lads, to go up there is to die. We've got armorsilk and zenblades. They'll kill you."

"Bladesinger Bartolo," Martin said, lifting his chin, "I'm not going home. You say there are too many for two bladesingers. Five more of us could turn the tide. No, listen." Martin shook his flaxen-haired head when Bartolo opened his mouth. "I haven't trained at the Pens since I was six years old just to go home when the going gets tough. What have we trained for, all these years, if it isn't for a day like today? I've got a sword, and I have my friends by my side. We need to do this."

217

Dorian met Bartolo's gaze and raised one eyebrow.

Bartolo sighed. "Who among you agrees with Martin?"

Every recruit raised his hand. Dorian chuckled.

"Then I thank you, lads. I . . ."

"Enough, Bartolo, just tell us how to kill them," Dorian said.

"All right," Bartolo said, his voice firming. "Here's how we're going to do it."

Bartolo and Dorian walked directly into the ambush, both with zenblades held out in front of them, poised to activate their armorsilk the moment they sighted the enemy.

It was close to midday, and the sun shone fierce rays down on the exposed mountain. Bartolo had considered using shadow but had discarded the idea; Dorian was too new, and there was no darkness to hide in.

Ahead, the walls at either side of the cleft loomed in Bartolo's vision. Looking up at the mountain face, he wondered how he'd ever climbed the sheer wall. He once more pondered the strange experience with the boulder, but whatever it was, it couldn't help him now. Bartolo and Dorian took three more steps, and still the enemy hadn't revealed themselves.

Dorian began to chant under his breath, and his armorsilk came steadily to life, runes lighting up on his hood, his chest, his arms and legs. Bartolo couldn't blame him, but he saved his breath, feeling the tension grow as he entered the gully.

With a series of grunts and roars, the enemy attacked.

Bartolo took only enough time to register their numbers: they were all here, and there was the necromancer sending them forward. These warriors had once been Petryans, he saw now, with swarthy skins and some wearing red, flat-topped hats. The symbols on their skins glowed softly, their white eyes showing eerie stares.

"Run!" Bartolo grabbed Dorian, and they sped back down the mountain away from the warriors.

The revenants were fast, and Bartolo opened his stride, pumping his arms as he sped across the loose gravel and dodged around bigger rocks, hoping he wouldn't stumble. Bartolo felt grasping hands on his back and whirled, cutting into a creature's side before resuming his run. He risked a glance at Dorian and saw the younger man's armorsilk once more dark as Dorian put everything into running.

Bartolo had laid his own ambush carefully. He sped between two huge boulders and ducked behind the rock on the left while Dorian whirled to the right.

The five recruits held their ground and took the first two revenants down with savage blows, sending blood and bits of skull flying in all directions. Bartolo activated his armorsilk and zenblade and charged back into the fray.

The gap between the boulders channeled the enemy, but those at the back circled around, and soon the seven Alturans would be pressed on all sides. Bartolo's voice came strong, rising in a deep baritone as he activated the fierce heat pent up in his zenblade and fended off a frenzied series of blows from two revenants. He cut off one opponent's limbs and tore a second revenant in two, leaping forward and taking off a head, rescuing Martin who was hard pressed. Dorian had his back to a rock and fought three at the same time, his wide eyes betraying his fear.

Bartolo saw Timo thrust deeply into a revenant's chest, but it simply snarled and lashed a fist into his face, moving faster than any human. The reedy recruit fell onto his back, and the creature leapt atop Timo's chest, grinning as it scrabbled at Timo's body, both hands squeezing the recruit's neck until Bartolo heard a resounding crack.

There was fighting on all sides now. With Timo down and Dorian pressed, Bartolo and the four other recruits fought in a circle, guarding each other's backs as they fended off lore-enhanced limbs with steel swords and courage.

Bartolo watched in desperation as Dorian's song faltered and his armorsilk dimmed. Bartolo couldn't leave the recruits; they were only still alive because of his whirling blade. Whenever a revenant came at them, Bartolo moved to meet it, protecting the recruits even as they protected his back.

As he fought, Bartolo looked up past the boulders and saw the necromancer, watching and guiding his minions. There were too many revenants for the Alturans to hold. Soon they would be overwhelmed.

Then in a flash of bright fire, the necromancer burst into flame.

Dorian spun on his heel in a move Bartolo had seen him practice a thousand times, throwing the revenants away as his fiery blade whirled in a flash of blue and purple.

Bartolo thrust into a burly warrior, but it only had the effect of enraging his opponent. Past the creature's shoulder Bartolo saw red robes, and a coiled ball of crimson flame smashed into the revenant. Sizzling flesh blackened in a heartbeat, and Bartolo's opponent fell.

A second ball tore through the air, sizzling with a sound like paper being torn as it bathed another revenant in liquid fire. The fireballs came fast now, and as the revenants turned to meet this new threat Bartolo leapt forward and took two heads in succession.

The last revenant moaned as two balls of flame struck it from different directions. Its skin crackled as the flame continued its grisly work, scorching the clothing to cinders and burning the flesh until runes could no longer be discerned, and then the revenant fell, just a dark lump on the rocky ground.

Bartolo lowered his sword, panting.

Petryan elementalists in red robes stood circled around the site of the battle, the cuffs at their wrists glowing.

A dark-haired woman stepped out of their midst, a red-robed elementalist with a white rope belted around her waist. She spoke a sequence to deactivate the devices at her wrists and then smiled wearily at Bartolo.

"Shani?" Bartolo said as he gasped.

"You're far from home," Shani said.

Bartolo looked around him. Aside from Timo, the recruits had escaped with cuts and bruises, but his men were alive. Bartolo knelt and put his fingers to Timo's neck, but the sightless gaze said enough.

"Men," Bartolo started, but he had to stop, coughing. "Men," he tried again, "some of you know my wife, Shani, an elementalist of Petrya."

The recruits exchanged glances. Dorian dropped his zenblade and looked at his shaking hands.

"They're pleased to meet you," Bartolo spoke for them. "On the mountain . . . That was you?"

Shani grinned. "We're not just wielders of fire. They call us elementalists for a reason. We saw a man in green armorsilk up on the cliff. He looked like he could use a hand."

As Bartolo panted, Shani's smile suddenly shifted to a frown. She came forward until she was directly in front of her husband and glared up at Bartolo's eyes. "You were out of your depth, bladesinger, and you know it."

"I had to . . ."

"Shut up," Shani said. "Don't ever do that again."

Shani put her arms around him, and as Bartolo felt her warmth close to him, he knew she was right. The arrival of the Petryans had saved all of their lives.

But even so, Bartolo had been right to try. He decided to save that discussion for another day.

"How?" Bartolo said.

"Our patrols found the ruins of Hatlatu. We tracked them here."

"Are there more Petryans . . .?"

"No," Shani said, "it's just us."

"The tower!" Bartolo suddenly pushed his wife away. "We need to raise the tower!"

"We saw it," Shani said. "It's on the other side of the pass. We were about to bring it back up when we saw you and came to help."

Bartolo instructed the recruits to stay with Timo's body and followed Shani and her fellow elementalists back up to the pass.

They swiftly found the three-legged tower, and after casting in wide circles, they finally found the prism, buried in a pile of rock, with green light seeping through.

Bartolo was exhausted, but he didn't rest until the tower was back up, with the signal shining fiercely. He felt relief flood through him as, looking into the southern lands from the mountain, he saw a satisfying wink of green light answer.

"They've called?" Shani said.

"Yes," Bartolo said. He took a deep breath. "We have to hurry. They need us, Shani. They need all of us. Will your elementalists come to Altura?"

Shani hesitated. "Yes. I don't care what the high lord says. I'll force them to come if I have to."

Bartolo gazed from the pass at the green forests of Altura.

He was exhausted.

But rest would have to wait.

28

Black smoke poured in two great spires from the coastline. The last refugees had left long ago, and now the free cities, built mostly of wood from the nearby forests, burned with a raging fire that wouldn't cease until every building was ash.

In the aftermath of the naval battle, a single ship limped to shore. The *Infinity* had lost a mast and was holed in three places, but it seemed Scherlic had kept his ship together long enough to break free from the clutches of the enemy fleet. He'd somehow managed to raise enough sail to outdistance the armada and make it to shore.

As Castlemere burned, Miro raised a reddened gaze to watch the ship. He stood on the beach, listening to the breaking waves contrast with the breaking timbers of Castlemere's falling buildings. The smell of burning wood filled the air; even the sea breeze couldn't banish it.

The *Infinity* came steadily closer as Scherlic brought his crippled ship to where clear water met the line of deep blue. Miro's eyes took in the broken timbers and fallen sails, holes in the sides and shattered prow. Scherlic's proud ship was a shade of her former self, yet even so, the shadow of night had sought to claim her, and she'd survived—the only vessel to do so.

A figure in green leapt off the side of the ship, and the man began to swim with strong strokes to shore. As soon as the bladesinger left the ship, Scherlic turned the vessel, and the *Infinity* limped farther down the coast. Miro waved, but his arm finally dropped to his side; he wasn't sure if the sailmaster waved back.

Miro watched as the bladesinger swam for shore. The man in green shook his head and stood when he reached the shallows, staggering forward before making better headway. Miro walked into the water to help him out, clasping his hand and putting his arm around the man's shoulders.

"Well met," Miro said. "You survived."

"Lord of the Sky, I don't know how."

"Come, I'll take you back to the encampment. We think they're going to commence their landing tomorrow."

"I tried, High Lord, but I couldn't see any ship being specially guarded," the bladesinger said. "If Sentar has essence aboard one of his ships, he isn't doing much to protect it. He sacrificed his own to destroy us. We took his flagship, and he simply moved to another."

The smoke from the burning city rolled over the killing ground as Miro took the bladesinger in a wide circle, skirting the red flags and leading him past the thick wall. The smoke-red eyes of the defenders followed them as they headed deeper into the encampment.

"Commodore Deniz?" Miro asked, holding his breath.

"Fallen," the bladesinger said. "I watched the fight through a seeing device. Deniz killed one of the commanders, a man whose flag was red with blue crossed swords, but fell himself, along with Bladesinger Willem."

Miro remembered Deniz describing Farix, the pirate king of Torian. The captured necromancer said there were two more of these so-called kings. Miro knew Deniz was a skilled swordsman, yet Farix had bested a bladesinger as well as Deniz.

"Here," Miro said. "Rest. Then go to High Lord Tiesto Telmarran. He will have orders for you."

Even as Miro mourned the loss of Deniz and the Veldrin and Buchalanti sailors, his mind turned to the coming struggle. Soon his men's courage would be sorely tested as they watched their friends killed and fought enemies who refused to die.

This was the worst time: the waiting. Miro knew that the longer he could hold, the more time there would be for help to arrive from the other houses.

Yet every day bought from now on would be a day bought with blood.

Miro and Beorn pored over a map of the rugged coastline as they waited to hear from Tiesto.

"They're not stupid," Beorn said. "They'll make landing either here"—he pointed at a place on the map east of Castlemere—"or here." He marked another place west of Schalberg, between the two cities. "My gilden's on the latter. Better beaches, shallower water."

"Do you think they'll have landing boats?"

"Who can say?" Beorn shrugged. "We've never fought a foe like this before. If we were fighting regular soldiers, of course I would say yes, but revenants?"

Miro voiced the one concern he didn't have a strategy for. "What are we going to do about Sentar Scythran?"

"I've told the men to concentrate their ranged fire on him, to try to weaken him. You never know; a lucky shot might get through."

Miro snorted.

"We'll have to put our trust in the Lord of the Sky," Beorn said.

"Are you saying we have to have faith, or do we hope Evrin Evenstar has something planned?"

"Both." Beorn grinned.

"High Lord?"

Miro and Beorn looked up as one of Miro's palace guards entered the command tent, a civilian at his side.

"What is it?" Miro asked.

"High Lord, this man comes from Sarostar. I think you should hear what he has to say."

Miro saw a solid man with thin hair combed over a bald pate.

"High Lord," the newcomer said gruffly, "I come from Bladesinger Bartolo."

Miro's eyes shot up. "Bartolo? Where is he? Dorian's also missing. Where are they?"

"There . . . there's been treachery. Some men tried to prevent our signal getting through to the lands in the east."

Beorn cursed.

"What? Tell me what happened?" Miro demanded.

"Some Tingarans swapped the real prism for a false one."

"Jehral," Beorn said. "He said he fought some Tingarans near the river. Now we know what they were doing there."

"Treachery," Miro spat. "I didn't even think of it." He pounded a clenched fist into his palm.

"Don't blame yourself—none of us could have known."

"But we could have guarded the towers."

"Guarded every single one of them?" Beorn snorted.

"High Lord," the bald man said, "Bladesinger Bartolo, he got it back up. The call went out. He went to check on the station at Wondhip Pass, and he sent me here."

"Scratch it," Beorn muttered. "All this time, wasted."

Miro sighed. He didn't have support from the Louans, from the Veznans, from the Petryans, Hazarans, Toraks, or Tingarans. The Buchalanti had done their part, and the Veldrins; now it was left to Altura and Halaran to hold back the tide alone.

"High Lord, may I fight?" the bald man said.

Miro tried to smile. "We won't turn you down. What's your name?"

"Fergus."

"Fergus," Miro said; the name was familiar. "Go and find a sergeant: one of the officers with a double-striped *raj hada*. Tell him to give you weapons and armor. Good to have you."

"Thank you, High Lord."

Fergus departed, but he'd only been gone a moment when High Lord Tiesto of Halaran entered.

"Miro, our scouts have been watching from the coast, and the dirigible pilot confirmed it. They're going to commence landing at dawn."

"Where?" Beorn asked.

"The beaches west of Schalberg," Tiesto said, coming forward to point at the place on the map Beorn had previously marked. "These defenses aren't exactly hidden. They'll make their landing far from here."

Miro's gaze returned to the map. If he could hold them at the beaches, they might still emerge relatively unscathed.

"Is there anything you need?" Miro asked Tiesto.

"Are you still going to be in the sky? I won't have your vantage, and once the battle starts . . ."

Miro nodded. "I'll be up in the dirigible. We'll coordinate, and I'll signal you if need be."

"I don't know how you can stand being up in that thing," Beorn said.

"I'd rather be up there than down here wondering what's going on," Miro said.

"Don't worry, Miro," Tiesto said. "If I can, I'll stop them."

Miro was pensive for a moment. "All right," he finally said. "We all know the plan. Tiesto, you have the command. Stop as many as you can on the beaches. Be ready to fall back to our strength here. We'll be ready for you."

"I'll leave now," Tiesto said.

"Good luck," Miro said.

"And you."

29

Ella waited with the forward guard as the rising sun revealed an empty beach. The only sounds were the crashing of waves and cries of gulls. Nervous, she dug her nails into her palms as she waited.

And then the sea was empty no more.

Ella felt a shiver of fear, her heart racing as tiny sails filled the horizon. The surviving ships of the enemy fleet faced no opposition as they carefully approached their chosen landing site; there was nothing any of the waiting defenders on the beach could do about it.

"Could at least be foul weather," Ella muttered.

"If you want me to respond, you should talk so I can hear you," Layla said.

Crouched beside Ella, the small Dunfolk healer was a comforting presence. Ella had chosen to wait with Layla rather than with Tiesto, who at any rate was preoccupied with his animators and constructs.

Layla scowled at Ella, her ruddy features crinkling. "Well? Are you in the habit of talking to yourself?"

"I said the weather is beautiful," Ella said. "I wish it wasn't. It'll make their landing easier."

"Clear skies help us see too," Layla said. "Would you rather it was raining and foggy, so you couldn't tell which of the men in front of you was a foe or a friend?"

Ella smiled. "You're right. Lord of the Sky, I'm scared."

Layla put her arm around Ella and squeezed her, the grip surprisingly firm. "I will always be with you," she said.

Ella let out a breath as she watched the ships grow larger in her vision, creeping inevitably closer to the coast. She could understand how Miro must feel; was any amount of preparation enough to face this? It felt like a doomed effort from the start, and they had yet to face Sentar himself.

A big warship, the foremost vessel at the point of a wedge of cruisers and motley barges, grew ever larger, and Ella fought to control her fear. She tried to tell herself she'd fought terrible enemies before.

"Remember, the plan is to wait until the landing begins in earnest, and to engage the enemy as they move through the water. We want to hold a line about knee deep. The drag of the water on the enemy should help us. We need our archers to pin them back while our swordsmen take their heads. Archers should concentrate their fire on the necromancers above all. We must stop as many in the water as we can."

"Ella," Layla said. "I know."

Ella realized she was speaking to hide her terror. The closest ship was still out in deep water, but Ella could now see a golden pennant flown next to a white flag that snapped in the wind. She saw a black design on the white flag that could have been a withered tree. It was the symbol of the Akari, but they'd inherited it in turn from the Lord of the Night.

Ella tore her gaze from the warship and then gasped.

A single, solitary figure stood at the water's edge.

Ella could swear he hadn't been there before. The man stood as if waiting and wore a sky-blue robe, belted at the waist with a golden cord.

Ella recognized the white hair and slightly stooped shoulders that were now, somehow, regal.

Evrin Evenstar stood alone to greet the enemy.

The advancing ships held off in the deep water, still several hundred paces from shore. It was as if time had stopped.

Ella held her breath.

Evrin's hands began to move.

Sparkles of light colored the air in front of him, twisting rainbows curling in among each other and threading together to form a startling platform. Evrin's hands shifted in the air; Ella guessed he must be holding a scrill, but if so, she couldn't see it. The trails of golden light whirled together, and Evrin took a step up. His hands moved faster now, faster than Ella thought possible, and Evrin took a second step forward, and then a third.

Evrin's voice couldn't be heard, as far away as Ella was, but she knew he must be chanting, calling on each rune as he trailed essence into the very air, connecting the new to the old.

Evrin built a glowing stairway, taking one step after another as he ascended. His creation took him past the shallows, then further still, to where the dark water met the light, and still he kept moving. He now stood high above the deep sea, and still he kept building, higher and higher, further out into the sea, as if trying to connect the white sand of the beach to the line of enemy vessels.

Evrin's stairway continued past the dark water and farther, to where the deep blue turned to black. He was now at an incredible height, and he stopped, looking down at the ships below while the whole world waited.

Ella tried to stand, but Layla clutched her arm, pulling her back down. "He has a plan," Layla said. "You are not part of it."

Evrin raised his arms to the sky as the watchers on the ridge looked on with mouths gaping wide.

Evrin called in a voice like a howl, and the thunder of his speech was easily audible to all below. It was a mighty, primal sound, a cry of rage, a bellow of pain, a summons.

"Sentar!" Evrin roared.

Ella clenched her fists, her knuckles white, as she caught movement from the ship with the golden pennant.

Ella watched as a figure in black rose into the air.

She'd heard so much about him, but it was the first time Ella had seen Sentar Scythran, the Lord of the Night, in the flesh.

Ella's gaze took in a man with red hair like Killian's, though Sentar's shade was deeper, the color of blood. The two men were too far away for Ella to see much more.

But as she watched Sentar floating easily in front of Evrin Evenstar, the difference in their abilities was driven home with sudden force.

Ella felt something terrible was about to happen.

———◆———

Evrin gazed at the face in front of him. How long had it been since he'd last seen this face? How many centuries had passed since he'd banished Sentar Scythran, Varian Vitrix, Pyrax Pohlen, and the rest of his brothers to the world they'd opened up with blood?

As high as he was, wind buffeted him, curling his robe around his body. Evrin stood with his legs spread and resisted the urge to look down into the deep water. In his right hand he held a golden scrill, a metal rod as long as his hand. His left hand was empty.

"Lord of the Sky," Sentar said, his lip curled in a sneer. "Human lover."

"Sentar, you killed the woman I loved, and you took away what I was. Still, we are brothers. End this madness. Learn to live with the humans."

"Live with the humans?" Sentar said. He tilted his head back as he laughed. "We're gods, Evrin Evenstar! We're as far beyond them as stars from insects. They swarm, they irritate, but we shine. We burn with power. Can you not feel the power, surging within you, filling your limbs with vigor? Oh," Sentar smiled, "I'm sorry, I just remembered. You cannot."

"They are too powerful for you now," Evrin said. "They've outgrown us."

Sentar looked back over his shoulder, down at the multitude of ships below. "The living will never defeat the dead. Every human I destroy feeds my war machine. Once I gain a foothold on this Empire, they will never turn me back. It will only end when I have resumed my rightful place. For humans, there is only death."

"A plague," Evrin said. "You and yours are a plague and nothing more. I should have killed you when I had the chance."

"Finally getting some courage, Lord of the Sky?"

"I sent you and the others to exile out of compassion, not out of any lack of courage on my part."

"You sent us to a nightmare world, to a fate worse than death."

"It was a world you found for yourselves. You deserved your fate."

"If you only knew, Skylord," Sentar spat. "If I had the power, I would revisit every moment of our brothers' suffering onto you."

"At least you finally acknowledge you aren't all powerful." Evrin smiled.

As Sentar opened his hands, Evrin spoke a series of swift words, and his robe shifted in nature. The pale blue developed a pattern, a mottling like the skin of a lizard as interlocking scales shifted up and down, coating Evrin's body and limbs, rising up Evrin's chin and covering his head.

A jagged bolt of black lightning shot from each of Sentar's hands, but splashed off Evrin's scaled armor. Sentar frowned and called on more of his power; each hand now projected two streams of dark fire, then three.

Evrin's armor began to smoke, but he chanted continuously, adding more scales to replace those that fell away. He pointed his empty left hand at Sentar and added two sequences to his chants, blending more inflections into his steady stream of activation runes.

A silver and gold bracelet appeared on his left wrist and a matching ring came into being on his index finger. The bracelet and ring flared brightly and a bolt of blue energy shot forward, followed by a second, and then a third. Sentar raised one of his palms in a warding motion and a field of solid air flattened in front of him, Evrin's beams diffusing across the field's surface.

Sentar's other hand continued with the stream of crackling fire, and Evrin called on more scales to replace those that now fell in a steady stream to the ocean below. He knew his robe wouldn't last long.

Evrin expended the energy of the twin devices on his left hand at a prodigious rate. He could see Sentar's protective field fading, and he increased the power of the bolts of blue energy to the limit.

Evrin felt heat touch his skin.

"Give . . . up . . . old man," Sentar said through gritted teeth.

Evrin's robe began to smoke and smolder. The skin at his chest, closest to the twisted streams of black lightning, began to sting, and now no more scales replaced those that fell into the water, striking the surface with a hiss.

"Last . . . chance . . ." Evrin gasped.

The blue robe caught fire. Evrin screamed in pain, and with the cry of agony he choked. His voice ceased chanting, and the robe began to disintegrate.

Evrin looked at the golden scrill in his right hand.

Everything until now had been a distraction.

"Finistratas," Evrin gasped the single word.

The scrill became a handle, and a long line of flickering blue fire, a strand of shining silver, now dripped from its tip, reaching down to the water below. Evrin lifted the handle and jerked his arm backward and then down. The blue line curled through the air, reaching around behind Sentar Scythran. The silver strand curled around Sentar's waist.

"Almothar," Evrin intoned.

The scrill fused to Evrin's hand. He could never let it go.

"Neveran."

Evrin's robe took on sudden weight; it was now as heavy as a mountain. Sentar's expression registered shock, and the onslaught of black lightning became stronger. Evrin's hair burst into flame.

Fighting the pain with all his strength, Evrin could only breathe the last of the activations sequences.

"Endara."

The golden stairway of ethereal light disappeared, vanishing as if it had never been.

Evrin plummeted, weighed down by his dragging robe, and in his right hand the golden scrill could never be released.

He'd built the device to do one thing, and one thing only. Evrin had built the coil of silver to grab hold of Sentar Scythran and never let go.

Sentar screamed as the two men fell through the air, writhing and kicking, with limbs flailing in all directions. Evrin hit the water first and Sentar a heartbeat later; immediately they sank.

Water was everywhere, light filtering through the surface but struggling to reach the depths as the two figures plummeted to the bottom. Evrin pulled with his right arm even as his lungs heaved and his body thirsted for air.

Sentar rolled over and over, trying to untangle himself from the glowing wire. Evrin grabbed hold of the man he'd once called brother and tried to hold him as the two men hit the sandy ocean floor.

Sentar attacked Evrin in a frenzy. Evrin felt hands clapped to his head, and excruciating pain wracked his skull and spine, filling his consciousness with fire.

Evrin's vision closed in until all he could see was a white tunnel with a warm golden light, beckoning him at the end.

His love called.

Evrin Evenstar, Lord of the Sky, followed her down the tunnel.

30

Ella watched in horror as the stairway of light vanished and Evrin and Sentar plunged into the water. For long minutes, only bubbles and hisses of steam indicated where they'd fallen.

Ella gripped Layla's hand with savage intensity. "Evrin!" she screamed. She was standing now, though she didn't remember getting to her feet.

All was silent. The onlookers at the beach, the distant ships preparing to unload their deadly cargos, all were still.

Then someone burst from the ocean, thrashing weakly. Ella's heart thudded with pounding jolts as she tried to see who it was.

The figure was black.

A boat sped out from the foremost ship. The reaching hands of gray-robed necromancers pulled the man in black clothing aboard, before turning back to the ships.

Ella waited, and waited. Long moments passed. A hundred heartbeats became a thousand.

But the old man never came to the surface.

Evrin Evenstar was dead.

"Evrin," Ella sobbed.

Layla held Ella back as she tried to pull free. Tears sped down Ella's cheeks as she desperately scanned the surface of the water, knowing her search was futile. The battle between the Lord of the Sky and the Lord of the Night was over. Sentar was evidently wounded, terribly so, but he had emerged the victor.

The ships came forward. The warship that Sentar Scythran had returned to retreated, and soon it was hidden by the line of encroaching vessels.

The line of ships passed the site of the battle and continued forward, crossing into the aqua-blue water. There were suddenly so many of them that they fought for space. With sounds of tearing and groaning, each vessel ran aground bow-first, tilting to the side as keels ground against the sand, sails hurriedly downed.

They had no landing boats: the revenants simply poured off the sides. Tiesto had a few cannon—they would have to abandon any brought here, so most were back with Miro—and thunderous booms split the air as he fired. Splinters flew from the ships and water fountained in great splashes, pieces of enemy warriors flying into the air. Still they came.

Six ships were now aground, and dozens more found gaps between them and made their own landings. Soon the line of enemy vessels crowded the beach; Tiesto's gunners suffered from no lack of targets.

Ella fixed her reddened stare back on the ridge and waited for Tiesto's signal. Constructs would sink in the water so this first charge would be made by infantry. Ella would fight with them.

Along the ridge the men in green and brown held their weapons ready. Fighters from the free cities nervously exchanged glances while the Dunfolk archers surrounding Ella readied their bows. Ella saw enchanters in green robes and bladesingers in armorsilk. She saw faces she knew: Jehral, the only man in black, waited near Tiesto's command center, and with surprise Ella recognized Fergus the ferryman standing not far away with a determined expression on his round face.

A clarion blared and a red light shone from the solitary dirigible flying high above, maintaining a position back toward Castlemere.

"Charge!" the defenders roared with a single voice.

Ella set her mouth with anger. She'd heard Miro speak of battle rage, and it was something she'd felt a few times herself: as the primate's army crushed the refugees at the Sarsen and at the prison camps in Tingara.

It was the rage that came when trying to right an incredible injustice.

"Go," Layla said.

Ella ran forward with the infantry as they charged.

The rush to the water's edge took an eternity and was over in a heartbeat. Ella ran with men and women defending their homeland from the darkest evil. There were thousands of soldiers, all well armored and prepared for what they were about to face.

The waist-deep water thronged with revenants.

Volleys of arrows sped overhead, plunging into the enemy warriors. Some wore ragged barbaric clothing, big men and women with double-bladed axes and heavy two-handed swords. Others wore the uniforms of their old regiments, lands across the sea now utterly destroyed. All were in advanced stages of decay, with lips rotted away to reveal yellow teeth, mottled black-and-blue rot taking hold of limbs and heads, and grotesque wounds on throats, faces, and bodies, revealing how they'd been killed, or how they'd refused to be put down since.

The defenders formed a long line in the knee-deep water. The crack of musket fire sounded from the ships, and some of the Veldrin defenders returned fire with their own barreled sticks. The arrows of the Dunfolk sprouted from enemy warriors, sending shoulders jerking back or tearing into throats, but making little impact; these warriors simply kept coming.

Ella held her wand in front of her with a shaking hand. The hazel wood felt warm in her palm, then hot as she activated it with a series of chanted runes. The prism of gold-flecked quartz sparked with yellow fire.

A snarling revenant, a woman with torn clothing revealing slashes across her breasts, shot out of the water in front of Ella. Ella sent a bolt of yellow fire into the woman's eye, and she went down.

The enemy struck the line in numbers, and the sounds of grunting and clashing steel split the air. The Alturan swordsman beside Ella thrust at a barbarian's neck, but the blow missed as the revenant swerved to the side. The Alturan made a second strike at his opponent's head. The barbarian's broadsword blocked the blow, but the Alturan's glowing blade cut through the steel, and another head went flying.

To Ella's right, a Halrana was having trouble with an enemy swordsman, a man who'd once been Veldrin by his blue and brown uniform. A bolt from Ella's wand shattered the revenant's skull into two pieces. The Halrana nodded his quick thanks.

Ella kept a wide circle around her, taking careful aim with each activation of her wand, making precision strikes to conserve power. Wherever she could, she helped the struggling swordsmen, but she could see the revenants' numbers now starting to tell. The Alturan beside her went down and Ella shifted, closing ranks with the next man.

Ella saw more beams of yellow fire in the distance and caught sight of Elwin Goss, Master of the Academy, with a wide circle of bodies floating in the water around him. Arrows continued to plunge into the revenants but the once decisive weapon could only slow this enemy; the necromancers stayed hidden in the ships. A volley of musket fire from the enemy vessels cracked, and the

Halrana on Ella's right fell with a hole in his chest. Once more Ella closed ranks.

Ella missed her next shot, and a revenant swung a spiked mace at her head. The warrior on her right blocked the blow and countered with a thrust into the revenant's face. The glowing blade tore through the snarling warrior's cheek, sending red blood in all directions.

Ella turned and nodded her thanks, seeing it was Jehral. He gave her a swift nod in return.

The line of defenders closed ranks again and again, and still the enemy kept coming, pouring from the ships, rising from the deeper water in an unending wave.

Ella heard a trumpet blast and looked at Jehral.

"Fall back," he panted.

Miro watched from the dirigible, carefully judging the moment when the enemy's numbers outweighed the defenders' power to hold them in the sea. He desperately wanted to be fighting down below, but he was working in close concert with Tiesto; their timing was critical.

More ships beached themselves along the shore toward Castlemere, and the line of defenders no longer covered the approach of all the clawing revenants. He couldn't allow the line to be outflanked.

Miro ordered the retreat.

He shone a light and saw Tiesto raise a flag, hearing a corresponding clarion blast. The defenders fought to hold off the enemy as every second man in the line stepped backward. Then the second line held while the foremost fell back. Miro prayed the retreat wouldn't turn into a rout.

Finally the defenders turned and ran. Miro's elite palace guard, held so far in reserve, rushed down to give them time to escape. The revenants that made it to the ridge fell to intense volleys of arrows as rail bows and Dunfolk archers peppered their bodies.

Miro watched to see what the enemy commander would do. With Sentar wounded, who was leading them?

Then Miro saw a tall man standing on the beach with a cluster of necromancers. He wore a blue shirt and a three-cornered hat with a white feather. This must be Diemos, the king of Rendar.

Diemos waved an arm, and the revenants formed up; they would wait to disembark all their warriors before making their next attack. It was what Miro would do himself.

Miro drew a shaky breath as he watched the breakers roll over the dismembered bodies of revenants, mingling them together with the fallen defenders.

So far Miro's defenders had faced stragglers, coming in from deep water in ragged numbers. The enemy had their beachhead now; the commanders and necromancers would form their warriors into an army.

More ships were unloading all the time. There was enough of a force forming up on the beach that any attempt to push them back would be suicide. Yet fully half their numbers were still on the ships. Tiesto's cannon continued to fire while mortars rained orbs on the beached vessels, but by necessity Tiesto's force was mobile, and Miro's strongest weapons were on the ridge guarding the approach to Sarostar.

Miro saw the danger in the growing numbers. He didn't want the defenders to become trapped on the ridge. Ella was down there. Every moment that passed would make retreat more difficult.

The enemy commander was clever and was waiting to establish his entire force on the beach. The horde on the shore was already so large, Miro struggled to encompass their numbers.

In moments their commander would hurl them against Tiesto's cannon.

"Fly a signal," Miro instructed the pilot. "Send in the constructs. Everyone else to pull back to the defenses at Castlemere."

A moment later there was a crash as the doors to the carts hidden in the forest burst open. Animators hurriedly climbed towers and placed tablets at their knees.

Ironmen and woodmen lumbered forward with odd, mechanical movements. The enemy hurriedly formed up, turning to face the new threat.

The constructs charged down from the ridge.

The ironmen glistened, black limbs shining as the light of early morning cast slanted rays on the steel. The polished woodmen held the left flank while ironmen held the right.

They smashed into the enemy, remorseless in their power. The golems and colossi were back at Castlemere, but this was the bulk of Halaran's military strength, unleashed in one mad charge. Hundreds of Halrana constructs became swallowed by thousands of revenants.

Miro gripped the rail as the animated fought the dead. Tearing his gaze away from the battle, he watched as Tiesto pulled the defenders back, leading the infantry and archers along the ridge until the foremost reached the start of Miro's long wall. Miro breathed a sigh of relief.

As the creatures of iron and wood battled the undead, soon the only people left at the ridge were the animators themselves, guiding their creations with touches of their controller tablets and spoken words. In a heartbeat, chaos overtook the battlefield, and the constructs' careful formation broke down.

Cannon boomed from some of the beached ships whose exposed sides faced the battle, tearing through constructs and revenants alike.

A group of revenants broke free and charged the animators on the bank.

Miro cursed. Even against the charge, the animators held their positions. Miro's heart went out to the courage of these men. Diemos, if the order was his, was clever.

Then something huge broke through the forest.

Miro saw a colossus stride forward in great lumbering bounds. Miro's heart raced; he'd thought all the colossi were back behind Castlemere. Squinting, he recognized the mighty construct, and in a moment Miro knew who the animator was.

Luca Angelo sat in his controller cage, guiding his colossus with words and gestures as he fought to defend his countrymen.

A great sword blazed in one of the colossus's huge hands. As the revenants rushed up the ridge, ready to crush the defenseless animators on their towers, a single stroke of the sword tore through a dozen bodies. A foot stomped on a revenant, and the colossus's free arm swiped at the ground, sending a bunch more flying through the air.

The ironmen and woodmen on the beach were now overwhelmed, their charge ended. The shallow waters heaved with broken bodies. The animators scrabbled down their ladders, and the brown-robed Halrana ran for safety, back toward Castlemere.

Luca Angelo swung the enchanted sword left and right, clearing the ground in front of him before moving deep into the horde. The immense blade tore through the enemy, but rather than breaking free from the onslaught, Luca fought on. His controller cage on top of the gigantic head sparkled with color. Miro held his breath as the colossus carved a path toward the man in the three-cornered hat.

Thunderous roars followed puffs of smoke as cannon fired.

A ball struck the colossus square in the chest.

The construct fell down on its back, but whatever Luca did, he managed to get the colossus back to one knee. Revenants climbed up the legs and arms but still the Halrana animator chopped into flesh with the huge enchanted sword, wiping out revenants in numbers, giving his countrymen the time they needed to escape.

Enemy warriors climbed up the limbs to reach the controller cage and tore it open. Swords stabbed in through the gaps in the metal and with a rumble the colossus once more fell on its back.

This time it was still.

Miro released a breath he hadn't realized he was holding as he wiped a hand across his face, watching as order returned to the enemy's ranks. More ships beached further away from Castlemere. Today's battle was over.

There were bodies everywhere, but with relatively few fallen defenders, at least there would be little fodder for the enemy's war machine. Miro knew the suffering it would cause his men to fight their friends. Miro and Tiesto had sacrificed the constructs, but they'd used them well.

He ordered the pilot to take him back to the defenses outside Castlemere.

The next attack would come soon.

31

Miro felt tension in every bone of his body as he sat in his command tent, staring at the canvas wall, waiting for the scouts to tell him of the enemy's approach.

The day passed slowly and inexorably, and then it was night. At dusk a scout told him the enemy had spent all day unloading. The attack would come the next day.

Another day, bought with blood.

Miro needed to hold. He needed to hold for reinforcements from the other houses. There were too many revenants. He knew he could never win unaided.

He missed Amber. He hadn't heard from her in an age. In a way, he was relieved that she was far from the battle, but he'd been expecting a message from her, and still none came.

Miro ate something and then he tried to sleep. He remembered Evrin Evenstar's sacrifice and felt the ache of sadness. Evrin had done something incredible: he'd hurt Sentar, and he'd removed the greatest threat of all, even if it was only for a time.

Miro hoped Sentar was mortally wounded. He hoped the Lord of the Night was in terrible pain.

As he tried to sleep, he remembered the last time he'd seen Amber, at Rialan Palace in Ralanast. He didn't know what he'd done to deserve her, but he thanked the stars every day. He thanked the Lord of the Sky.

He caught a few hours of snatched sleep, and then a low voice outside his tent woke him just before dawn.

"Miro." It was Beorn. "They're here."

Miro stood at the middle of the long wall, with Beorn by his side. In front of them another glorious day revealed the killing ground: a gentle slope of cleared earth heading down to the ruins of Castlemere.

"Tiesto is in place?" Miro said.

"On the far right." Beorn nodded. "Any last orders before I take the left?"

"Yes," Miro said. He met his lord marshal's gaze. "Stay alive."

Miro and Beorn clasped arms, and then Beorn left Miro standing with defenders on all sides, but alone. Miro thought about the times he'd made rousing speeches to his men. This time, no words came to his mind; they were fighting for their lives, for their families, and for their homes. They knew it as well as he did.

He followed the wall with his eyes, first to the left until it disappeared toward the distant shore, then to the right where he could just make out the barricade of fallen trees keeping the wall's flank firmly guarded by the forest. Each tower along the wall's length had a cannon sighted at the beach. There were eighty-six towers.

The killing ground stretched ahead. The red warning flags had been removed, and to walk into that area meant death.

Behind the wall, the majority of Miro's army lay in wait, formed three deep along the entire line. Dunfolk archers crouched behind their taller allies, and every two hundred paces a flying brigade of elite Alturan heavy infantry prepared to rally the defenders and close any breaches. Close to Miro's right was one of the gaps in the wall they'd left to enable the defenders to make sorties.

Then Miro heard it: calls and shouts, the sound of marching feet. A scout rushed forward to make his report.

"High Lord, they're forming up out of range."

Miro nodded but kept his eyes on the open expanse in front of him. "Thank you."

Miro gazed out at the white boulders, evenly spaced to aid his ability to make decisions. The farthest marked the extent of the range of his cannon. At the extreme limits of vision, he could now see the massed ranks of the enemy.

He wore his armorsilk, and his zenblade was in its scabbard, strapped to his back. The time for planning was now well and truly over. He would fight with the men.

A soldier coughed, and another turned his head and was violently sick. As the sun climbed the sky, the tension affected them all.

And then they attacked.

With a roar the horde came rushing forward, their numbers so great that even in massed ranks their line covered the entire length of Miro's long wall.

"Runebombs!" Miro cried.

The enchanters at the gaps rolled the glowing iron balls forward and then to the left, avoiding the murderous trenches hidden directly in front of the inviting spaces. As the slope began to take effect, the enchanters released.

At first the balls rolled so slowly that Miro tensed, thinking they would stop, but then they gathered momentum and soon hurtled along, heading inexorably for the enemy.

The horde was far enough away that men couldn't be distinguished one from the other; it was just a long line of attackers. Then the runebombs vanished into the enemy, swallowed by the multitude, and in unison they exploded.

The detonation was deafening, and all around Miro defenders put their hands to their ears. Great explosions of flame and sand shot into the air, and the destruction tossed bodies higher still. Miro wished he had more height; the wall was low and he couldn't see what effect the devices had. But after frequent use and with little essence, his one and only dirigible was no longer functional. From now on he would need to rely on his individual commanders.

The revenants filled the gaps left by the runebombs, and the horde kept rushing on. This was unlike any foe Miro had faced before; these weren't men whose spirits could break at the inevitable devastation coming their way. Only total annihilation would win or lose the day.

The rush of warriors reached the most distant of the white markers.

"Cannon!"

At every tower, Veldrin gunners opened fire, flames gushing from the mouths of the cannon as they unleashed their iron balls with a roar. If the detonation of the runebombs had been loud, the synchronized volley was thunderous. Smoke rose from each cannon, only to be blown back at the defenders by the constant sea breeze. Defenders visibly choked on the bitter smoke as the gunners at the towers launched a second volley. Miro pushed forward to stand close to the wall, peering through the smoke.

The cannon had taken their toll, but the enemy came on.

"Archers! Ranged volleys!"

The Dunfolk and Alturan archers drew back and pointed their bows into the air. In unison they released, and a cloud of arrows filled the air. Miro knew most of the arrows would pierce only flesh, but a few well-placed projectiles would strike eyes and unprotected parts of the face, burying themselves into the brains of the undead.

The cannon fired at will now, filling the air with shuddering blasts. Miro glanced back at the white-faced defenders and then out at the roaring mass of revenants. The attackers triggered the traps as they ran, the earth falling away to reveal deep spike-lined holes. Pounding feet triggered prismatic orbs buried and rigged with sensors. At every moment detonations tore holes in the enemy and brilliant lights sparkled across Miro's vision as explosions both chemical and magical ripped through the tide of warriors from across the sea.

Miro couldn't believe such chaotic destruction was possible. He'd built this killing ground, but even so, the raw power unleashed shocked him.

Yet still they came on.

Miro reached over his shoulder and drew his zenblade as he turned back to sweep his gaze across his men. He spoke a quick sequence that sent a ripple of fire along the blade and then raised the fiery sword high.

"Make some noise!" Miro bellowed.

To a man the defenders raised their weapons and roared their defiance. The sound of it carried along the line from one defender to another until every man screamed as loud as he could. Even above the pounding cannon and detonations in the killing ground, the sound of the defenders carried louder still.

Then with a gust of fresh air from the sea, the smoke cleared, and the revenants were at the last of the white markers.

"Orbs!" Miro shouted. "Every second man!"

All around him defenders reached down and clicked firing mechanisms into place as they threw the spherical Louan devices into the enemy. A multitude of glowing prismatic orbs sailed through the air to fall into the midst of the dark throng of attacking warriors. The thunder of the explosions combined with the roar of the cannon so that Miro wondered if any of them would ever hear again.

Miro just wanted them to live.

Then the revenants broke against the wall like a surging sea. The blockade was too low for battlements, but it meant the long swords of the Alturan infantry and the pole-arms of the Halrana could thrust forward with a greater reach than most of the enemy warriors possessed.

Knowing the battle would now be led by his officers, Miro concentrated on his section of wall. Just as he had planned, the revenants were funneled into the nearby gap. As intended, the temptation was too great to resist.

In front of the gap, an area fifty paces square vanished in an instant. The ditch was deep, as deep as six men were tall. The revenants poured into the trap and Miro knew the same thing would be occurring at all the other spaces.

Miro saw Master Goss roll a runebomb into the hole, and as the mass of the enemy and the horde's terrible momentum pushed more revenants tumbling forward, the device exploded.

Then a snarling face appeared in front of the wall, and Miro began to sing.

———————

Ella helped another enchanter roll their runebomb into the rapidly filling hole. Around her the battle was a chaotic crash of metal on metal, roaring defenders, thunderous cannon, and flashes of bright light. There was no way to see which way the battle was going. She could see her section of wall holding, but good men were dying at every instant as the attackers threw themselves against the low wall, climbing over each other to reach up to the higher defenders.

Ella ran, putting her back behind one of the towers as the runebomb detonated behind her. Peering around again, she saw revenants continue to fill up the now widened hole, clawing and scrambling, filled with the energy of glowing runes.

Ella climbed up to the wall and launched bolt after bolt from her wand, losing track of how many enemy warriors fell from the onslaught. Nearby she saw Layla calmly launch an arrow into a revenant's eye; the barbarian twitched and was still. Attackers now grabbed hold of the wall and pulled themselves up over the fallen bodies of their fellows. Swords hacked down, leaving wriggling hands abandoned on the stone.

Soldiers tossed orbs into the wide hole, each explosion sending blood and bits of flesh sailing through the air. Still the revenants poured into the gap; Miro's funneling strategy was working too well.

The hole swiftly became filled with twitching, climbing figures while the enemy warriors pushed from behind to plunge into the mess. A revenant made it past, and Ella saw High Lord Tiesto rush forward with a glowing sword to take the woman's head clean off. Another reached the tower, and Ella increased the power of her wand, even as she saw the prism dim, sending a beam of light to punch a hole in its chest.

Soon, Ella knew, the trickle would become a flood.

Looking to the left Ella cried out as she saw a score of tall barbarians climb onto the wall and clamber over to the inside of the defenses. A dozen of the elite palace guard shot forward to close the gap, but their strength simply wasn't enough. More revenants scrambled over into the breach as Ella sent flurries of golden bolts into their midst, but they moved so quickly she was having difficulty aiming. Sweat dripped down her brow, and her breathing was ragged. The pounding of her heart sounded louder than the roaring cannon on the nearby tower.

A figure in black threw himself against the barbarians. Jehral hacked and thrust at his enemy, but Ella could see he would soon be overwhelmed. And there was nothing she could do.

The ground began to shake.

Trees moved, and a colossus strode forward, knocking aside defenders and attackers alike, reaching down with its arm to smash and squeeze revenants into ruinous red. A second brigade of the palace guard arrived, and together they fought to close the breach. The colossus then moved to the gap between the walls and knocked down revenants as they climbed the hole to rush forward.

Couriers rushed along the line to take reports to the commanders. There was a moment of respite, and then Ella heard a trumpet screech: three long blasts.

Ella's blood ran cold when she heard the order to retreat.

Miro knew what he was doing, and he knew these defenses were lost.

Ella realized she hadn't heard the cannon for a while, and looking at the tower, she saw the pile of balls below the cannon was gone. Squinting at the next distant gap in the wall, she saw a colossus defending there also.

Bodies of Dunfolk, Alturans, Halrana, and free cities natives littered the ground, mingled with revenants, their runes sparking and fizzing as the energy left the corpses.

Past the front of the wall, at the distant edge of the killing ground, Ella saw the attackers regrouping for their next imminent wave.

"Fall back!" Ella heard the cry, taken up by the men around her. The soldiers grabbed weapons and ran.

Ella knew the plan; she and the other enchanters had their own part to play. They couldn't afford to let the cannon fall into enemy hands. The plan was to destroy everything. Miro didn't want his defenders facing their compatriots, brought back as revenants.

Ella rushed to the base of the tower and found the cube-shaped device. This runebomb wasn't designed to roll; it was made to destroy.

Already the wall was nearly devoid of men. Ella ignored the revenants now surging forward as she scanned the base of the wall and saw the fresh dirt marking where they'd buried barrels of black powder.

Ella placed her fingers on the cube and spoke the activation sequence.

She looked up at the colossus manning the gap. "Run!" she called.

Perhaps the animator didn't hear her. Or perhaps he decided to buy the defenders the time they needed with his life. As the enemy once more poured into the gap, the animator took his colossus to meet them.

Ella turned and sprinted back along the road toward Sarostar. Men and women in green silk ran at her side; the enchanters had played their part. Risking a glance over her shoulder, she saw the scrabbling revenants break against the colossus, clawing at the gigantic construct and climbing up the legs. More enemies climbed up to find the wall uncontested, roaring their triumph.

Behind Ella, the entire wall, at every part of its great length, fragmented in an instant as the buried explosives at the eighty-six emplacements blew in a detonation of dirt and flame.

The blast threw Ella flat on her face, and if she hadn't been wearing her enchantress's dress, she likely would have been killed. She picked herself up and glanced back.

They'd planned this carefully: Miro wanted to delay the enemy and rob them of potential new revenants. The earth had a new fissure, filled with rubble, an obstacle it would take the enemy days to clear.

Ella ran with the last of the stragglers, looking for the blockade she knew lay somewhere ahead.

Miro wasn't trying to hold his defenses; he was trying to buy time. Ella knew the next part of the plan: a rolling retreat, along the road to Sarostar.

32

The sound of dripping filled a constant counterpoint to the whirling thoughts spinning one after the other through Amber's head. She didn't know if it was night or day. The only guide she had to go by was the shining green prism, filling her every waking moment with dread.

She'd been in the cell for days, though it was hard to keep track of exactly how long it had been. She wondered how the search for Katerina, High Lord Grigori's daughter, was going. Her heart reached out the innocent girl; Sergei Rugar had probably killed the poor child.

Amber thought about the enchanters she'd sent north to Lake Vor. Would they come for her? She knew in her heart, though, that as soon as they saw the green light, they would rush back to Sarostar, skipping Rosarva. There would be no help coming.

Amber raised her head when she heard a heavy clanging, followed by the rattle of keys, and then the groan of metal against metal. Footsteps sounded moistly on the damp floor of the dungeons beneath the Borlag. Bright light suddenly assaulted her.

Amber shielded her eyes against the glare. Eventually the shining moved away from her face, and she blinked to restore her vision.

High Lord Grigori Orlov lowered the pathfinder in his hand. His eyes were red-rimmed and his clothes rumpled; he looked like he hadn't slept in days.

"Just tell me where she is," Grigori pleaded.

Amber looked for Sergei, but for once he wasn't present. Realizing her chance, she climbed unsteadily to her feet and approached the bars.

"Please," Amber said, "listen to me. You told Katerina she would be high lord after you, is that correct?"

Grigori frowned, his forehead creasing over his wide-spaced eyes. "It's common knowledge."

"Has Sergei Rugar told you how he feels about one day following a woman? Has he shared with you his ambition to become high lord himself?"

Grigori held up his hand. "Please, enough of your lies If you tell me where my daughter is, and she is unharmed, I will send you back to your people. Much as I would prefer to see you rot down here, I will make this pledge. Amber Torresante of Altura: Where is my daughter?"

"I don't know!" Amber said. "Your trusted lord marshal isn't what he appears to be. He's done this to discredit me and my people's call for help while also ensuring a woman can never rule House Vezna. You have to understand . . ."

"What's going on here?" a strong masculine voice said, and Sergei strode into the room, flanked by two of the palace guards. "Oh, it's you, High Lord."

"Sergei, your methods are not achieving results," the high lord said.

Lord Marshal Sergei looked at Grigori and then at Amber. "I am doing my best, High Lord. She's been fed nothing but water, and even then . . ."

"Starving her is not enough to restore my daughter!" Grigori shouted.

"Don't you think if I knew where she was, I would bargain with you?" Amber pleaded.

"Enough!" the high lord cried. He rounded on Sergei. "You've made her uncomfortable, nothing more. Alturans are known for their obstinacy. I want you to make her skin crawl. I want you to make her beg you for mercy. If you can get results without visible damage, more the better. But I'm asking you to find my daughter, Sergei, or perhaps your own head will roll."

The high lord was the bigger man, and he emphasized his points with a jutting finger prodded into Sergei's lean chest. The blonde-haired Veznan blanched, and when the high lord paused, he nodded.

"As you wish, High Lord," Sergei assented.

Grigori Orlov stomped from the room, taking the palace guards with him. Sergei and Amber were soon alone.

"I hoped he would be content with imprisonment," Sergei said. He shrugged. "I am sorry, Lady Amber, but I am going to have to make you scream for appearances sake. It's nothing personal."

Amber felt fear send cold fingers up and down her spine.

Sergei disappeared for several minutes.

Amber called out for help and looked for a weapon. She rattled the bars and thought furiously, but this dungeon was built to hold stronger captives than her.

All too soon Sergei returned with one of the dungeon guards by his side, a different sort than the proud palace soldiers, with a bare chest and big calloused hands. Terror surged through Amber's body as the guard looked her up and down and gave her an evil grin.

"You don't need to do this," Amber whispered.

"I'm afraid I do," said Sergei. "Open the cell," he instructed. "Take her out there, to the interrogation area." He inclined his chin in the direction of the green light.

Amber struggled against the guard, but it was no use. He carried her, kicking and writhing, and forcefully laid her down on her back on a hard wooden table. Her wrists were yanked together behind her head; she felt iron hoops conveniently located near her wrists and ankles, and the guard made swift work of tying her down. Amber's chest rose and fell with every heaving breath, and she cried out.

"Yes," Sergei said, "that's good. Scream so they all can hear." He looked down at her. "We're going to need to hear more than that, though. The high lord is no fool."

"Is she dead?" Amber said.

"Why, whomever do you mean?"

"Katerina. The high lord's daughter. You don't seem the type to kill a child."

Sergei glanced toward the heavyset guard. "Nice try, young lady. Now, it's time for you to tell me where she is."

"Don't even bother pretending," Amber said, feeling rage and terror course through her in equal measure.

"As stubborn as you are, the high lord's right about one thing. It wouldn't be wise to mark your flawless skin. It will be smarter to make you scream—and answer my questions—while leaving your body untouched. If Altura ever survives this enemy from across the sea, it will be much easier for us to invent some story to explain your death."

He ran a fingertip down Amber's cheek, and she flinched.

Sergei chuckled. "I've never held someone captive before. Particularly such a beauty. You know, I'm actually starting to enjoy it."

"My husband will gut you like a fish," Amber said.

"No, I don't think so. I think Miro Torresante has bigger things on his mind right now. He'll find another wife, one who will bear him a child of his own. Oh, that made you flinch, didn't it? Such a kind man, the Alturan high lord, to take on a son that wasn't his. I wonder if he'll be so kind when the mother is dead? What will happen to your precious child then?"

Sergei walked up and down Amber's outstretched length as he spoke, fingertips caressing her as he wandered. The guard looked on intently, his eyes flitting between Amber's face and her body.

Sergei suddenly vanished, leaving Amber dreading what would happen to her next. He returned a moment later, and now he held a glass jar in his hand. Sergei brought the jar close to Amber's face, and she saw black spiders, dozens of them, climbing over each other and writhing in agitation.

"We have many creatures in our forests," Sergei said. "The nettle spider isn't deadly, but it is known for the pain it causes, even though it leaves no mark."

Amber felt tears run down her cheeks.

"Scream, my pretty one," Sergei breathed.

Amber drew in a breath, and she screamed.

Katerina was hungry. Sergei only came to feed her once a day, and there was never enough food. She knew he didn't like her, and each time she ate, she sniffed at the food hesitantly before eating. Katerina knew all about poisons.

She knew she was in a house, with a dirt floor and a high ceiling formed by the two support trees leaning against each other, but she didn't know anything else about where she was. She knew it couldn't be far from her father's palace, but even so, she'd screamed and screamed until her voice was hoarse, and no one heard her.

When he'd first brought her here, Sergei had put a seed into the ground and sat Katerina nearby. He'd said it was a test, and Katerina had to be brave. That was before she knew he was a bad man. Crouching on his heels, Sergei leaned forward and dribbled some water from a flask onto the seed.

Katerina had grown worried when he shuffled away, giving her a wide berth. Then it had all happened very quickly. The seed sprouted a seedling, which became a vine, and the leaves on the vine became more vines.

Suddenly there was a vine crawling around Katerina, wrapping itself around her arms and legs.

Katerina had tried to get away; she'd been told to be brave, but there was a strange gleam in her father's friend's eyes. The vine pulled her down to the ground, holding Katerina fast.

Katerina knew that eventually the essence pulsing through the vine would kill it. How long would that take? She tugged and tugged at the tendrils wrapped around her limbs, but still she couldn't get herself free. Then Sergei left her.

She now looked down at her hands and flexed her fingers. Katerina had cried, that first day, but now she refused to cry. She was a Veznan princess, and she was determined to be strong.

Why had Sergei put her here?

Katerina's hands were mottled with pink splotches and tingled painfully. Every time she pulled on the vine, it responded by sucking her tighter into its embrace. Her wrists and arms hurt. Dozens of green tendrils wound their way over and around her fingers.

Something on the middle finger of Katerina's right hand flashed into her vision. It was the ring the nice lady from Altura had given her.

Katerina had an idea.

She wondered why it hadn't occurred to her earlier, but she'd been so scared, so alone, so trapped in the vine, that she'd forgotten all about it.

"*Tuhl . . .*" she said out loud. What was the strange word again? Katerina furrowed her brow and closed her eyes, but she couldn't remember.

She began to panic. Sergei would return soon, and he might take the ring from her.

Katerina took a slow, deep breath, releasing the air as she calmed herself. A princess of Vezna must be strong.

"*Tuhlas,*" she said. Nothing. "*Tuhlaranas.*" Still the ruby was dark.

Was it a trick? Had the woman deceived her somehow, like the man who once made a silver deen appear behind her ear?

"*Tuhlanas,*" Katerina said.

The symbols etched around the ring's circumference lit up with fire. The ruby sparkled and grew brighter and brighter as if shining from the inside. Katerina grinned and strained to touch the ruby to the vine. The living tendrils cringed and pulled away from the growing heat, but Katerina kept up her attack. The vine shied away from the bright stone and of its own accord unraveled itself from Katerina's arm. She kept pressing the ring to the vine again and again, freeing her limbs, wriggling herself out of the clutching strands.

Soon Katerina was free.

The girl stood and stretched, hearing her back crack as she felt blood return to her tingling limbs. She looked at the door, where a living lock held the wood fast.

Katerina stumbled to the door and set to work.

High Lord Grigori Orlov stood on the balcony outside his bedchamber and sighed. He gazed out at the moat surrounding the

Borlag and then at the Juno Bridge, the living walkway connecting the Borlag to the rest of Rosarva.

The Juno Bridge reminded Grigori of plants, which made him think of seedlings, which then led him to think about Katerina. Grigori's wife had died giving birth to Katerina, and his daughter was everything to him; he feared for her constantly. Veznan history was filled with intrigue and betrayal. When a high lord's son or daughter was kidnapped, it never ended well.

Everything living made him think of Katerina. A small sprout made him think about her fascination with seeds and seedlings. A dwarf tree made him think of how small she was, yet how quickly she'd grown. A crystal tree made him think about how fragile she was.

Grigori had to admit to himself: he was terrified. His only hope was that when Sergei finished with the Alturan woman, he would finally have the answers he demanded. Just a moment ago Grigori had walked down to the dungeons, close enough to hear her screams. He'd smiled in satisfaction before returning to his chambers. Amber Torresante would talk.

Grigori absently noted someone crossing the Juno Bridge, but whoever it was knew the password, and the bridge let him pass. He turned around and went back inside, once more looking into Katerina's bedchamber before heading back to his own. He fell down to his bed, lying on his back and staring up at the ceiling.

"Papa, what are you doing?"

The voice sent a tremor running through Grigori's body, stabbing into his heart with a sensation like being woken with a red-hot poker.

Grigori sat up. Katerina stood inside the doorway, looking at him with her head tilted. Tears had carved streaking passages through the dirt on her face, and he saw bits of leaf and dirt entwined through her clothing.

"Katerina. Katerina!" Grigori cried. He rushed over and pulled her close, holding her to his chest as tightly as he could. He held her at arm's length and scanned her body, grabbing hold of her limbs one by one and checking her for injuries, before hugging her again and again. Aside from some circular bruising on her arms and legs, she was unharmed.

"Where have you been? I've been so worried about you."

"It was him," Katerina said.

"Who, Katerina? Who?"

"Him! Please, Papa, keep me safe!"

Grigori pushed his daughter back by her shoulders. Terror filled Katerina's face as she pointed toward a figure in the doorway.

Sergei stood open mouthed, staring at them both with a face drained of all color.

Then Sergei reached for his belt, but he wasn't wearing his sword. Sergei's hand clasped on empty air, and he looked up at Grigori with shock.

"You!" Grigori roared. "It was you!"

Grigori swept his daughter out of the way and charged Sergei, knocking him to the ground. Katerina screamed as the two men rolled, first Grigori on top, then Sergei, then Grigori again. Each man fought to gain a stranglehold on the other, and it was an even match: Grigori was the bigger man, but he could sense that Sergei was fitter, better trained.

Suddenly Grigori was face down on the ground, with Sergei twisting his arms painfully behind his back. Grigori felt a heavy weight as Sergei pinned him to the floor, and then Sergei's hands were on his throat.

"I . . . will . . . be high lord," Sergei grunted as he squeezed.

Grigori gasped for breath, but all that came out of his mouth was a series of pops. Sergei's weight crushed Grigori's chest, and the squeezing on his throat increased intensity. Grigori needed air desperately; he felt darkness beckon.

Sergei cried out in pain.

As the hands came away from Grigori's throat and Sergei's weight fell away, Grigori drew in a deep breath of life-giving air. He saw Katerina with a ruby-set ring on her finger. Sergei held his hand to his eye. The ruby glowed with inner fire.

Grigori heard running feet, and four armed palace guards appeared, immediately taking in the scene.

Grigori pointed a wavering finger at Sergei. "Seize him!" the high lord cried.

The guards took hold of the former lord marshal. Grigori climbed to his feet. Katerina clutched her father's legs and began to sob.

Grigori recalled Amber's words—she'd tried to tell him the truth. As he realized she'd been right all along, Grigori thought about what he'd told Sergei to do.

"You." He pointed at one of the guards. "Come with me. The rest of you, hold him here. I will deal with this traitor myself."

Grigori ran through the palace, collecting soldiers as he went. He dashed down the steps to the dungeons and shouted for the gates to be opened. Keys chimed in shaking hands, and iron crashed as he passed through the sets of barred gates.

Green light bathed him in its glow. Amber lay on her back on a bench, and a dungeon guard glanced up in surprise.

"Get away from her!" Grigori shouted at the dungeon guard.

He rushed to Amber's side and brushed away a dozen scrabbling spiders. He ran his eyes over her, scanning the Alturan high lord's wife with concern.

She was blessedly unharmed.

"Release her. Now! Hurry up!"

Grigori held Amber's hand as she sat up, and he helped her off the bench. Her face was white, and Grigori remembered her screams.

"My Lady, I'm . . . I'm so sorry. How can you ever forgive me?"

Amber drew a shaky breath, and Grigori saw her gaze take in the red marks on his throat.

She was a long time in speaking.

"I've been through worse," she finally said, though her voice trembled.

"Tell me what I can do to make this right."

Amber fixed her gaze on the green light. She then turned back to Grigori, and the high lord of Vezna saw fierce determination in her eyes.

She told him.

33

Birds flitted from tree to tree, singing sweet songs to one another, filling the lingering silence. Insects hummed in the forest, buzzing and warbling as spring filled the brush with new growth and animal life.

The sounds of the forest were broken by the crash of metal on wood.

Hundreds of men worked together, and Miro worked with them. Each soldier held an axe in his hands, and they struggled in pairs to fell trees, one after the other, each coming down with a mighty crash of breaking branches and thudding trunks.

Every man worked in his armor, and although Miro felt sympathy for the infantry in their confinement of thick steel, armor took time to don, and Miro had to prepare for the unexpected. None complained, and Miro rotated the men to give them regular breaks. Not every soldier could work on the growing barrier at the same time; it would be too dangerous.

Miro leaned back and then smashed his axe into a sturdy tree close to the road while Beorn cut into his backswing. The triangular wedge gouged in the side of the tree grew larger with each cut, and then Miro could see the tree was about to fall.

"Stand back!" Miro cried.

With a cacophony of snapping wood, the tree fell down in the direction of the cut, adding its tangle of branches and foliage to the barrier.

"Come on," Beorn said. He panted and groaned. "I need a break."

The beaches were lost, and Miro and Beorn were at the first of seventeen defensive blockades spaced along the long road from Castlemere to Sarostar.

In front of them the massive barrier of fallen trees barred the way from the abandoned defenses. Back behind the blockade some men slept while others ate. Still others nervously rubbed at the hilts of their swords. Strange smells took turns wafting past: the scent of fragrant flowers, the tang of burned flesh, sea salt, melted metal, and above all, smoke.

Since the great explosion that had turned the walls and towers of Miro's once mighty defenses outside Castlemere to fissures and rubble, they'd retreated back to this blockade and worked at the obstruction. The last colossus still in operation hauled night and day, carrying fallen trees to add to the tangle, until the energy left its manufactured limbs. The last of Halaran's mighty colossi had now itself been added to the barrier.

As he and Beorn reached the wall of dirt, Miro's stomach rumbled. How could he eat at a time like this? Even so, the demands of his body grew in intensity. As if on cue, an outthrust hand shoved a bowl of something hot in front of his face.

Miro looked for a spoon, and with a grin and a shake of his head, Beorn handed him one.

"Thanks," Miro said.

"They'll clear it, slowly but steadily," Beorn said.

"How long, do you think?" Miro asked, talking through a mouthful of hot stewed meat.

"It's hard to say. Our scouts report they're building platforms to cross the fissure we left behind. Our archers harass them while they clear the trees."

The road was narrower than usual here—the reason they'd picked the place—which meant it was a small enough front for a third of Miro's army to wait here while another third under Tiesto waited at the blockade behind. The final third, along with the wounded, had been sent back to Sarostar.

"How are the golems and bladesingers?" Miro asked.

"They're keeping the forest clear. We were right—they'll come this way. The plan was a success. You did well."

"We all did well," Miro said. "We've bought time, with little loss of life. Time is what we need."

"Do you think help will come?"

"I have to believe it will. How goes the renewal?"

"Your sister and the other enchanters are back with Tiesto. We've already renewed the swords, and now they're working on the armor."

"But we've no more orbs. And few constructs—only the iron golems are left. No more tricks, eh, Beorn?"

"We'll hold them. We also have another helping hand."

Miro burned his mouth on the stew and waved his hand in front of his face. "What's that?"

"Winter is their element, but they came in spring. It's growing warmer every day. The necromancers will have their work cut out for them keeping the revenants going."

"Sentar is in a hurry. Wherever he is, he won't be happy at these delays."

Beorn swallowed a mouthful and then met Miro's eyes. "The Lord of the Sky came through. We owe Evrin Evenstar a lot."

"We do," Miro said. There was silence for a time, both of them remembering the old man, before Miro spoke again.

"Keep the scouts busy; we need to know when they're going to break through. Come on, let's get back to work."

———◆———

Three days passed and still the enemy worked at clearing the road. Miro lined the pikemen four deep along the blockade—little more than a dirt wall with a trench in front—while his best swordsman waited behind. The scouts now reported movement in between the fallen trees ahead. It wouldn't be long now.

Even so, every fallen tree would add to the delay. Miro and Beorn continued working side by side with the men, working so furiously now that mistakes were inevitable. They'd sent one man back to Sarostar with a crushed foot. Another soldier narrowly escaped being crushed, dashing to the side when the barrier resettled.

As Miro pulled back to allow Beorn to make a stroke at the biggest tree they'd worked on yet, he saw a familiar figure wave an arm to get his attention.

Miro withdrew to let another man take his place. He panted and walked back to meet the lean Hazaran warrior.

"Jehral." Miro nodded.

"High Lord," Jehral said. It was strange seeing the Hazaran on foot, without a horse. "I have an idea."

"Let's hear it," Miro said. "I'm all out."

"Do you still have black powder?"

"Yes, some."

"Do you have many of the iron balls?"

"Yes, but we destroyed the cannon."

"What about the cannon we had at the beaches when the landing first began?"

Miro met Jehral's gaze and then smiled. "Don't be coy, Jehral. You've scouted them?"

Jehral nodded. "It is difficult and the trees are extremely thick, but I forged a path through the forest to reach the beaches between Castlemere and Schalberg. I counted five brass tubes before I turned back. They are about half a day's journey."

Miro was pensive for a moment. The enemy would break through soon, but it would be worth the risk.

"You'll need four men to carry each cannon. Another twenty skirmishers."

"No, High Lord. Too much noise. No more than ten men."

Miro knew Jehral was right. With ten men Jehral would only be able to bring back two cannon, but even two would make a difference. "All right, Jehral of House Hazara, ten men. Leave right away."

Jehral sped away and Miro turned back to the huge tree. "Beorn!" Miro called. "Jehral's going to—look out!"

As Beorn turned at Miro's call, a falling tree nearby twisted and plummeted the wrong way, its tumbling path taking it into the mighty tree Beorn stood at the base of. Beorn's work was nearly done, and as one tree crashed into the other, the huge tree also fell.

Two trees came down, directly on top of Beorn, the second axeman, and Miro.

The trees fell slowly, but they were big.

Miro dived out of the way, but he was too late. Branches came down on top of him, smashing onto his back, pinning him face down to the ground. Miro took a knock on the back of his head, sending stars sparkling in his vision. But he could breathe, and as he shook his head to clear it, he realized he was unharmed.

Soldiers called out and rushed to help. Many hands reached forward to pull the branches away from Miro, and a Halrana held out a hand to pull him free from the tangle.

"High Lord!" the Halrana cried.

Miro ignored him and rushed back to the place he'd last seen Beorn, climbing over the entanglement. Thick tree trunks lay piled one on top of the other, a mess of green foliage and branches as thick as a big man's leg.

"Can you hear me? Beorn! Anyone!" Miro yelled. "Quick—bring axes!" he turned and shouted.

Miro saw the body of a man in a green uniform, crushed beneath the debris, white bone poking out of his legs and his torso squashed into a nearly unrecognizable shape.

"Beorn!" Miro called again.

"Down here," a hoarse voice came from below the tangle. Miro recognized Beorn's voice, which meant the dead man was the soldier who'd been assisting.

Soldiers arrived with axes. "High Lord, how do we cut him out?"

The pile shifted. A cry of pain came from below.

"We need to do something," Miro said. He turned and ran back to the blockade, dashing past wide-eyed soldiers who took in Miro's scratched and bleeding face.

Miro finally found what he was looking for. His zenblade lay in its scabbard, and he pulled the hilt in one swift motion, throwing the scabbard to the side.

He ran back to the site of the fall and called out again. "Beorn!"

"Still here," the weak voice came back.

Miro ran his eyes along the runes of the blade his sister had made for him. It had taken Ella a month to make this new zenblade since his return from across the sea. Controlling the activations was more complex than ever before, but this zenblade could cut through anything. Ella had demonstrated it to Miro herself. She wasn't a physically strong woman, but she'd shown it could cut through solid stone. At its limits, the blade's heat even melted the stone, leaving a wide triangular gouge when withdrawn.

Miro started his chant, his voice rising as fire traveled along the sword's length. He moved directly to the most powerful lore Ella had built into it, and suddenly the zenblade lit up with blue fire.

Miro didn't swing at the trees; he simply pressed down at the debris.

He grimaced and hoped Beorn would yell out if he came too close.

The zenblade burned so brightly that Miro struggled to look at it, squinting against the glare. It would drain at a prodigious rate, but Beorn was under there. His friend needed him.

Even without heavy pushing from Miro's sword arm, the blue fire cut through the green wood like butter. Taking their cue, the soldiers pulled the branches away as Miro cut through them. When he reached the trunks, Miro finally saw him. Beorn stared up at him with eyes filled with fear, his face white.

Miro couldn't say anything. He could barely hold his song together.

He pushed harder, and the zenblade cut into the topmost trunk with barely a sound. Beorn was pinned under both of the trunks— it was a wonder he was still alive—and Miro cut through the first and waited for a dozen soldiers to haul the log away before moving to the next.

Beorn had his eyes shut to the glare. Miro couldn't turn away from the blinding fire; he had to watch carefully, or he would strike his friend with the fierce heat.

Then he was through. Miro let his song fall from his lips, but he waited for the arcane symbols on the zenblade to completely fade before he cast the sword aside. Together with the men, Miro hauled the log away. Two more soldiers pulled the man out from under the tangled mass, and then Beorn was free.

Miro looked at Beorn in astonishment as his lord marshal climbed to his feet.

There was barely a cut on him.

"Lord of the Sky, you're a lucky man," Miro said.

"I thought it was my time for sure," Beorn said, shaking his head. "I've never seen power like that, not even from a zenblade."

"You can thank my sister yourself," Miro said. He clapped Beorn on the back. "It isn't your time, my friend. Not yet."

34

"Here they come!" Beorn roared. "Hold fast!"

The enemy finished clearing the road and immediately attacked. Miro felt his whole body tense as they rushed forward, filling the road, the attackers packed so densely that they were like a torrent pouring down a canyon.

The two cannon Jehral had brought back from the beaches boomed, and as tightly crowded as the revenants were, the blasts tore scores of warriors to pieces with every shot. The enemy ranks closed as swiftly as gaps opened, and now the gunners fired at will. Every shot told, but still they came on.

Miro had far fewer men manning a much weaker defense. He wondered how they could ever hold.

The attackers reached the deep ditch in front of the blockade, each warrior pushing those in front, sending their fellows to certain impalement. As they fell into the ditch, blood gushed from their mouths as the revenant warriors from across the sea fell onto the spikes. Bodies piled one on top of the other, and then they were over the ditch and climbing up the embankment. The first wave threw themselves against the sharp points of Miro's steadfast pikemen, and the second wave followed suit.

The rest kept coming, and then they were over. It couldn't be called a breach: the enemy broke the defenders in the first charge.

Suddenly revenants were everywhere, and Miro was in the thick of the fighting. Beside him Jehral swung a glowing scimitar, lopping off heads and limbs, while closer to the forest iron golems tore through revenant flesh. The pikemen dropped their weapons and drew swords. Miro's reserve smashed into the revenants, but even they struggled to hold the line.

There was chaotic fighting everywhere.

Miro called on the protective strength of his armorsilk, stiffening the shimmering material, and he sent power to his zenblade, turning it blue with fire. He danced among the attackers, slashing through bodies and sending splashes of crimson blood through the air in his wake. He fought with tired muscles and constant concentration as he chanted, feeling his breath come short, but pushing down the fatigue.

Miro saw a rotting head explode in front of him, and Ella was there, her dress as bright as his armorsilk as it turned enemy steel. She gasped activation sequences in her own deadly song, sending beams of yellow light through one revenant after another.

He sensed the Alturan palace guard—the best of his soldiers—fighting beside him, and knew the battle hung in the balance. One of the soldiers in green fell, and then another. Finally, Miro's fierce swordsmen slowly began to push back the revenants, but one of the enemy warriors held firm. Single-handedly, this warrior was turning back every attempt to reform the line.

An enchanter with a wand fell down, his hands clutched to his gushing chest. Another Alturan swordsman fell down with a cry of pain. Miro knew he needed to destroy this warrior.

Miro cut through a tall barbarian and in a single flashing image, his gaze took in the threat.

The warrior wore a blue shirt with a white trident sewn into the material. Holding a falchion in each hand—heavy single-edged swords with wide, powerful blades—he killed yet another swordsman with a crushing blow to the skull and then turned to face Miro.

Miro saw the three-cornered hat and the white eyes filled with blood. As Diemos, the pirate king of Rendar, fixed his stare on the high lord of Altura, he whirled, the twin blades casually cutting an Alturan in two, opening a space between Miro and himself. Miro felt chills along his spine as he knew he'd met his match.

Miro's song called more searing fire into his zenblade as he leapt forward. The twin blades flashed, slicing the air, and Miro ducked and then dodged to the side. The pirate king came to meet him, and their weapons clashed, sending blinding sparks into Miro's eyes, making him blink.

A falchion smashed into Miro's chest, and he grunted in pain. He met the next strike with the zenblade, forced to move quicker than he ever had before, and still the pirate king was faster.

Miro managed to get a thrust into the pirate king's chest, and his opponent roared as the sizzling steel penetrated his torso. Miro smelled burning flesh, but the blow that should have torn his opponent in half had little effect: the runes on this warrior glittered like stars in the night sky, beyond anything he'd seen on any revenant before. Sentar himself had made this one.

The two warriors ducked and sidestepped, blades cutting the air where heads had been moments before. Miro's song came strong, but he simply couldn't find a gap in his enemy's defenses. The falchions met the zenblade time and again, and Miro felt fire in his side as a falchion struck his armorsilk and tore the material. Heat washed from both the zenblade and the falchions. One solid strike, and Miro would be dead.

He sensed the battle around him even as he fought. The revenants began to surge forward, but with Miro occupying the indomitable pirate king's attention, the defenders took heart and rallied, pushing the enemy back once more. Bodies formed obstacles on the ground, making it difficult for Miro to dance out of the way of the pirate king's twin blades.

Blood turned the dirt to mud, and as Miro blocked an overhead cut from the red-eyed pirate king, he slipped.

Time slowed as Miro fell down to his knees, his zenblade falling from his grip. He raised an arm and blocked a glowing falchion with his naked armorsilk, grunting as the falchion struck with nearly enough force to break his arm, knowing that to cease his chant would be to die. The second falchion sizzled as it carved the air, in a direct line for Miro's neck. There was nothing he could do about it.

A newcomer in blazing armorsilk entered the fray and charged into the pirate king of Rendar. Taking the warrior by surprise the newcomer launched a flurry of blows at Diemos's head and chest. Miro picked up his zenblade and cut at the pirate king's legs, but his opponent deftly jumped out of the way.

Miro could see the fighter was a bladesinger, but he couldn't see his face, and even for a bladesinger this man was fast. Each blow of the whirling falchions was met with a blocking zenblade, and Miro looked for an opening in the flickering steel and sparks but couldn't risk harming the bladesinger.

Miro heard the man's baritone and knew who he was.

Bartolo.

Miro cut overhead at the pirate king from behind, yet still a falchion met his zenblade. Miro pushed down, and it was now a match of strength on strength. The pirate king held off Bartolo with a single falchion. With a crash like lightning, Bartolo struck home, directly into the revenant's heart. Miro continued to push, and the pirate king's arm relaxed for the barest instant. In a flash Miro brought his zenblade back and forward once more, swinging in a direct line for the neck. The pirate king moved out of the way, but Bartolo met the movement with his own blade.

Bartolo's zenblade smashed into the pirate king's skull, shearing it in half. The revenant slumped down to his knees and fell face first into the mud.

"We need to pull back!" Bartolo cried.

Miro saw that the attackers were gaining the upper hand.

"Retreat!" Miro shouted.

He and Bartolo fought to give the fleeing defenders space. Iron golems were suddenly by their side, and as the golems held the line, Miro and Bartolo turned and ran.

Risking a glance over his shoulder, Miro saw the golems fall one by one, swamped by the attackers. Then the river of warriors surged ahead. Miro put every thought to running, leaping over bodies as his breath ran ragged. He scanned the road ahead, looking for the next blockade where Tiesto waited, but the blockade was a distance away.

The enemy would reach them first.

Miro glanced at Bartolo and saw the fear on his friend's face. Bartolo pointed ahead and shouted something, but his words were lost in the din.

The two running bladesingers rounded a corner.

Miro saw figures in red robes. As he ran through the line of elementalists, feeling the breath of his enemies hot on his heels, a wall of fire rose up behind them.

Miro stopped when he reached safety behind the elementalists and turned, gasping and wheezing. He watched as fire took the revenants, hearing the terrible sound of sizzling flesh. It took time for the attackers to pull back from the flames, and in that time hundreds burnt to ash.

Miro grabbed Bartolo's arm and pulled him forward, clasping his arms around his friend's shoulders. "Where have you been?"

"Busy." Bartolo grinned. "Shani wanted a holiday at the beach, but instead I found you."

Miro scanned the red-robed elementalists.

"Behind you," Bartolo said.

Miro whirled and saw Shani, her hands in the air and an expression of concentration on her face as she guided the flames. He waited until her arms slumped at her sides and she deactivated the cuffs at her wrists, before pulling her into a rough embrace. "Petrya! You came!"

"No, Miro," Shani said, shaking her head. "There's only a few of us. I left the high lord in Tlaxor."

Miro felt disappointment like a blow, but his gaze took in forty elementalists, and he knew they'd lasted another day.

One more day, bought in blood.

———————————

Ella had a bowl on her knees as she washed blood from her hands and neck. She heard a throat clear and glanced up.

Shani stood with her arms crossed in front of her breasts, frowning down at her. Ella set the bowl down and leapt up to hug her friend.

"All that blood. How are you holding up?" Shani questioned her, holding Ella at arm's length.

"As well as any of us," Ella said.

"I found Bartolo at the pass. The signal's gone through, and I brought some friends, but I'm sorry there aren't more of us. I sent another message to the high lord but there's nothing more I can do."

"Don't be sorry," Ella said. "You came. That's enough."

"Lord of Fire," Shani said as she let out a breath, "how do you fight the dead?"

Ella sighed. "With hope and fear. With courage and death."

"Bartolo says your brother was almost killed."

Ella sucked in a breath, biting her lips, but tears welled at the corners of her eyes.

"Oh, Ella, I'm sorry. Miro's fine. I don't know when to shut up sometimes."

"There must be something more I can do," Ella said. "I feel so . . . powerless."

"What was that thing they fought? Bartolo said it wasn't like any revenant he'd seen before." Shani shook her head. "Two bladesingers, Bartolo and your brother . . . Ella, I've never seen better swordsmen. Yet that thing . . ."

"Sentar was the first to ever animate a corpse. He knows the lore better than anyone."

"Don't worry. The Hazarans will come."

"Even if Ilathor comes, do you really think they'll be enough?"

"Killian will come too. He won't leave us to hold alone."

"I'm not so sure. We didn't leave things on the best terms. Shani . . . Evrin told me Killian now has a woman in the palace."

"A woman?" Shani raised an eyebrow. She shook her head. "I don't believe it."

"It's true. I know who she is. Her name is Carla, and Killian loved her long before we met."

"You don't know the truth of it . . ."

"I know," Ella interrupted. "Evrin's dead, by the way."

Ella heard her own desultory tone as Shani's eyes showed her concern.

"I'm sorry about Evrin. Let's just focus on survival, shall we? Don't worry, Ella," Shani said. "I know you. You'll think of something."

35

The days grew longer and the air became warm and humid, night and day. Spring growth pushed through the forest floor, wildflowers filling the empty spaces and littering the landscape with color. The wind picked up, sending clouds in from the ocean.

Thunder rumbled overhead as the heavens turned gray.

It was the time of the rains.

Water poured from the sky in a flood, filling the air so it was hard to breathe. The winding road thickened with mud, making the going tough for defenders and attackers alike. It clamped down on the fires of the elementalists and wet the black powder. More than once a planned detonation became a fizzled failure.

Miro's defenders had performed miracles over the last weeks. His men fought and died, holding from one blockade to the next, felling trees, digging ditches, destroying each defensive wall in detonations of earth and flame as they retreated to the next. Each rearward action took place in the last breath, with the blockades blown in mighty explosions just as they were overrun. The valiant struggle left bodies piled high.

At each stage, wherever possible, the corpses of the Alturan and Halrana dead were destroyed rather than letting them fall into the enemy's hands. Often those wounded who couldn't run clutched runebombs with dying hands and lit fuses of powder kegs held between their knees, sacrificing their lives rather than allowing their dead selves to fight their comrades. The winding road from the free cities to Sarostar was a river of ash and blood, steel and mud.

Now they were at the seventeenth blockade, the last before the open ground and the final defenses at Sarostar.

Ella felt she was permanently wet. Her hair was tangled with filth and dirt, and she knew every defender felt as fatigued as she did. She now walked with heavy steps as she collected the dead defenders from the last bitter engagement. Shani worked beside her as they gathered the fallen and piled them in a ditch. Already the logs underneath were burning fiercely, despite the dripping rain. This was the worst part of Ella's job. She understood the need, but she hated it nonetheless. She and Shani, as well as the other enchanters and elementalists, were charged with burning the dead defenders.

At all costs Miro wanted to avoid adding to the enemy's strength. More than anything, he wanted to prevent his men having to fight their compatriots.

Ella looked for more bodies and then she stopped, fists clenching at her sides.

"What is it?" Shani said, coming over.

Ella stood over an older man with a round face and balding head. His eyes were closed as if he were sleeping, but his hands clutched a terrible wound in his belly.

"Fergus," Ella whispered.

Shani gripped Ella's shoulder. "You knew him?"

"A little," Ella said. She wiped water from her cheeks, tears mingling with the rain.

"Go," Shani said. "Let me do this."

"No," Ella said. "I'll do it."

Ella crouched and hooked her arms under Fergus's armpits. She heard a groan, and she nearly dropped him in surprise.

"Shani!" Ella cried.

Shani ran forward.

"He's alive!" Ella said. She set her mouth with determination. "Help me with him."

Together they dragged the weakly moaning man back through the defenders. Shani disappeared while Ella examined the gash in Fergus's stomach. Blood slowly seeped out between Fergus's fingers. The wound looked mortal.

Shani appeared a moment later with two men in white robes and a stretcher. Ella recognized the garb. Even the priests were doing their part.

"Here . . . that's right; we've got him, Enchantress. We'll take him from here."

Ella followed Fergus the ferryman with her eyes as they carried him away. She returned to her work, searching for more bodies, but at last there were no more. All were in the hole, burning to ash.

"I don't think we can last much longer," Shani said.

"I know," said Ella.

They both looked at the huddled defenders, not even trying to fight the rain, some sleeping even as droplets stung their cheeks. There were so few of them now. Miro had called up all the men from the defenses at Sarostar, and these were all that were left. How many revenants had they destroyed? Surely the attack couldn't keep going?

The scouts said they'd started discovering piles of revenants left back along the road. The defenders sometimes fought an enemy who simply dropped, becoming still as the light left the runes, sometimes crumpling as rot sunk in too much for the lore to function. It was their only sign of hope, yet they all held onto it.

"Where is Sentar, do you think?" Shani asked.

"It would be too much to hope he's dead. I don't know whether to be thankful or afraid that we haven't seen him."

"Their tactics have lost their edge since the death of the warrior your brother and Bartolo killed. Have you noticed?"

There were supposed to be three kings from across the sea, and they'd only defeated two, but nonetheless, Ella thought the necromancers must be in control now. Their strategy seemed to consist of hurtling forward, then regrouping, then throwing their revenants forward again.

"They'll wear us down anyway," Ella said.

"Ella, have heart," Shani said. "We'll get through. All it takes is one heroic act and we may still be saved."

"They're all heroes already," Ella said, casting her eyes over the defenders.

"Every last one of them," Shani murmured.

Ella suddenly looked up. "I have an idea."

Shani broke out in a smile, the first Ella had seen in weeks. "Good. That's the Ella I know."

"Keep Miro safe," Ella said. "I have to go. I might not be back for a while. Be safe!"

"I'll do my best," Shani said wryly.

Ella grinned and felt her friend's eyes on her back as she broke into a run.

Back toward Sarostar.

———◆———

Miro waited with Beorn, who flicked water from his beard. Nearby Jehral's eyes were closed; he was either resting or praying, perhaps both. Tiesto's shoulders slumped with exhaustion. A few paces away Bartolo stood with a bladesinger, Dorian, the youngest of their number.

Together they formed a core at the very front of the blockade. Behind them the men's eyes were lined with desolation and weariness, but Miro fought to stand tall and be a rock his men could count on.

They stood firm as once more the enemy charged.

"For freedom!" Miro cried as he held his zenblade over his head. His men gave a ragged cheer, and then the enemy poured into the ditch.

Once more scores of revenants fell willingly onto the spikes lining the base of the ditch, and their fellows climbed over their fallen. Once more Miro held the line as he sang with a voice hoarse from shouting, seeing fire light up his zenblade as he threw himself into the fray.

The defenders held, but the enemy kept piling up behind their own number, pushing those in front forward into the whirling blades. The rain fell in a continuous stream, mingling with the blood that cascaded down Miro's armorsilk.

The defenders held while the enemy charged, and charged again.

Miro saw Dorian go down as a revenant thrust a wicked spiked club into the young man's face. An enchanter in a green robe took his place, but then he went down too.

Men were falling everywhere.

"We must fall back," Beorn gasped.

"Guard my back," Miro said. He swiftly turned and waved an arm at the Petryan elementalists.

A wall of fire sprang up, but this was weaker than ever before. Miro looked on in horror as the revenants continued to run forward, even through the flames.

Their skin blackened and sizzled, but still the attackers pushed on. Miro knew the final blockade was lost.

"Back!" Miro cried. "Back to Sarostar!"

Unable to launch a coordinated retreat, the defenders simply turned and ran. This time there were no powder kegs or runebombs to slow the enemy. Men were cut down as they ran, and slowness meant death.

The running defenders cleared the forest, and now Miro saw the broad wall ahead. Behind it the tops of the highest buildings poked up.

This was Miro's city, his home.

There was no killing ground of hidden devices in front of the curved wall, simply a wide open space. It was strange to be running in the open. It felt like an eternity since Miro had last been able to see for a distance ahead of him without his vision being blocked by trees.

The iron gate stood wide open while the fleeing defenders poured through to find safety behind the walls, each man climbing up to fill the ramparts. But as he shot a glance over his shoulder at the pursuers, Miro saw that those bringing up the rear wouldn't make it.

"I'm going to make a stand here," Miro panted. "Get to the defenses."

"I'm not leaving you," Beorn said.

"Someone has to lead them!" Miro shot back.

Miro stopped and turned to face his enemies. Soldiers around him followed suit, and now the horde poured out of the opening road, forming a wide line. Miro caught Jehral's eye and nodded in the direction of the wall, but the Hazaran shook his head and also turned to face the enemy. Bartolo waited in fighting stance with Shani by his side. Tiesto roared with battle rage. As the mass of glowing revenant warriors filled the open space, no more than fifty men waited to hold them back.

Miro heard the thunder of hooves behind him, in the direction of the gate.

A trumpet blasted, and as he spun around, the first thing Miro saw was a big yellow banner with a desert rose. Flames filled the air, surrounding Miro and those with him with flickering fire, but he felt no heat, and the inferno caused no harm. The enemy warriors began to slow their mad charge and Miro saw necromancers in their midst, calling the attackers to order, fearful of the raging flame, though Miro knew it was illusory.

A tall bearded man on a great black stallion led a wedge of countless men on horseback, riders pouring one after the other through the gate. This was a battle on open ground, the kind the desert warriors of House Hazara liked best.

With relentless speed, thousands of horses galloped forward, and the black-garbed men on their backs waved their scimitars above their heads and whooped.

They struck the horde with a sickening crunch. Immediately, the necromancers saw the danger and tried to turn their revenants back into the more defensible ground between the trees. As the Hazarans struck hard and wheeled around to strike again, the revenants rushed back to the road in a flood. The leader of the desert warriors expertly turned his men after the second charge. The flames around the fifty defenders vanished as quickly as they'd appeared.

Kalif Ilathor Shanti pulled hard on the reins, and his stallion reared back, hooves clawing at the air. He formed his men in a long line between the fifty defenders and the trees, but for now the ground was clear, and the revenants didn't charge again.

"Back to the gate!" Miro cried.

With the Hazarans guarding their backs, Miro led his men through the open gate, the riders following them through. Finally, as the heavy iron gate closed shut, and three strong bars of iron were put in place in the slots, Miro lowered his sword and took a slow, shaky breath. He couldn't believe he was alive.

The kalif of House Hazara had answered his call.

Ilathor leapt off his horse and ran forward to embrace Jehral. "Lord of Fire, man, every time I see you, you look worse than the last."

"It is good to see you too, Kalif." Jehral grinned.

"Kalif," Miro said.

Ilathor walked forward, meeting Miro's gaze. "High Lord?"

Miro pulled Ilathor into a rough embrace and leaned forward, speaking close into the man's ear. He whispered hoarsely, and felt wetness on his cheeks as he looked past Ilathor's shoulder at the multitude of proud horsemen who'd come to his aid.

"Thank you."

36

"Why have you brought me here?" High Enchanter Merlon asked.

Ella took a deep breath. "High Enchanter, I know we haven't always been the best of friends, but I need you."

"You've never needed me before. In fact, you've always ignored my advice, rejected my opinions, scorned my strictures . . ."

"High Enchanter, please." Ella tried to smile, but it came out as a grimace. "This time we need to work together. I have an idea . . ."

"Enchantress," the high enchanter interrupted, "just tell me what you intend to do here."

He indicated the expanse of the Great Court. The Green Tower loomed overhead, the buildings that formed the Academy of Enchanters framing a strange scene of serenity compared with the carnage Ella had left behind.

"That's what I'm trying to do!" Ella glared at him, meeting his eyes. It was the high enchanter who broke contact. "I need . . ." Ella took a deep breath. "Please, High Enchanter, we need to make use of the purity sample."

High Enchanter Merlon's shaggy eyebrows shot up. His eyes narrowed. "What do you know of the purity sample?"

"I know that one of your duties is to test the essence that comes from Mornhaven. I know that you test the new essence against a supply you know is pure." Ella smiled. "I have friends among the faculty."

"We need it . . ."

"High Enchanter, it doesn't matter anymore. It is the only essence in quantity we have left. There isn't another drop, not anywhere in Altura. I've seen your work, and I know you deserve your position. For my idea to work, I need help, but I believe you have the skill to help me. Altura needs us."

"I will only fetch the essence if you tell me what you intend to do with it."

"Fine," Ella said. "But you're not going to like it."

When she finished telling him, High Enchanter Merlon looked at Ella as if he thought she were mad. But he agreed to make the attempt.

And Ella went to find some spades.

Jehral nimbly picked his way among the bodies to climb up to the ramparts in the southernmost section of the wall—one of the few places where the structure still stood. He found Ilathor staring out at the broken bodies below.

"The city is lost," the kalif said without turning around. "Sarostar will fall."

Jehral opened his mouth to disagree, but then closed it. The fighting over the last days had been bitter, with the last attack a furious assault that had culminated with the collapse of the majority of the wall. The revenants had felled trees and used the logs as rams, pounding at the stone rather than fighting the defenders.

The tactic had been successful.

The iron gate fell, flattened into the dirt, and the attackers had poured through the gap. Ilathor lost half his men in the counter-charge, the riders swallowed by the enemy's greater numbers. The Hazarans fought side by side with boys and old men. Most other Alturan and Halrana soldiers had fallen in the field.

Rain continued to fall in a relentless stream, but neither man acknowledged it. Thunder rumbled overhead.

"Where is Ella?" Ilathor asked.

"No one knows," Jehral said. "She hasn't been seen in days. I still can't believe you brought Zohra to this place."

Ilathor grimaced. "She wouldn't stay at home. An obstinate woman, your sister. She'll be safe at the palace. When the city falls, a fast horse will take her to safety."

"You think there is no chance of success?"

"None," Ilathor said. "Miro is a determined one, but Sarostar will fall. We must plan what our next step will be."

"You may go, Kalif, but I will not abandon them," Jehral said. "I have fought with these men for weeks. I will not say it was all for nothing."

The kalif turned to Jehral, and his lips curved in a smile. "I was worried you would say that. Never fear, Jehral. My honor will not let our allies be abandoned in their time of need. Only when the city is truly fallen will I take our warriors—those of us who survive—to safety. We must find the emperor and prepare a plan for throwing these creatures back into the sea."

"Yet Ella's homeland will be gone," Jehral said sadly, turning and gazing back at the pale stone of the city.

"Yes," Ilathor nodded, "I am afraid it will be."

"There you are."

Jehral heard a new voice and saw Miro climb up to the wall to join them. He seemed unaware of the blood splattered on his face, hands, and neck.

"Well? Tell it to me plain," Miro said as he surveyed the battlefield with them.

"One more charge," said the kalif, "and these defenses will be overrun."

"I know," Miro said.

Jehral's heart went out to the proud warrior. He'd planned and prepared, tried to gather support at the Chorum, and in the end it all came to nothing. They'd destroyed untold numbers of the enemy, no mean feat given the unholy strength of those they faced, but it hadn't been enough.

"So what do you intend, then, High Lord?" Ilathor asked.

"Your men don't like fighting on walls, do they?" Miro said.

"It is not our way."

"Then let's face them on the battlefield. One final charge. Kalif, if they make it past these walls and into the city, I release you from any obligation. You will need to tend to your own people and help fight to save the rest of the Empire."

Ilathor reached out and he and Miro clasped hands. Miro then turned to Jehral. "It's been an honor fighting by your side, Jehral of Tarn Teharan. I thank you for what you've done for my people."

"Miro," Jehral said, shaking his head, "even here, at the end, you face defeat with more honor than any warrior among my people. We pride ourselves on honor, yet no Hazaran faces his fate with more courage. You have my eternal respect."

A haunted look came to Miro's eyes, but vanished as quickly as it came. The wry smile returned. "We tried," Miro said. "They'll never say we didn't."

The kalif looked out at the forest. "They are readying for another assault. Let us form up in the open field, High Lord."

"The open field." Miro nodded. "I will gather the last of my men."

The Hazaran cavalry formed up on both flanks while the Alturans, Halrana, and Dunfolk formed a solid mass in the center. The defenders arrayed themselves in front of the rubble of the wall. They were the final barrier before Sarostar.

Ilathor led the horsemen on the left, and Jehral led the right. In the center, Miro stood with Bartolo and another bladesinger as Beorn grimly waited nearby with the infantry. Glancing over his shoulder, Miro saw Layla with the rest of the Dunfolk archers, an expression of fierce determination on the small woman's face.

The rain stopped as suddenly as it had started. The ground squelched with every footstep as the men moved into position.

Miro opened his mouth to speak, but he wasn't sure what he would say. The decision was taken away from him.

"Brace yourselves! Hold fast!" Miro heard Beorn roar.

The enemy charged.

Both groups of Hazaran cavalry rode out at the same time, peeling to the sides as Miro's men spread to hold the ground they'd left behind. The revenants hit the infantry with solid force, and every man fought to keep his slipping feet on the ground and hold firm.

"Forward!" Beorn cried.

Miro and Bartolo led the counterattack. The defenders followed the figures in blazing armorsilk as they drove a wedge into the heart of the attackers. Revenants screamed as they were torn apart by whirling zenblades and dismembered by flashing steel. Even with so few of their weapons now lit with the fire of essence, the infantry drove hard into their enemy.

Then the Hazarans struck from the sides, crushing attackers who'd been facing forward before they could turn to acknowledge the flashing scimitars of the horsemen. The Hazarans penetrated deep into the enemy ranks before wheeling back out to make another charge.

Ever more revenants poured from the road between the trees into the open ground. The attackers struck back, and the force of their momentum was too great to hold.

Suddenly soldiers in green and brown started falling on all sides. Revenants broke through the line to rampage among the Dunfolk.

Miro led his men to push the enemy back, and with a mighty effort Beorn managed to reform the line of infantry. Once more the cavalry charged, and this time it looked like the Hazarans couldn't get away.

"Hold the line!" Miro cried.

"Wait, look," Bartolo said, gasping as he regained his breath, pointing ahead at the forest. "The trees. Why fell them now?"

The tops of the foremost trees swayed, though there was no breeze. Miro heard the sound of breaking branches and then his eyes narrowed.

"Those aren't trees," Miro said.

Behind the revenant army, the forest came to life.

37

Amber immediately took in the battlefield. She saw the broken wall, now reduced to rubble, and the small knot of soldiers in the center of the field, the last of the army in green and brown. She watched the Hazaran riders charge the flanks and become embroiled with the revenants, unable to pull away. The battle was about to be lost.

She couldn't see Miro, or Ella. The field was littered with bodies; even those standing were covered in mud and blood. Amber's homeland needed her.

Amber clutched onto High Lord Grigori's shoulder and cried out. "We need to help them!"

Grigori nodded grimly and issued a series of swift commands.

The Veznans left the protection of the forest and charged.

Twenty Veznan nightshades and a thousand infantry pushed through the trees to smash into the army from behind.

Unarmed, Amber stuck close to the nightshades, weaving in between their legs as they plucked warriors up off the ground and tore the bodies into pieces like a child tearing petals from a flower. The Veznans carved a direct path for the defenders but soon even the warriors in orange became embroiled as the revenants' numbers told.

Amber could see horsemen to her left and right and infantry ahead of her. She saw a small group of bladesingers, whirling and dashing forward to push back the fiercest attacks and hold the line. The Veznans made it through to the Alturans, and the defenders gave a ragged cheer.

The battlefield cleared as the enemy pulled away and once more regrouped, while the defenders formed into a new line.

Amber's arrival had saved the moment, but it wasn't enough to save the day.

"Amber!" Miro cried, pushing through to her.

"I'm sorry," Amber said, "We came as quickly as we could."

"You did well," said Miro. "Lord of the Sky, I'm happy to see you." He pulled her close, ignoring the men around them. "I need you to go to the palace now. There are horses there. Take one and ride for Mornhaven."

"I'm not leaving you," Amber said. "Don't even suggest it."

"Amber, go. You need to take care of Tomas."

"Tomas is with Amelia. She knows what to do. She'll take him somewhere safe, and we can join him later."

Miro kissed her lips. "No. I need *you* to take care of Tomas, not Amelia."

"Here they come!" someone yelled.

"Go, please," Miro said.

"Come with me!" Amber said, tears running down her face.

"My place is here. I can't leave." Miro gave her a gentle push. Amber looked back at him one last time and then ran in the direction of the city.

Bartolo rejoined Miro's side. As the two men awaited the enemy's charge, hearts pounding and swords readied, time stretched out, and Miro saw that for the first time there weren't more warriors pouring out of the forest. They were facing the last of the force from the ships.

Scanning the line of defenders, Miro saw that even with the nightshades and fresh Veznan infantry, their numbers were still not enough.

They'd come so close.

"I wish my wife would leave too," Bartolo said.

"If I left, who would save your life?" Shani said beside him.

Bartolo rolled his eyes. "She rescued me at the pass. I'm never going to hear the end of it."

Miro smiled as he looked from one face to the other, remembering them. This was it: the end. They all knew it.

Scanning the battlefield, Miro saw the Hazarans now grouped together on the left. In that direction was the closest route out of the city. The kalif was being true to his word, and would fight this last battle, but he was preparing the way out. Miro hoped the rest of the Empire would succeed where he had failed.

Half the Veznan nightshades had fallen as they charged the enemy rear; even now Miro could see gnarled trunks twitching on the mud. The Veznan infantry stood side by side with Miro's soldiers.

Five houses had worked together to defend Miro's homeland. When had such a combined effort last taken place? More than likely when the humans first fought to depose the Evermen. Miro was glad he'd seen it in his lifetime.

Miro saw Beorn hold a sword in the air and fix him with a rare grin. In another direction Master Goss had one arm limp at his side, his green sleeve dripping blood to the ground, while his other hand clutched a silver wand. High Lord Tiesto Telmarran stood with the last of his soldiers. The Halrana were steadfast to the end.

Miro met Bartolo's eyes and nodded. He looked along the shining length of his zenblade. Ella had made it for him. He only regretted that he couldn't see her now.

Miro commenced his song.

The activation rune sparked first, the glow traveling to the next symbol along the blade, colors lighting each rune in turn until the zenblade shone with a brilliant gleam. Interspersed in the song were sequences to bring Miro's armorsilk to life, to cloak Miro's body and make him as ethereal as a shadow. Beside him he saw Bartolo's blade turn blue, and Bartolo's form also shimmered as his voice rose in a sturdy baritone.

The strange distortion of time ended. Everything became fast again.

The enemy charged.

Miro roared and threw himself at his foes. He ducked an axe and cleaved a tall barbarian in two. Weaving to the side, he shot up and tore a revenant woman in half. Fireballs smashed into enemies before Miro could reach them, and he saw Shani send sizzling balls of flame to strike into faces and torsos. Bartolo leapt and danced among the revenants as he cut through them. In all directions there was fighting, with Veznan soldiers in orange fighting beside Alturans in green, Halrana in brown, and Hazaran horsemen smashing in from the side.

Beorn led a charge to close a gap in the line, and then a huge revenant standing taller than the rest rammed his shoulder into the grizzled veteran and knocked him back. Beorn countered with his blade, but the revenant was faster, dodging and then thrusting a broadsword into Beorn's chest. The blade emerged from Beorn's back, and when it was withdrawn, blood gushed from Beorn's mouth.

Beorn's eyes widened with agony, but his scream was lost in the gurgle of blood as he crumpled to the ground.

Miro cried out and tried to fight his way to Beorn, but the press of the enemy kept him back. Master Goss of the Academy sent beams of golden light from his wand, but a rush of revenants swamped the enchanter, knocking him down to the ground, their axes and spiked maces breaking the enchanter's body into a red and green mess.

Miro fought like a man possessed, sending limbs and heads flying into the air with every stroke of his zenblade, but still they kept coming. Two nightshades smashed into the enemy in front of him, creating a momentary lull, and then Miro saw Shani.

She stood over the fallen form of a man in green and across the battlefield she met Miro's eyes.

The pain in her gaze told Miro enough.

Miro fought his way over, seeing Bartolo on his back with a shallow wound spurting blood through a tear in his darkened armorsilk. Seeing the fading runes, Miro realized Bartolo's armorsilk must have needed renewal, and he hadn't said a thing.

"Please," Shani begged, her eyes speaking volumes. "Please, Miro. Not like this."

Miro looked out at the battle and saw the attackers push forward relentlessly as the infantry fell back. Men fell, one after the other, and as Miro watched, the last of the nightshades crashed to the ground.

Thoughts whirled through his mind. The battle was lost. Bartolo was down. Shani needed him.

Miro made a decision, and he gave the order he never wanted to give.

"Back!" he cried. "Back to the bridges!"

As the defenders took up the cry, Miro picked up Bartolo's arms. "Take his legs," he gasped.

He sensed some of the infantry forming a defensive ring around him as they fled back to the city. The defenders fell as they ran; it was just too easy to cut a man down from behind. It wasn't a retreat; it was a rout.

They poured over the fallen rubble that had once been a defensive wall. Running and stumbling, Miro and Shani carried Bartolo through the buildings of Sarostar's workshops and warehouses. Miro saw two elementalists in red robes running with them.

Flames shot from the Petryans' hands back in the direction of the chasing enemy. The death cries of soldiers sounded in all directions, and the revenants surged through the western quarter of the city, butchering any of the living they found.

"Back to the bridges!" Miro heard the cry again and again. Across the bridges, on the other side of the river, lay the Crystal Palace and the Academy of Enchanters. Miro's only hope was that Amber and Tomas had already fled. At the nine bridges of Sarostar they might buy some time, but the city was lost.

"This way," Miro grunted, indicating with his head as he and Shani carried the heavy bladesinger. They turned a corner, and ahead Miro spied Victory Bridge, a wide span of stone crossing the bubbling green water below. Miro heard clashes of steel behind him and eerie singing as a bladesinger defended him and Shani. Then they were on the bridge, climbing the endless steps, stumbling along the broad path between two stone rails.

A soldier in green—Miro didn't even know his name—pushed past Miro at the apex of the bridge. "High Lord, give him to me. I'll take him."

Exhausted, Miro gave Bartolo's arms to the Alturan soldier. Only then did he turn and watch the destruction of his city.

The western quarter was overrun. Casting his gaze along the river, Miro saw defenders on all of the bridges he could see. Sarostar had no walls, but the nine bridges provided a defense of last resort. From the height of Victory Bridge, Miro saw thousands of fleeing defenders cross the bridges to the perceived safety across the river.

Many turned back to stand with their fellows until they thronged the bridges like Sarostar on a feast day.

Miro stood side by side with his fellow bladesinger and waited for the enemy to come.

As he panted, knowing his city was lost, Miro saw a flash of light, but it came from the wrong direction. It wasn't from a last prismatic orb, conserved until the end. It wasn't the fire of an enchanted sword.

It made no sense.

A bright light sparked, coming from the direction of the Academy of Enchanters. Suddenly, an arc of radiance reached into the air to climb the sky, crossing the river, a bridge of light and glowing runes.

Miro had seen this before: when Evrin Evenstar fought Sentar Scythran. He'd seen it at the ruins of the Bridge of Sutanesta.

Miro was forced to turn his attention back to the fighting as the horde rushed Victory Bridge.

38

Ella glanced at High Enchanter Merlon, seeing he was also at a loss for words as they took in the destruction they'd wreaked at the site of the Heroes' Cemetery. Upturned earth lay in piles beside each grave, the headstones strewn like victims of a fierce wind. In front of each marker a deep hole indicated where each man's burial site had once been. These final resting places were final no more.

A clutch of old men and women stood nearby with spades. Ella's desperation had called them out of their homes. The stubborn Alturans who refused to leave their city glanced at Ella with mixed apprehension and awe.

Shani's mention of heroes had sparked the idea.

Fifty of Altura's finest swordsmen stood upright beside their graves. Some were recently dead—the fallen bladesingers from the battle at the Bridge of Sutanesta—whereas others bore the marks of advanced decay. These warriors stood as they'd once stood in life: proud and tall, and they were undaunted by the wounds that had killed them. Each held a sword in his hand.

Ella had used the forbidden lore of the Akari to bring them all back. Every warrior's skin glowed with activated runes, and they stared at Ella with white eyes, already filling with blood. With High Enchanter Merlon's help, she'd raised them to once more fight for Altura in death as they had in life.

It was time to use the lore of the revenants against them.

"Why are we here?" one of the men who'd been buried in his armorsilk spoke. His voice was soft, more of a whisper. The others fixed him with their eerie stares and then looked back at Ella.

"Altura needs you," Ella said. "The high enchanter and I have brought you back to help in our greatest hour of need. You, who fell in battle to defend us, we are asking you to fight again. We need your help . . ." Ella choked.

High Enchanter Merlon called out a single activation rune: every sword in every hand was a replica of the others, even down to the inflection of the activation sequence.

"*Alitas!*" the high enchanter cried.

As the warriors' swords lit up with fire, Ella heard shouts and crashes. She rushed to the riverbank and looked across the water to the city's western quarter. She'd intended to run for the battlefield, but she saw she was too late. Making a swift decision, Ella dashed back to the high enchanter and snatched the flask out of his hands.

His eyes widened in surprise. It was the last essence in Altura.

Ella returned to the riverbank and cast her mind back to another river, at another time. She'd drawn from knowledge buried deep within her consciousness to build the runebridge. Her mind whirled as she thought about her falling city. Ella summoned power from deep within to calm her thoughts, and once more the lore came to her.

Ella dipped her scrill into the essence and began to draw. She drew the first rune on a flat stone, activating it to give the symbol form, and the second so swiftly the liquid hung in the air. She created the third rune, connecting it before the whole thing could fall. With each stroke Ella chanted, each symbol activated and floating in the air as she built the next. She worked in a flurry, furiously, and then she took a step forward onto the growing bridge.

Working faster now, Ella built step after step, ignoring the tumbling river splashing below. She climbed higher and could now see the enemy crowding the bank of the western quarter, barely held back by the defenders at the nine bridges.

Then Ella was descending back down to the opposite bank. As she stepped off her creation she looked back and waved her arm into the air.

With the swiftness of an arrow the dead heroes sped across the runebridge without pausing, glowing swords held in front of them. Fifty swordsmen —men who'd fought against the primate and served their house in the Rebellion—sped through Sarostar's western quarter with weapons held high.

As the last warrior stepped off the glowing bridge, it faded, as if it had never been.

Miro cut down two more enemies, and then suddenly he had no more to face. Down on the wide banks of the western quarter, a new force smashed into the enemy, a wedge of glowing light fighting with savage intensity. The revenants . . . dissolved . . . as the blur of whirling blades tore flesh into bloody components. There was no stopping this new arrival. Miro had been in many battles, and he knew it when he saw it. Nothing could impede a force like this.

As he watched from high on Victory Bridge, the wedge of warriors barely lost momentum as they sped through the revenants, leaving carnage behind them, tearing through enemy after enemy, leaving nothing but smears of red. Miro almost wiped his eyes as their efficient killing brought them closer. He had never seen anything like it, not even when his brother bladesingers had been at the height of their power.

Miro and the bladesinger with him exchanged glances. Miro raised his sword above his head. This was the moment that came once in every battle; the time to throw the dice and fight on even in the face of terror.

"Attack!" Miro cried.

He ran back the way he'd come, down Victory Bridge, and leapt into the fray. He fought to emulate the surging warriors, and poured his heart and soul into his song, feeling the zenblade come alive in his hands and seeing the armorsilk on his forearms shine with brilliance.

He tore through his opponents, and he heard another song join his own. Then he was fighting among them, and for the first time he realized who they were.

With wonder Miro recognized Bladesinger Porlen and Bladesinger Huron Gower, men he'd seen fall in the war against the primate. Runes glowed on their skin as their fiery blades tore through the revenants. They were indomitable, agile, as fast as a bird in flight; Miro's movements were slow and clumsy in comparison. The skills of these warriors, their lifetime of training and fighting, had combined with the lore of the Akari to create warriors beyond compare.

The revenants still fought on; this enemy wouldn't break—they would only stop when every last one was fallen. Yet Altura's dead heroes broke them the way a scythe cuts through wheat, dispatching them in numbers; even the horde couldn't touch this foe.

Then Miro heard a strange whirring sound overhead.

Looking up, he saw an incredible sight. The sky was full of dirigibles, hundreds of them clouding the sun as they shot overhead. Orbs rained down from their high sides, detonating one after the other, sending bursts of flame rolling through the alleys of Sarostar's western quarter, wiping out the surging horde, destroying revenants in numbers.

The Louan dirigible pilots, clean and sparkling in their blue uniforms, leaned out to call out to the defenders as they sped past. "The Legion is behind us! The Legion is coming!"

Taking heart, all of the defenders on the bridges surged forward to leap back into the fray. Miro roared with triumph as he cut down his enemies, and then, with a surge of joy, he realized something.

For the first time since the landing on the beaches, Miro had to search for enemies.

A knot of revenants countercharged, blocking the way forward, but then two tall black figures charged into their midst. Monsters of metal and cloth, with a thin red slit for eyes, for once they were fighting on the same side as Miro. A flail curled around a revenant, tearing it to pieces as a sword as dark as night stabbed through another. Lurching and twisting, the two Imperial avengers smashed through the cluster of enemy resistance.

Suddenly there were Tingarans in purple fighting side by side with men in green.

Pushing forward as the hail of orbs broke the horde into smaller groups, more avengers came to take the battle directly to the enemy's heart. Miro searched for opponents, but the attack was too much for the enemy; the last knot broke in a burst of red liquid, and then there were no more revenants to be seen.

Miro jumped up on top of a wall and climbed to a storehouse roof. Gazing out, he saw the dirigibles and Altura's heroes head farther out until they were past the city, and then past the rubble of the fallen wall. The wedge of glowing swords moved farther out, heading toward the forest, and then they were gone from sight altogether.

Miro felt tears running down his cheeks as he saw the dirigibles circle back toward Sarostar.

Sarostar, the city of the nine bridges, had made it through.

The Louans had come. The Tingarans had come.

As high lord, Miro's duty was to protect his people, to keep them safe from enemies. He'd known the enemy was coming, and he'd fought beyond all endurance.

Miro slumped down, falling to his knees on the storehouse roof, and his zenblade fell out of his hands; his armorsilk went dark.

Altura had survived.

39

With renewed vigor the allies scoured the land. And this time, no one died. Altura's fallen heroes hunted down the last of the necromancers and revenants until there were no more to be found. At the end, with Ella's help, the energy left the warriors' bodies, the runes faded, and then they were at peace again.

Ella ensured every last man was buried once more with honor. Word spread, and soon everyone knew it was Ella who, with High Enchanter Merlon's help, had brought back the bladesingers to fight again.

Ignoring their stares and murmurs, Ella searched for Miro. She went to the palace first and found Amber. After a brief embrace, Amber directed her to the city gardens, near the river.

Ella finally found her brother talking with a Louan artificer at the place where many of the pilots had chosen to set their dirigibles down.

Miro had his mouth open, an expression of consternation on his face, but whatever he'd been about to say, he stopped when he saw his sister.

"Ella," he said.

Ella pulled him close and held him hard. "You did it," she whispered into his ear. She felt wetness on her cheeks and, holding him back, she saw the glint of moisture in his eyes.

"You did it too," Miro said.

"No, Miro," Ella said, "it was you."

"We lost so many," Miro whispered.

"I heard about Beorn," Ella said. "I'm sorry. He was a good man."

"The very best," said Miro. He coughed and turned away, gathering himself before returning to his sister.

"So much destruction," said Ella, looking over the city.

"But we'll rebuild. We evacuated the free cities, and we'll rebuild Castlemere and Schalberg. It'll take a long time, but we'll get there."

"You'll do it." Ella nodded.

"There's one thing I don't understand, though," Miro said, "and I'm still waiting to find out." He turned to the short middle-aged Louan woman standing nearby, and his puzzled expression returned. "Artificer Touana, why did you come?"

"Why did we come?" Touana looked confused, glancing at each of them in turn. "I don't understand. We received your gilden, and we rushed your order through."

"Gilden?" Miro said. "What gilden?"

"Your agent brought it to us. What was his name . . . ? He was from the free cities. A strange name. Hermen, yes that's it. Hermen Tosch."

Ella stared at the Louan artificer. "What did you just say?"

"Hermen Tosch brought your gilden. Quite a lot of it."

Ella thought about her last words with the trader. Hermen had come through for them. He'd given up the wealth he'd taken a lifetime to accumulate, and he wasn't even here for her to thank him.

Miro smiled as he glanced at Ella. "You have some good friends."

"Bartolo," Ella suddenly said. "How is he?"

"Grumbling," said Miro. "Angry that he missed the last of the fighting."

"Sounds like Bartolo."

"I'm going to head back to the palace. Are you coming?"

"No," Ella said. "I think I need some time to myself."

"I understand. Don't be too long. The emperor's going to be here soon, and I'm sure he's anxious to see you."

Ella nodded and kissed Miro's cheek before leaving him behind. She walked through the city and crossed Singer's Bridge, her path taking her to the partly destroyed western quarter.

The inhabitants of Sarostar were returning in a steady stream, soldiers and civilians alike working together to pick through the bodies, some searching for loved ones and others piling revenants onto burning pyres. The battlefield was the worst, littered with bodies, but at least there were more enemy dead than allied soldiers: most of the fallen defenders had already been taken away.

Ella moved through the fallen, wishing she'd done more, sooner. Soldiers and citizens bowed their heads to her as she walked, but she wished they wouldn't. All of the fallen had parents and children, brothers and sisters. They would remember this day forever.

Then Ella saw a small body, incongruous among so many bigger corpses. Her heart skipped a beat as she rushed forward.

Ella knelt by the little woman, heedless of the mud and blood, and for a moment she could only put her hand to her mouth and stare.

Layla's small features made her look more childlike than ever before, yet her ruddy skin was now a sickly shade of yellow-white. Red liquid pooled beneath her body, mingling with the mud. Ella wanted her to look peaceful, but she didn't. She looked as if she'd died in pain.

Ella looked down at Layla's eyes, open and sightless, and as she closed the lids, she fought back a sob. She smoothed the hair back from Layla's brow.

Ella picked Layla up in her arms and stood. The Dunfolk healer's body was so light, it was as if the shell she was now had lost weight when life left her.

As Ella headed back to Sarostar with Layla clutched to her breast, she avoided looking at the deep wound across Layla's abdomen. Her friend deserved better than to die on the battlefield, on the very doorstep to the forest home she loved.

Ella was dimly aware of night closing in as she climbed a bridge and walked through the city. Lights came on at some of the windows, but still Ella walked, the load nearly weightless in her arms, her footsteps carrying her toward the Crystal Palace.

A tall bearded man in loose black clothing met her outside the gates.

Ilathor looked at the small body in Ella's arms before meeting Ella's eyes. "Ella," he said gently, "she's dead."

"No," Ella said, "she can't be."

"Let me take her from you . . ."

"No!"

Ilathor's arms dropped at his sides. "I am sorry for your loss."

"Please go," Ella said.

Ilathor sighed. "Just remember," he said, "I came."

Ella nodded blankly, and Ilathor walked away, leaving her holding Layla's body in her arms.

Ella had no plan, and she wondered what to do. The palace wasn't Layla's home. She should be with her people.

Ella left the Crystal Palace behind and walked through the city's northern quarter, finally seeing trees up ahead. She picked a path into the forest, moving deeper into the trees.

Suddenly, there was a little man standing in front of her. His features were wizened with age, and his limbs were scrawny.

The Tartana of the Dunfolk regarded Ella with sorrow.

"Leave her with us," he said.

Ella saw more Dunfolk emerge from the trees. The small figures came forward and took Layla from Ella's reluctant arms. As they vanished back into the forest, Ella realized she would never see her friend again. The Tartana came forward to take Ella's hand.

"Why did she have to die?" Ella said. She struggled to hold back the tears.

"She made a choice to stand with you. Many of my people did not. You must honor her choice. She is now with the Eternal."

"With the Eternal?" Ella cried. "What does that even mean? Show me the Eternal. Where is he—or she or it? Show me!"

"Layla touched the world with her spirit, and now her spirit will rejoin the earth. Miss her, yes. But please do not cry for her. Remember her with a smile." The Tartana grinned. "I knew Layla. She would like that."

"Must it be so hard?" Ella didn't know exactly what she was referring to.

"I know you, Ella, and I know the Eternal works within you, whether you realize it or not. You will continue your struggle because the world is out of balance. You can draw on that force whenever you feel lost or without courage. Trust in the Eternal, and you will have the strength to go on. Now, it is time for you to return to your people. We will bury her under a tree, and whenever you want, you can come to Loralayalana to speak with her."

Emotion threatened to overwhelm Ella again, but she pushed it down. "I want to speak with her now," she whispered.

"Before you can, the balance in the world must be restored. I see something in you telling me it will be you who plays a defining role in the new order to come. Go, Ella. Remember Layla with a smile. Fight for the life she died to protect."

Miro sat on the bed beside Tomas, watching the child sleep. He found he kept touching his son to see if he was real. Perhaps he was also reminding himself he was still alive. He looked up and saw Amber close the door behind her.

"How are you?" Amber murmured.

"Shh," Miro said, looking down at the child. "He's sleeping."

"Miro, listen to me. You have to grieve. Beorn was by your side since the beginning. He was the first officer to follow you after the defeat at Ralanast. He stood by your side as you took command at Mornhaven. He helped you liberate Halaran, and he was the first man to call you high lord."

Miro turned red eyes on Amber. "I am grieving. Can't you tell?"

"Please, husband, don't let this struggle change you. I'm your wife. I see all sides of you. I know you better than anyone, particularly those men who worship you, seeing you at the front of every battle."

Miro opened his mouth to speak, but no words came. He tried to cry but couldn't. Amber held him close as he thought about all the men he'd lost—so many it made the war against the primate pale in comparison. He thought about the fear that had been so constant he couldn't, even now, let it go. At the very end, he knew he'd given up. If Bartolo hadn't fallen and Shani hadn't needed his help, he knew he would have killed revenants until he fell under the weight of their numbers.

Miro tried, but he couldn't let the tears come. Instead, he drew in a long, shaking breath.

"Come on," Amber said, pulling him up. "Tomorrow we'll give Beorn the service he deserves. The emperor is here and he wants to see you."

As Amber led Miro away from Tomas's room Miro tried to ignore her eyes. "The Veznans," he said, "how did you get them to come?"

"It doesn't matter," Amber said. "I'll tell you about it some other time."

Miro nodded, but his mind was already whirling once more. He pulled away from Amber when he saw an enchantress, a woman in a green silk dress.

"High Lord?" she said when he touched her shoulder.

Miro gave her an instruction. "The green light," he said. "It's time to stop the signal."

"At once." The enchantress nodded and sped away.

Miro put on his high lord's face, and he went out to greet the emperor.

40

As the first evening stars sparkled high above Sarostar, the citizens turned out to give homage to the fallen. Carrying candles, the city folk walked in groups to stand together on the nine bridges, now scrubbed clean, the smears of red gone. Parents clutched children close, and husbands and wives held hands. The lights of the Crystal Palace began their evening display of colors, and the fountains shot high into the air, water reflecting the shimmering colors as it tumbled back to the ground.

Where riverboats once filled the green waters of the Sarsen, the river that wound through Sarostar's heart now became filled with rafts. The wooden platforms drifted ponderously through the city before the current took them south, where the river would eventually empty into the Great Western Ocean. A fallen defender lay on his back on each raft, a wreath of flowers clutched to his—or her—bosom, and all were sent on their final journey in this way, whether Alturan, Halrana, Hazaran, or Veznan.

Miro spoke, and afterward he never remembered the words he said. He only remembered his people shedding tears for the fallen, their eyes raised heavenward in gratitude to know they were alive.

As Amber took Miro's hand and led her husband back to the Crystal Palace, a man called out from the crowd.

"Thank you, High Lord."

Miro nodded to the man as words failed him. More calls came down from the bridges, and then a sigh rose from the common people, who wept even as they celebrated the survival of their home.

"Remember this moment," Amber said.

＊

That night, Miro and Killian assembled a hasty war conference at the Crystal Palace. With the rulers of four houses present, as well as the emperor, it was time to seek answers to grave questions and make important decisions about the future.

The biggest questions of all remained unanswered. Where was Sentar Scythran? Was the war over?

Ilathor and Jehral debated with Miro and Tiesto. Touana looked on with calculating eyes but said little. Grigori of Vezna looked repentant. Killian tried to keep the dialogue productive. Ella was conspicuously absent.

As the arguments became heated, Miro finally went out to the fountains to think. Looking east, in the direction of Halaran and Tingara, he felt the loss of Beorn more fiercely than ever. Drawing his gaze, the three-legged tower nearby loomed over the Crystal Palace. The pyramid of quartz at the apex was now dark.

Miro saw Killian, dressed in tailored clothing of black and gray, leave the palace and come to join him outside.

"Emperor, I must thank you again for coming," Miro said.

"We came as quickly as we could."

"The men took heart from your arrival. I don't think we would have won the day without the news."

"Hearts win battles, as well as minds," Killian said.

Miro turned to regard the new emperor. He didn't know Killian well, but there was something likeable about him. He appeared to

317

possess a store of wisdom despite his youth. Miro then realized the two of them were probably close to the same age. With all he'd seen, Miro felt like an old man.

Thinking about old men made Miro think about Evrin.

"I'm sorry about Evrin," Miro said.

"He gave himself that we all might live. I now believe it was his plan all along . . . to sacrifice himself to kill Sentar. I also believe he only showed a part of himself to the world, to us, and I think he never lost the guilt he felt. How is Ella?"

"Bad," Miro said. "We both lost loved ones. Have you spoken with her?"

"I haven't seen her."

Miro and Killian looked to the east, in the direction of Tingara together. "We should expect the worst," Miro said. "There were supposed to be three of these pirate kings, and we only fought two. There was no great store of essence. Sentar himself was absent. We haven't seen the end of it."

"I agree," Killian said. "With most of the Legion absent from Seranthia . . ."

Killian suddenly stopped speaking, and both men went rigid. The signal tower in front of them began to glow, the prism sparking from within until light radiated outward, shining with a bright, unquestionably fierce light.

Miro drew in a sharp breath. How could it be?

Someone was requesting help.

"Lord of the Sky," Miro whispered.

"The color . . . is it . . . ?"

"Yes. They're under attack."

The prism was white, the color of the Assembly of Templars. The color could only mean one thing: Aynar was under attack. Stonewater would be the next to fall.

"Could it be a ruse?" Killian asked.

"Only someone at Stonewater can put out the signal from the key reflector, and only the primate knows the activation sequence. For it to be false, either the primate would have to be turned, or someone with my sister's knowledge of lore would have to break the coded sequence."

"What do you think?" Killian said.

Miro let out a breath. "It's real. Evrin always told us to be wary of Sentar's cunning. And you, Emperor?"

"It can only mean one thing: he split his forces," Killian said. "This whole time we've been wondering whether it will be the east or the west, and in the end . . . it's both."

"Scratch it, we've only faced part of his army." Miro cursed. "Can Stonewater hold for long?"

"There's a division of the Legion there, as well as a few thousand templars."

"You know that won't hold them."

"No," Killian said. "It won't."

"I'm sorry," Miro said. "You've come here to help, and now it's the east that needs us."

"I have no regrets. I believe that anywhere the Empire is breached, we must go to help. When we leave, will you come?"

"Our forces aren't what they once were," Miro said, "but of course we'll come. No one should face this enemy alone."

"We must leave immediately."

"I know."

Killian stared up at the white light. "The Lord of the Night is at Stonewater."

———•———

Early the next morning, the Crystal Palace thronged with activity as plans were made for the journey east. The open ground outside the palace became trodden with hooves and soldier's boots; the officers and quartermasters huddled together making plans for food, shelter, and travel routes.

Miro watched as two groups began to form. They'd decided to split their forces. The Hazarans were by far the fastest and would ride for the Gap of Garl and Aynar. If Stonewater was fallen by the time they arrived—and that was likely, for the journey was long—then the Hazarans would harass and slow the enemy, delaying them until the second, slower force could make it across Halaran and through the Azure Plains to Seranthia. This second force, comprised of Tingarans, Louans, Halrana, Alturans, and Veznans, would hopefully reach Seranthia in time to boost the city's weakened defenses. Wherever he was, Sentar Scythran would be eager to reach the Sentinel.

"You know what you must do?" Killian appeared uncomfortable addressing the kalif of the Hazarans.

"Yes, Emperor. We will do our utmost to delay them until your arrival in Seranthia."

"I thank you, Kalif. The whole of the Empire is counting on you."

Ilathor nodded to Killian before walking over to speak with Jehral and a young Hazaran woman, finally mounting up on their waiting horses without another word.

Killian's face was white, and Miro could only imagine what he must be thinking. It wasn't a long journey from Stonewater to Seranthia, and they'd all seen how difficult it was to slow this particular enemy. Killian had traveled through the portal to the wasted land of Shar. He knew what would happen to Merralya if Sentar claimed victory against the Empire and brought his brother Evermen home.

Miro heard the rising clatter of approaching hooves, and men drew out of the way as a figure on horseback rode up. Miro was relieved when he saw Ella, her face set in a familiar mask of determination, but he could see that underneath she was having difficulty holding the mask in place.

Ella wore her green silk dress and held the reins of a second horse in her left hand. She looked ready to travel, with packed saddlebags and a knapsack on her shoulder.

"Ella," Miro said, walking up to stand beside her horse. "What are you doing?"

"The Hazarans will need help if they're going to delay Sentar's army for as long as we need them to. I'm lighter than any of the desert men, and I can ride faster, particularly if I change horses. The Akari will have seen Altura's signal, and Ada, Dain Barden's daughter, promised me she would convince her father to come. Their army should now be somewhere between Rosarva and Ralanast. I'm going to find the Akari, wherever they are, and divert them to Aynar so they can help the kalif and his men."

As Ella spoke, Miro saw Killian looking up at her with incredible intensity. By contrast, Ella avoided meeting Killian's gaze altogether, keeping her green eyes firmly on Miro.

Miro hesitated. "It's a good idea. But not on your own, Ella. Please—take someone with you."

"No one can ride as fast as I can," Ella said stubbornly.

"That's not true," a female voice said.

Turning to see who it was, Miro grinned as Shani stepped forward. "I can ride just as well as you can, and Bartolo's healing fine. I'm coming with you."

Ella opened her mouth and then closed it again, before smiling. "All right. You can come. Provided you can keep up."

"I'll have you know . . ." Shani began.

"All right," Miro forestalled her. "Three groups. Ella and Shani will try to find the Dain's forces and divert the Akari. The Hazarans will do what they can to slow the revenants. The rest of us will make all speed to Tingara. We know Sentar's eventual goal is Seranthia. We can't afford long good-byes, but our hopes go with all of you."

41

Time passed, days turning to weeks and the warmth of spring shifting to the long days and hot nights of summer. Across the Empire, fields ripened and careworn farmers prepared for the harvest; young birds grew to take their first flight; and men marched day and night, everyone heading east, always east.

With summer came scents, some sweet and filling the senses with delight, others rancid and repellent.

In Altura, with the last of the revenants incinerated, the scent of smoke and burning flesh finally came to be replaced with the fresh fragrance of summer flowers. A new odor wafted throughout Sarostar's western quarter: the smell of wood shavings and fresh mortar. Soon, with time, the free cities Castlemere and Schalberg would see the same transformation.

As always, in the icy north there was no smell at all. But with the army of Akari warriors heading south, the summer heat would begin to take its toll. The Dain's necromancers were busy.

In Petrya's north the Hazaran riders' noses were filled with dust and dung; with their horses traveling night and day there was little else to fill the senses.

In Seranthia the scent was fear. Stonewater must have fallen by now, and Aynar, the land of the templars, with it. Those who'd disbelieved the Alturan high lord's words now said they'd believed him all along. The shadow of night hung over the Imperial capital.

Fearful eyes looked out at the walled tower standing on the tiny island barring Seranthia's harbor. The Sentinel waited.

———◆———

At Stonewater, the spiritual heart of the Empire, a man in elegant black clothing clutched the stone wall at his side as he fought the buffeting winds to climb the last few steps to the summit of the mountain.

He scowled as he took in the worn decorations where once intricate designs displayed scenes of beauty. The steps themselves were rounded and broken; in his day the marble had been crisp and lustrous. Soon, he vowed, he would restore Stonewater to its former glory.

Finally, Sentar Scythran reached the summit, seeing the circular flat space crowning the mountain. He walked forward to stand in the middle of the plateau, high above it all. His crimson hair shone in the light, but the sun touched neither his ice-blue eyes, nor the streaks of black hair at his temples. He inhaled deeply and felt his spirits soar for the first time since he'd returned to Merralya.

The memories came flooding back. He remembered standing with his brothers, formed in a circle in this very place as they discussed the war with the humans. Pyrax Pohlen had suggested guarding the knowledge kept here with a barrier. Sentar spoke out against the idea, to suggest that the humans could win the war filled him with disgust at his brothers' cowardice. Yet Varian Vitrix agreed with Pyrax's suggestion: the vault, the temple-like chamber at the top of the mountain, kept many of their secrets. They took a vote, and the Pinnacle came into being.

The Lord of the Night now glared at the ruins of the vault, just a pile of fallen stones. Now the greatest works of lore would never be remembered.

But when Sentar Scythran brought his brothers back, things would be as they once were. They would restore Stonewater: the slaves would work night and day until it was more glorious than ever before. Together they would build new wonders, and with breeding humans kept captive, supplies of essence would be guaranteed. Once more they would open the way to new worlds, but this time it wouldn't be to go into forced exile. The next time they entered another world, they would be ready. Merralya would fall, and then world after world would follow. Perhaps another, more compliant race would come to provide fuel for the war machine. Nothing would stand in their way.

Sentar felt determination settle over him as he stood high on the summit of the solitary mountain that was Stonewater. He gazed out at the town of Salvation, a place he'd decided to leave standing. Most of Aynar's population had fled north, but many stayed to bask in his glory. Sentar now had priests and templars at his beck and call, and a few demonstrations of his power ensured everyone knew who their god was. He had taken back his rightful place.

In time, he would work to ensure only the dead were allowed to serve. But for now, it felt good to be loved.

His eyes again flickered to the ruined structure that had once stood at the summit of the mountain. Sentar's scowl slowly faded, for when his brothers returned, they would build as well as destroy. They would erect vats in every city of the Empire; they would breed the humans in numbers, and they would have a constant supply of essence and an endless source of revenant slaves.

He'd learned from Shar. Never again would he be in a position where there were no more bodies for the vats.

As he slowly turned and drank in the view, Sentar caught sight of approaching figures, climbing up the last few steps to meet him.

An older necromancer in gray robes led four templars, with two tall revenants bringing up the rear.

Sentar smiled and walked over to the templars.

"Kneel," Sentar commanded.

Three of the templars, all in white robes decorated with a black sun, fell to their knees. An older templar whose robe was lined with gold trim remained standing.

"Why do you not kneel?" Sentar inquired.

"I am the primate. And you are no god," the plump old man said.

"Then why are you primate?" Sentar sneered. "I am the Lord of the Night! Who do you worship now?"

"We don't worship; we ponder. We teach. The force that makes us know right from wrong doesn't come from outside—it comes from within. It is something we humans have developed, and continually strive to understand." The primate's eyes saddened. "It took us too long to learn this."

Sentar lunged forward and gripped the primate around the neck. The three templars whimpered and cowered, but even with Sentar's hand on his throat, the primate simply rested his weary gaze on Sentar.

"You had your chance," Sentar said to the primate. "Renrik," he spoke to the necromancer. "Toss your knife at the feet of our three friends here."

A short dagger clattered to the stone. The three kneeling templars looked down at the knife with fear before returning their wide-eyed gaze to Sentar.

"Now, there's just one knife, and there are three of you," said Sentar, glancing down at them with his hand still clutching the old primate's throat. "Whoever ends this one's life first can live and serve me. The rest of you . . . well, you'll see."

The three kneeling men exchanged glances, and then there was a mad scramble as they fought each other for the knife. The youngest of the three elbowed one of his fellows in the face and then punched the other in the gut. He grabbed the knife and from a kneeling position, he thrust into the belly of the struggling old man in Sentar's grip.

Blood spurted out from the wound, staining the young templar's white robe. The red liquid slid off Sentar's own clothing, unable to cling to the fabric.

"Now, use the knife on your fellows," Sentar said as the primate writhed and moaned. "Be still!" he said to the dying old man, whose twitching was making it difficult for Sentar to maintain his hold.

After another scrabble filled with grunts and moans, the other two templars were dead. With a heave of his lore-enhanced muscles, Sentar lifted the wriggling primate higher and then tossed him into the air.

Renrik had seen this all before, but the young templar was awestruck as Sentar chanted and called forth elemental air from his hands, whirling the primate above all of their heads. Finally Sentar threw him sailing over the edge of Stonewater's summit, tossing the old man from the mountain without bothering to watch him fall.

"Who am I?" Sentar demanded as he dusted his hands.

The young man in white robes bowed down to the ground in a satisfying way as the dripping knife fell out of his hands. "You . . . you are the Lord of the Night."

"That is correct. What am I?"

"A god."

"Excellent. You can live. Your first order is to clean up this mess."

"At once, Nightlord."

"Renrik, come with me."

The exercising of his power gave Sentar a sense of satisfaction, banishing his disgust at the sight of what the humans had done to Stonewater with their misuse and neglect. Sentar walked to the border of the plateau and felt the wind tear at his shirt as Renrik joined him at the edge.

"Do you think they fell for it, Renrik?" Sentar asked the leader of his necromancers. Sentar smiled; he was in a good mood. "Are they leaping around this Empire with no plan of where to go next?"

Renrik played with the circle of bones around his neck as he spoke. "Who can say, Nightlord?" Renrik said. "We'll only know when we reach Seranthia."

"Divide and conquer," Sentar said. "Divide, and divide again. Splitting our fleet was as a stroke of genius, was it not?"

"It was, Nightlord."

Rejoining the second naval force had also given Sentar a chance to recover from his battle with Evrin Evenstar, though he didn't say it. The voyage had been long, but it had been time used well. He was ready.

Sentar had built lore into his ships that kept them cool and prevented the revenants from rotting away, even as they sailed past the Hazara Desert and into the Gulf of Aynar. Unchallenged, he'd disembarked the revenants close to Stonewater while the fleet, now much swifter with loads emptied, set sail again for Seranthia.

There hadn't been much of a defense mounted at Salvation or Stonewater. The templars and Tingaran legionnaires had fought with desperation, but in the end Sentar was victorious, as he knew he would be.

"We now enter the next phase of the plan," Sentar said. "I want you to lead the army—all of the warriors we have here at Stonewater—north. Take the king of Nexos, Gorain, with you. He is a capable general and a strong fighter; few can stand in his way. Your goal is to draw them to you. Lay siege to Seranthia. Tie them up. While we've been fighting here, the fleet will have rounded the cape and will now be awaiting my arrival on the eastern coast. I will defeat their navy, open the portal, and bring my brothers home. This emperor will have to choose between defending his capital and trying to prevent me reaching the Sentinel. The humans are nearly done as a force. Only we will prevail."

"As you will it, Nightlord." Renrik bowed.

Sentar Scythran once more gazed out at his new lands. He would wipe the human-built city of Seranthia from the face of the world, but Stonewater would form the heart of the new order.

The thought of standing in this very place once more with his brother Evermen filled him with excitement. They would acknowledge that Sentar had been right all along. They would know they had been correct to put their trust in him to guard the portal. Sentar would be supreme, even among his kind.

"One force for the west," Sentar said. "By now, Altura is conquered. One force for the east, led by you, my trusted Renrik. A third and final force for Tingara's harbor and the portal, led by me. Divide, and divide again."

"Yes, Nightlord."

"Renrik, I must ask you: Will the Akari, who were once my people, join in the fight against me? Or will they serve again?"

"They will side with the Empire, Nightlord."

Sentar frowned. "Against me? Even in the face of inevitable defeat?"

"Those necromancers who would follow are already with us. But I have a plan, Nightlord. There is one in their number I have turned to our cause. The Akari will be neutralized."

"Excellent, Renrik. You are ahead of me for a change."

"It is my will to serve." Renrik bowed.

"And Renrik?" Sentar frowned down at the plain. "Those shining lights offend my senses. Send some men to those towers; knock them all down."

"I will see it done."

42

Ella and Shani rode into the border town of Mourie, located between Halaran and Loua Louna, the hooves of their horses clattering on the cobbled stones, fatigue pulling at their shoulders.

It was market day in Mourie, a scene of strange normality as men and women in a variety of costumes hurried to and fro with goods in their hands and pouches of gilden at their belts. The scurrying townsfolk turned and stared in astonishment as Ella pushed her mount in between the drudge-pulled carts and picked her way around the stalls. Most had never seen a horse before, and the two women gathered attention as they rode to the market's heart.

The town square was framed by a tower and a cluster of buildings. Ella rode directly for the center and pulled up, her horse whinnying as she pulled on the reins to draw it to a halt.

"Oh no," Shani muttered under her breath. "Here we go again."

Ella pointed her hand in the air, and a beam of bright golden light shot out of her wand. The townsfolk screamed and gasped; she had their attention.

"People of Loua Louna and lands far from here, I have news," Ella called.

Soon there were hundreds of people around them as the crowd gathered to see what this strange young woman had to say.

"You may have heard about the enemy from across the sea. If you have not, then be warned, for this enemy is unlike anything our Empire has faced before. I come directly from Altura, my homeland, which has only survived a great onslaught by the barest margin, thanks to the combined efforts of the houses. The free cities are gone. Sarostar is partly destroyed. I am Ella Torresante, and Miro, high lord of Altura, is my brother."

The people gasped as they heard the news, exchanging glances as women pulled children close, and all wondered how this affected them.

"We fight a force of ultimate evil, bent on destroying every house, not just Altura, but Loua Louna as well. This enemy will not rest until the Empire is gone."

Ella paused to take a breath and frowned as she caught Shani rolling her eyes.

"We now know that the battle for Altura was just part of the struggle. We believe we only faced a part of their forces in the west. A second force traveled by ship to the lands in the east. Their next target became clear when Aynar sent a call for help, but it was a call we were unable to answer. By now the enemy has undoubtedly conquered Stonewater."

The gasps were clearly audible now. Faces turned white and men growled.

"Soon my brother, the high lord of Altura, and the high lords of Vezna and Halaran, will pass this way. With them is Killian Alderon, your emperor. They go to stop our enemy before he can conquer Seranthia. I don't need to tell you, if Seranthia falls, the rest of the Empire will soon follow."

Ella's gaze swept the market, roving over the growing crowd. These people would pass the word, and soon everyone in Mourie and beyond would hear the news.

"When they come, I ask that you help. Gather your weapons and your men, and follow where your emperor leads. We don't battle for Altura, nor do we fight for the survival of Seranthia. We fight for the Empire. Please, I beg that you do your part."

"Who is this enemy?" someone called.

Ella considered her words. "It is an army of revenants, led by rebel Akari necromancers. Their leader is a man of the utmost evil." She paused to let her words sink in. "Which brings me to my next purpose. The Akari are our allies, and their own revenants may help to hold back the tide. Have they been seen in this area?"

As before, Ella saw only shaking heads and blank looks. She would have to continue her search.

Ella reared her horse back, sending the hooves kicking at the air before her mount once more regained its footing. She nodded at Shani, and they sped from the market, all eyes on them as they left.

———

Ella and Shani rode along narrow trails, through forested glens and down wide roads, heading north into the wild lands the Akari would have to pass through on their way south. Ella made the same speech at every town and village. Sometimes her words were received with fright; other times people challenged her with rattling swords and cries of rage.

They traveled as swiftly as possible, desperate in their search, always with the fear in their minds that they would miss the Dain's force altogether. Perhaps the Dain hadn't seen the signal. Or perhaps he'd seen it and hadn't come.

Even with remounts, they couldn't gallop all the time. Ella took care to ensure they spared their horses. If they lost a mount, their mission would suffer.

"Ella," Shani said as they walked the horses alongside a grassy bank beside a thin stream. "I just want you to know, I don't think it's true."

Ella tore her gaze from the trail. "What's not true?"

"About Killian having a love back in Seranthia. I don't think it's true."

Ella sighed; she wished she'd never told Shani. "What makes you say that?"

"I saw the way he looked at you back in Sarostar. You'd have to be a fool not to see it. It was the look of a man in pain. A certain kind of pain, if you get my meaning."

"It doesn't matter," Ella said. "We've got bigger things to worry about."

"What's more important than love?"

"Safety," said Ella. "Freedom. Life."

"You're wrong," said Shani. "Bartolo would give his life for me, and I for him. Do you doubt me?"

"No, but . . ."

"It's love that binds us together. Even if we rarely acknowledge it, it's love for our fellow humans, even those we don't know, that makes us risk our lives to fight for the Empire."

"Fine," Ella said. "I get your point."

"Do you? Ella, love is a risk. It takes courage, and it takes work, but it's all worth it in the end. Every time something goes wrong, you can't shy away. You need to face things head on."

"Like facing an enemy?" Ella smiled.

"Like everything else in life," Shani said, her expression as grave as Ella had ever seen her. "You're brave in so many ways, but when it comes to love, you're as timid as a dormouse. I understand you're afraid of being hurt, but that's part of the process. Every time Bartolo goes into battle, I'm so scared I can hardly breathe. But I wouldn't have it any other way. Do you understand what I'm saying?"

"Shani, he knows about Ilathor. I saw his eyes; he'll never forgive me. And now he has Carla. She was his first love. I'll never compete."

"Talk to him!"

"I'll think about it," Ella said. "There's another village ahead. Let's see what they have to say."

The villagers told them about a large army passing through. Ella couldn't believe the relief she felt to hear them describe tall, blonde-haired warriors with pale skin and endless ranks of eerie white-eyed revenants.

Ella pushed Shani and herself harder now, riding from before dawn until after dusk. After two more days they passed a fallow field next to a series of pastures, and with night setting around them Ella saw a multitude of twinkling lights that could only be campfires.

"Who goes there?" a tall sentry challenged the two riders.

Ella breathed a sigh of relief to see he was a living Akari warrior. More sentries came up to join them, and soon they faced a cluster of warriors carrying axes, hammers, and two-handed swords.

"I'm Enchantress Ella Torresante of Altura, and this is Elementalist Shani of Petrya," Ella said. "We need to see the Dain."

The sentries conferred, and a moment later half a dozen warriors formed up around them as the two women dismounted, leading Ella and Shani through the camp. Ella passed necromancers in gray robes and tried to relax her tensed muscles: these were friends, she reminded herself. Lord of the Sky, she struggled to shake how much they looked like the enemy.

Seeing the revenants actually wasn't as bad; the enemy revenants came from the lands across the sea, a motley horde collected from all over those conquered lands. These revenants were calm and orderly, universally Akari, with gray uniforms and precise movements. Ella managed to steady herself after a time. The memories of the fight for Altura were a month old, but they were as fresh as if they'd occurred moments ago.

Ella and Shani halted outside a white pavilion, open at the sides, evidently a space the Dain used for receiving visitors and making plans. Revenant servants took their horses, and then Ella ducked her head and entered the pavilion, with Shani following close behind.

Dain Barden Mensk of the Akari sat at the head of a table of whitewashed wood. He leaned forward over a map while a commander spoke to him in low tones.

"Enchantress Ella of Altura and Elementalist Shani of Petrya," a soldier announced.

Dain Barden glanced up and frowned. Ella felt the familiar chill along her spine as he looked at her with penetrating blue-gray eyes. Tall, even for his people, and muscled more than any man she'd seen, Dain Barden pulled on his forked beard, playing with the silver thread woven through. His long white hair was braided at the back of his head, and the lines in his brow were cruel and forbidding.

"Ella," the Dain said, "finally some news. The fact you are far from your home says much. How fares Altura?"

Ella took a deep breath. "Dain, Altura stands, but only just. We turned back the enemy, but with great loss of life. The forces of Altura and Halaran are shadows of what they once were. The free cities are gone."

"But you turned them back?" the Dain said. "Good. We can go home."

"You don't know, then?" Shani asked.

"Who is this?" Dain Barden scowled.

"She is Shani, an elementalist of Petrya and a friend. We've been searching for you for weeks."

"Tell me, what is it we don't know, Ella?"

"Our enemy is crafty and divided his forces. While we were tied up fighting in Altura, he continued by sea to the lands in the east. A month ago Stonewater requested help. We can only assume that, while they would have held for a time, by now the land of the templars has gone to the shadow."

Dain Barden's eyes went wide. "And Seranthia?"

"That's why we're here," Ella said. "With the emperor and most of the Legion marching back from Altura, along with the rest of our forces, the emperor asks . . . he requests . . . your help. Your force is in a position to delay the enemy until he can bring the Legion back."

"Where is the enemy now?" one of the Dain's commanders spoke.

"Most likely somewhere between Aynar and Tingara."

"And what stands between the Lord of the Night and his goal?" Dain Barden said.

"The Hazarans."

"Those desert men? Three years ago we were fighting them, and now you want us to help them?"

"It is the only way to save the Empire. We've been outmaneuvered, Dain. If the emperor hadn't come to Altura's aid, we would have fallen, yet by doing so he's left Tingara exposed."

"I'll think on it," Dain Barden said.

"Let's head back to Ku Kara—" the commander began.

"I said I'll think on it!" the Dain growled.

Ella and Shani swapped glances. Ella knew it wasn't the time to press the proud Dain, but she also knew that without the Akari, the Hazarans were doomed to fight the enemy alone.

Ilathor and Jehral had come through for Altura. True to their word, they'd fought for Ella's homeland and had lost a great many men.

Now it was Ella's turn to come through for her friends.

335

"Leave me," Dain Barden said. "Someone will find you tents. I need to think."

"Of course," Ella said.

She and Shani nodded and left the Dain of the Akari staring down at the map on the table, though his eyes had the look of a man seeing something else altogether.

As they left the pavilion behind, Shani turned to Ella. "That's the first time we've met. Is he normally like that?"

Ella hesitated. "Gruff, yes. But there's something affecting him."

A steward in a gray uniform came forward. "Ladies? Would you care to follow me?"

Ella turned to the steward. "Is Ada here? The Dain's daughter?"

The steward paled. "She's . . . unwell."

"Unwell?" Ella said. "Can I see her?"

The steward hesitated and then nodded. "I will show you. Be warned, it isn't pleasant."

He led them past campfires and clusters of tents to a structure larger than the rest, with a wide space left around it, as if the Dain's warriors were reluctant to make their camp too close. As they passed through the entrance, Ella saw it was an infirmary tent. Her gaze took in dozens of cots, all lined up in rows.

Every bed had an occupant, and the sick people were mostly Akari men. Moans of pain sounded from many as they writhed and gripped their bedding. Others appeared to be comatose.

Ella and Shani followed the steward along a row, past a cot where an older man with a lean frame lay on his back. His head was strangely bald in wide patches, and his eyes were closed. If it weren't for the rising and falling of his chest, Ella would have thought he was dead. At the next cot a younger man gasped in pain and clutched at his stomach, red blood showing between his teeth. Patches of bare skin also showed on his scalp.

Ada was on the next bed.

The Dain's daughter was taller than Ella and older, with hair so pale it was close to white, and brilliant blue eyes. Ella looked down at the proud Akari woman in pity. Half her hair had come out, leaving ragged clumps, and her eyes were closed, though even in sleep her face was wracked in a grimace of pain.

"Please don't wake her," the steward said. "She rarely sleeps. If she does, it is a blessing."

Ella wanted to squeeze Ada's hand, but instead she bowed her head. She no longer wondered why the Dain had been so upset. Ella stayed for a while and then nodded that she wished to leave. Passing the rows of wretched Akari once more, Ella waited until they'd left the infirmary before she spoke in hushed tones.

"So many . . . What's wrong with them?"

"We don't know. It started just two weeks ago, mainly striking the necromancers. Many are in that tent, but we've buried dozens along the way. I'm not sure if you understand our lore . . ."

"I know something about it," Ella said.

"Well, as you know, our draugar need tending, and they need necromancers to control them. Our necromancers started to get sick, and Ada stepped in to help. As the Dain's daughter she's been trained in our arts. Now she is sick too."

Ella's brow furrowed. "Is it only necromancers?"

"Only those who've spent a lot of time with our draugar, yes."

Ella thought about the things she'd learned from the alchemist's book. "Corpses carry many diseases . . ."

The steward shrugged. "It is beyond me. I'll find you somewhere to sleep tonight," he said. "Enchantress . . . if you can help us get to the bottom of this sickness, we would be grateful."

Ella nodded. "I'll do what I can."

She exchanged glances with Shani. The Hazarans needed the Akari's help.

But it appeared the Dain had problems of his own.

43

The tension in Seranthia was palpable. The terrified citizens barricaded their homes, nailing planks across doors and windows so that the tap of hammers formed a pattering background noise to any walk through the city. The markets were all but devoid of food; stockpiling had led to a shortage of everything.

Once again Seranthia's fate would decide that of the Empire.

Yet this time was different. When the allied force led by Altura had freed Seranthia from the grip of evil, leading to the defeat of High Lord Moragon and Primate Melovar Aspen, the city's conquest had come to be seen as liberation as prosperity and pride eventually returned to the city, culminating with the coronation of a new emperor.

This time the enemy was feared by all. The Alturan high lord had warned them, and his words had been proven true.

Refugees from Aynar trickled into the city, each bearing terrible tales of death and wanton destruction. They said this enemy was unbeatable. Vats were being erected in Aynar, and the revenants would keep coming until they'd achieved total victory.

The enemy now had a foothold in the lands of the Empire. The Lord of the Night was coming for Seranthia.

Rogan Jarvish sighed and rubbed at his eyes as he sat in his study in the Imperial Palace and made notes on a map of the city and harbor. He had a meeting with the Tingaran marshals later in the day and would present his plan for the city's defense.

Rogan had faced many enemies, and it took time to take their measure, but he now knew Sentar's style. Rogan knew that the enemy force—which must even now be somewhere between Tingara and Aynar—would attack the city's landward side. Meanwhile, their navy would attack the harbor. Sentar's strategy was to distract them, to tie up their forces, while he went for his main objective: the Sentinel.

As Rogan marked dirigibles on his map, he heard heavy footsteps. The footsteps grew louder, and then with sudden force the door to his study crashed open. Rogan glanced up in astonishment. He saw a Tingaran officer he didn't recognize.

"Ever heard of knocking?" Rogan growled.

The officer brandished a sealed scroll in expensive purple-edged paper and thrust it into Rogan's face. "Rogan Jarvish, I bring new orders. I regret to inform you that you are hereby dismissed from the army."

"What?" Rogan spluttered, rising from his seat.

He took the scroll and broke the seal. The decree was curt, summary. It was signed by the Tingaran Council of Lords.

"We'll see about this," Rogan muttered.

He pushed past the officer and felt seething rage build up, heat rising to his cheeks. Passing through the marble-floored palace corridors, he finally found the Tingaran marshals, meeting in the war rooms. It was a meeting he hadn't been invited to.

"What's the meaning of this?" Rogan demanded, holding out the scroll. "Marshal Trask?" he spoke to a Tingaran officer he usually got along with.

"Rogan," Marshal Priam spoke instead, "your influence affected the emperor's judgment, making him take most of the Legion from Tingara to go to Altura's aid."

"That's not true!" Rogan spat. "I've always acted in your best interests. Taking the Legion was his decision, and I still maintain it was probably the right one. If they gained a foothold in Altura . . ."

"They instead gained a foothold in Aynar, right on our doorstep. You saved your homeland, Jarvish, but at our expense. The Council of Lords met this morning and they took our recommendation. You won't be playing a part in the city's defense."

"I'm sorry, Rogan," Trask said.

"Scratch you!" Rogan said, throwing the scroll down to the table. He loomed over the table as the men drew back, their eyes fearful. "I'm tired of defending sound decisions to bureaucrats. I'm done with all of you."

"We thank you for your service," Priam said. He affected a conciliatory tone. "Go home, Rogan. You're old."

"Old?" Rogan felt heat come to his cheeks as his fury rose. With an effort he tried to calm himself.

"You have a wife and son. Go back to Altura. We will manage without you."

Rogan Jarvish paced the length of the High Tower, the tallest structure in the Imperial Palace, open on all sides. He clenched and unclenched his fists as he walked, turning on his heel at the end of every dozen steps.

His gaze swept over the vista; his vantage was all encompassing. In front of him he could see the harbor and the walled tower enclosing the Sentinel; and when he next turned, on the landward side the gray Wall loomed over the buildings to guard the city. Even the Wall wasn't high enough to block the view of hills surrounding the Empire's capital.

Rogan fumed.

He'd been arguing with the Tingarans for weeks, and it seemed they'd taken matters into their own hands. Rogan wanted to send troops to Tingara's south, to buy them all time for the emperor to return, and to provide cover for the multitude of fleeing refugees. Instead, the Tingarans wanted to abandon the people of Aynar to their fate. They would now have their way, and the remainder of the Imperial Legion would stay on high alert in Seranthia.

A few days ago, the white light of Stonewater's distress call had abruptly ceased to shine from the towers. In the end, the decision was taken away. The land of Aynar, home of the Assembly of Templars, had fallen.

Rogan heard soft footsteps and glanced back at the stairs to see Lady Alise approaching. He stopped in his tracks and took a deep breath, smoothing the wrinkles from his frown and calming himself.

Rogan gave Alise a small bow in the eastern manner and was slightly amused to see her touch her lips and forehead like an Alturan.

"I'm sorry, Rogan. I heard about what happened. There was nothing I could do. How are you?"

"I don't think it's that I was dismissed, although telling me to my face would have been more honorable than sending a man with a scroll. It's that they blame me for everything, from the emperor's departure to the fact that half the Buchalanti went to Miro's aid. No one likes being a scapegoat."

"I understand," Alise said. "Don't be bitter; they're simply scared."

"I know," Rogan said. "Maybe they're right. Maybe I am old. But I'm not going home. When the time comes, I'll fight, and this time I won't have to stay back with the officers."

"My influence is waning," Alise said. "It's hard without Killian. I worry for him."

"I'm worried too," Rogan said. "I left my wife and son in Altura."

"I'm sure they are well," Alise said.

"That's what my head tells me," Rogan said. He barked a laugh. "But a piece of paper in my hands would be better."

Alise smiled thinly. "Do you think we're ready?"

"Ready? No. Miro had the better fleet, but we know they were defeated, easily if the reports are true. First Altura called for help, and then Stonewater. We know Sentar Scythran is attacking on multiple fronts. All we can do is try to hold Seranthia and hold the harbor against a naval attack on the Sentinel."

"Is there anything more we can do?"

Rogan fixed his gaze on Seranthia's harbor. He could see the ships of the Imperial Navy as well as several Buchalanti vessels, keeping guard around the walled tower enclosing the statue.

"There's something you can do, yes."

"What is it?"

"You will need to convince the others, but I don't think it will be difficult. There's no use waiting for the end. Seranthia was his goal all along, and the fall of Stonewater only proves it. I think we should send out the call. Let's light the purple signal."

"I'll see it done," Alise said. "What will you do?"

"I'm going to dig out my armorsilk," Rogan said. He grinned. "It's time for an old man to get back into shape."

44

"Slow the enemy," Ilathor muttered to Jehral. "Slow the enemy," he repeated. "More easily said than done, my friend."

Reined in on a broad ridge, the two men watched the revenant horde covering the plain in front of them, coating the land like an insect swarm. A month of hard riding and here they were; they'd found the enemy somewhere in Tingara's south. If this army reached Seranthia before the emperor, the city would fall.

"We need to bite at their flanks and flee before they can give chase," Jehral said. "Forming up to resist our charges will slow them. We can also put barriers in their way: trenches and rock falls, perhaps get some logs . . ."

"What do Hazarans know of digging trenches?" Ilathor said.

"We can learn, Kalif."

"It is our skill on horseback that is our greatest strength, not scrabbling at the earth like Toraks."

"Still, Kalif, I think . . ."

Ilathor stood up in his stirrups and called out. "Form up in a line! We will charge their western flank."

"Kalif, the men are exhausted. Perhaps one night's rest . . ."

"Jehral, I have given the order. Come, fight by my side, my friend."

"Yes, Kalif," Jehral said.

Thousands of horsemen rode up to line the ridge, riders formed up side by side in one long line.

"They know we're here," said Jehral.

"Then let them tremble."

Ilathor held his sword aloft and his men followed suit, until every desert warrior clutched a curved scimitar above his head.

Jehral prepared himself, rehearsing the activation sequence for his weapon, practicing techniques in his mind that would decapitate enemy warriors with heavy slashing blows.

"Charge!"

Ilathor waved his scimitar over his head and kicked his stallion into a gallop. Jehral spurred his gelding to keep up, and soon the thrill of the charge filled his spirit. Hooves thundered across the hard ground. Riders in black and yellow roared as they sped forward, their steeds eating up the earth as they rushed in a line that rapidly became a wedge, with the kalif leading from the point of the spear.

Jehral saw the kalif deftly nudge his stallion in a slight direction change and realized Ilathor was heading for the cluster of black flags. Jehral saw their leader—a man in black-and-white checkers, wearing a three-cornered hat—call out a series of orders as he turned his men to face them. Jehral's eyes widened. The man in black was a revenant, but he behaved like a man.

With a heavy sense of dread, Jehral remembered Miro's story of fighting Diemos, the king of Rendar. They'd never faced the last of the three kings. This must be Gorain, the king of Nexos. The revenants in black and white uniforms around him were his men.

The Hazarans struck the enemy with their relentless charge, screams of men and horses filling the air and the ring of steel on steel clanging like temple bells. The enemy fell under the scimitars, and the horsemen surged ahead to fill the widening gap.

Then Jehral saw Ilathor ahead, embroiled in the fighting, dispatching his enemies with strong blows of his muscled arm, but caught in the thick of the fray.

"Kalif," Jehral called, "pull back!"

Jehral wasn't sure whether Ilathor heard him or not, but the kalif continued pressing through the uniformed revenants, his knees on his stallion's flanks taking him ever closer. Ilathor charged in a direct line for the black pirate king.

The battle slowed to a vicious series of images, snarling revenants lunging up at the riders and Hazarans slashing with curved blades as Jehral fought with all his energy to reach the kalif. He felt revenants pressing him on all sides, grotesque visages tilted to look up at him to be met with crushing blows of his enchanted blade. He slashed down at a revenant, cleaving through its head, and then dispatched a tall warrior on his other side with a deep cut into the neck and chest. Jehral spurred his gelding forward, but the revenants were everywhere.

Jehral saw the pirate king counter a blow from the kalif. Gorain's moves were smooth and graceful as Ilathor then narrowly blocked his riposte. Jehral's heart pounded as he saw the kalif was outclassed. This warrior moved as quickly as a bladesinger.

The man in black and white grabbed the stallion's bridle and pulled down, hard. Ilathor jerked back on the reins to bring his steed back up, but Gorain grimaced and thrust up at the kalif with a glowing sword of thin steel.

Ilathor screamed as the blow struck the center of his chest, and then he slumped in the saddle.

"The kalif!" Jehral cried.

Jehral felt the revenants give ground as the Hazarans pushed forward to reach their leader. A brave horseman smashed his mount into the pirate king, but the rider was met with flashing steel that took the head off his mount. The man fell and Gorain's followers hacked at the Hazaran's body. Jehral finally reached the kalif and cut away the clawing revenants as he took hold of Ilathor's reins in his hand. He wheeled and with a sense of relief felt the stallion come with him.

"Fall back!" Jehral said. The men took up the cry around him, and with a valiant effort the Hazarans pulled free of the enemy's grip and wheeled back out of the fray. They rode at full gallop, and their slower enemy didn't give chase.

The horses fled with frantic terror, but Jehral didn't halt the mad flight until they'd reached the safety of the temporary camp in the hills. He swiftly issued orders from the saddle, relieved when the men didn't question his command.

As Jehral reined in at the camp, he saw Zohra rush forward. He slipped off his horse and took Ilathor in his arms. Together with another warrior, they carried the stricken kalif back to his tent as Zohra hovered around them.

Lying Ilathor on his back in the center of his tent, Zohra tore Ilathor's clothing back to reveal an ugly wound in his chest. Blood spurted out of a gash the length of a man's hand.

"Bring me clean cloth and boiling water, and fetch my bag from my tent," Zohra instructed. "Quickly!"

Jehral leapt to do her bidding.

He didn't want to think about what would happen if the kalif died. The tribes were fractious, and there were no other candidates for the leadership of House Hazara.

Jehral didn't want to think about the fate of Ilathor, his friend.

He exited the tent, and the tarn leaders came rushing forward.

"What news?"

"Is he dead?"

Jehral held up a hand. "He has been wounded. My sister is treating him. He will live." He hoped the words were true.

"What do we do?"

"I am taking command," Jehral said. He directed his gaze at the first of the tarn leaders. After a long pause the man slowly nodded. Jehral looked at each in turn until all had nodded.

"We will follow you while the kalif recovers," Saran of Tarn Salima said.

Jehral nodded. "Our strategy is to harass the enemy to slow them. There will be no more wild charges. We must fight this foe with cunning and guile. We must conserve our men and bring them out of each battle ready to face the enemy again at a moment's notice. Do you all understand?"

"Yes, Jehral of Tarn Teharan."

"Good. Then let's get to it."

Two days later, Jehral returned to the camp with blood on his hands and an arm heavy from wielding a sword. With the kalif wounded, the desert warriors had consented to his leadership, though he knew it would be a different case if Ilathor died. Without the kalif's strong rule to be counted on in the future, the tribes would once more fragment.

Jehral was succeeding at his task. He was managing to slow the enemy, but if Ilathor died, he knew nothing would stop these men going home to the desert.

A Hazaran's first concern was always for his horse, and Jehral's gelding looked as fatigued as he felt himself. He removed the saddle and under blanket while the horse slurped at a bucket of water. Jehral ran a short-toothed comb over his horse's coat, removing dust, blood, and bits of flesh and bone.

Hobbling the gelding, Jehral took the bucket away, lest he drink too much, and washed the blood from his own face and neck, finally scrubbing his hands to remove the last vestiges of red, before hurrying to the kalif's tent.

Jehral stopped in the entrance as he looked in.

Ilathor was awake.

Zohra had a cloth pressed to the kalif's brow, and they were talking softly. The kalif's color had returned, and though he moved with care, it seemed he would live.

Jehral watched for a moment as his sister said something and Ilathor's lips curled in a smile. She tilted her head back and laughed, and then she leaned forward and kissed the kalif's brow.

Jehral smiled. He left Ilathor in his sister's care and went to tell the tarn leaders the good news.

45

Summer in the Azure Plains meant flies. They swarmed over the camp, harassing the men, getting into mouths and noses, sucking at the moisture at the corner of their eyes. Maggots writhed in the meat, and weevils poked up through apparently sealed barrels of grain.

Miro's hand moved constantly in front of his face as he sat in his command tent, poring over the endless rows of figures. It was hot in the tent, and the trickles of sweat running down his face seemed to attract more of the infuriating creatures.

At least the heat would take its toll on the enemy.

Miro turned his attention back to the numbers in front of him. They told him how much flour was spoiled and how much he still had available to make bread for his men. Another sheet described the state of weapons and armor. He read over the number of miles they'd traveled each day and the projections for their arrival in Seranthia. He had the reports of the scouts in one pile and the reports of the injuries his men had sustained in the frantic descent down to the Azure Plains in another.

The figures wavered and blurred in his vision.

They'd set a frantic pace, collecting more men as they led the allied army through Halaran and Loua Louna, and now they were finally in Torakon. The men were exhausted, and the foraging parties needed to hunt. Though it was only afternoon, they'd made camp early and given the soldiers of the Empire an opportunity to rest one final time before the final push to Seranthia.

"Can I help?" Miro heard a voice, and glancing up, he was surprised to see Killian enter the tent.

Miro smiled wryly. "Do you know how often I hear those words?"

"Not often, I'm guessing," Killian said.

Killian walked over to Miro's desk and glanced down at the papers. "Let me assume something—and no insult intended: you're swamped with detail."

"How do you manage?" Miro asked. He felt the loss of Beorn with a fierce hollow sensation in his chest. "I don't know where to begin."

"Your problem is that you need to learn to delegate," Killian said. "Once again"—he grinned—"no insult intended."

Killian came around to scan the contents of Miro's desk. "I can see reports mixed up with logistics. Provisions mixed up with arms. Take the load off, Miro. You need assistance."

Miro waved a fly from his face. "But who? Beorn used to take care of all these things."

Killian took the sheaf of reports from the scouts. "Have you named a new lord marshal?"

"No . . . not yet."

"Then do it. Which of your commanders spent a lot of time with Beorn?"

"Marshal Scola, Marshal Corlin . . ."

Even saying the names made Miro feel better.

"Who should be lord marshal?"

"Marshal Scola," Miro said without hesitation.

"Good. Give him the military briefs. Have him bring the important items to you. Now, who among your commanders is good with logistics?"

"That's where I struggle," Miro said. Then an idea came to him. "Amelia was excellent at provisioning Sarostar during the city's defense. Would that . . .?"

Killian smiled. "Good choice. Have duplicates of the scouting reports sent to Amelia. She can also concern herself with foraging and the like. Who can help you with lore?"

"Amber," Miro said.

"See?" Killian grinned. "Sometimes the people you need to help you are closer than you think. Have your new lord marshal delegate the rest of the responsibilities."

"Poor Beorn," Miro said, running his eyes over the reports. "He carried so much of the weight, and I never even thanked him for it."

"He knows," Killian said. He patted Miro's shoulder. "Wherever he is. But Beorn delegated, just like you're doing now."

Killian turned back to the tent's opening and poked his head out of the entrance. He spoke to someone outside. "Please fetch Marshal Scola, Marshal Corlin, Lady Amelia, and Lady Amber to the high lord's tent."

"How did you become such an expert?" Miro said when Killian returned.

"I had help," Killian said. "Rogan Jarvish. A big bureaucracy in Seranthia. Perhaps my mother, most of all."

"Killian?"

"Yes?"

"Thanks."

"None of us are perfect, Miro. It pays to remember that."

An hour later Miro left his tent, feeling something close to peace for the first time since Beorn's death. He wondered if holding onto the workload was his way of memorializing his former commander and friend. Even so, it felt good to let go.

The blue haze on the endless horizon made the plains appear to go on forever. There was perhaps an hour left of daylight, and Miro intended to return a favor with one in kind.

It couldn't hurt to have some fun along the way.

He weaved through the tents, and his men nodded to him as he greeted them by name. Leaving behind the green uniforms of the Alturans and the brown tabards of the Halrana, he finally found the significantly larger encampment of the Tingarans.

Compared to Miro's men, the legionnaires sparkled as fresh as warriors could be. They glanced up at Miro but took no special note of his appearance; he'd changed to simple clothing. Most of them hadn't yet fought, and though they were as tired as the rest, these men looked ready to do battle at a moment's notice. To a man they would be anxious to return to Tingara and defend their homeland against the horde. Miro empathized with them, and he would do his part. The Legion had come to support Altura, and Miro always repaid his debts.

As he approached the Imperial compound, guards stepped forward, but Miro held his ground, meeting their eyes until they finally realized who he was and drew back. He spotted a grander tent than the rest and found Killian sitting on a log with a nearly empty plate on his lap.

"Eating alone?" Miro said.

Killian chuckled as he looked up. "It's a nice change from the Imperial Palace."

"Finish up," said Miro. "Come with me."

Killian raised an eyebrow, but he set the plate down and followed Miro out of the camp. It took a long time before they exited the perimeter, curious glances following in their wake, but Miro didn't stop until he'd found a wide clearing beside a stream, a reasonable distance from the encampment.

Miro then turned to Killian and showed the emperor what he held in his hands: two wooden practice swords.

"You have the strength and the agility," Miro said. "You just need to know the movements."

"Sword practice?" Killian said. "I don't need . . ."

"Every man should know how to use a sword," Miro said. "You never know when lore will desert you. Trust me, I was in the lands across the sea with no zenblade or armorsilk, and without my training I would have died."

"Why so far from the men?"

"You don't want them to see you beaten, do you?" Miro grinned.

"So sure of yourself, aren't you?"

"You haven't seen me fight," Miro said.

He tossed one of the swords to Killian, who deftly snatched it out of the air.

"Let's start with a classic move: the feint and thrust. Let me see your stance."

Shaking his head, Killian formed an awkward fighting stance.

"Turn your body to the side; that way you present a smaller target," Miro said. "Good. Now keep your elbow bent and your arms limber. Watch my eyes and my feet above all; don't focus on my hands. With training, you'll block without thinking."

Miro leapt forward and smashed his wooden sword into Killian's exposed side. The almost indiscernible symbols on Killian's body lit up with fire in response to the blow. Killian made a clumsy attack, and Miro ducked under the outstretched arm to thrust again at Killian's chest, striking harder this time. Still, Killian didn't even grunt in pain.

"A challenge?" Miro said, lightly panting.

"I can't help it." Killian smiled and shrugged.

"Never fear. I always like a challenge."

Miro sped forward to launch a flurry of blows, finally angling his leg behind Killian's ankle and pushing Killian to fall flat on his back.

"You need to move faster," Miro said. "But to know how to move, you need to read your opponent. Let's go again."

Killian climbed back to his feet, his brow now wrinkled in frustration.

"Look how I'm holding my sword," Miro said. "Copy me. Yes, that's it. Now copy my posture. Stand more relaxed. Now, you try an attack."

Killian shuffled forward and made a cut at Miro's eyes. He suddenly stopped the blow and changed his attack, instead thrusting at Miro's chest.

"Good. Feint and thrust. Now let's try a riposte. Block my blow, and then thrust under my attack."

Miro cut overhead, and the two wooden swords clattered together. Killian nimbly cut underneath Miro's extended arm, sending a blow at Miro's abdomen.

Miro sucked in his stomach, drawing back before the blow could strike home.

"When the time comes to strike, don't hesitate. It's the most common mistake I see. You have the advantage, so seize it!" Miro tossed away his sword. "Let's see if you can strike me."

Killian grinned, his eyes glinting, and the emperor's training began.

46

As Ilathor recovered from his wounds, Jehral continued to deploy his own tactics against the enemy. He led sortie after sortie, and worried that when Ilathor's health returned, the kalif would once more lead wild charges. If Jehral's command would soon be taken away, he wanted this time to count.

He built deep traps and long ditches in the enemy's path and closed canyons with boulders. He diverted rivers to block their passage and built fires so they couldn't see in the smoke. For every real diversion, Jehral ensured there was a false one. Interspersed with every labor of effort, Jehral had the Hazaran elders create confusing illusions of cloud and fire.

Attacking the flanks, harassing the horde, Jehral slowed the enemy's progress to a crawl. Yet the distance to Seranthia shrank each day. The scouts said they were now just a week's travel from the city.

Giving half of his men some much-needed rest, Jehral now led a smaller group after discovering an opportunity to hunt down some stragglers. The scouts reported that a splintered force of revenants had vanished between two jagged hills.

As he passed under the heights, Jehral scanned the tops of the cliffs even as he kept his men in a careful skirmishing line. The crowded hills became a canyon, and Jehral cursed that he hadn't scouted more carefully. The past few victories had been easy.

He saw the trap too late.

Revenants sprang from the sides of the canyon and in a mass at the front, closing in on all sides. To continue forward would be to die.

The enemy commander was learning.

"Turn back!" Jehral cried. "Retreat!"

Wheeling his mount, Jehral turned his men back the way they'd come. Even as the horsemen spun around, revenants leapt forward to pull men from their horses, tearing into them with weapons and bare hands. Jehral charged into the encirclement, cutting into the enemy as he tried to break free of the ambush.

"To me!" he called.

Finally, Jehral broke free, but risking a glance over his shoulder he saw he'd left men behind, entangled with the enemy. Jehral cursed; there was nothing he could do to help them. He spurred his horse forward, hearing the thunder of hooves behind him as the survivors flocked to his call.

Then Jehral saw more of the enemy ahead, closing the canyon completely. A new force of revenants formed a solid wall, pikes bristling in front of them. Jehral tried to charge, but his horse shied away from the barrier.

The bristling wall of pikes moved forward inexorably.

Jehral's horse wheeled, spinning as the gelding tried to find a way out. Jehral struggled to take control of his mount as his desert warriors formed a cluster around him, all looking for escape. But there was none.

Behind Jehral, the enemy continued relentlessly down the canyon. In front of him the pikemen gathered momentum, trotting now in disciplined ranks. Jehral raised the glowing sword Ella had gifted him high above his head.

The pikemen broke around the cluster of Hazaran horsemen like water parting around a rock. As Jehral watched in stunned surprise, they continued their charge.

Jehral saw tall warriors with braids and gray tabards. Soft light glowed through their armor as they ran past, leaving Jehral and his men behind, smashing into the force charging down the canyon.

Jehral turned in wonder and watched as revenant fought revenant. Finally, there was a foe equal to the task, and the warriors in gray pushed relentlessly forward.

The enemy broke.

They turned and ran to draw away from the fight: the hunters had become the prey. The narrow canyon gave the pikes an unquestionable advantage, and the enemy retreated to save their force to fight another day.

"Jehral!"

A slim woman in green ran forward, and Jehral's eyes went wide with astonishment as he recognized Ella's pale blonde hair and green eyes. Only then did the pieces fit together as Jehral realized the Akari had come to his aid.

"Where is the kalif? Are you all right?" Ella asked.

Akari necromancers ran past and called their units back. The pikemen maintained their formation, but the enemy didn't charge again.

Jehral saw a huge man leading the Akari and recognized Dain Barden Mensk. He saw Shani standing nearby.

Jehral deactivated his scimitar, and his arms slumped at his sides.

——◆——

As the Akari bolstered the thinned numbers of the Hazarans, they all made camp in a naturally fortified position while their scouts kept a wary eye on the enemy.

Jehral told Ella about Ilathor's wounding, and Ella went to visit the kalif of House Hazara.

During the defense of Altura, Ella hadn't spoken with Ilathor, but she was now filled with fear. He was her friend, and she couldn't bear the thought of him being hurt. The guards stood aside to let her past, and Ella stepped tentatively into the tent.

Immediately, she felt relief when she saw that Ilathor was sitting up and his color was strong. Zohra, Jehral's sister, sat at the side of his pallet, a bowl of dried fruit in her hands.

"I came as soon as I heard," Ella said. "What happened?"

Ilathor smiled ruefully. "I got ahead of myself. I should listen to Jehral more."

"That's a good idea." Ella returned his smile.

"Zohra," Ilathor said, "could you please leave us?"

Scowling at Ella, the young Hazaran woman nodded and rose. She bent down and kissed Ilathor's forehead before leaving the tent.

"What was that about?" Ella said.

"Ella, please come and sit by my side."

Ella knelt in the place Zohra had vacated and took Ilathor's hand. "What is it?"

"There is something I need to speak with you about. It . . . it is hard for me to say."

Ella began to grow worried. "Your wound . . ."

Ilathor barked a laugh. "No, it is not about my wound, although nearly losing my life has brought some truths home to me. Truths I think I was reluctant to see."

"What are you saying?"

"I do not wish to bring you pain, but I am a plainly spoken man. Ella, I want to release you."

"Release me?"

"I wish to release you from any obligation you have to me. Zohra and I . . . love has blossomed between us. She is right for me—I know it in my heart. I am sorry. I will always care for you, and I will always be your friend. Even now, looking at you brings fire to my blood, but I now believe love between the two of us was never meant to be, much as it pains me to say it."

Ella looked down at the ground, breathing in and out as Ilathor anxiously waited to see her reaction, and then a slow smile spread across her face. Ella felt as if a great weight had been lifted from her shoulders. She squeezed the kalif's hand.

"Ilathor," she whispered, "I'm so happy for you."

"You are?" he said.

"I will always be your friend, and I'll never forget that you came to help my homeland in our time of need. There is no obligation between us, and I can see Zohra is right for you."

"I cannot tell you how much joy it brings me to hear you say that. You are not upset?"

"I'm happy," Ella said. She grinned. "Just tell her that she doesn't need to hate me."

Ilathor laughed, and then winced and clutched his chest. "I will tell her."

"Ella?" Shani poked her head into the tent. "The Dain wants to see you."

Ella stood and her hand fell out of Ilathor's.

She looked down at him fondly, and then she realized she and Ilathor were friends, and that was enough.

———◆———

"Ella," Dain Barden said without preamble, meeting her eyes, his expression grim. "Once, I gave you my help. Now I am asking for your help in return."

"I've tried," Ella said, guilt wracking her. "I'm no healer, nor am I an expert with revenants. I can't find out what ails your daughter and your necromancers."

"Then help us in another way. Many of our draugar are wounded and need tending. You know our lore, and we are now down to just a few necromancers: Aldrik, whom you know, and three others. Six more have died. I need you to go to Aldrik and offer your services."

Ella knew she was in Dain Barden's debt. He had allowed her to learn his people's lore, and now he needed her help. "Of course," she said.

"Good. I thank you. We need to regain our full strength if we're to help out here and hold for the emperor's arrival." The Dain summoned a guard. "Take the enchantress here to Aldrik. He knows her and is expecting her arrival. And Enchantress?"

"Yes?"

"Use that mind of yours. See if you can find the source of this illness, and stop it."

"I'll do my best," Ella promised.

The Akari guard led Ella to a large square tent, set aside from the rest. Entering, Ella walked past scores of slumped revenants, most standing, some prone on the ground. At the center of the tent, four gray-robed necromancers each hovered over an iron table. A fifth table was empty.

A revenant lay on its back on each of the tables. Each necromancer had a scrill in his hands and worked with concentration as he renewed the runes around the wounds, closing the deepest gashes, mending the broken bodies. Smoke sizzled up in thin plumes as they worked, and each necromancer kept his head tilted to the side. Their eyes were shadowed with exhaustion.

Aldrik, a plump necromancer and Ella's former teacher, looked up as Ella entered. "The Dain told me to expect you," he said. "Can you help?"

"What do you need me to do?"

He ceased working and carefully placed his scrill in a holder. "It's a simple task, but it is time-consuming, and there aren't enough of us to tend them all. Take a draug and lie it down on your bench. The deepest wounds break the matrices and prevent the lore from functioning, so the runes must be drawn over again. When you are finished with one, move onto the next. Any questions?"

"No," Ella said. "I understand."

She walked over to the clustered warriors—many of the revenants staggered as the lore struggled to keep them animated—and took a tall man by the hand, resisting the urge to cringe at the cold touch of his fingers. The huge warrior regarded her with a white-eyed stare but allowed her to guide him to the workbench.

"Lie on your back," Ella said.

The revenant complied, and Ella breathed a sigh of relief. She found a set of tools on a stand nearby, but she looked about for essence.

"Here," Aldrik said, coming forward to hand her a vial.

Ella ran her eyes over the warrior's body. His bleached leather armor was torn wide open, revealing a broad chest with a palm-sized hole at her heart. She could see where the matrices were broken, and without thinking too much about what she was doing, she took a scalpel and cut away the torn flesh before using needle and thread to sew the gash closed.

Ella then fitted gloves over her hands and dipped a scrill into the vial of essence. She held it in the bottle for a single breath and then withdrew the scrill and touched it to the flesh. Ella began to draw over the rune structures, fixing the lines, reconnecting the whorls and bridges. A hissing sound came from the tip of the scrill, and a thin stream of blue smoke rose into the air. Ella tilted her head as she worked, wrinkling her nose at the scent.

It smelled even worse than usual.

Ella put the thought out of her mind as she concentrated on the task at hand. She knew that every warrior she sent back to the field was a warrior who would challenge Sentar's minions.

Ella felt good to be working, the fear and sadness melting away as she concentrated. As she devoted all her effort to her task, Ella thought about the illness striking the Dain's necromancers. Her primary theory was that the rot in the bodies was causing those who spent the most time with the revenants to succumb to diseases lodging in the corpses. By working with the necromancers, Ella could discover if any of the revenants were especially putrid.

She examined the body she currently tended. It didn't seem any different from the revenants she'd seen before. Ella pondered. Surely the Akari were more experienced than she and knew what they were doing?

Aldrik came over to inspect Ella's work and then nodded. "Well done, Enchantress. Please, there are many more. If we work all night, they will be ready to fight on the morrow."

Ella nodded and found another broken body to mend.

47

The next morning, Ada, Dain Barden's eldest daughter, was dead. Unable to watch the red-eyed Dain standing over the body of his child, Ella left to find Aldrik.

She entered the square tent, now empty except for the plump necromancer, and surprised Aldrik as he tinkered with something near a workbench. He shot Ella a guilty glance as she saw him set down a vial of essence.

"The Dain's daughter is dead," Ella said.

"That's terrible news," Aldrik said. "I should go and offer my condolences."

He made to push past her, but Ella stopped him with a hand on the sleeve of his gray robe.

"What's killing your necromancers? Have you seen anything like this before?"

"No, Enchantress. Nothing like it."

He tried to get past her again, but once more Ella held him fast. "Hold on. What were you doing?" Ella asked curiously.

"Preparing for the next round of draugar to tend, Enchantress—nothing more."

"The essence you had in your hand," Ella said. "Can I see it?"

Aldrik barked a laugh. "What are you talking about? You are far from home, Ella, and this is my domain. Do not challenge me in my own place of work."

"Give it to me," Ella said.

"Why?"

"There's something going on here. Nothing in the bodies strikes me." Ella thought about the strange smell of the smoke when she'd been working the previous night. "It might have something to do with the essence."

Harrumphing, Aldrik walked back to the shelf and reluctantly handed Ella the vial. Ella removed the stopper and sniffed cautiously at the mouth of the bottle. Essence itself was odorless, but she could definitely smell something else.

"There, can I have it back, Enchantress? The essence is needed . . ."

Ella could read people, and Aldrik was definitely acting suspicious.

"I'm just going to take this to my friend Shani," Ella said.

Aldrik sighed. "Do what you will; it is none of my concern. Just bring it back."

Ella turned to depart, but the sound of movement made her look back over her shoulder.

Aldrik held a scalpel in his hand. He looked at Ella with wild eyes.

Ella backed slowly away. "Aldrik. What are you doing?"

"You should have kept your mouth shut," Aldrik spat. "You're dead, at any rate."

As Ella opened her mouth to cry out, the necromancer lunged at her. The scalpel cut at her neck, but Ella flinched and the blade only scraped against her enchantress's dress.

"Guards!" Ella cried out.

She dodged out of the way as Aldrik lunged at her unprotected face. Ella dashed to put an iron table between her and the necromancer.

Ella heard querying voices from outside.

An expression of panic crossed Aldrik's face. He looked around in desperation, and then his gaze settled on another vial of essence. He dropped the scalpel and picked up the bottle, removing the stopper, and Ella drew back, terrified of what he might do.

"What have you done?" she said.

"He made me," Aldrik whispered. "I am no traitor."

"Who made you? Please, Aldrik, just tell me what you did."

"The essence," Aldrik said. "It's tainted. You have to understand—I had to!"

"Why, Aldrik? What could make you do such a thing?"

"They took my sister!"

"Where is she? Stop this, Aldrik. I'll help you get her back."

"There's no getting her back. She's with him, now."

"There's always a way!" Ella cried.

"He said if I do this, he won't take her legs as well."

As Aldrik's words filled Ella with horror, she heard a noise, and two Akari warriors rushed into the tent. Ella saw the two men struggle to make sense of the scene.

Then Aldrik stood tall and looked at Ella sadly. He lifted up his hand.

"No!" Ella shouted.

Aldrik poured the contents of the vial over his head.

———◆———

After explaining Aldrik's betrayal to the Dain, Ella found Shani waiting outside the Dain's tent.

"There are terrible rumors going around. Ella, what happened?"

"It's over now," Ella said.

"Are you all right?"

"I'm fine. One of the Dain's necromancers somehow tainted the essence. The Dain thinks Renrik, a senior necromancer who used to be one of his closest advisors, is behind Aldrik's betrayal. Apparently, Aldrik's sister went missing not long before the Dain's army left Ku Kara. Aldrik had been acting strangely, but there are many reasons to act odd these days."

"Lord of Fire, what a mess."

Dain Barden strode out of his tent. "Enchantress, I've given this thought. We don't have the strength or the ability to fight a series of protracted battles. I've made a decision. We're going to draw them out and expend the last of our draugar to hold them as long as we can."

"Are you sure . . . ?"

"I'm sure," the Dain said, wiping a hand over his face. "I expected danger, but I should have expected betrayal. Now my daughter is dead."

"I'm sorry I couldn't do more."

Dain Barden composed himself. "Are you sure you are all right? I am sorry. I put you directly into harm's way."

"I'm fine," Ella repeated.

"That brings me some relief. Tell the kalif our plan, and take your friends to Seranthia. We'll hold them here."

After the Dain's pronouncement swarthy Hazarans scurried back and forth as the horsemen prepared to depart. Ilathor's men gathered the barest amount of supplies; they would leave their tents behind and make all speed to Seranthia.

As Ella collected her few possessions, Shani poked her head into the tent.

"Here," Shani said, handing Ella a metal plate with a piece of bread and a hunk of cheese. "Eat it—that's an order. It's probably the last food we'll get for a while."

Shani vanished again, and Ella gulped down the food as she packed to the noise of whinnying horses and shouting men.

The plate was soon empty, and Ella couldn't help but look at her reflection in the shining steel. Her face was grayed and drawn, her green eyes haggard. She was still shaken by the encounter with Aldrik and only now realized how close she'd come to being splashed with deadly essence.

She ran her fingers through her pale blonde hair, trying to untangle the mass of knots and restore some semblance of order.

Ella's heart gave a lurch as she looked at her hand. She'd torn free a clump of hair. The golden strands came out as easily as loose thread.

She remembered the scent of the essence as she'd drawn runes with the tainted liquid Aldrik had handed her, working for hour after hour, the smoke rising into her nostrils for an entire night.

Ella bowed her head, and as realization dawned, she dropped the plate in horror.

She remembered Ada's body at the end. Ada's hair was gone, and her face bore the marks of terrible pain. The Dain had spoken in desultory tones, explaining Ada's last moments to Ella, hoping the knowledge would help. He'd said Ada clutched at her stomach, screaming in pain as she coughed red blood.

None of the stricken had survived; even now only a few still lived, writhing in the makeshift infirmary, more of a place to die than anything else.

And now Ella had the taint herself.

48

As the summer sun cast shining rays on the hills surrounding the city of Seranthia, a long line of Hazaran warriors rode down the hills to the open gates. They'd slowed the enemy, but too many saddles were empty.

Ella glanced at Ilathor when she heard his voice. The kalif rode gingerly, and Ella knew bandages circled his chest under his desert garb, but he was leading his men once more.

"Close the gates!" Ilathor called as they rode in. The Hazarans took up the cry as they spurred forward.

The enemy could only be a few days behind them. Dain Barden of the Akari wouldn't hold them long.

Entering the city with a feeling of intense relief, riding with Shani by her side, Ella was surprised to see that all looked quiet in Seranthia. She'd seen so much blood and death that she wondered if she'd ever banish the terrible images from her vision.

Rider after rider passed through the gates, slowing as they began to move among the city folk. Ella glanced back over her shoulder as she heard a groaning sound, and when the last of Ilathor's men entered, she saw Seranthia's iron gates swing inexorably closed, smashing together with a mighty clang of metal on metal. It felt good to be inside the city, guarded by the Wall.

Seranthia's denizens rapidly cleared way for the riders, staring up at them with wide eyes. Ella turned to say something to Shani, when she felt a sudden pain in her stomach and clutched at her chest, a grimace spreading across her face. Her horse shied and whinnied before Ella once more got her mount under control.

"Ella?" Shani said, concern in her eyes.

Ella fought down the pain and smiled, taking her hand off her stomach. "I'm fine," she said.

"Are you sure?"

"Yes," Ella said, "I'm fine."

What had Sentar tainted the essence with? How did one set about altering essence in the first place? Ella knew that for all she'd learned, there was so much more to understand about the liquid.

She wondered how long she would last. She'd seen the terrible pain Ada had been in. Ella didn't want to spend her last moments like that.

"Let's get you to the palace," Shani said.

"And a hot meal." Ella smiled.

Shani fixed Ella with a penetrating stare. Ella knew her friend; she wasn't fooled.

The hooves of the horses clattered on the stones as they rode along wide streets and past narrow alleys, through the district of Fortune, until they reached the Grand Boulevard.

Ella held back the pain as she saw the towers of the Imperial Palace ahead.

"Ella?" a voice came from the other side of the door.

It was morning, and Ella gulped, forcing the bile back down into her stomach. She was sitting at a table, rummaging in her satchel, taking out scrills and lining them up on the wooden surface. She couldn't bear the thought of eating, and if someone was bringing food, she planned to send that person away. "Yes?"

Shani opened the door to the small bedchamber they'd given Ella in the palace, and glanced in. Her nose wrinkled as if she smelled something bad. "There's news."

"What is it?" Ella said.

"The Buchalanti scouts have sighted the enemy fleet. They're going to attack the city by both land and sea."

Ella glanced up. "How long?"

"Not long. I'm going up to the High Tower. Rogan's there and he wants to see you. Will you come?"

Ella took a deep breath and then nodded. "Of course," she said.

Shani filled her in with the details she'd gleaned from Rogan as they climbed up the stairs to the palace's higher levels.

There had been early skirmishing, out in the Tingaran Sea, and they'd already lost two storm riders, in return sinking a dozen enemy vessels. Sentar's tactics had changed from those employed at the free cities: rather than looking for a place to land, he was throwing his ships at any vessel coming close. His most powerful warships clustered around the center while the rest rushed ahead to do battle. Sentar was protecting his center; the sailmasters said that much was clear.

Ella and Shani reached the top of the High Tower, and Ella saw Rogan turn to greet her. His gray hair looked disheveled, but he'd lost none of his stature, and he looked leaner than ever. As Rogan said something in greeting, another spasm clutched Ella's chest with searing pain. Ella gave Rogan a halfhearted wave and moved to the rail, anxious to avoid his gaze.

Ella saw that with the naval battle expected to take place at any moment, dirigibles were being sent out to hover over the docks. The ships of the Imperial fleet clustered around the Sentinel while the graceful Buchalanti vessels sailed in circles on the flanks.

Then the distant horizon filled with ships, sails growing larger with every passing instant. Ella had only heard Miro's accounts of the titanic clash in the deep waters of the Great Western Ocean. Seeing the naval battle slowly unfold in this way was terrifying.

Ella sensed Shani and Rogan come to stand with her at the rail, and none of them spoke as they watched the armada approach. The island barring the harbor looked vulnerable; the Torak-built wall surrounding the statue suddenly wasn't enough. From this distance the sturdy ships of the Imperial fleet looked puny, and most of the Buchalanti vessels weren't much bigger.

The huge warships built in the lands across the ocean drew closer, and the defending vessels looked smaller still.

The city sounded the alarm as a dozen ships of the Imperial fleet and six Buchalanti vessels went out to meet them.

Ella almost couldn't watch.

Puffs of smoke rose up from the ships, and it soon became impossible to see through the thick clouds. Rogan passed Shani a Louan seeing device, but Ella declined.

The pain in her abdomen grew greater with every passing moment. Ella now leaned hard against the rail, a hand on her hip and another on the stone. Each puff of smoke and blast of cannon sent a wracking shiver through her stomach, clenching her bowels, blurring her vision.

More of her golden hair had fallen out in the morning. Soon she wouldn't be able to hide it. Ella felt fatigued in a way she never had before.

"Two Buchalanti ships are down," Rogan said. "There goes another."

The clouds of smoke now surrounded the tiny island, rising to cloak the walled statue. Now and then the wind tore holes in the clouds, and Ella saw big warships bearing down on the defending vessels, rows of cannon opening up fire in solid broadsides.

An enemy cruiser drew up between two Imperial ships, and then Ella flinched as a thudding boom resounded throughout the harbor. The cruiser exploded, vanishing in a single instant, becoming a boiling blur of flame and ash. Even as she struggled against the pain, Ella recognized the signature of black powder.

"He must have filled his ships with explosives," Ella murmured.

"He's sacrificing them. He doesn't care if he destroys his entire fleet," Rogan said.

"How can you stay so calm?" Shani said.

"Calm?" Rogan said. "I'm terrified."

Shani turned and then gasped. "Look," she said, pointing. "Back at the hills."

As she whirled to look back at the landward side of the city, Ella saw the revenant horde pouring down the slopes of the hills to surround the city.

The city now sounded the call to arms, a heavy deep blare that shook the ground and sent tremors through Ella's belly.

"We're now under siege," said Rogan.

"They're sending the dirigibles out to the harbor," Shani said.

Scores of floating wooden balloons glowed with shades of blue, emerald, and gold as they headed out from the docks in the direction of the Sentinel.

"I hope they can succeed where our navy can't," Rogan said.

Above the site of the naval battle, a speck rose from the smoke of war to fly high into the sky. The tiny figure hovered in the air, waiting as the dirigibles approached.

"It's him," Ella whispered.

She remembered witnessing the final battle between Evrin Evenstar and Sentar Scythran. The vision of Evrin screaming in pain as his flesh blackened was forever burned into her consciousness. Ella again felt the terror that had coursed through her as she'd watched black lightning pour from Sentar's hands. Her heart thudded in her chest as she recalled waiting for Evrin to surface. But he never did.

Ella suddenly grabbed the Louan spyglass from Rogan and trained it on the black figure.

"They need to pull back," Ella muttered.

The dirigibles were close now, drawing up to the heat of the battle. The figure in the sky slowly moved to meet them at their own height.

A jagged line of bright energy suddenly shot from the black figure to strike the foremost dirigible. The balloon flared up to meet the storm of fire, and for long seconds Ella held her breath as the lore of the Louans fought off the attack.

The dirigible exploded. Ella couldn't help but think of the pilot.

"Isn't there something we can do?" Shani whispered.

"Against that?" Rogan said as Sentar Scythran bathed the next dirigible in fire. The roar of the next explosion overshadowed even the blasts of the cannon below. Rogan glanced at Ella. "There's only one among us who can face him."

"And he left to rescue Altura," Ella said.

"He left for you," Rogan said, so low she could only just hear it.

The dirigibles at the rear now tried to turn back, and it became Sentar's turn to play hunter. He followed after them, as if gleeful, his awful power making one after the other burn in the sky, falling down to the sea in ash and fire.

Ella took the seeing device away from her eyes. She couldn't watch any more.

Smoke now enveloped the whole harbor, rising up high into the sky, clouding even the sun.

"I need to go," Ella said.

She turned and staggered as she walked, leaning against a stone column for support.

"Ella!" Shani said.

"I'm fine. Let me be!"

Ella pushed away from the column and descended down the steps, clutching the wall as pain wracked her senses, clawing at her abdomen, leaving Rogan and Shani watching her as she fled the destruction in the harbor.

------❖------

The human ships stubbornly resisted Sentar's encroachment, darting out of the way of his attacks and veering off to turn and fight again. He was losing ships too fast to count, and the humans had learned to be wary of the explosive devices stuffed into the hold of every one of his vessels, yet he knew it was just a matter of time until he achieved dominance of the harbor. Why fight the inevitable? Humans were nothing if not obstinate.

Sentar stood with legs apart, close to the prow of his cargo ship, the vessel that had to be protected at all costs. He frowned as a huge explosion nearby caused water to smash against the sides of his ship, splashing his face with cool seawater. That one was a touch close.

Sentar spread his arms at his sides and once more rose into the air, climbing the sky until he was again high above it all, with a view of the entire battle. He'd lost a multitude of warships, but what did it matter? He no longer cared whether Renrik and Gorain enjoyed success leading the attack on Seranthia's walls. His target was so close, he could reach out and touch it.

Looking ahead, Sentar saw with satisfaction that just one human ship remained. Even as he watched, one of Sentar's cruisers drew close to the glowing Buchalanti dreadnought, and the two vessels exchanged fire.

Foolish.

Sentar's cruiser exploded as her magazine detonated, destroying the last defender in the conflagration, and as the dreadnought sank below the waves, the harbor was now his.

Sentar's ships drew forward to surround the tiny island. The humans had walled the Sentinel, but against his power and his cannon, the wall wouldn't last long, even enhanced as it was with the lore of these so-called builders of Torakon.

Sentar Scythran could now take his time.

He would order every cannon trained on the wall around the statue. If any more ships came, his warships would blow them out of the water. If more dirigibles came to bomb him, he would roast their crews alive.

Night would fall soon, but the bombardment would go on.

The Evermen would soon be home.

49

Ella's chamber in the Imperial Palace contained a soft bed, but Ella didn't sleep that night, and she doubted few of Seranthia's inhabitants caught their night's rest. Their city was doomed: revenants now occupied the land around Seranthia unchallenged, and the Imperial fleet guarding the harbor had been utterly destroyed. The Buchalanti storm riders, blue cruisers, and dreadnoughts were all gone. The Tingarans had seen many of their dirigibles burned out of the skies and were now saving the remainder for the Wall. Throughout the night bodies from the naval battle washed up to the docks, nudging against the wooden pilings as if trying to garner attention.

Nevertheless, she readied herself in the morning, washing her face, neck and hands, settling her green enchantress's dress over her body, looking at her face in the mirror and staring back into her own eyes.

Ella brushed her hair, and still more of the pale golden strands came out with her comb. Her bones ached. The pains in her stomach now struck her with agonizing regularity.

There was a knock at the door.

Without waiting for her answer, the door opened and Rogan Jarvish stepped into the room. Not for the first time, Ella felt sad to see him as an old man. Lines of care wrinkled his face; his hair was entirely gray; and his scars had faded to become part of his skin. Ella's eyebrows rose when she saw he wore his armorsilk.

"You might be able to fool others, Ella, but you can't fool me," Rogan said. "What's wrong?"

Ella stood and made to leave the room. "I'm going to go and do what I can . . ."

"Tell me," Rogan said, taking hold of her shoulders. "You asked Alise for essence. What do you intend? Is it something to do with being unwell? Shani thinks you're hiding something. She told me there was a terrible sickness moving through the Akari necromancers."

Ella looked up at Rogan; he was as tall as Miro and loomed over her. "I have to do something. I have a greater chance of success working alone," she said.

"Do what?" Rogan demanded. He didn't let go of her shoulders. Ella could have sent a shock through her dress to burn his hands, but the last thing she wanted to do was hurt him.

Ella met his gaze. "We've all seen it. There's a cargo ship Sentar is protecting. It's undoubtedly where he has the essence he needs to open the portal. We need to sink that ship."

"And how do you plan to do that?"

"With every bit of skill I possess," Ella said simply.

"Alone? Ella, what will I tell your brother if you fail? Which you will."

"I have to try," Ella said. "I've been watching the Sentinel. He's already uncovered the top of the statue. I have to destroy his essence."

"I can't let you do it," Rogan said.

"Rogan," Ella hesitated briefly, but she decided to tell him. "I'm dying."

"What?" Rogan gasped. His hands fell from her shoulders.

"I'm dying. Shani was right. I've been . . . tainted. I saw what it does. Already it's a struggle to stand straight and speak to you. In a few days," Ella said, "I'll be dead."

"You don't know that . . ."

"I know! I'm no fool. I'm not lying to you."

Rogan circled the room and sat heavily on the bed. "Who else knows?"

"No one. And I want it to stay that way."

"What do you propose to do?"

"I'm going to sink that ship."

"There could be a cure . . ."

"There's no cure," Ella said. "Or if there is, Sentar Scythran is the only one who knows of it. We don't understand essence. None of us do—not the templars and not the loremasters. No one can fix this."

"You never know—"

"I'm going to do this. You can't stop me."

Rogan nodded, his mouth moving without speaking, and Ella was surprised to see tears at the corners of his eyes.

"Do you want to see Shani? She's helping out on the Wall, along with the other elementalists."

"No," Ella said. "She's needed there. Please don't tell her."

Rogan nodded, and for a time there was silence.

"May the Lord of the Sky go with you," he finally said.

"Thank you," Ella said. "He will."

⁂

Ella was fully aware that with every passing moment more of the wall around the Sentinel was being destroyed, more of the statue revealed; yet she also knew that she stood a much greater chance of success in the night.

She spent the day alone in her rooms, creating the lore she would need for when darkness came.

In the early afternoon there was a soft knock at her door, and when she opened it Ella found a paper packet on the threshold.

Opening the packet Ella found willow bark, sable root, and blue pine powder. Even as she looked down at the sedatives—no doubt from Rogan—pain trembled its way through Ella's body, but she couldn't afford to have her reflexes slowed, not now.

It was a sweet gesture, but Ella put the medicinal herbs to the side. Instead, she fought the pain, her forehead creased in concentration as she spent the day renewing her wand and working on the items she would need, lore she'd never tried before.

When she was done, Ella examined her work.

She held her two silver slippers in her hands, items that would help her when night came. Ella ran her eyes over the symbols she'd drawn throughout the day, checking the matrices, the activation rune, the whorls and bridges. She turned the slippers over to check the soles, muttering to herself as she rehearsed her plan in her mind.

She'd never tried anything like this before, but she'd never been this desperate.

Ella put the slippers on her feet and took a shaky breath as she looked at the vial of essence Lady Alise had procured for her, essence that smelled the way it should. Her set of scrills sat in a row beside the vial, and next to the scrills were her protective gloves. She could always do more, but Ella couldn't wait. Every passing moment sent more pain wracking her body and revealed more of the Sentinel to the world.

She didn't plan to throw her life away, and she would do her utmost to escape unscathed, but at least her illness gave her the courage and determination to see the task through.

Looking out the small window, Ella saw that it was night.

She left the palace before her courage deserted her.

The staccato thumps of the cannon resounded like rumbles of thunder, rolling into the city from the harbor. Wearing her hooded enchantress's dress and silver slippers, Ella quietly exited the Imperial Palace, careful to stay out of the way of the officials dashing to and fro. She passed through the great hall and out of the main entrance, the guards nodding and making way for her as she exited through the barred iron gates.

Ella walked through Imperial Square as clouds flitted overhead, dark storm clouds that echoed the mood in the city.

As she headed down to the harbor, it began to rain.

Ella lifted the hood over her head and heard the patter of droplets on the streets, soon sounding in splashes as the rain formed puddles. Ella thanked the heavens, feeling determination in every fiber of her being. The rain was a blessing, for together with the darkness it would help hide her from her enemies.

Reaching the docks, Ella saw soldiers and civilians alike clustered around the wharves, taverns, and shipyards. To a man they stared out at the harbor, huddled under the eaves of the buildings as they flinched with every boom of the cannon. Flashes of light flickered again and again. A gush of bright energy lit up the far side of the harbor, followed by a shattering crash. In the sudden glow, Ella saw the statue revealed along with the wreckage of stone blocks falling outward.

She hoped Sentar would use all of his power to destroy the wall. She hoped he would be distracted enough for her plan to work.

Ella walked as far along a pier as she could, until she stood at the water's edge. The heavy rain bounced off her, splashing into the waters of the harbor with a steady tinkle. The plumes of flame at the mouths of the warships' cannon regularly lit up her destination.

For what she planned, conditions were perfect.

Ella looked down at her feet. She called out an activation sequence. *"Arias-lutanas!"*

The silver slippers flared up, a fiery glow traveling from each symbol to the next faster than the eye could follow. The runes shone with blue and green, so bright it hurt Ella's eyes to look at them, and even against the falling rain, the shine would be visible at Ella's destination.

"Arias-lutanari!"

The next sequence dimmed the runes, sending the light into itself, until the slippers only glowed softly green-silver, like phosphorescence glistening on the waves of the open sea.

Ella took a deep breath, feeling her heart race. She prayed her plan would work. She'd performed some successful tests in the washbasin. The sea should be the same, shouldn't it?

Ella sat down on the pier, her legs dangling, and raised her left foot out over the water. She placed her foot onto the glistening surface.

Her left leg wobbled as the cushion of air under the slipper slid on the water. Still sitting on the pier, and realizing there was only one way to find out if she'd been successful, Ella placed the other foot onto the water. She pushed down tentatively with her right leg, noting with some relief that the platform of air was evidently big enough to support her weight.

Ella pushed off the dock, and then she was standing on the water.

She nearly lost her balance and fought the urge to sit back on the pier. Seeing the destruction of the wall around the Sentinel brought home the urgency of her task, and when she considered her fear, combined with her pain, she knew that to back down now would be to fail.

Ella lifted her left leg and took a step forward. She took a second step, and she realized that it was easier to maintain her balance if she kept moving. Ella then made a dozen steps, resisting the urge to look back until she'd walked far enough over the water that she knew she wouldn't turn back, and then she glanced over her shoulder.

Onlookers stood on the pier, watching her in amazement, completely ignoring the rain. A man raised a hand in front of him, as if in greeting or farewell, and the others followed suit.

Ella turned her attention back to her destination, and then she began to think about her dress.

It was a dark night, and the rain helped, but the green silk would still shine in any light, particularly when Ella drew close to the flickering destruction in the area around the Sentinel.

Ella started to chant, pouring all of her concentration into the constant hum of activation sequences she'd built into her enchantress's dress. She didn't concern herself with protection or heat. Ella wanted to become invisible.

She wore black gloves on her hands and had pulled her hood to hang low over her face. Each step took her closer to the flashes of fire, and she now saw the scattering sparks as the lore of the builders fought both the force of black powder and the energetic onslaught of the Lord of the Night's power.

Ella glanced down at her sleeves as she walked across the water, developing a comfortable rhythm of splashing steps and chanted runes. She was satisfied; she could see through the sleeves to the dark water below.

Real thunder sounded overhead, barely able to be heard over the shattering sounds of energy unleashed, and the rain picked up strength. Ella now felt each tap against her back with force, feeling her shoulders bow down under the weight of rain and the agony of pain in her body. But she was grateful for the storm, for it hid the imprints of her footsteps in the water. A clear night would have meant discovery.

The hulking vessels grew larger with each step, and Ella's blood pounded in her ears with a steady staccato. The words came from her lips between gasps as her stomach clenched, this time with excruciating force, but she couldn't stop her chant or she would be seen. Ella thought about the bodies of the sailors washed up to the docks. She remembered Evrin's battle against Sentar Scythran. She again saw the devastation of Shar.

She filled her mind with these thoughts; they were all that gave her the strength to go on.

Ella skirted around a huge Veldrin warship, fear momentarily cutting through her constant chant, but she gathered renewed strength as her training and experience reasserted itself. Black figures scurried on the decks, and the vessel quivered with each broadside of the rows of cannon. As she rounded the ship, Ella saw the crumbling wall around the Sentinel, with bits of stone fragmented all around the perimeter of the island. She looked for Sentar Scythran but couldn't see him.

An inner ring of warships clustered around a central vessel. These ships had been left out of the fight, their purpose to instead provide protection to the center of the circle. Ella made each step carefully now, though the slower speed made it harder for her to keep her balance.

Looking down, she saw that the phosphorescent glow of the symbols on her slippers had dimmed. It was impossible for Ella to know whether her lore would last; she could only hope.

The figures on these ships didn't scurry; they stood and watched, peering out at the night. Ella spotted necromancers in gray robes and revenants standing guard. As she passed under the side of a warship, she glanced up and saw the white face of a peering man as he scanned the sea.

He looked down, and Ella stopped moving, reducing her chant to a whisper.

The muscles in her legs ached with raw pain; first her left leg and then her right began to tremble.

If she fell, she would sink. They would see her splash, and she would fail.

Ella's left leg gave way as she slipped.

50

At the same time that Ella slipped, a greater explosion than any before split the air, filling the air with thunder, and Ella heard a huge crash. The peering necromancer turned to look at the Sentinel, and Ella scrabbled and splashed at the water, finally righting herself.

Not looking to see whether she'd been spotted, she sped forward, passing under the warship's prow and beyond before a chill struck her.

She'd forgotten to continue chanting. She was in the open, able to be seen with the most casual of glances.

Her heart hammering, Ella looked at the bright green sleeve of her dress in horror. The constant fire and resulting sparks on the walls shone from the glistening silk.

Ella calmed herself and started again. She forced down the ache in her limbs and the clutching pain in her belly. She fought the fatigue and the pounding headache in her temples that was even now shifting to the front of her head.

Ella gasped the runes in between breaths of air. She was between the protective circle and the hulk of the cargo ship in the center. She couldn't stop now; she had to go on.

She reached the side of the cargo ship, wheezing, but she never stopped her constant chanting, and with a surge of relief, Ella realized she'd made it.

She tilted her head back, looking up to the ship's rail, scanning for a way to climb up.

As she peered up from under her hood, Ella caught the gaze of a pale-skinned man with gray robes and a hooked nose.

The necromancer's eyes widened with surprise as their eyes met. He opened his mouth to call out, and Ella's hand darted into the pocket of her dress.

She moved faster than she'd ever had to before, pointed her wand, and interspersed a single word into her chant. Ella released a bolt of golden energy into the air, directly into the necromancer's mouth.

He cried out and fell forward, tumbling through the air to hit the water with a splash, only a few paces to Ella's left. Against the roar of the cannon and the shatter of stone, the sound might have been lost, but the attack on the wall around the Sentinel was a mixed blessing, for though it drowned out sound, it provided light.

Ella didn't wait to find out.

She swiftly scanned the side of the cargo ship. Lord of the Sky, it was massive. Ella saw matrices of runes covering the beams on the sides, with not a single part of the surface left bare. The protective symbols gave Ella confidence. Sentar had expended a great deal of precious essence to give this ship the strength to endure cannon fire and the blasts of prismatic orbs.

She'd come to the right place.

Starting to wobble, Ella picked up pace once more, skirting the side of the ship as she tried to find a way up. As she sped along the huge vessel, Ella finally spotted a rope hanging down to the water. She ran now, each footstep sinking into the water. She saw that each splash her slipper made sank deeper than the one before it. The power was leaving the runes.

As she approached the rope, her footsteps were sinking several inches. She had to jump for the thick hemp and grab hold, just as she looked down and saw the runes she'd drawn on the slippers fade altogether.

Ella didn't wonder how she'd get back to Seranthia. She was going to die anyway. The important thing was to complete her objective.

She was forced to abandon her chanting as she climbed the rope, pulling her body up with arms already weak. She groaned in agony, each exertion a supreme effort of will. The next moments passed in a blur as she reduced her concentration to this one task. She forgot about the fact that she would be visible once more, and about her own danger, even her fear.

Ella had to make it on board Sentar Scythran's cargo ship.

She finally clutched onto the rail, grabbing hold with her other arm now, and threw her body over the edge to tumble down onto the deck.

Something heavy and metallic smashed down onto her enchantress's dress, sending a fountain of sparks flying in all directions. Ella rolled onto her back and looked up into the white-eyed stare of a revenant. He was a tall barbarian, holding a double-bladed axe, with a horned helmet and ragged furs on his torso.

"*Sahn!*" Ella called forth a bolt of energy from her wand. Her aim was awkward, but the yellow beam of light tore a head-sized hole in the revenant's chest. The creature moaned and then fell.

Ella climbed to her feet and once more activated her dress's shadow ability, chanting as she scanned the decks, looking for a hatch—anything that would lead her down into the vessel's belly.

She heard shouts and cries but ignored them, ignoring even the shadowed figures dotting the deck as she spotted a closed hatch.

Ella sped to the hatch and yanked it hard.

It was locked.

She raised her wand and the metal lock vanished in a glow of fierce yellow light. Ella heaved again, and the hatch burst open. She threw herself down the opening, grabbing hold of the ladder at the last instant and narrowly avoiding a broken leg as she fell sprawling onto the deck below.

Essence. Ella had to find the essence.

There were barrels everywhere, all sealed tight with a metal clasp. Ella fumbled at a latch and opened the top of a barrel.

Black liquid greeted her. She sniffed, and it was odorless, the way essence was supposed to smell.

Ella reached into the pocket of her dress and pulled out the destructive cube. She hesitated. The cargo ship was huge, and she had to be sure of success.

Ella left the barrels and found another hatchway leading down into the bowels of the cargo ship. As she descended she saw more barrels, stuffed into every crevice and filling every compartment.

Deeper. She still needed to be deeper. Gasping and panting, she ran along the corridors, heedless of the shouts she heard back the way she'd come, forced to sacrifice the shadow ability of her dress as her breath ran ragged.

Ella hauled open yet another hatchway, and then she was in the great hold. The entire length of the ship was filled with barrels, piled high, one on top of the other.

"*Lot-har,*" Ella said, activating the cube and throwing it down in the vessel's lowest point.

Ella began to count to ten.

One.

She climbed back up to the next deck above, tripping over the edge of the hatch in her haste. Ella sped along the corridors looking for the way up.

Two.

Ella wondered if she was lost; she'd been so consumed with finding the hold that she hadn't been paying attention.

Three.

She finally found the next ladder and began to climb up, but fell away as a snarling face and white eyes peered down. A series of bolts from her wand flew into the creature's head and torso, and it fell down the ladder to crumple at its base.

Four.

Ella's heart raced and her blood roared in her ears as she ignored the fallen revenant and climbed the rungs, muscles burning as she raced up to the next deck. She smelled sea air and the burned tang of black powder. The last exit to the open deck wasn't far.

Five.

Pain clutched at her stomach, overriding all thoughts of counting, consuming her consciousness as a thousand needles pierced every part of her body. She screamed against the agony and fought it down, running for the ladder to the open deck and climbing, feeling cool air against her skin.

Ella sent a series of bolts from her wand through the hatch, heedless of how much she drained the wand. She rolled out onto the open deck and crouched as she took stock, knowing she had to get far from the cargo ship as quickly as possible. How much time had passed? The danger wasn't the detonation of the cube, as powerful as it was. The danger was in the essence itself. It would spill into the water, and though it would merge with the sea, anyone caught in the thick black liquid would die.

As Ella scanned the ship, looking for the fastest route to the side, her gaze flickered to the Sentinel. The wall was gone. The statue was exposed.

A black figure landed on the deck beside her.

Light suddenly bathed the ship, revealing the scene, and Ella saw a bright sphere rise from an outstretched hand.

For the first time, Ella met the ice-blue stare of the Lord of the Night. She couldn't look away from his eyes; he didn't scowl or glower, but simply looked at her with a dead gaze that made her feel insignificant. His blood-red hair was slicked back to his head, and faint silver swirls of runes decorated his hands, face, and neck. He was as tall as Killian, which meant he looked down his nose at Ella, and though his shoulders were broad, he was slim rather than muscular.

"I know you. Ella, you must be," he murmured. "Ella of Altura, sister of Miro. Tell me, Ella, what are you doing on my ship?" Sentar's eyes narrowed. "What have you done?"

Ella opened her mouth to speak her defiance or to activate the blinding power of her dress.

Ten.

The ship blew apart underneath their feet. Decks heaved upward with titanic force as the cube fed on the essence around it, adding to its destructive power. The explosion wracked the vessel, shattering the timbers, launching Ella and Sentar upward.

But the Lord of the Night wasn't finished with her.

Even as the deck heaved, Ella felt a hand go around her neck, taking hold of her throat, robbing her of breath. The detonation of the cargo ship filled the sky with a cloud of smoke and flame, but Ella felt herself lifted higher still, and she realized her eyes were closed and opened them.

If Sentar Scythran's face had been expressionless, it was now twisted with rage. He clutched Ella's neck and rose high into the sky, above the circle of destruction, as high as the clouds and still ascending.

Ella saw him look down at what had once been his cargo ship, filled with the essence he needed to bring his brothers home. The power of the explosion surprised even Ella. Only beams of blackened timber would be left, for now it was all flame and destruction. Sentar screamed in rage and glared at Ella as he took them up while she gasped and choked, her lungs starved for air.

The city of Seranthia became a small circle of glowing lights, and still Sentar climbed higher, dangling Ella in his grip while her legs twitched and her feet scrabbled at nothing. Finally, just above the shifting clouds, he stopped. Even the harbor was now an expanse of black, ships indistinguishable, only the occasional tiny flash indicating the cannon blasts.

They were so high that wind tore at Ella's hair.

"You've just delayed the inevitable," Sentar spat. "Nothing will stop me from crushing your race, and everyone you hold dear will feed my vats. I will once again get the essence I need, and it will be bought with the blood of all those humans seething in the city below. You think you've dealt me a blow? Then think again. Before I release you, I want to hear you beg for your life."

The grip on Ella's throat relaxed slightly. Ella gasped in a breath of air, filling her lungs as her chest heaved.

Ella met Sentar's dead eyes with her own stare. "We'll stop you," she said. She looked down from the height. She was dead anyway. "Let me go."

"With pleasure," Sentar Scythran said.

He released his hand from Ella's neck, and she fell.

Ella's limbs twisted, clawing at the air as she rolled over and over, plummeting through the sky.

The great fall happened in heartbeats. Ella's life flashed in front of her eyes. She saw the face of Brandon Goodwin, then Lady Katherine, and then her brother's awkward movements from the bruises he'd taken at the Pens. Ilathor's face swam in front of her, and Shani's, and she remembered the mad charge into Tlaxor, capital of Petrya. The devastated world of Shar was more of a blur than a memory, but one face came to dominate her vision, clear above all. Ella saw Killian.

As the water came up to meet her Ella gasped a series of activation sequences. Her dress hardened around her, and rather than fiery heat, she projected a cushion of air.

Ella smashed into the water, directly in the midst of the cargo ship's remains.

She immediately sank, her speed so great that even the pocket of air couldn't prevent her plunging deep into the sea. Something inside her body broke with a crack.

Ella's eyes shot open with the pain. Her vision became a series of flickering images. The light cast by the shining runes of her dress revealed the murky sea. Wooden beams and bits of metal and rope drifted downward. Sinking barrels were everywhere, many of them intact.

Many weren't.

Black liquid clouded the depths, the essence meeting the salted seawater and rushing past in the swirls and currents.

In the midst of it all, Ella felt her vision close in, and she fell into darkness.

51

The army rushing through Tingara's west passed tall, three-legged towers glowing with purple light, and though the single color didn't offer any information, it told every soldier that Seranthia was under attack. It gave them hope that the city still held.

Then, still a week from Seranthia, the allied army came across a battlefield. This was a place where the dead had fought the dead, and with only broken revenants filling the landscape, even Miro had never seen anything like it. As the creatures hacked at each other, trying to destroy their foes by decapitation or loss of limb, the result was a horror Miro hoped never to see again.

No one wanted to linger, and Miro and Killian kept the slower men moving as they looked for survivors and put down any still twitching.

Miro scanned the endless field of corpses and tried to make sense of what had happened.

"The Akari made a stand here," he said to Killian. "You can see over there where they fought in a circle that grew ever tighter as their numbers were thinned. They fought to the end. Needless to say, the Akari did not emerge victorious."

"So the revenants of the Akari are gone, all of them." Killian said as he scanned the battlefield. "Come on—there's nothing to see here. We should catch up to the men."

Miro nodded and opened his mouth to call his personal guard away from the bodies, when he saw a commotion in the distance. A couple of Tingaran legionnaires crouched at the center of a circle of dead Akari warriors, waving their arms to attract attention.

Miro and Killian exchanged glances.

As the two men stepped around the mangled bodies, the corpses became so thick Miro was forced to step on the occasional arm or torso. Finally, the legionnaires made way, and Miro saw a warrior in armor of bleached leather being helped to his feet.

Miro eyes widened as he recognized the huge man, close to seven feet tall, with long white hair and silver thread woven through his forked beard. His eyes were closed, but he stood, and his breathing was strong and even. Blood welled from several places on his chest.

"It's the Dain," Miro said.

"Quick, fetch a stretcher!" Killian called.

"I don't need a stretcher," the Dain growled, opening his eyes.

"Don't be a fool," Miro said.

"No!" the Dain said. "I can walk on my own two feet." The Dain wobbled, but he drew in a deep breath and straightened. "I'm fine."

"Dain," Killian said. "We're marching hard, and you need attention. I'm ordering you to get seen to."

"No one gives me orders, lad," the Dain said. "My apologies," he corrected, putting a hand to his temple, "Emperor."

Even among all the carnage, Miro smiled and shook his head. "He's a tough one," he said.

Killian's lips twitched. "Dain, we're marching for Seranthia at best speed. If you can keep up, you're welcome to join us. First, however, you're going to get those wounds looked at. Then you can tell us what happened here."

"All right, lad," Dain Barden said.

"Emperor." Miro coughed.

"All right, Emperor," the Dain of the Akari muttered.

—◆—

The ground-eating pace continued as the army of soldiers from across the Empire put their heads down and marched. The long column wound over the dusty plain, flies buzzing at the corners of eyes and vermin-ridden food eaten while walking. Those in front were lucky, but the men behind choked on the dust raised by the boot heels of their fellows. Soldiers remarked that they'd never seen so much dust in Tingara. It was proving to be one of the hottest summers in memory.

Against all admonishment, Dain Barden Mensk marched with them, grumbling and fending off men with bandages and needles even as Killian instructed the best of their healers to give him care. Miro didn't know whether to be surprised to see the Dain actually manage to keep up.

True to Killian's words, they didn't sacrifice the speed of their march. The men were down to four hours' sleep, walking in a long column from before dawn until the middle of the night.

It was morning, and Miro was at the head of the column, walking by the emperor's side, when the first scouts returned from Seranthia.

"What news?" Killian demanded.

"Emperor, the city is surrounded and under siege."

"The enemy—how many are there?" Miro asked.

Dain Barden had said their numbers were almost beyond counting, but Miro prayed some might have fallen to the heat.

"It's hard to say," the scout reported. "There are two forces: one larger force assaulting the Wall with ladders, and a second infantry square formed up in ranks outside the gates. Those assaulting the Wall are impossible to count. We've estimated the numbers of the infantry square at the gates . . . perhaps ten thousand."

Miro muttered to Killian. "Even that's too many."

"We've sent men to check on the harbor, but we can assume the fleet is defeated, with Seranthia under attack on all sides. They're smashing the gates with battering rams, and they're scaling the Wall. The defenders are barely holding on."

"Will we make it in time?" a new voice spoke. Turning, Miro saw Dain Barden come up to meet them, a two-headed war hammer at his belt. The huge leader of the Akari's face was pale, but he stood tall.

Killian nodded to the scout.

The scout hesitated. "There's no way to tell. If it weren't for the mortars and dirigibles, the city would have already fallen. I saw several breaches along the Wall only barely reformed. There are Petryan elementalists on the ramparts supporting the Legion, but the defenders won't hold out long."

"We need to push on," Killian said. He looked back at the long column of soldiers, stretching behind to the distant hills. "Double time!" he called.

A horn blared, two sharp successive notes, and the army picked up pace, the sound of clomping boots filling the air.

"Dain," Miro said, "are you sure you can still keep up with us?"

"I'll crawl if I have to," Barden said. "There's one among the enemy. I saw him across the battlefield, and I mean to see him dead. Renrik, his name is, and he was once one of my inner council, the most senior of my necromancers. He's to blame for the death of my eldest daughter."

Killian fixed his gaze firmly ahead, and even he began to pant at the wearying pace. He spoke to the Dain without turning. "You didn't mention this before. What happened?"

Dain Barden wiped sweat from his forehead. "Not much to tell. There was a betrayal, and I lost my daughter as well as nearly all my necromancers. Your sister uncovered it, High Lord. The enchantress said our essence was tainted."

"Ella?" Killian's eyebrows went up.

"Yes. At any rate, short of necromancers, we were forced to make our stand. I sent the Hazarans ahead, and Ella went with them."

Miro glanced at Killian and could almost see the thoughts crossing his face. Ella's path had once more crossed Ilathor's.

"Did any of your people make it out?" Miro asked.

"I sent our living home, but I stayed. A few of my necromancers stayed with me. They're all dead."

"Is there anything else you can tell us?" Killian said.

"I fought one of them, a strange one. This warrior was unlike any draug I've seen. He had his own set of followers, all wearing checkered black and white, and on his head was a bizarre hat with three corners and a black feather. I've never faced an opponent of his caliber, and I never wish to again."

"Miro?" Killian said.

Miro was pensive for a moment before answering. "He is the last of three kings, renegade rulers from across the sea. Sentar himself brought them back to the world of the living."

Killian's eyebrows went up. "How do you know this?"

"We captured one of the enemy necromancers off Castlemere. I lost a friend, Deniz, as well as one of my best bladesingers to the first of them, but they killed him. The second bested me on the retreat to Sarostar."

"He bested . . . you?"

"Only the fact that Bartolo came to my rescue enabled us to defeat him. This last revenant, this . . . king . . . his eyes will be filled with blood."

"That's right," the Dain said, nodding.

"He behaves like a man—plans strategies and gives orders. He remembers all the swordsmanship he learned in life, but his abilities are now supplemented by incredible speed and the ability to go on when a living man would fall."

"Who is he?"

"Deniz said his name is Gorain."

They marched in silence, each man thinking his own thoughts, concentrating on the sapping energy of the frantic pace. The army now wound along a well-maintained paved road, and Miro began to see familiar features. The soldiers kept up the burning intensity of the march, hour after hour.

And then a scout came running. "The city lies ahead!"

The column stopped.

Immediately, they heard cries and screams, thudding booms, and crashing stone.

"Call up the command!" Killian directed.

Soon a circle of nobles and officers stood around Miro, Killian, and the Dain. Miro nodded to the Alturan commanders, Lord Marshal Scola and Marshal Corlin. Tiesto was there, along with two Halrana commanders. High Lord Grigori stood with a Veznan marshal in an orange uniform. Touana of Loua Louna looked from one face to the next. Miro saw Bartolo standing with Amber a short distance away.

"I brought you all here to make our final plan," Killian said. "Right now, as we speak, Seranthia is under siege. We must make all haste to break the siege. If we can combine our attack with a sortie from the city, we stand a much greater chance of success."

Miro looked on in wonder as Killian spoke. He'd come to know the young emperor on the long journey from Altura, and a friendship

had developed between them, but he'd never seen the emperor—
only the man. Killian had almost seemed too . . . gregarious . . . to
lead the harsh land of Tingara and the fractious new Empire.

Miro realized he'd been wrong in his estimation. Where this
man led, people would follow.

"We know that inside the city are the Hazarans and our legionnaires. We have avengers and meldings and Louan dirigibles, both
here and in Seranthia. If we time it right, we can still scourge this
darkness from the Empire. Our swords must be sharp, but our wits
must be sharper, for the enemy is at the gates, and they're climbing
the Wall . . ."

Sharp swords. The Wall.

Miro had an idea.

"Emperor," Miro said. All eyes were suddenly on him. Miro
gulped. Part of him thought it was a mad plan, but even as he ran
it through in his mind one more time, he decided to get Killian's
opinion. "Can I speak with you for a moment?"

Killian frowned, but he nodded, and Miro peeled away from
the group to walk to a cleared patch of dirt where they wouldn't be
heard. Miro crouched on the ground and waited.

"Well?" Killian said, squatting beside him. "What is it?"

Miro reached over his shoulder and drew his zenblade. The
steel made a whispering sound as it came out, and Miro laid its
length on the ground in front of him. He was a tall man and wore
the zenblade on his back. It was long, and its entire surface was
inscribed with arcane symbols. The zenblade was a work of beauty,
a thing of terrible power.

"Ella made this zenblade," Miro said. "It's the most powerful
ever created."

Killian glanced down at the huge sword. "I can imagine that."

"As I understand it, we have two problems to deal with.
One is the mass of revenants formed along the base of the

Wall, forcing their way up with ladders. The scouts tell us they're disorganized revenants, but they'll soon open a breach nonetheless. The other is the infantry square outside the gates, the more disciplined of the two forces, led by Gorain. I have an idea, a way we might be able to neutralize one of those problems, but at a cost."

"Let's hear it."

"You're going to think it's crazy, and it will need your help, but hear me out."

"Miro, just tell me."

Miro took a deep breath.

He told him.

Killian shook his head as the two men rose to walk back to the circle of commanders, but he'd agreed to Miro's proposal. Miro wasn't sure who was crazier—Miro for suggesting the idea or Killian for going along with it. He only hoped it would work.

"You know this plan leaves the army without either of us to lead it?" Killian said, stopping to look Miro in the eye.

"I know," Miro said.

"Who would you have lead them?"

"Tiesto," Miro said without hesitation.

"Any other contenders?" Killian asked.

"No," Miro said.

Killian nodded, and the circle made way for the two men to rejoin the group. "The Alturan high lord and I have put together a strategy, a way that the two of us might be able to make a difference. Whether we succeed or fail, your task is the same. You must try to break the siege, and we will do our best to ensure you have support from the inside."

Miro scanned the onlookers; he saw nods and heard murmurs of assent.

"But," Killian said, "I won't be here to lead you."

Every set of eyes was on the emperor.

"Someone must get into the city to speak to the defenders and time the attack. I am the only one who can do so, and I have my own duty to fulfill in order to protect the Empire from our foe." Killian turned as he spoke, looking at each face in turn. "One among you must make the overall decisions if you are to have any chance of success. Miro and I will have our own tasks to accomplish."

Killian paused to take a breath.

"Is there one you trust with this duty?" Killian asked.

Miro's eyes widened. He'd expected Killian to nominate Tiesto.

Outside the circle, Miro saw Amber's eyes on him. She knew nothing of his mad plan.

High Lord Grigori Orlov of Vezna stepped forward. "I will follow Tiesto Telmarran, high lord of Halaran," he called.

"I will follow the high lord of Halaran," Lord Marshal Scola said.

"He has my vote, for what it's worth," said Dain Barden of the Akari.

"And mine," Touana spoke up.

Killian fixed his gaze on his Tingaran marshals.

"If it is your wish, Emperor," said one of the big men with the shaved heads.

"It is," Killian said. "High Lord Tiesto Telmarran, you're in charge. By my decree, the army is yours to command, the orders yours to give."

Tiesto scanned the crowd. "I thank you for your support. We will need to form up, but the city needs us, and the longer we wait here, the greater the chance we'll be spotted by the enemy. We will attack when we hear your clarion."

Killian nodded. "I'll coordinate those in the city and tell them help is on the way." He spoke with fierce determination. "We can still win."

Miro nodded at Bartolo. "Bartolo, can I speak with you? I will need your help, more than at any other time."

Bartolo came forward. "Of course."

Miro tried not to see Amber's worried expression.

His plan was insane. But it was worth the risk.

His zenblade was the key.

52

Killian took his thoughts away from the army and instead focused on what he needed to do. Miro's plan was mad—*mad!*—and could lead to terrible destruction for Seranthia, even as it held the hope of victory. Killian would have to use every bit of skill from the training he'd received at Evrin's hands. Miro's part would be more dangerous still.

"Well done," Miro said.

"With what?" Killian was puzzled.

"With Tiesto's nomination. They thought it was their idea."

Killian shrugged. "Something my mother taught me. She says that if you know in advance how someone will decide, and it's what you want to happen, then tell them the decision rests with them. They'll appreciate the trust you place in them, even though it costs you nothing."

Miro shook his head and grinned. "Remind me never to sit at the bargaining table with your mother."

"Are you two done?" Bartolo said. "Come on. We've got a war to win."

Killian, Miro, and Bartolo left the army behind them and ran toward the city, keeping clear of the tall hills and instead skirting along the gullies and far sides, their path always taking them closer to the crashes and thuds of the battlefield.

It was mid-morning, moving toward midday, and the three men finally took cover in a copse of trees as they regarded the gray stone of the Wall in front of them and prepared to make their approach.

Miro and Bartolo both looked fit and lean in their green armorsilk. Killian's eyes kept involuntarily flickering to Miro's zenblade before looking at the man himself.

"When you cut a tree, which way does it fall?" Miro said, evidently noticing Killian's attention.

Bartolo grimaced. He'd been brought in on the plan, but his expression said enough. Even so, he'd promised to do his part. Bartolo was needed to protect his friend. Killian could tell at a glance that Miro trusted Bartolo with his life.

"In the direction of the cut," Bartolo said. "Most of the time."

Miro grinned. "That's why sometimes you need to give the tree a push."

Killian glanced from one man to the other. "Are you ready?"

"We're ready," Miro nodded.

"Good luck," Killian said. "When you hear the city's clarion, you'll know it's time. I don't know how much of a difference I can make, but I promise you I'll try."

"That's all any of us can do," Miro said.

"Find Shani," Bartolo said. "Trust me, she can help."

Killian put out his hand and shook hands first with Miro, then with Bartolo. He left the copse of trees and stepped out into the open ground. With the two Alturans watching, Killian took a deep breath and spread his arms. Chanting a series of activation sequences, Killian rose into the air.

Wind buffeted his face as Killian climbed high in the sky, for the first time gaining a full appreciation of the struggle being fought for the city. Even now, glowing orbs rained down on the revenants below, pouring like hail from the Wall and dirigibles alike. The warriors of the enemy horde leaned incredibly long ladders against the Wall and swarmed up as soon as they were placed. The ladders were too long to be pushed back by pole-arms, and the defenders could only wait until the enemy reached the top before the struggle could begin.

On the thin ramparts, Tingaran legionnaires fought side by side with avengers and black-clad Hazarans to cut down the enemy.

Killian's people were dying. Every land of the Empire was his to protect. They needed him.

He tilted forward now and moved his arms slightly to propel his body through the air. He sped over the surging revenant army and heard the crack of muskets as some of the enemy took shots at him. He felt a small sting, barely noticeable, as a ball hit his chest, bouncing off without harm.

Killian thought about the other man who had these powers. Where was Sentar Scythran? It was too much to hope that the injuries Sentar sustained at the free cities had removed the Lord of the Night from the struggle.

Killian passed over the Wall and saw eyes staring up at him in astonishment and fear. With his fiery-red hair and black clothing Killian could have been the enemy they'd all been dreading, but he'd made sure to wear his purple cloak, and the nine-pointed star on his chest covered his torso, boldly proclaiming who he was.

The cries turned to cheers, and Killian slowed his motion to hover fifty feet over the narrow ramparts, barely wide enough for two men to pass each other and dizzyingly high. Looking down, he saw Hazarans standing side by side with Tingaran legionnaires. Avengers scanned for enemies with red glares, and common citizens fought with trained warriors. More than any other color, purple filled the length of the Wall.

"I have returned!" Killian roared.

"Emperor!" the shouts followed in his wake.

Killian traveled over the city, and the call was soon taken up in the streets of Fortune and the alleys of the Tenamet. The slums and market districts roared up at him as he passed overhead.

"Emperor!"

———◆———

The news of the emperor's arrival traveled like wildfire throughout the city. The defenders on the ramparts took heart and threw back the latest charge with renewed vigor. The cowering citizens left their barricaded homes to share the news.

The jubilant voices carried to the Imperial Palace, but Shani shrugged them off; she had bigger things on her mind.

Shani sat on the side of a bed, and once again she pulled back the covers to reveal the body of the young woman with pale golden hair.

Ella lay comatose.

Shani wiped tears from her eyes as her gaze took in what had happened to her friend.

When the morning tide had brought Ella's body in to the docks, some people recognized her enchantress's dress and pulled her out of the water. Then others arrived and said they'd seen her at the harbor the previous night, miraculously walking on water.

They'd told Shani the story with wide eyes. Everyone not fighting on the Wall had witnessed the destruction of the huge cargo ship, though none had realized its significance. Even so, the people at the docks knew Ella had done something to make a blow against the enemy, and they decided to take her body to the palace. Shani had met them and carried her limp form back to her rooms.

Ella was near death.

Under the covers, Ella wore just a sleeveless white shift. Shani once more ran her eyes over her friend's skin. It was uniformly tinged a sickly blue color. Even Ella's face was blue, and Shani kept touching Ella's cheeks to see if she was frozen. But the blue wasn't from the cold.

Shani and Rogan had pieced it together, and as an elementalist, Shani knew what it was.

Shani set the covers back down and resumed stroking Ella's cheek. She didn't know what else to do. She knew she should be back at the ramparts, fighting alongside Ilathor, Jehral, and her fellow elementalists, but she couldn't leave Ella. Not like this.

Shani heard running footsteps, and suddenly the door crashed open. Her eyes shot up as she saw the last person she expected to see.

Killian, emperor of Merralya, stared at her with frightened eyes.

"What happened?" Killian cried. He rushed to Ella's side. "I heard. How is she? What's wrong with her?"

Shani considered her words before turning to Killian, who nearly quivered with pent-up emotion. "Killian, you need to listen to me. When we were with the Akari, she was affected by poison an Akari traitor put in her essence. I had my suspicions, but I didn't know for sure until Rogan told me this morning." Shani met Killian's pain-filled eyes. "No one affected survived. No one."

"I don't understand. They said something about Sentar's essence . . ."

"She did it, Killian." Shani sighed. "She destroyed Sentar's store of essence. Ella knew it was dangerous, but she also knew she was dying. Last night, she went out, all alone, and she did it. He can't open the portal now."

"Why does her skin look like that?" Killian placed his hands on Ella's forehead and cheeks. "Is she cold?"

"It's essence poisoning," Shani said. "Where essence touches the skin, it turns it blue."

Killian's face went white. "Essence poisoning?"

"Ella destroyed a ship filled with essence. I know the signs. We can only assume it came into contact with her skin."

Ella's chest was barely moving. Killian put his ear to her lips. "She's breathing."

"For now."

"How is she here? How can she still be breathing? What will happen to her?"

"I don't know," Shani said simply. "I'm sorry, but I don't expect her to live."

Killian straightened, his face twisted with anguish. "It should have been me."

"She was dying even before she destroyed Sentar's essence," Shani said. "You can't blame yourself."

Killian leaned forward to brush his lips across Ella's forehead. "I'm so sorry," he whispered, so that Shani could only just hear him. "I should have been there."

Shani heard a sudden blast. It was the city's clarion, sounding the call to arms. Shani wondered at the sound: they were already fighting for their very survival. "What's happening?"

Killian couldn't take his eyes off Ella. Shani read the expression of a man in terrible pain.

Killian visibly shook himself. "We have to go," he said. "Shani, I need your help."

"With what?"

"I need you to come with me to the Wall. Help me gather the other elementalists. We need you. I'll explain it to you on the way."

53

Ella didn't know where she was.

She stood on a path made of neatly fitted stones. The path stretched ahead as straight as an arrow until it vanished into the hazy horizon. The air felt hot and heavy, weighing down on her, and looking up, she saw the sky seethe with storm clouds, shifting hue from gray to red, plunging down to greet the land but shooting back up again as if shying away from making contact.

Ella frowned in puzzlement. How had she come to be here? She heard a rumble but knew it didn't come from the clouds, and turning around she saw that behind her the path continued back in the opposite direction, but shadows danced on this horizon, shadows that launched streaks of flame into the air and erupted with smoke.

A second sound carried forward from the shadows: the clunk of marching boots, and Ella felt a surge of fear when she saw the flash of steel as spears and swords poked through the flame.

The shadows were moving along the path, picking up speed as the thunderous footsteps grew louder, heading inexorably forward, toward Ella.

Ella's heart began to race. She knew that the enemy was approaching. If they caught her here, she would die.

Ella began to hurry forward, glancing back over her shoulder with every few steps.

In all directions the horizon blurred, impossible to focus on. An angry purple haze coated the land, as if seeping up from the ground itself. Ella looked for features, anything to break the monotonous landscape, but saw only a rocky, barren wasteland.

Her footsteps were heavy, and she felt tired, but she hurried fearfully on. Her hair fell in front of her face, and she pushed it away, her eyes widening when she saw golden tresses tumble through the air, though she'd only touched her hair with the lightest caress.

Looking back, Ella saw with relief that she'd outdistanced the enemy. They were still there, at the limit of her vision, back behind her, but the detonations weren't as loud now, and she could no longer hear the marching.

She wondered how she would ever get out of this place.

Ella pinched the skin on the back of her hand and grimaced. Wherever she was, she could still feel pain. She looked at her bare arms and then down at her body. She wore a plain white dress, sleeveless and short, and her bare feet moved silently on the smooth paving stones.

Ella squinted ahead again, shading her eyes from the glare, though there was no sun in the sky. To the left: there was something there, beside the road. It was a building of some kind.

Checking to confirm her pursuers were still far behind, Ella progressed along the road until she drew close to the structure. She decided to investigate.

It was a wooden house, more of a shack really, with crumbling steps leading up to a rickety porch. A post outside the house proclaimed its name.

"'Mallorin,'" Ella said, reading the sign.

Ella stood at the bottom of the steps and gazed up at the house. Then she heard a voice from outside the building, and looking to the rear, she saw trees clustered around a muddy pool.

Ella crept around the side of the house until she could see.

A little blonde girl sat on her knees at the edge of the puddle, a scooped bowl in her hand. She submerged the bowl in the water and then lifted it out. She grinned.

"Come along, tadpoles," the little girl said. "Your pool's drying up, and you need to get to the river." Ella watched the muddy girl climb to her feet, holding the bowl carefully in her hands as she began to walk. "Don't jump, it's a long way down."

Ella spotted movement in the nearby trees. A woman stood watching, hidden by the forest. She had ivory skin and wore an embroidered dress, with jewelry at her throat. The woman smiled as she watched the little girl, though tears spilled down her cheeks.

Ella looked back over her shoulder as she heard crashing sounds and the shouts of men and cries of women. She couldn't stay here long: the thudding explosions were again louder, and once more she could hear marching boots.

When she returned her gaze to look forward, both the woman and the child were gone.

Leaving the side of the house, Ella walked over to once more stand at the foot of the steps. She hesitated, knowing she should leave, but she felt she was searching for something, and she began to climb.

Reaching the top, Ella crossed the porch and pushed open the thin door to look into the house's interior.

Three chairs stood around a table, though only two were occupied. An old man sat with the same little girl, and each had a plate and knife and fork in front of them.

"Now, Ella. Pick up the fork in your left hand," the old man said to the little girl. "Hold it like this. Do you see how I'm holding it?"

Ella watched the small girl struggle to copy the old man.

"Good," he said. "Now pick up the knife. You always hold the fork with your left hand and the knife with your right."

Ella smiled as she saw the old man reach over to adjust the child's grip.

Then she heard another explosion, and the sounds of pursuit urged her on. She closed the door to the house and walked back down the steps.

A young boy with a shock of black hair strode toward where Ella stood. He was scowling as he stared right at her. He had a savage red mark to the left of his mouth.

"What happened?" Ella heard a voice behind her, and she saw that the little girl was behind her on the steps. The boy wasn't looking at her; he was looking at the girl.

"I got into a fight," the boy said.

"Why?"

"Because people say stupid things."

"Did you have to fight?" the girl asked.

"Sometimes there's no other way. I don't care what they think of me, but it's important what I think of myself."

Ella stepped away from the steps and watched as the boy and girl spoke.

"I don't want you to fight," the girl said.

The boy sighed. "Neither do I."

Ella heard the clash of steel against steel, and looking back toward the road, she could now make out individual soldiers, terrifying men with black armor and sharp swords revealed in the occasional gaps in the smoke. Another boom came from the enemy, and Ella heard the sound of splintering wood combine with the roar of flames.

When she looked for the two children, the boy and girl were gone.

Ella decided to go back to the road. As she walked away from the house, she suddenly saw the little girl in front of her holding a stack of books precariously piled in her arms. The roar of fighting men grew louder, and the girl glanced apprehensively over her shoulder and tripped.

Books fell everywhere as the girl fell down to her knees.

"Here, let me help," Ella said.

She knelt and began to gather the books, placing them side by side on the ground. Reading the spines, Ella saw every topic imaginable covered, from language to the study of weather, to mathematics, to lore.

The girl went completely still, and Ella saw her face turn completely white.

"He's here," the girl said.

Ella felt cold fear shiver down her spine, and following the direction of the girl's gaze, she saw a man step out from behind the house.

He shifted as he walked, changing appearance and stride, even bearing, as if two men existed in the one body. He was an old man in a gold-trimmed white robe with a black sun on the breast, an emaciated frame, and stick-thin arms. The old man's skin was dead, wrinkled like parchment, and his eyes were dark and intense, the stare of a fanatic. He held a dagger in his hand.

Then he flickered and changed. Now he was a slim middle-aged man in elegant clothing of dark velvet, diamonds set in chrome at his cuffs and a silver chain around his neck. His hair was blood red, and his eyes were the shade of blue frost. As he walked, something wet and liquid dripped from the tips of his fingers, pattering to the ground with each step. Ella saw it was blood.

"Please," the little girl said, looking imploringly at Ella. "Don't let him get me."

Ella scooped the little girl up in her arms and ran.

Expecting at any moment to feel hot breath on her neck, Ella left the house behind her and rushed back to the paved stones of the road. Risking a glance behind her, Ella saw the cloud of smoke and flame surge ahead. The house was gone, as if it had never been.

The menacing figure still walked toward them.

"Please," the little girl whimpered.

"I'll protect you," Ella said.

Ella's heart pumped as she ran along the road, away from her pursuers, heading into the haze. She was forced to set the girl down and instead held her hand, pulling her along as they ran from the encroaching darkness.

The blonde girl was surprisingly fast and kept pace with Ella, no faster and no slower than she was herself. Her little hand fit snugly into Ella's palm. The task of protecting the girl gave Ella a sense of purpose she hadn't felt before.

They ran, and now the man was at the front of the cloud that was the enemy. He was one of them, and the threat stronger than ever before.

A blurred shape appeared through the mist, a triangular mass at the end of the road, lying directly ahead.

Ella saw it was a mountain.

"Quick," Ella said to the little girl. "We'll be safe here."

The mountain came at them all at once, a stepped pyramid of dark stone looming down, solid and indomitable.

"There'll be a chamber at the top," Ella panted as she led the girl up the steps. "They can't hurt us there."

"I'm scared," the little girl whimpered.

Ella's legs burned with fatigue, and sweat dripped down her brow. Wet strands got in the way of her vision, and she impatiently brushed them aside. At her touch, the hair came out in a big clump. Ella looked at the strands in her hand in horror and flung them away.

Ella climbed step after step, surprised that a girl so small could keep pace with her. Glancing back, she saw that the enemy had reached the base of the mountain, the man running forward to lead the charge. He brandished the dagger and snarled as he dashed up the steps, his white robe twisting around his thin frame, though there was no wind. He smoothed back his slicked hair, and symbols on his hands and neck glowed with fire. Ella shook her head and returned her gaze to the front, desperately searching for the chamber she knew was here.

The man was nearly on them. Ella reached the dark opening and turned wide eyes behind her as she saw him lunge up the mountain. Ella heard his hoarse breathing and saw the dagger in the man's hand speed through the air, not aimed at her, instead shooting forward at the little girl.

Ella pulled the girl into her arms, and she launched herself up the final step and into the dark opening.

Ella fell.

Suddenly there was nothing in her arms: the girl was gone. Ella screamed as she plummeted endlessly through darkness, her limbs writhing and her vision conjuring a hard floor coming up to meet her. She ran out of breath and gasped before screaming again. She screamed, emptying her breath three more times before she realized she was face down on the ground.

Ella struggled to make sense of it. She'd been falling, and now she was on the ground. She lifted her head. Where was the little girl?

Ella was in a cavern, and though there was no source of light, she could easily discern the craggy walls and smooth stone floor. She rose to her feet and, tilting her head back, could only see a black void above, a shadowed height disappearing endlessly to the limits of vision.

There were two side tunnels leading from the cavern, one large and one small.

Ella walked toward the entrance of the smaller tunnel and peered inside. This tunnel was walled, with blocks of stone fitted next to each other to fill the arched ceiling. The tunnel glowed with blue light, and it turned at the end. Deciding to see what lay after the turn, Ella walked inside.

Her bare feet made no sound on the stone, and the air was cool and dry. She rounded the corner, and still the tunnel stretched on. Ella walked for an age as the tunnel bent left and twisted right, heading deeper and deeper into the rock.

Ella frowned, tilting her head to the side as she heard a strange clinking and bubbling. As she rounded the next corner, Ella stopped and stared.

A man in a black robe had his back to her, and Ella saw a symbol on the back of the robe: a triangle bounded by a double circle. A bench stood against the wall of the square room, and Ella saw smoke pouring from the mouths of bubbling glass flasks, with pipes leading from one vial to another. Jars lined the wall, each containing a colored liquid or powder.

Ella cleared her throat, and the man turned.

He was old, with kind eyes and a high forehead. Ella saw he held an open book in his hands, the pages yellowed with age.

He closed the book with a snap and scowled at Ella.

"I told you," he said. "Everything is poison; there is poison in everything. Only the dose makes a thing not a poison."

"I . . . I don't understand," Ella said.

"Listen! Everything is toxic, and small amounts of things considered poisonous can do good, while large amounts of safe substances can kill. For every bad there is good."

"Please . . ." Ella said.

"You aren't listening!" the old man roared at her.

Ella turned on her heels and fled. She ran back down the winding passage, gasping as her bare feet slapped against the stone, until she finally stood back in the wide cavern.

Ella leaned against the wall to regain her breath.

Shaking her head, trying to clear it, she resisted the urge to sob. She didn't understand any of this. What was happening to her?

Ella was frightened of what she would find in the larger tunnel. But she had to find out what was in there.

She walked over to the entrance.

Where the last passage had been walled, this tunnel was rough and jagged, as if naturally formed. Golden light welled from inside, and with each step forward Ella found herself feeling strangely at peace. This tunnel didn't turn and twist, it continued on straight ahead, but with all the outcrops and hanging formations, she couldn't see what lay ahead.

Ella heard the sound of masculine breathing, back the way she'd come.

She stopped in her tracks and looked fearfully back behind her.

The man appeared from between the rocky walls. Where he walked the golden light changed to darkness, and every footstep filled the tunnel with shadow. He brought the shadow with him, and Ella knew that if he swallowed her in that darkness, she would never see light again.

Ella began to run, her chest once more heaving. She opened her stride and dashed through the passages, taking cuts and scrapes from the sharp stone. The man ran with her, chasing her, and Ella's spine crawled at the thought of her unprotected back.

Ella heard her name, and someone suddenly stood in front of her, barring the way.

She saw it was a small woman with ruddy skin and crinkled features. She was nonetheless pretty in a way, and she had a bow in her hands, pointed past Ella's shoulder. A soft mantle of white fur rested on her shoulders.

"Get behind me," the woman said. "I will keep him from you."

Ella rushed to reach safety behind the small woman and turned to look back. The man growled and sneered as he stood in the shadows where the golden light couldn't reach him. He didn't come any closer.

Ella realized she knew the woman's name.

"Layla," Ella said. "What are you doing here?"

"You summoned me," Layla said.

"How?"

Layla shrugged, even as she kept an arrow drawn on the bowstring, sighted at the man. "I was enjoying myself, hunting, climbing, swimming, sharing laughter with my people, and then I was here."

As Ella watched, the man drew away, taking his shadows with him. Layla lowered her bow.

"I've missed you," Ella said. She met Layla's green eyes, and Ella felt tears well at the corners of her own.

"You need to take better care of yourself," Layla said. She ran her eyes up and down Ella's body and raised an eyebrow. "Your hair. Is that a new fashion among your people?"

Ella laughed, though it hurt. "No."

"I have missed you too. But do not blame yourself. We are each responsible for our own actions."

"What am I supposed to do?" Ella said.

"If you want to keep running, then that is your choice. I will guard here, and I will keep you safe."

"What lies ahead?"

"Your destiny."

"Can I wait here with you?"

"No, Ella. I do not have the power to stay here long. If you choose to run, then you must go now."

"Will I see you again?"

"You will always see me. If you want to be close, come to the Dunwood, and visit my tree. But I will be everywhere. I will be in the wind that moves through the trees, and the water flowing through the rivers. The clouds will bear my name, and I will be carried down with the rains to continue the cycle. Now go."

Ella opened her mouth.

"Go," Layla repeated.

Ella reached forward to touch her friend, but her grasp caught only air. Layla smiled at Ella sadly, and Ella left the Dunfolk healer behind.

The golden light grew stronger the further Ella wandered down the tunnel. She once more felt the sensation of peace, and with it came a feeling of being tired. Ella wanted to sleep, and she knew that when she did, it would be the sweetest sleep she'd ever had. She was weary. Soon, she would rest.

The tunnel narrowed and Ella passed through the close walls to see the tunnel widening once more, forming another cavern.

Ella raised a hand to shield her eyes. An arched opening at the cavern's end shone with radiant light. The feeling of tiredness and tranquility was now so strong she could no longer resist it, and Ella knew it stemmed from this arch.

She stepped into the cavern and walked through the center, ignoring everything else as she approached the light.

When she was directly in front of the arch, she felt an incredible sensation of peace. It surged through her body, sending a tingle through her limbs, and Ella realized the pain was gone. While she looked at the light there was no more agony, only joy.

"Ella," she heard behind her.

Ella turned in surprise as she heard the voice. For the first time her gaze took in the entire cavern. Jewels of all colors sparkled from the rocky ceiling, reflecting the golden light. A beautiful centurion tree with glistening green leaves stood over a wooden bench, branches drooping down.

Ella drew in a sharp breath.

An old man in a sky-blue robe sat on the bench, and Ella's eyes widened as she saw he had a little girl on his lap, her hair pale blonde and her eyes sparkling emerald. He set the girl off his lap and rose to his feet as he once more spoke her name.

His white hair was flecked with ginger, and his soft beard was dotted here and there with red. His intensely blue eyes looked at Ella with the utmost kindness and compassion as he stepped toward her.

"Evrin," Ella whispered. "What are you doing here?"

"I'm here because you're here," Evrin Evenstar said.

Ella looked down at the little girl, whose hand was clasped in Evrin's. "Who is she?"

"She's you," Evrin said.

Ella's senses reeled, and suddenly she was the girl, the girl was she. She looked out through the little girl's eyes, and then Ella closed her eyes and opened them, and the girl was gone. Evrin's hands were now empty.

"I remember," Ella said.

"That is good. But tell me, my dear," Evrin said. "What do you remember of lore?"

Ella spoke with a trembling voice. "Runes are drawn with essence. Different runes combine to give objects properties they didn't possess before."

"What makes someone a master of lore?"

"Learning," Ella said. "Experience. Wisdom."

Evrin shook his head sadly. "You never did understand, though you came close to the source three times." He came forward and put his finger at Ella's breast, close to her heart. "Power comes from within. Only when you realize this, will you become the master of yourself, and then you can become what you've always wanted to be."

Ella saw Layla enter the cavern to stand by Evrin's side.

"She knows it," Evrin said, indicating Layla. "But then again, her people were always close to the truth."

"What truth?" Ella said.

"You've always believed everything should have a rational explanation, and you've struggled to explain the things you don't understand. You can't explain away love, my dear, it doesn't work like that. Nor can you explain intuition, or the strength to go on even through the darkest struggles."

"I don't understand," Ella whispered. "Why can't you just tell me?"

"Because these things are for each of us to learn on our own. They can't be taught or explained, which is the point of what I'm trying to say to you."

Ella turned to look at the archway of golden light. Once more the feeling of restful peace came over her.

"You can go that way, yes, and you deserve it, that is true."

At the other end of the cavern, from where Ella had come, the entrance darkened with shadow. The man stood at the cusp of the cavern, watching and waiting, filled with menace.

"Or you can fight," Evrin said. "It will mean discovering the source of your strength in the face of utter darkness. You will either find yourself, or you will perish."

"We must go," Layla said to Evrin.

Evrin nodded. He turned back to Ella. "I have faith in you, my dear. But when you make your choice, remember: if you choose to fight, the battle will be more difficult than any you've ever faced before."

Evrin and Layla both turned to the light-filled tunnel, and as they walked, they began to fade. They became translucent with each step, and the centurion tree and wooden bench also faded.

"Don't go," Ella pleaded.

"Trust in yourself," Evrin and Layla whispered together.

Evrin looked one last time over his shoulder back at Ella, and then he and Layla walked through the archway, into the light.

The man in black now stepped forward into the cavern, half-filling it with shadow as he snarled, clenching and unclenching his fists.

Ella looked longingly at the light, and then at the darkness.

She chose to fight.

54

Tiesto Telmarran stared white-faced down at Seranthia as the rumbling horn blast sounded the call to arms from behind the city walls.

It was time.

Smoke rose to cloud the battlefield, rolling up from the mass of heaving enemy warriors below. They pressed against the stone wall and swarmed up ladders, seemingly oblivious as the dirigibles emptied their last loads of orbs, their pilots desperate to keep the assault parties clear from the tall heights.

Fear threatened to overwhelm Tiesto as the responsibility pressed down on his shoulders. He kept his back straight, forcing himself to breathe, and he promised himself he would rise to the task. The clarion meant it was time to engage the enemy. Tiesto had to lead his men to victory. His task was to defeat the savage revenants below.

It was midday and the sun blazed with fierce heat. The revenant horde clustered up against the Wall, scrabbling madly, heedless of the raining destruction. In complete contrast, the second force waited in front of the gate in disciplined ranks, ready to charge when their opportunity came.

The enemy commander's strategy was simple: to open a breach, either by climbing up to the city using their long ladders or by pounding at the gates with their iron-tipped battering rams. Where a strong breach opened, the infantry square would follow.

As the clarion blast hung in the air, Tiesto scanned the hills behind him to see his army ponderously making its way up to the crests of the hills. He cursed every second that passed. Returning his gaze to the city, he saw the handful of dirigibles taking fire from muskets below. The pilots finished releasing their deadly hail and returned back to the city, but not before a dirigible suddenly fell into a spiral, plummeting to the ground and crashing in a shower of sparks.

A gust of wind blew the stench of the battlefield up to the hills, and Tiesto momentarily recoiled. As the summer sun took its toll, the rotten bodies that fought the natural order of things to keep moving were falling to putrefaction.

"Ugh," a nearby bladesinger said, putting his hand to his mouth.

Couriers in brown, green, blue, purple, and orange ran in all directions, fetching orders and making reports.

"The grenadiers need more time to come forward."

"High Lord Grigori reports his men are ready."

"The Legion awaits your command."

"Do you want my infantry up front?"

"Yes! Hurry!" Tiesto said.

"We can't wait much longer," Dain Barden said, standing nearby.

"I know," Tiesto muttered.

"It's madness, charging the infantry square and ignoring the revenants at the walls."

"Enough," Tiesto said, surprised at his own ability to voice down the huge Akari warrior. "We have our orders."

Looking down at the infantry square, sizing up those he would soon be fighting, Tiesto saw a cluster of enemy warriors in black-and-white-checkered uniforms at the front of their ranks. Narrowing his vision, he thought he could see a warrior in a three-cornered hat.

"Gorain," Dain Barden said, noting the direction of his gaze. After the space of ten heartbeats he spoke again. "We've been spotted."

The warrior in the hat waved an arm, and the revenants under his command began to turn to face the threat from the hills.

Tiesto swore.

He'd lost the advantage of surprise. Gorain waved his arm again, and the ranks of revenants wheeled.

"Why aren't we attacking?" someone cried.

"Miro also said to wait for the light," Tiesto said.

"We need to charge now!" Dain Barden urged.

"We wait!" Tiesto turned and glared at the huge warrior.

Dain Barden grumbled but backed down. His eyes continued to rove over the battlefield. "Ah, there he is."

"Who?" Tiesto asked.

"Renrik." Tiesto saw Dain Barden point toward a gray-robed necromancer on the left flank of the infantry square.

"So many of them," someone said.

"I don't see any light!" someone else muttered.

"On your command, High Lord Tiesto. We're ready."

"Good," Tiesto said.

But he still waited for the light Miro had promised him.

Disciplined order came to the revenant army as Gorain and the necromancers formed them into a longer line, more of a rectangle than a square. As he waited, Tiesto counted along the files until he'd passed one hundred. He then repeated the same process as he counted the ranks.

"I count ten thousand, give or take," Tiesto said.

"This won't be easy," said the Dain.

Tiesto shaded his eyes from the glare as he waited for the promised signal. Surely Miro wouldn't let him down?

A sudden pinprick of light sparked at the base of the Wall, on the extreme right-hand side of Tiesto's vision. The light grew brighter and brighter until it outshone the sun, though it was midday. Tiesto's heart began to hammer. A second horn blasted from the city, as if responding to the light.

Tiesto tore his gaze away from the light and instead focused on the force formed up in ranks in front of him. The emperor had been clear: Tiesto was to concentrate on this enemy above all else.

"Let's do this," the Dain said.

"Send word. *We attack!*" Tiesto roared.

Heralds sounded the advance, and the huge army moved relentlessly forward, tired men pushing down their fear and instead summoning their reserves of strength to make this last surge for Seranthia.

Tiesto led from the center while the other high lords and marshals each commanded a formation of warriors: Tingaran legionnaires, Louan grenadiers, Halrana pikemen, and Alturan heavy infantry. Beside Tiesto, the Dain took the huge two-headed hammer from his belt, an almost eager look on his face, and two nearby Halrana muttered prayers as they advanced.

The thud of marching footsteps turned to thunder as the allied army picked up momentum. Tiesto felt both the thrill of the charge and the fear of death overwhelm him in equal parts, but soon even those feelings were replaced by something more primal, the raw emotion of a man charging into battle.

The space between the two formations grew smaller, and now both forces were running at each other, revenants charging the soldiers of the Empire, the men of Tiesto's army charging back.

The two forces hit.

Everything fell into chaos.

55

"This is mad," Bartolo muttered.

"If it has a chance of success, we have to try. Quickly, they have yet to see us," Miro said. "I need you."

"I'm here. Don't worry. I'll keep them from you."

"This is going to draw them like moths to a flame," Miro muttered. "Here goes."

Miro held his zenblade in two hands and looked at the solid gray stone of the Wall. He'd seen his zenblade cut through men without pausing. The zenblade could cut through steel, even through enchanted blades.

Miro's zenblade could also cut through stone. And if he drew on all of its power, as he planned to now, it would melt a fissure twelve inches high.

Miro drew in a slow, deep breath, his heart pounding in his chest, threatening to leap out of his mouth. He spoke an activation sequence and immediately followed with another, and then a third, until he was chanting.

Fire sparked from one rune to the next, traveling along the length of the blade, sending a rainbow of colors along the glistening steel. Miro's voice rose as the light grew in intensity, and now he was singing, his voice rising, drowning out all other sound, until all he could hear was the sound of his own voice. He resisted the urge to focus on the activation sequences; to lose his song would be to fail.

The light grew brighter until the zenblade was a solid bar of fire.

Still Miro called on more power, bringing forth the incredible new abilities his sister had imparted to his zenblade, heedless of how much he drained his weapon's energy.

Miro now held a rod of intense blue flame. His hands shook; the width of the blue light was wider and longer than the steel, the runes projecting the energy outward but protecting Miro's hands. He could no longer look at his zenblade. To gaze at the blade would blind him.

Miro's song came strong and even. He leaned forward and pushed.

Miro thrust his zenblade into the gray stone of the Wall.

Sparks fountained in all directions as the stone melted from the pressure of Miro's thrust and the incredibly fierce heat. Bits of fiery rock splattered onto Miro's armorsilk and burned his hands, but he pushed away his fear, ignoring the pain on his skin. He couldn't call forth his armorsilk to protect him, and he instead concentrated on his weapon. He felt the zenblade push in, meeting resistance, but then molten red poured from the Wall.

Still Miro pushed. He cut a gouge into the Wall, and finally his arms were outstretched and he was reaching into his own newly created hole.

Fighting down the pain of his burns and his own fear, Miro let his song run free. He began to walk along the length of the Wall.

Miro took three steps, and then a dozen more, all the time cutting into the stone, nimbly dancing out of the way of the bright yellow molten rock. He was unable to think of anything else, his task completely consuming him, and he continued to walk, faster now.

He had quizzed Killian about the thickness of the Wall. It was a mad plan, but in theory it should work.

Miro's plan was to bring the Wall down on top of the revenant horde.

He remembered his earlier words: a tree should fall in the direction of the cut. Lord of the Sky, if the Wall fell the wrong way, disaster would follow. Miro hoped Killian had cleared the ramparts as agreed.

As he traveled along its length, Miro was distantly aware of Bartolo protecting him from the relentless attack of the revenants. Blood and hot sparks splattered onto his back in equal measure. He was now in the midst of the enemy warriors fighting each other to climb ladders and throwing themselves against Bartolo, the only man standing between Miro and certain death at their hands.

He was now at the gates.

Miro continued his song, cutting through the wood and iron, until he reached the other side of the gates.

He pushed on.

Even through the immensity of his task, Miro saw the runes on the zenblade begin to dim. He had no way of knowing if he would make it to the end of the Wall's great length. He could only pray.

Bartolo screamed in pain, distracting Miro from his own song. Miro choked and began to lose his rhythm.

Miro breathed in gasps. He fixed his memory on the tranquility of the Crystal Palace. He remembered Tomas, and thought of his homeland.

The song returned.

Even as Miro worked, he was aware that they were in the thickest of the fighting. Revenants threw themselves at Bartolo again and again, and the whirling bladesinger's baritone rose in contrast to Miro's tenor as Bartolo kept them back.

And then they were through the fighting, and past, to the Wall's far side.

The two men were close to completing their circuit of the Wall when Miro's zenblade went dark.

Miro lowered his arms, feeling raw pain scream all over his body, from the burns on his hands and the terrible fatigue in his muscles.

Miro's song faltered, and he took stock of where he was.

He looked up at the Wall.

It hadn't worked. Miro thought he could hear groaning, but the Wall still stood.

"Where now?" Bartolo gasped. A revenant charged, and Bartolo swiftly cut through its body. "We should get away from here."

"Where else?" Miro panted. "Into the battle."

56

Killian had recalled the defenders from the Wall, and the ramparts would soon be empty. When the enemy realized there was no resistance at the top of the Wall, they would begin to climb over, and the city would be overrun.

Killian now stood in the center of a long line of elementalists, close to forty of them. To his left, a hundred paces away, he could see Shani, her eyes on him. Another elementalist stood the same distance away on his right.

Seranthia's buildings didn't press close to the Wall, and there was a cleared swath of ground following the long line of gray stone.

Killian had no idea if this would work.

He waited: Miro would need time to play his part. How long he needed to wait, though, Killian didn't know. He only knew he needed to be down here, with the elementalists. After the second clarion blast, he counted his breaths, and then he decided it was time.

Killian's heart raced, and his breath came in short gasps. He steadied his nerves as he stared up at his city's main defense.

The defense he was about to try to bring down.

For once freed of his responsibilities with the army, Killian brought himself into the trance-like state he'd sometimes used on the trapeze or the tightrope.

"Walking a tightrope," he muttered to himself. Much of his life seemed to feel that way.

Killian pointed his hands in the air and spoke a swift activation sequence. A line of fire shot into the sky, where the elementalists would see it.

Glancing to his left, he saw the cuffs at Shani's wrists flare up in a bright array of colors. On his right, the next elementalist followed suit.

Killian didn't need cuffs. He clapped his hands together and then made a pushing motion at the Wall as he summoned the wind to do his bidding.

He chanted in rapid tones as he pushed, condensing the air in front of him and throwing it against the stone. Along the line the people in red robes would be calling forth their own elemental air. Killian could feel the concussive waves he created stretching and tightening. His hands were pushing at nothing, yet he felt he was heaving the weight of the entire Wall.

Killian started to feel failure: his task was foolish, impossible. But then an eerie wind began to develop. Soon it grew to become a howl. Gusts tore at his clothing. Swirls and flurries of dust and litter spun through the air, dashing against the stone.

Then the Wall started to groan.

Killian pushed harder now. He wasn't sure if what he was doing was making a difference or whether it was the elementalists. Perhaps the Wall was falling under its own weight.

Either way, it was visibly tilting now.

As the wall began to lean, for a moment Killian thought it was going to fall the wrong way, back toward the city, and he would be responsible for the destruction of much of Seranthia.

But the incline grew steeper, and even over the sound of the howling wind and his own chanting Killian could hear the crunch of stone that had stood in place for centuries, disturbed and angry as the Wall tore itself free.

Killian roared and pushed harder. Looking at his outstretched hands, he saw his runes begin to dim, but he continued relentlessly. He suddenly knew in his heart that he was making a difference, and he chanted, calling on everything Evrin had taught him about the elements.

Killian heard a strident female voice as Shani pushed with him. Killian's voice rose in a shout, and he felt he could hear every other elementalist working with him in concert, every one of them calling on the wind.

The Wall tipped forward. It moved faster now.

With a sound of terrible thunder, the length of stone crashed. The trembling grew stronger, and the roar of breaking stone became impossibly loud until it stunned the senses. The ground shook in a mighty quake, and a cloud of dust rose to obscure everything as the Wall flattened the ground in front of Seranthia, crushing every plant and animal in its path.

Killian felt triumph course through him. Glancing at his runes, he saw he'd drained much of his power, but they'd done it.

He stretched his arms out at his sides and rose into the air.

Dust covered the ground, and for a moment Killian couldn't make any sense of the upheaval in front of the city. He rose higher into the sky, and higher still, and then he could see the immense cloud of powdered stone and dirt where the Wall had fallen.

Nothing could have survived that destruction.

Killian only hoped Miro and Bartolo had made it out in time.

Rising higher still, Killian saw the heaving battle underway between the allied houses and the infantry square. If this last force could be defeated, the day would be won.

The fighting surged back and forth, but Killian felt a chill as he saw that Tiesto would be outflanked at any moment. He prepared to launch himself at the enemy and do whatever he could to help out, when something, a shiver of awareness that couldn't be explained, made him look back at the harbor.

What he saw made him gasp.

It was incredible, impossible.

Killian realized he was needed elsewhere even more than he was needed at the battlefield below.

Killian now knew where he could find Sentar Scythran.

57

Removed from command, Rogan Jarvish stood in his armorsilk, waiting inside the city gates.

He felt frustrated. Aside from hearing the order for the defenders to leave the Wall, he had no idea what was happening outside the city, nor what the reason for the order was. He assumed they would soon be sallying from the gate to try to link up with the allied army outside.

And Rogan planned to fight.

He walked back and forth, a solitary splash of green among the ranks of purple, as he looked to the gates, wondering when they would open.

Rogan heard men gasp as a line of fire appeared in the gate. It traveled from one end to the other, cutting through the wood and iron, reaching the end and disappearing. Rogan watched in astonishment.

He looked to the soldiers, but they were as confused as he was. Still they waited.

Then a wind came up. It was a wind unlike anything Rogan had ever experienced. It buffeted his body, ripping at his clothing, and then it began to push at him from behind.

What was happening?

The fearful Tingaran legionnaires muttered and exchanged wide-eyed glances. Soon the muttering ceased as they were forced to concentrate on standing upright. Rogan crouched and felt the wind push at him. His feet slipped forward of their own accord. Some incredible lore was at play. Rogan only hoped it came from his side and not the enemy.

Then Rogan's eyes widened and blood drained from his face as he saw the unthinkable happen.

The Wall, that great gray presence never absent from view at any quarter of Seranthia, began to wobble.

Slowly, inexorably, the indomitable height of stone began to fall forward. Soldiers cried out as they saw the unfolding destruction. Time slowed and Rogan's awareness became heightened as the Wall tumbled forward, and now its own weight pulled it down, speeding toward the ground, and with a mighty roar of crashing stone and tumbling earth, it fell.

The soldiers pressed their hands to their ears as the fall of stone covered all other sound. The ground heaved beneath Rogan's feet and dust rose in an all-encompassing cloud, covering the entire city.

In front of Rogan and the men who stood with him, the gates simply fell away, vanishing into the swells of dust and vaporized stone.

Rogan saw the kalif of the Hazarans struggle to control his stallion as it reared again and again. Finally, Ilathor got his mount under control.

As Rogan tried to make sense of it, he realized what they'd done. It was a terrible risk—and a great victory. Even as the fall crushed the swarming horde, the city's primary defense was gone.

The thunder gradually subsided, leaving an eerie silence in its place, and then one man's voice rose to break the sudden stillness.

"The city's defenseless!" Rogan called to the men around him. He didn't want to think about the fate of anyone who'd been below the Wall when it fell. "I'm not waiting anymore."

Rogan gazed around and met the eyes of Marshal Trask, standing hesitantly in his armor with bands of purple. "Are you with me?" Rogan said.

Trask nodded. "We will follow, Blademaster."

"Kalif?" Rogan called to Ilathor.

Ilathor nodded and drew his scimitar, speaking an activation sequence, sending fire along the length of the curved steel.

"Follow me!" Rogan cried as he ran forward, the men around him taking up the cry. *"Attack!"*

Rogan began to sing in a low chant, leaping over the fallen rubble and heading straight into the cloud of dust. He easily outdistanced the slower Tingarans and saw horses on all sides as the desert warriors deftly jumped the rubble and led their mounts into the heart of the opaque storm of dirt and powdered stone.

Then there was yellow dust on all sides, and Rogan coughed and choked, struggling to breathe. He was forced to cease his chanting and instead concentrate on dodging around the blocks and darting between horses as he ran forward.

It was unlike any battle he'd ever been in.

It was impossible to see. The dust was so thick, it filled his nose and mouth. Rogan gasped for fresh air but kept running, pushing his aging body through the mass of horses and littered stone. Beside him a horse tripped on a block, and its leg shattered with a sickening crack, propelling the rider out of the saddle. Rogan helped the Hazaran stand and saw with relief that he was unharmed, but Rogan kept running, knowing that if the revenants made it through the dust cloud, the city would be theirs for the taking.

It would be a massacre.

A man rushed out of the cloud, heading directly for Rogan, and he held a huge two-handed sword above his head. Taking in the glow of runes and the white-eyed stare, Rogan choked a series of runes and sent fire into his zenblade, though his armorsilk stayed dark. He ducked under the overhead blow and thrust into the neck, flicking his wrist to sever the spinal column. The revenant warrior fell, and then Rogan was in the heart of it.

Revenants and horses were everywhere in a chaotic confusion of spraying blood and rolling dust, figures appearing and disappearing in the haze. Rogan cut down enemy after enemy, gasping the sequences for his zenblade and armorsilk, seeing his blade light up with fire and then dim again as he coughed. He saw enemy warriors swarm forward to leap on top of the horsemen and drag the desert men from their saddles, hacking and slashing at the bodies before turning to the next.

He continued to move forward as he fought, lunging ahead after he dispatched each foe, leaping on top of the stones to gain height and thrust down at the revenants as they threw themselves at him and he cut them down.

Then Rogan was clear of the dust.

Suddenly, he burst free into fresh air. He could see the hills surrounding Seranthia, and below the hills the plain was filled with soldiers of the Empire, clashing with a heaving mass of formed-up revenants.

The soldiers of the Empire were outnumbered.

Rogan sucked in a lungful of air as he fought to regain his breath. He saw a glowing spear at the front of the allied army; they could only be Alturan infantry and bladesingers. The point of the wedge struck deep into the heart of the enemy, but even they couldn't break through, and like the horns of a bull, the flanks of the horde came out to envelop them.

Rogan scanned to the left and right. He was alone. The defenders of Seranthia were fighting in the dust cloud.

He fixed his gaze on a cluster of uniformed revenants and saw the warrior who led them, clad in black-and-white checkers. Rogan regained his breath and once more commenced his song.

He ran forward, and fighting alone, Rogan Jarvish threw himself at the enemy's rear.

58

Sentar Scythran climbed up the stairs and emerged from the glowing stairway at the Sentinel's base to stand once more in the open air.

Rage coursed through him.

After the wretched enchantress's destruction of his essence, he'd entered the chamber inside the Sentinel and once more examined the portal, desperate to find some way to open the gateway and bring his brothers home.

But to open the portal he would need essence.

Sentar calmed his rage, feeling clarity return to his thoughts.

Fortunately, he knew just where he could find some.

He'd left necromancers in Aynar, their task to build vats and raise more revenants, to gather essence in quantity for just such an eventuality.

Sentar had cunning. If one strategy failed, he always had another prepared.

Huge blocks of stone clustered around the base of the pedestal, remains of the wall that had enclosed the statue. Freed of its encumbrance the Sentinel now stood proud and tall.

Sentar looked up at the statue and smiled.

The portal wasn't the greatest relic the Evermen ever devised. It was the Sentinel in its entirety that took the combined powers of the Evermen to create. The portal was just one part.

Sentar walked away from the legs until he could stare up at the torso, and leaning his head back, he could see the great head, the noble cast of its features, and the regal aspect to its eyes, nose, and mouth.

The Sentinel had one arm raised to point somewhere in the distance, as if giving homage to the bright sun, or trying to touch the stars.

Sentar felt his seething emotions replaced with satisfaction. He could hear great crashes and explosions from across the harbor, the sounds rolling out from the city, but he didn't care about the fate of Renrik, or Gorain, or his revenant army.

They were just a distraction. The power was his.

Sentar lifted his arms at his sides and chanted under his breath. He rose into the air. It was time to show the humans how much power he had.

Sentar ran his eyes over the statue as he climbed the sky. He saw the huge, powerful legs, and the thick torso. He passed the broad shoulders and gazed up at the gigantic head.

Sentar rose until he was level with the statue's head. He floated forward until he was looking at the flowing hair, held back by a crown.

A single rune decorated the crown.

Sentar ceased his chant but continued to float. He began a new chant. Even for the Lord of the Night, this chant was complex.

He first spoke a single activation sequence. The rune on the crown lit up with a soft emerald glow. Sentar remembered the Sentinel's genesis, feeling the power he and his brothers had given this, their greatest creation.

Sentar's voice rose in a steady stream of words and inflections. He opened his mouth to call the sequences loud and clear, feeling a surge of triumph as the millions of tiny symbols inscribed and hidden all over the statue came to life. Rainbows of color flickered and danced in his vision. A steady hum filled the air, a low sizzle of energy.

Sentar's arms dropped to his sides.

The Sentinel's eyes opened.

Sentar felt savage joy course through him. He had woken the giant. Only one of the Evermen, a god, could commune with this, their most powerful creation.

Looking into the huge eyes, Sentar spoke. "Sentinel. Remove yourself from the pedestal."

Glancing down, Sentar smiled as he saw a line of green fire spark around each foot. With a groan, first one knee lifted, and the foot below came away from the pedestal before setting itself back down. The second foot followed suit.

The Sentinel thrummed with power. The raised arm lowered, and the statue regarded Sentar with a look that could have been called inquisitive.

"Sentinel, take yourself from here. Go to Stonewater."

The arm came up again, the statue slowly turned, and this time the statue pointed south, toward Stonewater. In the direction of Sentar's place of power.

"Yes. To Stonewater." Sentar had a sudden thought. "But first, Sentinel," he said, "I have another task for you." Sentar pointed at Seranthia. "Destroy that city."

The arm swept around once more as the Sentinel turned and pointed at Seranthia.

Sentar tilted his head back and laughed as the Sentinel turned to face the city. With heavy, ground-shaking steps, it moved forward, its size belying its agility as it stepped off the pedestal and reached the water's edge.

The Sentinel kicked its legs and launched itself forward, over the clutter of the stones, landing in the water and plunging below the surface. Sentar rose higher into the air, feeling pleasure when he saw the vibrant colors shining up from below the harbor's depths. The glow moved forward, and Sentar floated in line to follow it from above.

As it grew closer to the docks, first the crown crested the water, and then the head. The Sentinel's shoulders were now above the surface, with Sentar following from behind.

Sentar frowned.

A figure stood at the docks, as if waiting the Sentinel's arrival. Sentar took in the fiery red hair and black clothing, the nine-pointed star on the man's chest. His eyes narrowed as he sped forward.

59

"Sentinel," Killian said. He didn't know how he knew the relic would understand him, but he could see awareness in the glowing eyes. "Go back. Go from this place."

The eyes shifted, fixating on Killian as he felt a tremor of apprehension run though his body. Would the Sentinel acknowledge him as one of the Evermen?

"Go east," Killian said, pointing out to where the harbor opened up onto the Tingaran Sea. "Do not stop until you reach land."

Standing on the edge of the dock, feeling the wooden planks firm beneath his feet, Killian held his breath.

The shoulders shifted; the head turned back around. Once more the Sentinel sank beneath the water, leaving a surging whirlpool as it subsided.

Killian heard a roar of rage an instant before he saw him. There was a blur of motion, and then Sentar was suddenly beside him on the docks, barely a dozen paces away.

Killian felt his own anger rise. All of the destruction could be laid squarely at the feet of the self-proclaimed Lord of the Night. This man had killed Evrin Evenstar. He'd destroyed the lands across the sea and ravaged Ella's homeland. Sentar was responsible for untold deaths across the Empire, people Killian was supposed to protect.

Even as he seethed, Killian took in Sentar's appearance in macabre fascination. His hair was dark red, the color of fresh arterial blood, and slicked back to his head. Streaks of black hair at his temples, and black clothing to match. But more than anything, it was his eyes that drew Killian's gaze. They were dead, expressionless, with an icy stare that filled Killian with dread.

Killian drew on his anger even as his heart thundered in his chest, using the rage to banish his fear.

Evrin had described Sentar Scythran as the most dangerous opponent Killian would ever face. The Lord of the Night was at the height of his power. Killian's own runes were faded, drained from the struggle at the Wall.

The two men locked gazes, eye to eye, neither of them breaking contact.

"Leave my city alone," Killian said.

"*Your* city?" Sentar sneered. "You are a god. You don't have a city—or an empire; you have a world! Why fight me? Together we can easily defeat them all."

"I once followed another's dreams of glory," Killian said. "Never again."

Killian began to chant, allowing his body to rise in the air as he spoke. The farther they were from the city, the more chance his people had of avoiding further destruction.

Sentar climbed the sky with him, the two red-haired men circling each other, only a stone's throw apart.

"We will let you join us," Sentar said. "We will give you a kingdom, and you will rule your humans however you see fit. The wolf does not huddle with the sheep. You have no idea of your true potential."

"I know enough," Killian said. "I survived Shar."

Sentar raised an eyebrow. "You were there? Impressive. Tell me, Killian—Emperor—how did you enter the portal?"

Killian realized his error. He'd just revealed to Sentar that they'd found a way to open the portal.

"Or did someone open it for you?" Sentar continued. "Perhaps the young enchantress? Tell me, Emperor, how is she? As much as I enjoyed holding her life in my hands, I enjoyed taking it more."

With a cry, Killian opened his hands and shouted a quick series of activations. Four twisting lines of black lightning poured from his palms and stabbed at Sentar Scythran.

The Lord of the Night held up his palm and a hazy field of energy appeared in front of him, deflecting the attack, sending the lightning scattering off to the sides like rain off a shield.

Killian bit the words off as he muttered sequence after sequence and changed the nature of his attack, sending a solid spout of fire from his hands to strike Sentar's defensive barrier.

Sentar's lips moved soundlessly, calmly, as he fended off the onslaught. Then, without warning, he dropped.

Sentar's body plummeted through the air, and then he flew back up to launch balls of flame one after the other at Killian, from underneath. Killian projected his body out of the way, tumbling through the sky out of control. Sentar tracked him with his hands, sending fiery spheres one after the other until first one and then another splashed against Killian's body.

Killian's runes lit up as they fended off the attack, and he wheeled to once more draw level with his enemy.

High in the skies above Seranthia, the battle between the two Evermen began.

60

At the forefront of a wedge of the strongest fighters, Tiesto threw himself at his opponents, sending limbs and heads in all directions as he whirled into the fray. He was dimly aware of fighting all around: Tingaran legionnaires launching disciplined charges into the ranks of the enemy; avengers tossing revenants high in the air; soldiers from across the Empire marching forward in unison, pushing their opponents back before stepping forward once more.

Tiesto was too embroiled to issue orders to the high lords and marshals, but he could see each column working together to guard the flanks of the other, neither surging too far ahead nor holding back in cowardice.

Yet neither army gave ground easily, and Tiesto sensed the allied forces meeting heavy resistance, and then the revenants began to push back. The two long lines faced each other, but the enemy's ranks were deeper, and this gave them the strength to hold. The revenant line was longer, and began to stretch to the left and right, beginning to envelop Tiesto's army in its longer arms.

Even as he cut down snarling foes, Tiesto could see the great cloud of dust; this cloud was now the only barrier between the horde and the streets of Seranthia. The Wall had fallen moments before, stunning them all. Spotting a huge block of stone, Tiesto pushed down his fear and leapt forward, dispatching a barbarian warrior with two successive blows before climbing up on top of the block to gain a vantage.

He had only the briefest instant to gauge the flow of the battle, but he could see this last disciplined force was simply too strong. Not only was Tiesto losing his men faster than they were taking down the revenants, when they were finished with Tiesto's army, Scranthia would be next.

"Renrik!" Tiesto heard a bellow, and he saw the huge Dain of the Akari charge a square of revenants protecting a necromancer in their center.

Even weakened, Dain Barden was an indomitable force. Each swing of his hammer smashed heads and bodies into pulp, and he fought alone, unaware or uncaring of the fact that he was surrounded by enemies on all sides. He stood as high as the tallest of the barbarians, and his muscled arms wielded his weapon with savage strength. His armor of bleached leather was torn and covered in blood, but the Dain had only eyes for his traitorous necromancer, the man it had all started with, when Sentar visited the Akari, long ago.

Tiesto tore his eyes from the Dain's struggle as a group of revenants came close, but his men pushed them back, and he once more scanned the battlefield.

Dain Barden was now two men from the gray-robed necromancer, and then one. He killed the last revenant with a crushing blow to the skull, and then Renrik turned and fled.

The Dain snarled as revenants came between him and the fleeing necromancer, and then there were so many flashing blades that Tiesto could no longer make sense of the struggle.

Looking farther out, Tiesto saw Hazarans trickle out of the cloud of dust, the desert warriors choking and gasping, and then the trickle became a steady stream of riders. Directly in front of Tiesto, a cluster of three Tingaran avengers broke through the enemy ranks, flails whirling, giving Tiesto a moment's respite.

As Alturan heavy infantry with glowing armor and swords surged to follow the spearhead into the enemy's heart, Tiesto heard a man calling his name.

"Tiesto!"

Tiesto turned and saw Bartolo pushing forward, blood splattered on the man's face and hands.

"Where's Miro?"

"I lost him. Look! Back at the hills!"

Tiesto turned back to the hills and saw a long line of red. A huge flag flapped in the breeze, and Tiesto recognized the teardrop and flame.

"It's the Petryan advance guard!" Bartolo cried. "The Petryans have come!"

"They're too far away." Tiesto grimaced. "We'll lose the battle before they get here."

Sweeping his gaze across the clouds of dust and engaged men at every point of the line, Tiesto had an idea.

"Bartolo, go and find the kalif. The Hazarans are coming out of the dust on our right. If you can't find Ilathor, find Jehral. Tell him to gather his horsemen and ride up to the hills. Fetch the Petryans and bring them down to the battle."

"What if Ilathor refuses?"

"Make him!" Tiesto growled.

Bartolo grinned. "All right."

As Bartolo sped away, Tiesto once more saw the danger at his flanks. The three avengers had all fallen, revenants hacking down at them as they writhed.

Tiesto saw the enemy preparing a countercharge at the gap left by the avengers and, realizing the danger, saw it was time to make his own attack.

"To me!" Tiesto cried.

He waved his single-activation sword high above his head and leapt back into the fray with renewed vigor, signaling his intent with the fiery line of his sword. Soldiers of all nations gathered to his call, roaring and shouting in defiance.

61

Miro fought.

Lost in the dust, Miro looked for Bartolo, but he couldn't see much at all. His zenblade was completely dark, and without the power of Ella's lore, the long blade became heavy and difficult to wield. Miro concentrated on his armorsilk, chanting for protection and shadow, and with the battlefield a confused melee of powdered stone and screaming warriors, he simply looked for opponents, throwing himself at enemies as quickly as they came.

He fought by running, flicking his sword to the left and right as he charged, knocking as many back with his shoulder as he did with his blade. He poured activations into his armorsilk, his voice rising and falling with each stroke of the bright steel, and each cut at a warrior was met with a cry, the sharp sword slicing through flesh and bone. Penetrating deep into the ranks, he realized he was among the toughest of the enemy warriors, revenants in black-and-white checkered uniforms, and these were skilled swordsmen, many carrying enchanted weapons.

Soldiers of all nations fought and died on all sides. It was the most chaotic struggle Miro had ever fought in. Dust came and went, obscuring the city and then revealing the enemy's endless numbers. An Alturan on Miro's left fell as a gash opened in his throat, and a Veznan on his right died as a warrior in black tore his body in two. Two more soldiers filled the spaces they left, but were in turn cut down.

And then it was only Miro.

Glancing around, he saw the allied attack had faltered; he was the only one of the charging men still among the cluster of uniformed warriors.

Miro saw Gorain himself.

A space had opened around the pirate king of Nexos. The revenant in his black and white garb held a sliver of purple light, an enchanted blade, as long as a zenblade and wielded with precise skill. Opposing him, a tall man in shining green silk whirled to meet every strike, his own blade crashing against his enemy's with each darting parry, every feint and thrust.

The two swordsmen circled each other, stepping in and out like trained dancers, carving the air between them in a deadly flurry of blows. They moved so quickly Miro couldn't see any opening for either warrior to take. This was swordsmanship of the highest order.

Only when the tall man in green blocked a strong overhead blow and grimaced as his muscles strained with effort, did Miro see the gray hair and scarred face.

The warrior in shining armorsilk was Rogan Jarvish.

A steady song came from Rogan's lips, the zenblade seething with energy as he darted forward and leapt back, spun on his heel and thrust before ducking and cutting at Gorain's legs. Rogan's blade found an opening and smashed into his opponent's side, but the runes on the revenant's skin warded off the blow with a sound like a lightning strike.

Desperately trying to find his own opening as he drew in, Miro watched as Gorain launched a counterattack, a series of slashing blows aimed at Rogan's head and torso. Rogan grimaced as he met each attack with a flashing parry, giving ground as he drew back, and now Gorain's back was to Miro.

Miro saw his chance. Thrusting his darkened zenblade at the pirate king's exposed back, Miro's eyes widened with shock as Gorain was suddenly there to meet him, moving incredibly fast to knock Miro's blade to the side and spear his purple blade into Miro.

The purple fire met the armorsilk and tore through the runes, breaking the lore and splitting the fabric. Miro screamed as he felt the steel penetrate his abdomen, but he rolled his chest away even as the blade came forward.

Rogan saw Miro's plight, and the old blademaster threw himself at Gorain, slicing and slashing, striking twice at the revenant's body. Still the runes warded off the blows.

Miro felt at his chest and looked at his hand, dripping red. Rogan feinted at Gorain's face, and as the revenant drew back, cut once more. Rogan's zenblade sliced through the pirate king's left arm at the shoulder, sending the limb flying through the air.

Rogan coughed and choked, and Miro saw the older man's breathing was labored, his face gray.

Snarling with rage and pain, Gorain spun into Rogan's overextended frame and made a reverse thrust into Rogan's chest.

The pirate king of Nexos roared in triumph as his purple blade penetrated through the armorsilk and continued through the center of Rogan's torso. Miro cried out as steel emerged from Rogan's back.

The light in Rogan Jarvish's eyes darkened, and the strength left his legs. He collapsed to the ground as blood spurted from the deep wound.

Miro felt rage fire his blood. He charged into the pirate king, smashing his shoulder into the revenant. He crashed his blade again and again into Gorain's sword, and when the pirate king expected another overhead swing, he fell to one knee and thrust with every bit of strength he possessed into the revenant's stomach. His zenblade met the resistance of the runes.

Miro's zenblade shattered.

But Miro had positioned his body as he'd intended. He dropped his broken sword and grabbed the hilt of Rogan's zenblade, still hissing and blazing with power. From one knee, Miro thrust Rogan's sword directly upward.

The point hit the underside of the pirate king's chin and continued, thrusting toward the brain. Miro grunted with effort as he pushed, his muscles straining as the zenblade fought the protective power of the revenant's runes.

Rogan's zenblade won.

Gorain's head exploded. As the last of the pirate kings died its final death, the light faded from Rogan's sword.

Miro moved to stand over Rogan. He was an island in the chaos as enemies came at him one after the other, and each time Miro fought better than he ever had to cut them down with Rogan's darkened blade. Blood dripped down Miro's chest, his arms felt like lead, but he fought on.

No enemy was going to make him move from this place.

No one.

62

High above Seranthia, waves of terrible energy cascaded across the sky as the two Evermen fought a battle that would only end with one of their deaths.

Killian dove under an assault of blue lightning and sent his own flurry of fire from his hands, chanting constantly as he launched coiled yellow spheres at his opponent.

But Sentar was fast.

He darted out of the way of each successive ball, flitting through the air and then laughing as he bathed Killian in a sudden cascade of fire.

Glancing down at his hands, Killian saw that only half of the runes on his skin still glowed brightly, the rest starting to dim. Drawing on the skills he'd learned fighting wraiths on the nightmare world of Shar, he clapped his hands together and sent a wave of concussive air toward Sentar, tossing his opponent back through the air. Sentar righted himself, and Killian saw Sentar's runes had also dimmed, but Killian had made fewer strikes.

The difference in their skill was apparent. Sentar was the more experienced fighter.

Sentar shouted a sequence and opened his palms. A vertical sheet of black energy filled the air, and with a pushing motion, Sentar sent the sheet forward. Killian warded it with his palms in the way Evrin had shown him, scattering the sizzling black energy around him.

Killian decided to gain height and spread out his arms, shooting into the sky. But Sentar was there to meet him, and this time both men held one palm to create a defensive shield and pointed their other hand to launch twisting spirals of fire. Killian's red fire splashed against Sentar's shield while the Lord of the Night's blue fire cascaded against Killian's own barrier.

Both men chanted, and Killian's brow furrowed with concentration, matching Sentar's own expression of intense absorption.

Killian's shield started to thin as it pushed back closer to his body. He felt heat begin to reach through to his skin, at first with a sensation of discomfort and then shifting to burning pain. Killian's shirt began to smoke. Sentar's face grew triumphant.

The battle was similar to a sword fight, the spirals of fire like piercing blades. Remembering Miro's training back in the Azure Plains, Killian moved his arms and turned side on, feeling immediate relief as his body presented a smaller target.

But the relief was momentary, and Killian knew he had to do better or he would die.

Recalling his own training as an acrobat, Killian dropped his attack, and even as Sentar brought his other hand forward to launch a second blast of blue fire, Killian shot up again into the air. He poured all of his power into speed, performing a complete loop in the sky to come up behind his opponent and crash into Sentar's back.

The breath shot out of Sentar's chest as Killian wrapped his arms around Sentar from behind and began to squeeze. Robbed of his ability to chant, Sentar grunted, and Killian sent a wave of lightning across his body. He saw the runes on the back of Sentar's neck dim and then one symbol after another fade altogether.

Killian squeezed with every ounce of his lore-enhanced strength. But rather than having Sentar by the neck, he only had him around the chest, and the strength it required for him to hold on was taking its toll on Killian's own runes.

He saw several symbols on his arms fade.

Sentar took a deep, gasping breath and spat out a series of activations. Sentar's body lit up like a flame, and Killian screamed as his arms burned. Killian could no longer hold on, and Sentar kicked out, sending him tumbling through the sky.

Killian's training once more saved him as he corrected his wild spin, and both palms came up to ward off the next assault. As lines of energy shot from Sentar's hands, Killian chanted to keep the defensive field up, but once more felt it pushed back as still more runes faded, and now barely a third of the symbols on Killian's body still glowed.

Sentar met Killian's level as he kept up the relentless attack, streams of blue fire pouring from his palms. Killian saw his enemy's dead eyes regard him with disdain, and he knew he was finished.

Killian felt a sudden lurch as the power to stay in the sky left him.

The drop took them both by surprise. Killian rolled and twisted as he plummeted down to meet the city below, his arms and legs scrabbling at the air.

Looking down, he saw he was somewhere between the city and the harbor. In the space of a heartbeat, the wooden docks came up to meet him with incredible speed.

At the last instant Killian gasped a series of activations and instead of crashing through the docks, he smashed hard into the wood, bouncing and rolling along the surface as agonizing pain filled his senses. Rising to his hands and knees, Killian shook his head and took in the scene.

Fire raged on a nearby shipyard, threatening to take hold of the city if it caught onto the next building. A Tingaran soldier directed a chain of people with buckets to fight the blaze, but his astonished eyes were now on Killian.

The soldier ran toward his emperor.

"No," Killian choked. "Go. Run."

The soldier was only a dozen paces away when Sentar landed gently on his feet behind him, unnoticed by the legionnaire. Sentar's hand shot forward, and he took the big Tingaran by the neck. Sentar squeezed, and with a snarl and a horrible crunch, he tore the soldier's head from his neck. Blood spurted into the air.

The Tingaran's body fell down, and his sword clattered to the wooden planks. Sentar threw the Tingaran's head at Killian's feet.

The people by the fire screamed and began to run.

Sentar smiled and whirled, launching fire at the fleeing people, taking them down in bright bursts of flame. He then turned back to Killian.

On his hands and knees, Killian looked down at the head, seeing the Tingaran's wide eyes and feeling rage burn within. As Sentar came close, Killian leapt forward with all his remaining strength, flying through the air to bring his fists down on top of Sentar's head.

His physical attack took his enemy by surprise as the twin blows struck home. Sentar reeled but struck back with a blast of air, throwing Killian twenty paces before he fell to the ground. Sentar probed his jaw and rubbed at his temple while Killian climbed back to his feet.

The two men faced each other.

"What a barbaric method of attack," Sentar said.

Killian's chest heaved as he glared at his enemy. Sentar spat a tooth out of his mouth and smiled, his teeth tinged with blood.

"Face me like a man," Killian panted, attempting to steady his breathing as he straightened, clenching his fists at his sides.

"Unfortunately for you, I won't descend to your level," Sentar said. "I am not a man." His icy stare was filled with menace. "I am a god."

Killian tried to dodge to the side, but Sentar was faster. Black lightning wrapped around Killian's body.

The glow of runes left his limbs.

Killian cried out in agony as his body convulsed, forcing his teeth together until he tasted blood. He was standing, but the only thing holding him up was the lightning, and when Sentar lowered his hands, Killian fell back to the wooden planks.

"I will make your death slow," Sentar said.

Killian tried to think, but his mind was filled with pain.

"But not too slow," said the Lord of the Night.

63

As the battle for Seranthia raged, every soldier knew that with the Wall gone the city was defenseless. The men fought with desperation, but even Amber could see the outcome was inevitable.

Outflanked, the allied army became surrounded. The last men standing fell inward against the press from the front, sides, and now behind. The once disciplined ranks of the allied army gave way to the formation of a defensive circle. There was no more use in strategy or tactics; this was simple survival.

Amber scanned the soldiers even as she was pressed inward. She searched for Miro, but he was nowhere in sight. The stormy dust in front of Seranthia still clouded her vision. Amber wished she could be with her husband. The war would soon be over.

The soldiers at the boundary fell, and the circle tightened. Those taking turns to rest in the center, the wounded and the tired, were pushed to the edge and fell in turn. The avengers were all down. The dirigibles had fled, their supplies of prismatic orbs exhausted. The last of the grenadiers had fallen long ago.

The expected sortie from the city had faltered in the dust.

Amber suddenly found herself at the perimeter, and once more she launched bolts of golden fire from her wand, though she could see its runes dim and knew it wouldn't last much longer. Revenant warriors clawed and grasped at her, and she fought them off with precision strikes, but still they kept coming. An Alturan fell at her left, his hands futilely trying to hold back the red blood spurting from his throat, and a Veznan in orange came to take his place but fell in turn.

The circle tightened again, and Amber's wand went dark.

She fell back from the boundary, and a Tingaran legionnaire in glowing armor took her place. Gasping and shivering with fear, Amber saw High Lord Tiesto grimace as he darted in and out of the enemy ranks. Bartolo and another bladesinger fought like whirlwinds, their song the only thing giving the defenders heart as they held their ground against the pressure.

More defenders fell, and the men began to look for somewhere to run. Amber could see their courage had failed them.

But they were in a circle, and there was nowhere for them to go.

Amber knelt and picked up a fallen Alturan's bloody sword. She took a deep breath. She knew nothing about wielding a sword, but she was determined to die fighting. Perhaps her enchantress's dress would give her some advantage.

As Amber prepared to leap back into the fray, she felt an intense longing for her homeland. She wanted to see her son. She looked one last time, back at the distant hills, in the direction of Altura.

Something appeared on the ridges.

First one speck sped over a crest and down toward the battlefield, then another. Suddenly, there were hundreds of horsemen thundering down the hills, galloping with savage speed. Each horse bore two riders, one in black and yellow, another in red, the color of flame.

The riders drew up to a shuddering halt just outside the battlefield, where the revenant horde surrounded the circle of defenders. Petryan elementalists leapt off horseback and formed a long line, hundreds of them.

Even through the haze of the battle, Amber saw the cuffs at their wrists light up with fire as they linked their power in a way she'd never known was possible.

Bright light traveled from one elementalist to the next, darting from wrist to wrist, and then the elementalists lifted their arms.

A wall of flame rose up, spreading to fill the air along the length of the elementalists. The wall rolled forward, and through the conflagration Amber saw the elementalists step forward in unison, moving the wall ahead of them, sending it speeding ahead like the detonation wave that rushes from a huge explosion.

The wave rolled over the revenants in a fury of heat and flame, and Amber turned her head away from the sight.

From the other direction came the thunder of hooves.

The Hazarans smashed into the enemy, horses crushing revenants beneath their hooves and warriors slashing scimitars into sinew and bone. A revenant ran straight onto Amber's sword. The hilt fell from her limp fingers, and then suddenly the wave of heat reached the defenders.

Men whose spirits had been crushed suddenly had no choice. There was only one direction they could go: away from the flames.

It was a rout and a charge all at the same time. The soldiers fleeing the flames rushed into the mass of the enemy, and the strength of their momentum met the relentless force of the horses, crushing the revenants in the middle like a block of iron between a hammer and anvil.

Even as she was carried with the soldiers, Amber felt a breeze on her cheeks, and then the wind picked up pace until it was a gale. The wind tore through the battlefield, blowing away the cloud of dust in one great sweep.

There were suddenly Tingarans everywhere.

"The Legion!" Amber heard the cry. The soldiers who'd fought in the dust to keep the helpless citizens from the enemy had finally broken free of the cloud. Now thousands of huge men with heavy armor and shaved heads fought among them. There was no order to it; everyone was all mixed in together, but for once their numbers were far greater than their opponents.

Amber was carried up in the frenzy, unable to break free. As she was pushed, she desperately searched for Miro.

In the distance she saw Dain Barden, gasping and panting as he sat on the ground. At his feet was the broken corpse of a gray-robed necromancer. The Dain of the Akari didn't look like he was going anywhere anytime soon.

Finally, Amber found him.

Miro was kneeling by a body. From his armorsilk the fallen man was a bladesinger, and his skin was white as snow, drained of all color, the blood that had once filled his veins pooling around him.

Amber saw Miro also had a wound on his chest, but he appeared unaware of the blood running down his armorsilk in rivulets.

"Miro," Amber cried as she ran to his side.

He looked up at her with haunted eyes. Amber put her hand to her mouth.

The fallen man was Rogan Jarvish. His eyes were closed, as if he were sleeping.

Together, Amber and Miro struggled to stanch his terrible wounds.

64

Ella floated in an empty void. Her consciousness was somewhere far from her body, tossed in eddies and currents like a leaf in the wind. She could barely recognize her thoughts for what they were, each disappearing before it could be properly formed.

She remembered a cavern and a fight to the death against a creature of pure evil. Just when she'd thought she'd achieved victory, the cavern had vanished, and now she was here.

She was dimly aware of voices, and she heard her name. One of the voices, a strong, masculine voice, was familiar.

Killian?

Ella tried to say his name, but then the wind came up, and she was suddenly far away again.

She fought to come back to the place where there was thought. The swirling gusts tore at her every time she tried to press forward, and try as she might, she couldn't return.

Ella drifted for a time.

Then with force, more sounds came to her. Shouts and explosions, and a colossal fall, the sound of a mountain crashing down.

And then Ella's thoughts shattered like pieces of glass, tumbling away with her fear. She saw a radiant light and fled to it, and with a soft sigh she once more felt peace and harmony settle over her awareness, but she'd felt this sensation before and she fought it as much as she'd fought her fear. She struggled as the ethereal wind picked up pace, tearing at the last glimmers of knowledge about who she was.

Ella tried to cry out, but her voice was taken from her, along with her ability to think.

Ella needed something to ground herself. The thoughts whirled through what remained of her being, and she discarded each in turn. Then a thought came that Ella seized with the desperation of a drowning child clutching onto a rope.

She thought of an old man with kind blue eyes, and first she concentrated on his face. When she had it firm in her mind, she felt the ethereal wind settle down. As she pictured Evrin's face, she drew away from the light and knew she needed still more to hold on to.

She remembered Evrin's words. What would save her wasn't experience or knowledge, for the struggle she faced wasn't anything she'd ever gone through before, and it wasn't something she could think her way through.

Ella instead drew on her courage.

Rather than searching the void, she searched within herself and felt a thread of power blossom from somewhere deep inside. Ella took hold of the thread and felt her awareness grow until she could suddenly hold onto more than one thought at once.

The wind picked up as she tried to seize more from the well of power. The gust grew in force until it howled and shrieked, trying to block all thought from forming, overwhelming her with the deafening sound.

Ella fought, but she was growing weak, and the more she became aware, the more the wind tore at her, threatening to throw her far from the golden light of peace and instead send her screaming into the void.

Ella tried to calm her fear, but again she needed something to ground herself. She then realized what her visions had been trying to tell her.

Ella remembered seeing herself as a child, and her mother, Katherine, by her side in a way Ella had never known in memory, but she knew in her heart was real. Brandon Goodwin, her old guardian, hadn't just taught her manners, he'd brought her up, and many of her values were his. She saw Miro, even as a boy, telling her that sometimes the only way was to fight.

Ella focused on the faces: Evrin, Katherine, Brandon, Miro. The wind stilled.

She reached down inside herself and drew on more of the thread of power.

The wind was a gale, and then a storm. As Ella's memories came, it tore at her, threatening to rip the thread of power away from her grip. Ella knew she had to fight it with every bit of strength she had.

Ella took hold of more of her inner power, bunching it together, hauling on the shining radiance, pulling herself down to the ground.

Even as she perceived a strange feeling of wakefulness, Ella felt the wind come at her from all directions at once. She was in the middle of a vortex, and it was spinning her, around and around, over and again. Ella felt herself losing her way, and her thoughts began to fragment.

She focused on more faces: Layla's smirk, Shani's glare, Rogan's look of concern. She brought more people to the front of her consciousness: Amber, Jehral, Bartolo, Ilathor, Amelia, Tapel, Tomas . . .

Ella focused on Killian. She saw the warm smile that touched even the corners of his eyes, and she heard his laugh. She wanted to hear that laugh again.

She knew that she couldn't let them down. She couldn't vanish into the void or rise up into the soft golden light of peace.

Ella used her love to bring herself home.

The wind died down, and Ella took hold of the thread of power with the last shreds of her courage. Rather than let the wind toss her away, she accepted it. Rather than hauling on the radiance, she imagined the power inside her, a well of strength that was there to draw on whenever she needed it.

And then the power was inside her.

⸻

Ella opened her eyes. Blinking, she saw daylight pour through the open window. She was in her personal bedchamber in the Imperial Palace, lying on her back under the covers. She pushed the covers aside and stepped out of the bed.

She cast her eyes around the chamber and saw her set of scrills lying side by side on the table, a vial half-filled with essence resting next to the tools.

Ella felt strange. It wasn't an unpleasant sensation; it was more of a tingling that spread from the tips of her toes to the back of her neck and everywhere in between. She turned to her mirror and her eyes widened.

Ella's skin shone with health and vitality. Her hair—her hair!— fairly glowed, straight and lustrous, falling down nearly to her waist where before it had only just covered her breasts. She wore a sleeveless white dress that left her feet and calves bare.

Ella caught her own eyes in the reflection of the mirror, and they sparkled back at her.

She smiled.

65

Killian flew through the air to come crashing against the hard wooden wall of the burning shipyard, smashing the planks to splinters. Pulling himself shakily back to his feet, he saw Sentar Scythran walk toward him, taking his time, drawing out the moment of his revenge.

"Your enchantress destroyed my essence, but there will be more," Sentar said. "There is always more essence as long as there are bodies to feed my vats. My army is but a distraction. What does a god need with an army? None of you can stand against me—not Evrin Evenstar and not you. All alone I can dominate your species. The humans are mortal, yet we, Emperor—we are immortal. And you chose to throw it away!"

Killian looked frantically around the docks for a weapon. Every rune on his body was nearly faded. He spotted a steel sword resting on the planks. The head of the Tingaran soldier sat nearby, fixing Killian with his pain-filled stare.

"You've failed, Emperor. Only you had the power to stop me, but it was always an uneven contest. What do you know of the Evermen? I have lived for over a thousand years. What skill do you have? Only what Evrin Evenstar could teach you in a comparative second. You were never going to defeat me. It was always a foregone conclusion."

Killian spoke an activation sequence as he leapt forward and shot a weak ball of flame from one hand. Sentar laughed as his warding hand fended off the blow. Though more than half the runes on Sentar's body had dimmed, it was a puny strike.

Killian rolled and flame struck the wooden planks of the dock where he'd been a moment before. His fingers brushed the Tingaran's sword, but blue fire enveloped him. Once more he felt himself picked up. Once more he was completely under Sentar's control, and there was nothing he could do about it.

Sentar walked forward as he flicked his wrists and turned Killian to face him. Killian's back arched, and his head tilted back as his feet left the ground. The blue fire brightened, and Killian screamed with pain as his clothing again began to smolder.

Killian's pain diminished as Sentar ceased his chanting to speak, but Killian knew that in moments the agony would return in force.

"I've had my fun," Sentar Scythran said.

Killian's feet returned to the ground, and he collapsed onto his back, powerless to do anything about his own helplessness or even to brace his fall, the pain in every part of his body so strong he could barely think.

"Now it's time for you to die. Know this, Emperor. I will grind your people to dust. When I am finished with you, this world will be next."

As Sentar loomed over him, Killian turned his head, refusing to meet Sentar's icy gaze. He instead looked past the Lord of the Night's shoulder.

Killian's eyes went wide.

Ella stood behind Sentar Scythran. Yet she had changed. She was . . . different.

Ella's pale blonde hair shimmered nearly to her waist, parted in the middle, but at her left temple there was a fiery swath of red, a streak that began at her crown and cascaded down along the entire length of her hair.

She wore a plain white sleeveless dress, devoid of decoration, and her feet were bare. Yet though her dress was unadorned, her skin was covered in faint silver symbols, fresh and intricate, coating her neck, arms, legs, and feet.

Frowning at Killian's stare, Sentar whirled. For once, the Lord of the Night was without words.

"You're no god," Ella said softly. "You never were."

Sentar's mouth worked, but no sound came out.

"You were simply lucky," Ella said. She spoke calmly, as if instructing a child. "An ancestor of yours survived the touch of essence. I know it wasn't you who survived, for survival takes incredible strength."

"It's not possible." Sentar was rocked. His mouth gaped open as he struggled to make sense of it.

"I know," Ella said, each syllable deliberate, and the evidence was there for Sentar to see.

Killian climbed unsteadily to his feet, and Sentar didn't stop him.

"There is a difference between power and strength," Ella said.

"You're human, Sentar," Killian said. Sentar swung his head to face him.

"We all are," said Ella.

Sentar screamed, and it was a sound of such anguish that it split the air like thunder.

"One more thing," Ella said.

She spread her palms, and Killian saw a myriad of tiny symbols, runes shining with glittering silver.

"The emperor here wasn't the only one taught by Evrin Evenstar."

Sentar spat commands one after the other as Ella began to chant. Flecks of moisture erupted from his mouth as he snarled each activation sequence, an expression of hate distorting his face. He brought his hands forward, and twisted veins of blue fire shot out, but Ella's red fire was there to meet it, and the two streams of magical energy entwined, igniting the air between them.

The two streams of fire collided, and the burning air in the middle pushed first toward Sentar, then toward Ella, and then back toward Sentar again.

Ella's expression was calm as she chanted, but Sentar's was wild with rage. First one, then another symbol on Sentar's palm began to fade. Ella's voice rose in pitch and intensity, and she added more streams of blue energy to the air in front of her. She pushed with her arms, sending Sentar's feet sliding along the dock.

Ella's body began to glow as her runes shielded her from the searing heat. She glowed brighter and brighter until Killian couldn't look on.

Sentar's runes darkened one after the other, and his black velvet shirt began to smoke. The cuffs at his wrists started to melt, and the chain at his neck sizzled against his skin. Ella pushed forward again, and the central zone of superheated air moved inevitably closer to the Lord of the Night.

Sentar screamed.

Killian picked up the sword.

He recalled Miro's instruction. Miro said that when the time came, he couldn't hesitate to strike.

Killian leapt forward, and as the last of the runes on Sentar's body darkened and Sentar's hair caught fire, Killian struck with all of his strength, thrusting into Sentar Scythran's back.

Killian pushed and felt the last of the Evermen's lore leave his body along with his life. The blade met little resistance and emerged from Sentar's chest.

Ella's hands dropped.

Killian pulled out the sword, and Sentar Scythran cried out one last time, a gasping wheeze that exited his body along with the dripping blade.

The Lord of the Night crumpled, his eyes staring wide, dead before he hit the ground.

Killian lowered the dripping sword, red with blood, and crouched at Sentar's side.

The Lord of the Night's eyes were wide and unblinking. Otherwise, the dead stare hadn't much changed.

66

Miro woke and groaned as he felt pain in his stomach. He tried to free his hands, but they were trapped by another's grip. He writhed around until he heard a soothing voice.

"Shh," Amber said. "You've been wounded. Don't try to move."

"What . . . ?" Miro said, looking wildly around him.

He was in a bedchamber with the familiar marble floor and slate and timber walls of the Imperial Palace. An open window let in a steady breeze. It was evidently nighttime.

"It's over," Amber said soothingly. "You're safe. You're in the palace."

"How long?" Miro said.

"Two days."

Miro suddenly shot up and tried to throw off the covers. "Rogan!"

Amber pressed down on his arms. "Miro, listen to me. He's very badly wounded. They're saying he might not make it. Right now he's being tended by the emperor's best healers, but it doesn't look good."

"I have to see him," Miro said.

"You will. But they don't want any interruption right now, and you need to rest. He lost a lot of blood, and they're trying to save his life. You've lost a lot of blood too."

Miro sank back to the bed, his limbs feeling weak and mind thick. "How . . . ?" he began and then coughed and cleared his throat. "How am I here?"

"The Petryan elementalists arrived at the battle. They burned the revenants. Lord of the Sky, I've never seen anything like it. They blew the dust away, the Legion regrouped, and we hit the enemy. I found you with Rogan."

"I remember," Miro said. His dark eyes were shadowed.

"You were trying to help Rogan, but you were wounded yourself. Bartolo and Tiesto helped me bring the two of you back here."

"And the enemy?"

"The Petryan infantry arrived at the city soon after. They'd marched after receiving Stonewater's distress call. Sentar Scythran left necromancers in Aynar to build more vats and raise more revenants. The Petryans freed Stonewater and Salvation, clearing the land as they marched for Tingara and Seranthia."

Miro's eyes went wide. "Sentar!" he once more tried to sit up.

"He's dead. We have his body, and we're showing it to the people, letting them see that one of the Evermen can die just as easily as any other human."

"Dead? How?" Miro's breath caught. "Killian. He did it?"

"No," Amber said, and Miro's eyebrows went up. "Well, yes. But he had help."

"Help?"

Amber smiled. "I'll let you see for yourself. Don't be shocked when you see her."

Amber rose from the bed and went to the door. Opening it, she spoke to someone outside, and then she entered with Ella behind her.

"Ho, Miro," Ella said, smiling.

Miro's mouth dropped open. Ella's pale blonde hair shone in the golden light of the room's nightlamp. But she had a streak of strawberry red at her left temple, an inch wide line framing her face and falling down nearly to her waist. Her green eyes were now tinged with blue, like emeralds glinting within sapphires. Rather than her silk enchantress's garb, she wore a dress of sky blue, thick and supple material that fit her better than the cloth of an enchantress ever had.

"Ella . . ." Miro spluttered. "You . . ."

"I'm still the same." Ella grinned. "I've just grown, that's all."

Amber's eyes moved from one face to the other. She looked like she was fighting to keep a smile from her face.

"How?" Miro said. "Lord of the Sky, I keep saying that."

"Do you remember the alchemist Tungawa's dying words to Amber?"

"'Everything is toxic; it is the dose that makes a thing a poison,'" Miro said. "I think that was it."

"I think he knew he was onto the biggest secret of all. There's so little we understand about essence. It gives objects incredible properties. It can bring the dead back to life. Elixir can be made from essence, turning a deadly substance into something that gives longevity and powers of rejuvenation. I think that's the first hint we should have had that the history of the Evermen was tied to essence."

"You . . . you're like Killian now?"

"Yes," Ella said simply. "Killian and I defeated Sentar Scythran together. In the end, I wonder if he didn't let himself die. The knowledge that he wasn't a god must have been the most painful blow of all. Yet, for a change," she grinned again, "this is something I can't explain. Aldrik, one of the Dain's necromancers, tainted the Akari's essence. I didn't even know essence could be tainted, and I became sick." Ella grew serious. "So sick. The pain was . . . it was terrible. I knew I was going to die. When I destroyed Sentar's supply of essence, I fell into the sea, and some of that essence was mixed up with the seawater."

"Ella was affected by essence poisoning," Amber said. "They took her back to the palace, and everyone thought she was going to die."

"I dreamt," Ella said. "Evrin came to me, and he told me I had to fight. But it wasn't fighting that brought me back, it was thinking of you two, and everyone else I loved. There was . . . a light. It was beautiful. But I made a decision. It wasn't yet my time."

Miro spoke slowly, struggling with the words. "I have heard of this," he said, "from soldiers who've been close to death but survived. The mind struggles to make sense of the changes to the body and invents gods and demons, tunnels and lights."

"That's what I would have said before it happened to me," Ella said. "But now I don't feel so sure. I know the Evermen weren't gods, and the stories of flying through the clouds, healing the sick and bringing people back to life come from those who struggled to make sense of their powers. But long ago, Layla told me about the Eternal, who works to keep balance in the world. I don't know if there's an Eternal, but there's something out there, and it enabled me to survive."

Miro and Amber exchanged glances.

"I have to say, Ella. That doesn't sound like you at all."

"Maybe that's a good thing," Ella said.

"I'll reserve judgment," said Miro. "And please don't fault me if I continue to believe the things I see with my own eyes."

"I won't." Ella smiled.

"Where's Killian?" Amber asked.

"He's setting the city to rights, helping the wounded get attention, hunting down wandering revenants."

"Have you spoken?" Miro asked.

"There's still a lot to do. He's the emperor and he takes his responsibilities seriously."

"He does," Miro said, "but that doesn't mean the two of you don't need to talk."

Ella stared out the window, as if unwilling to meet Miro's eyes.

"I still can't believe it," Miro said. "Your hair . . . your eyes. Does this mean anyone can become like you now?"

"I wouldn't recommend it," Ella said. "If someone's willing to go through what I did, then perhaps they deserve their reward. It's not like there was any logic to it. If I hadn't been affected by the tainted essence, would I have survived essence poisoning? What effect did the seawater have, and how much essence was in it? I just have to trust that these things worked out for a reason."

"Now that really doesn't sound like you," Miro said.

"Do you remember when you'd started training at the Pens, you used to come home with bruises from the other boys?"

Miro frowned. "I remember."

"You told me that sometimes there's no other way but to fight. Do you remember that?"

"I do."

"See?" Ella said. "It's me."

"Of course it's you," Amber said, pulling Ella into a quick embrace.

"Ella," Miro said, "will you talk to Killian?"

Ella stood, ignoring Miro's question. "I need to go and see if there's any news about Rogan. Before I go, can you tell me something?"

"What is it?" Miro said.

"The alchemist, Tungawa. Was he old, with a high forehead and crinkles around his eyes, and did he wear a black robe with a triangle bound by a double circle?"

Miro and Amber both nodded.

"Think on this," Ella said. "I saw the alchemist when I dreamt. If they were just visions invented by my mind, then how did I know that, if neither of you told me?"

Ella smiled and exited the chamber, leaving Miro and Amber open mouthed.

67

Another day of waiting for news of Rogan passed, another day of setting the city to rights.

Ella sat on her bed holding a note in her hands. The paper was heavy and edged with gold. Her hands shook and her heart raced, thudding in her ears with a steady beat.

Ella's hands fell down to her lap, and she closed her eyes.

For a long time she fought to calm her breathing as she thought about the message.

Hearing a knock on the door, she opened her eyes and called out. "Come in."

Miro entered, and Ella immediately came to her feet. His face was pale and filled with anguish.

"What's wrong?"

"It's Rogan," Miro said. "I think you should come now."

Putting the note aside, Ella followed her brother along the marble-floored corridors of the palace to an antechamber.

Dread sank into Ella's stomach as she looked at the door to the next room, where the healers had been tending Rogan. Sunlight shone through the open window, but the mood was somber.

Amelia spoke in low tones to a middle-aged woman, evidently a healer, with a satchel over her shoulder and blood on her smock. Bartolo stared out the window with Shani by his side, her arm clutched protectively around her husband. Ilathor and Jehral stood together in a corner, their heads close together. Lady Alise made way for Miro and Ella to enter.

All eyes turned to the two newcomers as they approached.

Ella felt sudden fear clutch at her chest as she saw their expressions.

"What's . . . what's happening?"

"He wants to speak with you," Miro said, his eyes indicating the closed door. "You need to go in."

Ella met Amelia's red eyes and fought to control her ragged emotions. Ella drew in a slow, steady breath, exhaling before breathing in again.

"Go," Miro said.

Ella felt their eyes on her as she crossed the room. The dozen paces were suddenly an interminable march, each footstep an effort. She reached forward to touch the handle and pushed the door open, eyes on the floor as she entered the room and closed the door behind her.

Ella smelled the sweet stench of sickness.

She lifted her eyes.

The room was dark and the curtains were closed; only a nightlamp activated at the lowest setting giving Ella enough light to see by.

Tables lined the wall, and Ella fought an involuntary gasp as she saw bloody bandages and flasks of brown liquid. The sole other piece of furniture was a bed.

Rogan Jarvish lay on the bed.

He looked old, older than Ella had ever thought he could appear. The pallor of his skin matched his gray hair, and he appeared to be having difficulty breathing.

Ella couldn't fight it anymore. She sobbed and fell to her knees beside the bed.

"Ella," Rogan whispered. "You've changed."

"I'm still the same," Ella said through her tears.

"I know," he said. "I've been watching you since you were small. Even though you never knew it, I've watched you grow. Your mother and I were friends. We spoke about you together. She loved you with a burning passion. She wanted you to have a normal, happy life, even if it meant she couldn't be with you. Through her, I came to know you. I came to love you."

Ella felt tears spill out of her eyes, streaming down the sides of her cheeks. She breathed in gasps between sobs and couldn't control herself no matter how hard she tried.

"Take my hand," Rogan said.

Ella looked over his body for the first time. The blankets came up to his waist, but Rogan's chest was black with oxidized blood, evil darkness spreading through the cloth wrappings around his torso.

Ella reached forward and took Rogan's hand. His palm and fingers were cold, though the room was warm.

"Don't cry," Rogan said.

Ella wiped at her cheeks with her free hand. "Is it bad?"

"I've taken worse." Rogan's voice was hoarse. "But that was as a younger man. We all grow, and we all age."

Ella knew Rogan as an indomitable force. Her breathing ran ragged as Rogan closed his eyes for a time, and then he opened them again.

"Do you believe that with age comes wisdom?" Rogan asked.

"Sometimes," Ella said.

Rogan tried to laugh but fell into a coughing fit. Ella wondered if she should fetch help and started to rise, but Rogan's surprisingly firm grip pulled her back down.

"That's you, lass. Always one to tell the truth. You're right; I wasn't wise to fight, not with Amelia and Tapel to take care of. But here I am."

"If you didn't fight, Miro could be dead on the battlefield," Ella said. "Rogan . . . thank you. I'm so sorry."

"Enough of that." Rogan sighed. "Listen, lass. I have something important to say. Will you heed me?"

"I . . . I will," Ella said.

Ella's vision closed in as sadness overwhelmed her. She realized Rogan was saying good-bye.

"I may not always be wise, but I know you. I know you sometimes better than you know yourself." Rogan broke off with another cough. "Occasionally, Ella, you have to take a chance on life. You grew up an orphan, and you were all alone in the world when Brandon died. You've always accomplished everything on your own; you had no other choice. You're brave and intelligent, but you're also a fool and a coward."

Rogan's words shocked her. He wasn't holding back. "I'm sorry," Ella said through her tears.

"Don't be sorry," said Rogan. "You haven't had an easy life. I want you to do something for me. Talk to Killian, Ella. Tell him the truth. Tell him all those things he doesn't know about you, the secrets that you think are yours alone. Then let him talk, and listen, girl—listen well. Will you do that for me?"

Ella nodded.

"Good," Rogan said. "Come here." He kissed Ella's cheek, and she kissed his in return, feeling his skin cold on her lips. "I love you, girl, as does your brother, and all your friends. But there are different kinds of love. There is the love a man bears for his woman, and the love a parent bears for a child. You need to find that out."

Rogan drew a shaky breath, and Ella saw tears gleam at the corners of his eyes.

"Now go," Rogan said.

Ella stood and looked down at him. "Rogan," she whispered, "I love you too."

"I know," he said.

Ella left the room and closed the door behind her. Her vision was a blur between her tears, and she was barely aware of crossing the room to stand beside Shani and Bartolo. Shani took Ella's hand, her face filled with concern.

Miro entered the room after Ella, and he was gone a long time. He finally came out and looked at Amelia. "He wants to speak with you," Miro said.

Amelia entered to speak with her husband, and she was also gone for a long time. Finally, Amelia came back out of the room. She looked at Ella, and her reddened eyes met Ella's for a moment.

Ella gasped as Amelia shook her head.

"Please, everyone leave," Amelia said. "I want to be alone with him now."

68

"Shani," Bartolo said as he entered their room and closed the door behind him.

"Hello, soldier," Shani said, arching an eyebrow. Lying on the bed, she raised her burgundy dress to her upper thigh. "What is it? Come to give homage to the goddess of love?"

Bartolo sat next to his wife on the bed. "I want to be serious."

Shani sighed and sat up to sit cross-legged beside him on the bed.

Bartolo took a deep breath. "We need to talk."

"Here we go." Shani rolled her eyes.

"Please, Shani, this is hard enough as it is." Bartolo took Shani's hands in his own. "The war is over. Where are we going to go? I have a life in Altura, and you have a life in Petrya. Which will it be? I don't want to be apart from you anymore. Frequent visits aren't enough. The position of blademaster is there for me in Altura, if I want it. No one else can do it."

"Blademaster?" Shani said.

Bartolo nodded. "There are recruits who need training. Altura needs bladesingers. After the war with the primate, we never regained the numbers we once had. One day we may face another enemy, and we need to be prepared."

"Do you think it would be difficult for a bladesinger to wear the cuffs of an elementalist?" Shani grinned.

"Shani, please, I'm trying to be serious."

"So am I. Perhaps we could both be teachers. It's about time we began to share lore between the houses."

"But can you leave your homeland?"

"That's the question, isn't it?"

"Shani!"

"I'm playing with you, bladesinger. You make it too easy."

"Just speak plainly. Will you come to live with me in Sarostar?"

"Listen," Shani said gravely. "I love my homeland. But Petrya's a harsh land, and change will only come about slowly. They're talking about building a new road to properly connect Altura and Halaran to Petrya, rather than using that treacherous Wondhip Pass."

Bartolo nodded. "Of course I would expect you to visit your homeland, and I'd come with you. I want to get to know your lands, just as I want you to come to know mine."

"There's also something else we'll need to consider," Shani said. "Petrya's no place to raise a child."

She met Bartolo's eyes, gazing at him meaningfully as she smiled broadly. Bartolo looked at her and frowned in puzzlement, and then his eyes widened. His mouth dropped open, and he looked down at Shani's belly and then up at her.

Shani nodded.

Bartolo's grin spread slowly across his face, dimpling his cheeks and crinkling at the corners of his eyes. "I'm going to be a . . ."

"Yes," Shani said.

Bartolo's deep laugh rumbled throughout the palace.

69

Jehral stood at the highest point of the Imperial Palace, feeling the wind on his cheeks and gazing out at the sea. He ran his eyes over the rebuilding already underway at the docks and lifted his stare to scan the still waters, eventually resting on the empty island where once the Sentinel had barred the harbor. The great statue was gone now, and no one, not even the emperor himself, knew where it was. Stone blocks surrounded the pedestal. The air was warm, but the eerie emptiness of the island made him shiver.

Jehral thought about the Empire's future. As he gazed at the placid harbor, fishing boats appeared as if out of nowhere, heading out to make a day's catch, and the scene was of such wonderful normalcy that Jehral watched their white sails for a long time.

He turned, suddenly feeling a strong desire to look west, though the desert was far from this place. The Wall was gone, and rumor had it that the emperor was going to leave it that way. The Wall had long been a symbol of suppression; the last emperor had executed dissidents by throwing them from its summit. Seranthia, as capital of the Empire of Merralya, was going to be an open city.

Past the city's perimeter, patrols of soldiers were returning while others headed out to take their place. Several plumes of smoke indicated where the bodies of the revenants were being burned in piles. The fallen of all the houses were being gathered, and a new graveyard was going to come into being just outside the city. Everyone had lost someone they loved; yet the Empire had endured. The war with the Evermen was over.

Behind him, Jehral heard a throat clear.

Ilathor stood watching him with a strange expression on his face, an apprehensive cast that Jehral had never seen before. The kalif had recovered from his wounds, and he now stood proud and tall. His cloak of black and yellow billowed in the breeze and he stroked the carefully trimmed beard on his chin as he opened his mouth to speak and then closed it.

"Kalif." Jehral bowed with a flourish.

"Jehral . . . may I speak with you, my friend? Are you . . . busy?"

Jehral fought to hide an expression of bemusement. "I know it may appear that way," he said with a wry grin, "but my time is yours. Of course we can speak, Kalif."

"I am just Ilathor today, my friend. I have come . . . to ask you something."

Jehral nodded. "Yes, we are all packed and ready to go. We will have to travel home overland, but there are many here who will share our journey for a time."

"No," Ilathor said. He hesitated. "It is something else."

"Ahh," Jehral said. "You have come to ask me about the signaling system. The emperor has agreed to keep it in place. In fact, he has some ideas for supplementing it. The artificers of Loua Louna have agreed to attack the problem and work with the Alturan enchanters. Combining the lore of the houses, we may be able to devise a new system of instant communication."

"No, my friend." Ilathor's expression grew pained. "I wish to speak with you about something else."

"What is it, Kalif?" Jehral said, spreading his hands.

Ilathor's expression said he could finally see the twinkle in Jehral's eye.

"You are making sport with me?" Ilathor wondered, shaking his head.

"I am." Jehral laughed. "I know why you are here. Yes, of course you can marry my sister, my friend. I look forward to calling you brother."

Ilathor grinned, a childish smile Jehral had never seen before, and the two men embraced. "And I you, brother."

They drew apart and Ilathor's expression once more grew sincere. "There is one other matter. I have one final request to make."

This time Jehral didn't know what Ilathor was going to say.

"The Alturans have the concept of a lord marshal. He is a ruler's closest advisor and ranks above the other nobles. He tells the truth when it needs to be told. The title catches on my lips, however. I prefer to use a word that already exists among us: vizier. Will you be my vizier, Jehral? Together there is nothing we cannot achieve. Please say yes." Ilathor drew back when he saw Jehral hesitate. "What is it?"

Jehral struggled to frame his thoughts. "You want me to tell the truth when it needs to be told?"

"Yes, Jehral. That is what I want."

"Then, Ilathor, sometimes you are a fool. Your heart takes over your mind, and you are brave, but sometimes it takes more than courage to win the day."

The kalif's brow darkened and he scowled, ready to speak words of anger. Then, as quickly as they'd come, the lines left his forehead and he grinned.

"I asked you for the truth." Ilathor smiled wryly.

Jehral realized what he'd said. "I apologize, Kalif. I should not have . . ."

Ilathor held up his hand. "Yes, you should. Always speak your mind, brother. I will not always agree with you, but I will listen."

"Then yes," Jehral said. "I will be your vizier."

The two men looked westward for a time. The summer sun was hot, and in the far distance, heat waves shimmered from the hills.

"Come, Jehral. Let us make preparations to go from this place. The desert awaits."

70

Ella glanced at the note in her hands and then looked down, her eyes following the winding path to the copse of trees below.

"This is the place," she whispered to herself.

She was somewhere between Fortune and the market district. It was easy to miss the grove, hidden as it was by a row of tall buildings on a ridge of land. Yet the directions had been precise, and Ella's heart told her she'd come to the right place.

Ella's pulse raced as she walked with tremulous steps down the path.

The path led her down the hillside and wound between the trees, taking Ella deeper into the grove. It was narrow, and Ella passed under branches heavy with foliage, smelling moss and hearing the sounds of the city banished completely.

Ella arrived at an iron fence, hidden in the depths, previously obscured from her view.

She looked through the bars of the fence, and her breathing quickened as she saw the crumbled house. It was fallen into complete disrepair, the roof caved in and timbers strewn one on top of the other.

Her hands shaking, Ella read the note one more time.

Ella,

Some time ago, you received a legacy from your mother that enabled you to enroll at the Academy of Enchanters. The Eternal, or whomever we look to for the twists of fate, blessed Merralya on that day. Now, as I entrust you with my legacy, I hope and pray my final gift to you can have a similar result. There is none other I would rather entrust.

I now go to bring peace to my conscience, for I intend to end Sentar Scythran's evil once and for all. I do not expect to survive. I will soon be rejoined with my love, wherever she may be.

I give you my sanctum. No feet other than my own have ever crossed this threshold. I told you I have no home, and that is true. I once told you that when in Seranthia, I always stay with my friend Barlow at the Cedar Palace, and that was a lie.

I will tell no more lies.

On the reverse side of this message are directions to my sanctum, as well as instructions for revealing the structure and passing my wards.

I believe your journey has only just begun. Learn from my mistakes. Be truthful always. Fight for what you know is right.

You have my eternal love and respect.

I am better for knowing you.

Evrin Evenstar

Ella glanced up once more at the iron fence and dilapidated house. Following the line of the fence, she walked until she came to a barred gate, as high as her shoulders, sealed shut with a rusty padlock.

Ella crouched down and picked up a stone, tucking some strawberry tresses behind her ear as they fell in front of her face.

She tossed the stone over the gate, her eyes following its arc. With a sudden flash of flame the stone vaporized, leaving nothing to fall back down to the ground.

Ella moved her hand slowly forward and felt it grow warm as she passed the boundary. Before long the feeling became uncomfortable and she drew her hand back.

Ella smiled and shook her head.

She spoke a word and the gate . . . changed. The rusty padlock vanished, to be replaced by an intricate silver lock covered with runes of enchantment. Only the iron bars were the same. Ella spoke a second word, and with a click the lock opened, the gate swinging open.

Ella stepped through and closed the gate behind her, seeing it once more shift until it was again bound by a rusty padlock.

Gazing at the ruined structure, Ella raised her hand in front of her and spoke three words aloud.

In a heartbeat, the dilapidated house was gone. In its place was a cottage with three steps leading up to a porch and a white wooden door with an oval glass window in the center.

Ella felt excitement creep upward along her spine as she walked up the steps to stand in front of the door. She nearly cried out in astonishment as a face appeared in the oval window.

She realized she wasn't looking through the window; the face was a projection, hovering in empty space and scowling as he looked out.

"Who goes there?" Evrin said. "Ah, my dear, it's you." His glare shifted to a grin. "Welcome."

Ella wiped tears from her eyes as she smiled. How long had he known she would come here? Seeing Evrin's face like this only reminded her how much she missed him. She'd lost so many friends.

Ella pushed away thoughts of Rogan. She couldn't face that. She wasn't ready.

"Welcome to my sanctum," Evrin said. "Everything here is now yours. I have a few instructions. Drink the wine; don't keep it until it goes bad. Use my recipes, but only when you're in good company. And be careful whom you share the lore with, but"—he smiled—"I know you will be. My home is now yours, my dear. As you know by now, there are no schools of lore. All power comes from the one source, and that source is inside you, inside your brother, your people, and inside every living thing. Perhaps you will learn things the Evermen at the height of their power only dreamt of. Perhaps you will open the pathway to new worlds, or cure the ills of this world. That is for you to decide. Be well. And tell my descendent I expect him to treat you in the manner you deserve."

Evrin's face vanished, and Ella sighed. She knew whom he was referring to.

Killian.

Ella spoke the last of the activation sequences Evrin had given her, and the white door opened. Ella stepped inside, and of its own accord the door shut behind her.

Somehow the small cottage was cavernous inside. Ella was in a sitting room with shelves filled with books lining every wall, other than where a solid leather armchair rested next to a cold hearth. She saw an arch leading to another room, and stepping through, she found a dining room, also filled with shelves of books in addition to the square table and seating for four.

Another chamber was a large workroom, with a few vials of black liquid neatly spaced on the shelves alongside a bewildering array of scrills. A long bench filled the length of one wall. Stacked books stood piled on a side table beside three black cubes covered in tiny symbols. A golden egg sat on a stand, and a dozen wands of all shapes and sizes lay on another shelf. Gems filled a bowl, and bracelets and rings hung on hooks. Tall, bizarre devices Ella couldn't categorize clustered against the wall.

Ella left the workroom and found a kitchen, a huge room filled with knives, pots, and pans. Near the kitchen a set of steps led down to a cellar, and expecting more works of lore, Ella was surprised to see racks of wine bottles, neatly ordered and categorized with scribbled tasting notes.

"Alturan silversweet. Dessert wine. Plum and nutmeg overtones. Delicious with chocolate pudding," Ella murmured as she read one of the descriptions. She smiled, shaking her head.

There was so much of Evrin's personality in this place. Ella was filled with sadness and comfort in equal measures, and she felt closer to the old man than she ever had before.

Climbing the steps out of the cellar, she went back into the sitting room and began to scan the shelves. So many of these books' pages were made of the strange metallic fabric Ella had seen in the Lexicons and the book that had led the primate to the hidden relic.

As she drank in the sight of all the knowledge, Ella felt frayed nerves began to settle and ragged emotions calm.

When Brandon had died, she'd buried herself in her studies at the Academy of Enchanters. After Killian vanished into the portal, Ella had again thrown herself into her work, going to Mornhaven to help Evrin build the new machines that would once more give the Empire essence.

Ella had lost too many friends: Evrin, Layla, and now Rogan. She didn't want companionship. Ella wanted knowledge. She needed lore.

Finally, Ella allowed herself to think of Rogan, testing herself, seeing if she could bear the loss. The pain was raw and jagged.

Ella's breathing began to catch and she pushed the thoughts down. Selecting a book from the shelf she read the cover. *Of Plants and Animals.*

Ella sat in the leather armchair and began to read.

Soon, the pain melted away.

71

Winds of change swept across the lands of the Empire.

New essence rolled out in drudge-pulled carts from the catacombs under Mornhaven. This time priority was given to the houses that had sacrificed the most.

Though they weren't part of a house, and preferred the glint of gold to the glow of runes, the proud people of the free cities even received their own allocation. The unexpected wealth would go a long way toward rebuilding Castlemere and Schalberg.

Councilors Lauren and Marcel decided to appoint a new joint mayor to oversee the work and renew the ties of trade that the free cities depended on. Hermen Tosch grumbled, but he finally agreed—in return for concessions for his new trading company.

The winds swept away the last odors of decay.

———◆———

In Seranthia, a contingent of tough Tingaran legionnaires halted outside a sprawling manse stretching from the edge of Fortune down to the harbor's edge.

Killian waited impatiently while his captain called through the barred iron gate to summon the owner of the manse, Lord York, one of Seranthia's wealthiest nobles. As the hired guards on the other side of the fence ran to find their master, Killian looked at the nervous man at his side.

Lord Osker combed his fingers through the thin hair covering the bald patch on his scalp. He looked frightened.

"You're certain?" Killian asked. "Lord York is the one?"

Osker licked his lips but nodded decisively. "I've known for some time."

Killian scowled. "Then I'm not going to give him a chance to get away. Stand back."

The legionnaires stepped away from the iron gates at Killian's command. The emperor spoke a series of activations and moved his hand in a vertical cutting motion. A flash of bright light flickered from his palm, slicing through the bar holding the gates closed.

Two legionnaires hauled the gates wide open.

"Find Lord York," Killian called, waving to send his men forward. The legionnaires swept past the emperor, crossing the grounds and dashing into the grand structures.

Entering the manse, Killian ran his eyes over the opulent property. Beautiful statues dotted the grounds, spaced around spilling fountains lit up from underneath with the glow of multihued nightlamps. He had no doubt that the manse's grounds would be stark compared with the decadence of the interior, but Killian had no desire to continue inside.

He was angry enough as it was.

As Killian waited, glancing at his companion and pacing the area, he wondered what to do with Lord Osker. His mother, Alise, had unearthed Osker, though she hadn't explained to Killian how she'd found out that the lord belonged to the Melin Tortho, the most powerful of the streetclans. Killian had promised Osker that he would spare his life in return for information leading to the architect of the plot to abandon Altura and assassinate the emperor. And here they were.

Anxious to avoid punishment, Osker had told them everything he knew, yet he had abused a position of trust in the Imperial Palace and certainly wasn't without guilt. Killian thought about his mother's discovery and mused. Perhaps it was time for a new convict to arrive on the island that Alise had once been exiled to. Perhaps there was a place for the Isle of Ana after all.

Killian looked up at a commotion and saw six of his legionnaires leading a thin man in purple velvet out of the manse's main entrance.

"What is the meaning of this?" Lord York demanded as Killian's men dragged him forward.

Killian waited until the hook nosed noble was directly in front of him before speaking. "Lord York, you are under arrest for treason. You will be given a fair trial, but let me be clear; we will uncover all of those involved in the plot against my life and the plot to abandon Altura."

"This is preposterous," Lord York spluttered, his eyes seeming to pop out of his head.

"We shall see, Lord York. Or should I say, Tortho."

The winds of change moved on.

In the city of Sarostar, a young boy helped a hobbling middle-aged man leave the infirmary and walk along the wide stone road leading toward the river.

"You don't need to help me, lad," Fergus grumbled. "My wife'll be here soon."

"She knows I'm here," Tapel said. "She's waiting at the river."

Fergus leaned on Tapel as he felt the stitches on his wounds tighten. Even so, he felt better, whole again. He looked forward to resuming work.

When they reached the foot of the Tenbridge, Fergus held up a hand. "Hold on a moment. Just let me see my city."

Fergus drank in the sight of Sarostar, seeing the Crystal Palace cycling through its evening colors, the famous nine bridges cascading down the bubbling Sarsen one after the other. But most of all, he saw the people.

A couple of old men fished from the apex of Victory Bridge, each of them holding a steaming mug that could only be cherl as they chatted, their attention more on each other than their rods. A pair of lovers walked hand in hand on the Tenbridge. Fergus knew the boy; he was training to be a stonemason.

There were faces he knew and faces he didn't, but with time, he would come to know many of them, their hopes and dreams, trials and tribulations. Fergus had taken a terrible wound, but he was alive. The Lord of the Sky had blessed him and given him many more years with his nagging wife and unruly children. He longed to be home with them, but he took a moment to sweep his gaze across his beloved Sarostar.

He thought about the one who had saved him and taken his broken body from the barricades to be healed. Fergus the ferryman planned to one day find her and thank her, even if it took his whole life.

They said she was a determined young woman, with green eyes and pale yellow hair.

An enchantress.

72

Ella stayed in Evrin's house for weeks, only surfacing to venture to the nearby bakeries and markets for the barest sustenance, just enough to get her through another day of study.

She found still more rooms filled with books: they filled Evrin's bedchamber and even his wardrobe. Ella snuggled deep in the armchair and read, clearing all other thoughts from her mind. There were lifetimes of knowledge here. Ella planned to accumulate as much as she could.

Ella lost track of time. Sometimes she woke before dawn; other times she slept until late in the afternoon.

Soon she planned to enter Evrin's workroom. It was time to test out some of the things she'd learned.

Frowning as she tried to understand a particularly difficult treatise on the various forms of light—apparently some light could even be invisible, Ella looked up in annoyance as she heard a loud curse from somewhere outside the house.

She moved to the door and waved her hand in front of the wood, muttering a swift series of activations. The door became transparent and Ella could look out, though she knew whoever it was couldn't look in.

She put her hand to her mouth as she saw who it was.

Her heart began to beat rapidly.

How had he found her? Should she open the door?

Ella drew in a shuddering breath and summoned her courage.

She pulled the door open.

Ella stepped out, walking down the steps to stand in front of the cottage, and she knew that to the newcomer she'd appeared as if out of thin air.

Killian yelped and jumped backward as he saw her. He was nursing his hand, which it seemed he'd burned trying to get past the gate.

Ella touched her hand to the red part of her hair. It was a few shades lighter than Killian's fiery color.

Killian looked at her in astonishment. Ella spoke a word and the gate swung open to allow him through.

"What is this place?"

"It's Evrin's sanctum," Ella said. "You wouldn't believe—"

"I've looked everywhere for you," Killian interrupted. "I've searched far and wide. If you didn't have to eat,"—he shook his head—"I would never have found you."

His expression was filled with raw emotion, and seeing him like this filled Ella with fear. Yet there was another emotion curled up within the fear, struggling to break free.

Ella hadn't seen him since Sentar's defeat. He'd left immediately to do what he could for the city, and after using her new abilities to help wherever she could, Ella had followed her own path.

Ella knew Killian had his love, Carla, somewhere in the city, a woman Ella had no desire to meet. She knew he hated her for the relationship she'd had with Ilathor. Back in Seranthia, before Sentar's arrival, Ella had thought something could work between them, but now Ella didn't want to be close to anyone. The pain wasn't worth it.

"Killian . . . I—"

"Ella, don't talk; just listen. I know the life you've had," Killian said. "I've had the same life. We can't always have the best childhood, but when we grow up, we're given a chance. We can start all over again. We get to form our own family, and this time we can get it right."

Ella felt tears form in her eyes, and she sought escape. She looked back at the house and then at Killian again. His blue eyes burned with feeling.

Killian stepped forward and reached out to touch Ella's lock of red hair. "We have to take a chance. You and I were meant to be together. Do you know another word for chance? Fate."

"How do you know?" Ella whispered.

"Know? I don't know it, I feel it."

"I can't. I've lost—"

"I know," Killian said. He held out his hand. "You don't have to be alone anymore."

Ella looked into Killian's eyes, and suddenly all thoughts of Evrin's sanctum left her.

"Come with me," Killian said, still holding out his hand. "Please."

Ella made her choice.

She stepped close to him, and she felt his larger hand enfold hers. She followed Killian through the gate, and it shut behind them with a soft click.

The knowledge could wait.

───────◆───────

Ella and Killian walked together up the winding path, strolling through the streets of Seranthia, past the markets and down to the docks.

At first they walked in silence. Ella opened and closed her mouth several times, but she didn't know where to begin.

With a feeling of terrible sadness, Ella realized she'd nearly broken her promise to Rogan. She'd said she would talk, but she'd done what she always did and fled to knowledge. She owed Rogan more than that.

As she and Killian reached the water's edge, both staring out over the still expanse of glistening ocean, Ella finally began to talk. She told Killian about the true nature of her relationship with Ilathor, and he told her about what had happened with Carla.

Ella shared herself, and Killian listened, just like he had when they first met in Sarostar on the banks of the Sarsen.

For hours Ella and Killian simply talked, watching the sun fall down toward the horizon and seeing the first stars come out at night.

Finally, as the warm summer breeze blew across the rippling water, the reflected stars saw the couple standing close together, sharing their innermost feelings. Ella summoned every reserve of her courage to do something she'd never done before.

Ella told Killian she loved him.

73

High above Seranthia's harbor, a small park spread to the edge of a low cliff. It was the perfect place to watch the stars come out, with a view of both the docks and the sea. A long bench of worn wood with a high back sat close to the drop, and there were people sitting on the bench, drinking in the view.

Miro stretched and then leaned back against the seat, before something caught his eye.

"Look who it is," he said.

Miro pointed to a place on the edge of the docks where two people stood together, looking out over the water, huddled close as they spoke. One was a man with fiery red hair that reflected the lights of the city and the stars. The other was a slender young woman with pale hair cascading down her back, shining silver in the evening light.

Miro watched as Killian put his arm around Ella and she placed her head against his shoulder.

"He loves her," Amber said.

"I know," Miro said. "And she loves him too."

"It's about time." The third person on the bench spoke in a rough, gravelly voice. "She's going to kill me when she finds out. Was it really necessary?"

"If that wound couldn't kill you, then you've got nothing to fear from my sister," Miro said, grinning. "We all agreed to it, but it was my idea. Trust me, if anyone needs a push, it's her."

"And the proof is right there in front of us," said Amber.

Miro and his two companions watched the lovers in silence as each of them thought their own private thoughts. Miro considered how far they'd all come. He thought about all the friends he'd lost, but also the friends he wouldn't have made without the wars. Creation followed destruction in the strangest ways.

Miro wondered what was next for Ella. That was for her to decide. He knew where his home was.

"I'm thinking about Tomas," Amber said. "I miss my son."

"Me too," Miro said.

Miro returned his gaze back to Seranthia's harbor. There would be a lot of work to do when he arrived back in Altura, but compared to worrying about defenses, rebuilding his homeland was a task he relished.

He would pour every resource into restoring Castlemere and Schalberg to their former selves. He would help the Veldrins find their way home.

But most of all, he would spend time with his family. Miro and Ella had both grown up as orphans. Amber and Tomas were Miro's chance for a fresh start.

Miro's vision returned to his sister and her love. They didn't look like they would be moving for a long, long time.

"How do you think you'll like retirement?" Miro asked.

"Like it?" Rogan said. "Nothing will give me greater pleasure than spending my days fishing on the Sarsen."

"Or dropping by the Pens to offer some advice," Amber smiled.

Rogan snorted. "Come on," he said. "Let's go home."

ACKNOWLEDGMENTS

I've thoroughly enjoyed writing the Evermen Saga. It's been an incredible journey, and like the characters in my books I've been fortunate to make some friends along the way.

Huge thanks go to my editor, Emilie, and the team at 47North, for excellent guidance, support, and assistance with every aspect of development and publication. Thank you also David for believing in me.

Thanks go to Mike for tireless efforts developing the manuscript, and Mark and Peta for all your help with the tough parts.

Most of all, in this, the last book in the series, I wish to highlight that none of this would have been possible without the readers who supported me from the beginning. Without you, Enchantress would still be gathering silicon dust on a hard disk and the relic would still be hidden.

Thanks to all of you who've reached out to me and taken the time to post reviews of my books.

My final thanks I reserve for my wife, Alicia.

I will be ever grateful for your constant support.

ABOUT THE AUTHOR

 James Maxwell found inspiration growing up in the lush forests of New Zealand, and later in rugged Australia where he was educated. Devouring fantasy and science fiction classics at an early age, his love for books translated to a passion for writing, which he began at age 11.

He relocated to London at age 25, but continued to seek inspiration wherever he could find it, in the grand cities of the old world and the monuments of fallen empires. His travels influenced his writing as he spent varying amounts of time in forty countries on six continents.

He wrote his first full-length novel, *Enchantress*, while living on an isle in Thailand and its sequel, *The Hidden Relic*, from a coastal town on the Yucatan peninsula in Mexico.

The third book in the Evermen Saga, *The Path of the Storm*, was written in the Austrian Alps, and he completed the fourth, *The Lore of the Evermen*, in Malta.

When he isn't writing or traveling, James enjoys sailing, snowboarding, classical guitar, and French cooking.